Her Greek Proposition

LYNNE GRAHAM

MICHELLE SMART

TARA PAMMI

MILLS & BOON

First Published in Great Britain 2020
By Mills & Boon, an imprint of HarperCollins*Publishers*
1 London Bridge Street, London, SE1 9GF

GORGEOUS GREEKS: HER GREEK PROPOSITION © 2020
Harlequin Books S.A.

A Deal at the Altar © 2012 Lynne Graham
Married for the Greek's Convenience © 2017 Harlequin Books S.A.
A Deal with Demakis © 2014 Tara Pammi

Special thanks and acknowledgement go to Michelle Smart for her contribution to the *Brides for Billionaires* series.

ISBN: 978-0-263-29828-4

MIX
Paper from
responsible sources
FSC C007454

FSC
www.fsc.org

This book is produced from independently certified FSC™ paper to ensure responsible forest management.

For more information visit: www.harpercollins.co.uk/green

Printed and bound in Spain
by CPI, Barcelona

A DEAL AT
THE ALTAR

LYNNE GRAHAM

CHAPTER ONE

'WHAT do I want to do about the Royale hotel group?'
The speaker, a very tall and well-built Greek male with
blue-black hair, raised an ebony brow and gave a sardonic laugh. 'Let's allow Blake to sweat for the moment…'

'Yes, sir.' Thomas Morrow, the British executive who
had asked the question at the behest of his colleagues,
was conscious of the nervous perspiration on his brow.
One-on-one encounters with his powerhouse employer,
one of the richest men in the world, were rare and he
was keen not to say anything that might be deemed stupid or naive.

Everybody knew that Sergios Demonides did not
suffer fools gladly. Unfortunately, priding himself on
being a maverick, the Greek billionaire did not feel the
need to explain the objectives behind his business deci-
sions either, which could make life challenging for his
executive team. Not so long ago the acquisition of the
Royale hotel group at any price had seemed to be the
goal and there was even a strong rumour that Sergios
might be planning to marry the exquisite Zara Blake,
the daughter of the man who owned the hotel chain. But

after Zara had been pictured in the media in the arms of an Italian banker that rumour had died and Sergios's curious staff had not noticed their boss exhibiting the smallest sign of annoyance over the development.

'I took the original offer to Blake off the table. The price will come down now,' Sergios pointed out lazily, brilliant black eyes glittering at that prospect for more than anything else in life he liked to drive a hard bargain.

Purchasing the Royale group at an inflated price would have gone very much against the grain with him, but a couple of months ago Sergios had been prepared to do it and jump through virtually any hoop just to make that deal. *Why?* His beloved grandfather, Nectarios, who had started his legendary business empire at the helm of the very first Royale hotel in London, had been seriously ill at the time. But, mercifully, Nectarios was a tough old buzzard, Sergios thought fondly, and pioneering heart surgery in the USA had powered his recovery. Sergios now thought that the hotel chain would make a timely little surprise for his grandfather's eightieth birthday, but he no longer had any intention of paying over the odds for the gift.

As for the wife he had almost acquired as part of the deal, Sergios was relieved that fate had prevented him from making that mistake. Zara Blake, after all, had shown herself up as a beautiful little tart with neither honour nor decency. On the other hand her maternal instincts would have come in very useful where his children were concerned, he conceded grudgingly. Had it not been for the fact that his cousin's premature death had left Sergios responsible for his three young children, Sergios would not even have considered taking a second wife.

His handsome face hardened. One catastrophe in that department had been quite sufficient for Sergios. For the sake of those children, however, he had been prepared to bite the bullet and remarry. It would have been a marriage of convenience though, a public sham to gain a mother for the children and assuage his conscience. He knew nothing about kids and had never wanted any of his own but he knew his cousin's children were unhappy and that piqued his pride and his sense of honour.

'So, we're waiting for Blake to make the next move,' Thomas guessed, breaking the silence.

'And it won't be long. He's over-extended and underfunded with very few options left,' Sergios commented with growling satisfaction.

'You're a primary school teacher and good with young kids,' Monty Blake pointed out, seemingly impervious to his eldest daughter's expression of frank astonishment as she stood in his wood-panelled office. 'You'd make the perfect wife for Demonides—'

'No, stop right there!' Bee lifted a hand to physically emphasise that demand, her green eyes bright with disbelief as she used her other hand to push the heavy fall of chestnut-brown hair off her damp brow. Now she knew that her surprise and disquiet that her father should have asked her to come and see him were not unfounded. 'This is me, not Zara, you're talking to and I have no desire to marry an oversexed billionaire who needs some little woman at home to look after his kids—'

'Those kids are not his,' the older man broke in to remind her, as though that should make a difference to her. 'His cousin's death made him their guardian. By all accounts he didn't either want or welcome the responsibility—'

At that information, Bee's delicately rounded face only tightened with increased annoyance. She had plenty of experience with men who could not be bothered with children, not least with the man standing in front of her making sexist pronouncements. He might have persuaded her naive younger sister, Zara, to consider a marriage of convenience with the Greek shipping magnate, but Bee was far less impressionable and considerably more suspicious.

She had never sought her father's approval, which was just as well because as she was a mere daughter it had never been on offer to her. She was not afraid to admit that she didn't like or respect the older man, who had taken no interest in her as she grew up. He had also badly damaged her self-esteem at sixteen when he advised her that she needed to go on a diet and dye her hair a lighter colour. Monty Blake's image of female perfection was unashamedly blonde and skinny, while Bee was brunette and resolutely curvy. She focused on the desk photograph of her stepmother, Ingrid, a glamorous former Swedish model, blonde and thin as a rail.

'I'm sorry, I'm not interested, Dad,' Bee told him squarely, belatedly noticing that he wore an undeniable look of tiredness and strain. Perhaps he had come up with that outrageous suggestion that she marry Sergios Demonides because he was stressed out with business worries, she reasoned uncertainly.

'Well, you'd better get interested,' Monty Blake retorted sharply. 'Your mother and you lead a nice life. If the Royale hotel group crashes so that Demonides can pick it up for a song, the fallout won't only affect me and your stepmother but *all* my dependants…'

Bee tensed at that doom-laden forecast. 'What are you saying?'

'You know very well what I'm saying,' he countered impatiently. 'You're not as stupid as your sister—'

'Zara is *not*—'

'I'll come straight to the point. I've always been very generous to you and your mother…'

Uncomfortable with that subject though she was, Bee also liked to be fair. 'Yes, you have been,' she was willing to acknowledge.

It was not the moment to say that she had always thought his generosity towards her mother might be better described as 'conscience' money. Emilia, Bee's Spanish mother, had been Monty's first wife. In the wake of a serious car accident, Emilia had emerged from hospital as a paraplegic in a wheelchair. Bee had been four years old at the time and her mother had quickly realised that her young, ambitious husband was repulsed by her handicap. With quiet dignity, Emilia had accepted the inevitable and agreed to a separation. In gratitude for the fact that she had returned his freedom without a fuss, Monty had bought Emilia and her daughter a detached house in a modern estate, which he had then had specially adapted to her mother's needs. He had also always paid for the services of a carer to ensure that Bee was not burdened with round-the-clock responsibility for her mother. While the need to help out at home had necessarily restricted Bee's social life from a young age, she was painfully aware that only her father's financial support had made it possible for her to attend university, train as a teacher and actually take up the career that she loved.

'I'm afraid that unless you do what I'm asking you to do the gravy train of my benevolence stops here and now,' Monty Blake declared harshly. 'I own your mother's house. It's in my name and I can sell it any time I choose.'

Bee turned pale at that frank warning, shock winging through her because this was not a side of her father that she had ever come up against before. 'Why would you do something so dreadful to Mum?'

'Why should I care now?' Monty demanded curtly. 'I married your mother over twenty years ago and I've looked after her ever since. Most people would agree that I've more than paid my dues to a woman I was only married to for five years.'

'You know how much Mum and I appreciate everything that you have done for her,' Bee responded, her pride stung by the need to show that humility in the face of his obnoxious threatening behaviour.

'If you want my generosity to continue it will *cost* you,' the older man spelt out bluntly. 'I need Sergios Demonides to buy my hotels at the right price. And he was willing to do that until Zara blew him off and married that Italian instead—'

'Zara's deliriously happy with Vitale Roccanti,' Bee murmured tautly in her half-sister's defence. 'I don't see how I could possibly persuade a big tough businessman like Demonides to buy your hotels at a preferential price.'

'Well, let's face it, you don't have Zara's looks,' her father conceded witheringly. 'But as I understand it all Demonides wants is a mother for those kids he's been landed with and you'd make a damned sight better mother for them than Zara ever would have done—your sister can barely read! I bet he didn't know that when he agreed to marry her.'

Stiff with distaste at the cruelty of his comments about her sister, who suffered from dyslexia, Bee studied him coolly. 'I'm sure a man as rich and powerful as Sergios Demonides could find any number of women willing to marry him and play mummy to those kids. As you've correctly pointed out I'm not the ornamental type so I can't understand why you imagine he might be interested in me.'

Monty Blake released a scornful laugh. 'Because I know what he wants—Zara told me. He wants a woman who knows her place—'

'Well, then, he definitely doesn't want me,' Bee slotted in drily, her eyes flaring at that outdated expression that assumed female inferiority. 'And Zara's feistier than you seem to appreciate. I think he would have had problems with her too.'

'But you're the clever one who could give him ex-

actly what he wants. You're much more practical than
Zara ever was because you've never had it too easy—'

'Dad…?' Bee cut in, spreading her hands in a silenc-
ing motion. 'Why are we even having this insane conversation? I've only met Sergios Demonides once in my
life and he barely looked at me.'

She swallowed back the unnecessary comment that
the only part of her the Greek tycoon had noticed had
appeared to be her chest.

'I want you to go to him and offer him a deal—the
same deal he made with Zara. A marriage where he
gets to do as he likes and buys my hotels at the agreed
figure—'

'*Me*…go to *him* with a proposal of marriage?' Bee
echoed in ringing disbelief. 'I've never heard anything
so ridiculous in my life! The man would think I was a
lunatic!'

Monty Blake surveyed her steadily. 'I believe you're
clever enough to be convincing. If you can persuade
him that you could be a perfect wife and mother for
those little orphans you're that something extra that
could put this deal back on the table for me. I need this
sale and I need it now or everything I've worked for all
my life is going to tumble down like a pack of cards.
And with it will go your mother's security—'

'Don't threaten Mum like that.'

'But it's not an empty threat.' Monty shot his daughter an embittered look. 'The bank's threatening to pull
the plug on my loans. My hotel chain is on the edge of
disaster and right now that devil, Demonides, is playing a waiting game. I can't afford to wait. If I go down

you and your mother will lose everything too,' he reminded her doggedly. 'Think about it and imagine it— no specially adapted house, day-to-day responsibility for Emilia, no life of your own any more...'

'*Don't!*' Bee exclaimed, disgusted by his coercive methods. 'I think you have to be off your head to think that Sergios Demonides would even consider marrying someone like me.'

'Perhaps I am but we're not going to know until you make the approach, are we?'

'You're crazy!' his daughter protested vehemently, aghast at what he was demanding of her.

Her father stabbed a finger in the air. 'I'll have a For Sale sign erected outside your mother's house this week if you don't at least go and see him.'

'I couldn't...I just *couldn't*!' Bee gasped, appalled by his persistence. 'Please don't do this to Mum.'

'I've made a reasonable request, Bee. I'm in a very tight corner. Why, after enjoying all my years of expensive support and education, shouldn't you try to help?'

'Oh, puh-lease,' Bee responded with helpless scorn at that smooth and inaccurate résumé of his behaviour as a parent. 'Demanding that I approach a Greek billionaire and ask him to marry me is a *reasonable* request? On what planet and in what culture would that be reasonable?'

'Tell him you'll take those kids off his hands and allow him to continue enjoying his freedom and I think you're in with a good chance,' the older man replied stubbornly.

'And what happens when I humiliate myself and he turns me down?'

'You'll have to pray that he says yes,' Monty Blake answered, refusing to give an inch in his desperation. 'After all, it is the *only* way that your mother's life is likely to continue as comfortably as it has done for years.'

'Newsflash, Dad. Life in a wheelchair is not comfortable,' his daughter flung at him bitterly.

'And life without my financial security blanket is likely to be even less comfortable,' he sliced back, determined to have the last word.

Minutes later, having failed to change her father's mind in any way, Bee left the hotel and caught the bus home to the house she still shared with her mother. She was cooking supper when her mother's care assistant, Beryl, brought Emilia back from a trip to the library. Wheeling into the kitchen, Emilia beamed at her daughter. 'I found a Catherine Cookson I haven't read!'

'I won't be able to get you off to sleep tonight now.' Looking down into her mother's worn face, aged and lined beyond her years by illness and suffering, Bee could have wept at the older woman's continuing determination to celebrate the smallest things in life. Emilia had lost so much in that accident but she never ever complained.

When she had settled her mother for the night, Bee sat down to mark homework books for her class of seven-year-olds. Her mind, however, refused to stay on the task. She could not stop thinking about what her father had told her. He had threatened her but he had also told her a truth that had ripped away her sense of security. After all, she had naively taken her father's continuing financial success for granted and assumed that he would always be in a position to ensure that her mother had no money worries.

Being Bee, she had to consider the worst-case scenario. If her mother lost her house and garden it would undoubtedly break her heart. The house had been modified for a disabled occupant so that Emilia could move easily within its walls. Zara had even designed raised flower beds for the back garden, which her mother could work at on good days. If the house was sold Bee had a salary and would naturally be able to rent an apartment *but* as she would not be able to afford a full-time carer for her mother any more she would have to give up work to look after her and would thus lose that salary. Monty Blake might cover the bills but there had never been a surplus or indeed a legal agreement that he provide financial support and Emilia had no savings. Without his assistance the two women would have to live on welfare benefits and all the little extras and outings that lightened and lifted her mother's difficult life would no longer be affordable. It was a gloomy outlook that appalled Bee, who had always been very protective of the older woman.

Indeed when she thought about Emilia losing even the little things that she cherished the prospect of proposing marriage to a very intimidating Greek tycoon became almost acceptable. So what if she made a fool of herself? Well, there was no 'if' about it, she would make a colossal fool of herself and he might well dine out on the story for years! He had seemed to her as exactly the sort of guy likely to enjoy other people's misfortunes.

Not that he hadn't enjoyed misfortunes of his own, Bee was willing to grudgingly concede. When her sister had planned to marry Sergios, Bee had researched him on the Internet and she had disliked most of what she had discovered. Sergios had only become a Demonides when he was a teenager with a string of petty crimes to his name. He had grown up fighting for survival in one of the roughest areas of Athens. At twenty-one he had married a beautiful Greek heiress and barely three years later he had buried her when she died carrying their unborn child. Yes, Sergios Demonides might be filthy rich and successful, but his personal life was generally a disaster zone.

Those facts aside, however, he also had a name for being an out-and-out seven-letter-word in business and with women. Popular report said that he was extremely intelligent and astute but that he was also famously arrogant, ruthless and cold, the sort of guy who, as a husband, would have given her sensitive sister Zara and her cute pet rabbit, Fluffy, nightmares. Fortunately Bee did not consider herself sensitive. Growing up without a father and forced to become an adult long before her time as she learned to cope with her mother's disability and dependence, Bee had forged a tougher shell.

At the age of twenty-four, Bee already knew that men were rarely attracted to that protective shell or the unadorned conservative wrapping that surrounded it. She wasn't pretty or feminine and the boys she had dated as she grew up had, with only one exception, been friends rather than lovers. She had never learned to flirt or play girlie games and thought that perhaps she was just too sensible. She had, however, for a blissful few months been deeply in love and desperately hurt when the relationship fell apart over the extent of her responsibility for her disabled mother. And while she couldn't have cared less about her appearance, she *was* clever and passing so many exams with distinction and continually winning prizes did, she had learned to her cost, scare off the opposite sex.

The men she met also tended to be put off when Bee spoke her mind even if it meant treading on toes. She hated injustice or cruelty in any form. She didn't do that fragile-little-woman thing her stepmother, Ingrid, was for ever flattering her father with. It was hardly surprising that even Zara, the sister she loved, had grown up with a healthy dose of that same fatal man-pleasing gene. Only her youngest sister, Tawny, born of her father's affair with his secretary, resembled Bee in that line. Bee had never known what it was to feel helpless until she found herself actually making an appointment to see Sergios Demonides...such a crazy idea, such a very pointless exercise.

Forty-eight hours after Bee won the tussle with her pride and made the appointment, Sergios's PA asked him if he was willing to see Monty Blake's daughter, Beatriz. Unexpectedly Sergios had instant recall of the brunette's furious grass-green eyes and magnificent breasts. A dinner in tiresome company had been rendered almost bearable by his enticing view of that gravity-defying bosom, although she had not appreciated the attention. But why the hell would Blake's elder daughter want to speak to him? Did she work with her father? Was she hoping to act as the older man's negotiator? He snapped his long brown fingers to bring an aide to his side and requested an immediate background report on Beatriz before granting her an appointment the next day.

The following afternoon, dressed in a grey trouser suit, which she usually reserved for interviews but which she was convinced gave her much-needed dignity, Bee waited in the reception area of the elegant stainless-steel and glass building that housed the London headquarters of SD Shipping. That Sergios had used his own initials to stamp his vast business empire with his powerful personality didn't surprise Bee at all. Her heart rate increased at the prospect that loomed ahead of her.

'Mr Demonides will see you now, Miss Blake,' the attractive receptionist informed her with a practised smile that Bee could not match.

Without warning Bee was feeling sick with nerves. She was too intelligent not to contemplate the embarrassment awaiting her without inwardly cringing. She was quick to remind herself that the Greek billionaire was just a big hulking brute with too much money and an inability to ignore a low neck on a woman's dress. She reddened, recalling the evening gown with the plunge neckline that she had borrowed from a friend for that stupid meal. While his appraisal had made Bee blush like a furnace and had reminded her why she usually covered up those particular attributes, she had been stunned by his apparent indifference to her beautiful sister, Zara.

When Beatriz Blake came through the door of Sergios's office with a firm step in her sensible shoes, he instantly recognised that he was not about to be treated to any form of charm offensive. Her boxy colourless trouser suit did nothing for her womanly curves. Her rich brown hair was dragged back from her face and she wore not a scrap of make-up. To a man accustomed to highly groomed women her lackadaisical attitude towards making a good impression struck him as almost rude.

'I'm a very busy man, Beatriz. I don't know what you're doing here but I expect you to keep it brief,' he told her impatiently.

For a split second Sergios Demonides towered over Bee like a giant building casting a long tall shadow and she took a harried step back, feeling crowded by his sheer size and proximity. She had forgotten how big and commanding he was, from his great height to his broad shoulders and long powerful legs. He was also, much though it irritated her to admit it, a staggeringly handsome man with luxuriant blue-black hair and sculpted sun-darkened features. The sleek unmistakeable assurance of great wealth oozed from the discreet gleam of his thin gold watch and cufflinks to the spotless white of his shirt and the classy tailoring of his dark business suit.

She collided with eyes the colour of burnished bronze that had the impact of a sledgehammer and cut off her breathing at its source. It was as if nerves were squeezing her throat tight and her heart started hammering again.

'My father asked me to see you on his behalf,' she began, annoyed by the breathlessness making her voice sound low and weak.

'You're a primary school teacher. What could you possibly have to say that I would want to hear?' Sergios asked with brutal frankness.

'I think you'll be surprised...' Bee compressed her lips, her voice gathering strength as reluctant amusement briefly struck her. 'Well, I *know* you'll be surprised.'

Surprises were rare and even less welcome in Sergios's life. He was a control freak and knew it and had not the smallest urge to change.

'A little while back you were planning to marry my sister, Zara.'

'It wouldn't have worked,' Sergios responded flatly.

Bee breathed in deep and slow while her white-knuckled hands gripped the handles of her bag. 'Zara told me exactly what you wanted out of marriage.'

While wondering where the strange dialogue could possibly be leading, Sergios tried not to grit his teeth visibly. 'That was most indiscreet of her.'

Discomfiture sent colour flaming into Bee's cheeks, accentuating the deep green of her eyes. 'I'm just going to put my cards on the table and get to the point.'

Sergios rested back against the edge of his polished contemporary desk and surveyed her in a manner that was uniquely discouraging, 'I'm waiting,' he said when she hesitated.

His impatient silence hummed like bubbling water ready to boil over.

Beneath her jacket, Bee breathed in so deep her bosom swelled and almost popped the buttons on her fitted blouse and for a split second Sergios dropped his narrowed gaze there as the fabric pulled taut over that full swell, whose bounty he still vividly recalled.

'My father utilised a certain amount of pressure to persuade me to come and see you,' she admitted uncomfortably. 'I told him it was crazy but here I am.'

'Yes, here…you…are,' Sergios framed in a tone of yawning boredom. 'Still struggling to come to the point.'

'Dad wanted me to offer myself in Zara's place.' Bee squeezed out that admission and watched raw incredulity laced with astonished hauteur flare in his face while hot pink embarrassment surged into hers. 'I know, I told you it was crazy but he wants that hotel deal and he thinks that a suitable wife added into the mix could make a difference.'

'Suitable? You're certainly not in the usual run of women who aspire to marry me.' Sergios delivered that opinion bluntly.

And it was true. Beatriz Blake was downright plain in comparison to the gorgeous women who pursued him wherever he went, desperate to attract his attention and get their greedy hands on, if not the ultimate prize of a wedding ring, some token of his wealth. But somewhere deep in his mind at that instant a memory was stirring.

'Homely women make the best wives,' his grandfather had once contended. 'Your grandmother was unselfish, loyal and caring. I couldn't have asked for a better wife. My home was kept like a palace, my children were loved, and my word was law. She never gave me a second of concern. Think well before you marry a beauty, who demands more and gives a lot less.'

Having paled at that unnecessary reminder of her limitations, Bee made a fast recovery and lifted her chin. 'Obviously I'm not blonde and beautiful but I'm convinced that I would be a more appropriate choice than Zara ever was for the position.'

A kind of involuntary fascination at the level of her nerve was holding Sergios taut. His straight black brows drew together in a frown. 'You speak as though the role of being my wife would be a job.'

'Isn't it?' Bee came back at him boldly with that challenge. 'From what I understand you only want to marry to have a mother for your late cousin's children and I could devote myself to their care full-time, something Zara would never have been willing to do. I also—'

'Be silent for a moment,' Sergios interrupted, studying her with frowning attention. 'What kind of pressure did your father put on you to get you to come here and spout this nonsense?'

Bee went rigid before she tossed her head back in sudden defiance, wondering why she should keep her father's coercion a secret. Her pride demanded that she be honest. 'I have a severely disabled mother and if the sale of the Royale hotel chain falls through my father has threatened to sell our home and stop paying for Mum's care assistant. I'm not dependent on him but Mum is and I don't want to see her suffer. Her life is challenging enough.'

'I'm sure it is.' Sergios was unwillingly impressed by her motivation. Evidently Monty Blake was crueller within his family circle than Sergios would ever have guessed. Even Nectarios, his grandfather and one of the most ruthless men Sergios had ever met, would have drawn the line at menacing a disabled ex-wife. As for Beatriz, he could respect her honesty and her family loyalty, traits that said a lot about the kind of woman she was. She wasn't here for his enviable lifestyle or his money, she was here because she didn't have a choice. That was not a flattering truth but Sergios loathed flattery, having long since recognised that few people saw past his immense wealth and power to the man behind it all.

'So, tell me why you believe that you would make a better wife than your sister?' Sergios urged, determined to satisfy his curiosity and intrigued by her attitude towards marriage. A wife as an employee? It was a new take on the traditional role that appealed to him. A businessman to the core, he was quick to see the advantages of such an arrangement. A paid wife would be more likely to respect his boundaries while still making the effort to please him, he reasoned thoughtfully. There could be little room for messy human emotion and misunderstanding in such a practical agreement.

'I would be less demanding. I'm self-sufficient, sensible. I probably wouldn't cost you very much either as I'm not very interested in my appearance,' Bee pointed out, her full pink mouth folding as if vanity could be considered a vice. 'I'm also very good with kids.'

'What would you do with a six-year-old boy painting pictures on the walls?'

Bee frowned. 'Talk to him.'

'But he doesn't talk back. His little brother keeps on trying to cling to me and the toddler just stares into space,' Sergios told her in a driven undertone, his concern and incomprehension of such behaviour patent. 'Why am I telling you that?'

Surprised by his candour, Bee reckoned it was a sign that the children's problems were very much on his mind 'You thought I might have an answer for you?'

With a warning knock the door opened and someone addressed him in what she assumed to be Greek. He gave a brief answer and returned his attention to Bee. Something about that assessing look made her stiffen. 'I'll think over your proposition,' he drawled softly, startling her. 'But be warned, I'm not easy to please.'

'I knew that the first time I looked at you,' Bee countered, taking in the sardonic glitter of his eyes, the hard, uncompromising bone structure and that stubborn sensual mouth. It was very much the face of a tough guy, resistant to any counsel but his own.

'Next you'll be telling me you can read my fortune from my palm,' Sergios retorted with mocking cool.

Bee walked out of his office in a daze. He had said he would consider her proposition. Had that only been a polite lie? Somehow she didn't think he would have given her empty words. But if he was seriously considering her as a wife, where did that leave her? Fathoms deep in shock? For since Bee had automatically assumed that Sergios Demonides would turn her down she had not, at any stage, actually considered the possibility of becoming his wife…

CHAPTER TWO

Four days later, Bee emerged from the gates of the primary school where she worked and noticed a big black limousine parked just round the corner.

'Miss Blake?' A man in a suit with the build of a bouncer approached her. 'Mr Demonides would like to offer you a lift home.'

Bee blinked and stared at the long glossy limo with its tinted windows. How had he found out where she worked? While wondering what on earth Sergios Demonides was playing at, she saw no option other than to accept. Why queue for a bus when a limo was on offer? she reflected ruefully. Had he come in person to deliver his negative answer? Why would he take the trouble to do that? A man of his exalted status rarely put himself out for others. As a crowd of colleagues and parents parted to give Bee and her bulky companion a clear passage to the opulent vehicle self-conscious pink warmed her cheeks because people were staring.

'Beatriz,' Sergios acknowledged with a grave nod, glancing up from his laptop.

As Bee slid into the luxury vehicle she was disturbingly conscious of the sheer animal charisma that he exuded from every pore. He was all male in the most primal sense of the word. Smell the testosterone, one of her university friends would have quipped. The faint tang of some expensive masculine cologne flared her nostrils, increasing her awareness. She felt her nipples pinch tight beneath her bra and she went rigid, deeply disconcerted by her pronounced awareness of the sexual charge he put out. Her shielded gaze fell on his lean masculine profile, noting the dark shadow of stubble outlining his angular jaw. He was badly in need of a shave. It was the only sign in his otherwise immaculate appearance that he was nearing the end of his working day rather than embarking on its beginning. Aware that her hair was tossed by the breeze and her raincoat, skirt and knee-high boots were more comfortable than smart, she was stiff and awkward and questioning why because as a rule her sole concern about her appearance was that she be clean and tidy.

As the limousine pulled away from the pavement Sergios flipped shut his laptop and turned his arrogant head to look at her. His frown was immediate. She was a mess in her unfashionable, slightly shabby clothing. Yet she had flawless skin, lovely eyes and thick glossy hair, advantages that most women would have made the effort to enhance. For the first time he wondered why she didn't bother.

'To what do I owe the honour?' Bee enquired, watching him push the laptop away. He had beautiful shapely hands, she registered, and then tensed at that surprising thought.

'I'm leaving for New York this evening and I would like you to meet my children before I go.'

'Why?' Green eyes suddenly wide with confusion, Bee stared back at him. 'Why do you want me to meet them?'

A very faint smile curled the corners of his wide sensual mouth. 'Obviously because I'm considering you for the job.'

'But you *can't* be!' Bee told him in disbelief.

'I am. Your father played a winning hand sending you to see me,' Sergios fielded, amused by her astonishment, which was laced with a dismay that almost made him laugh out loud. She was a refreshing woman.

Her well-defined brows pleated and she frowned. 'I just don't understand…you could marry anybody!'

'Don't underestimate yourself,' Sergios responded, his thoughts on the enquiries and references he had gathered on her behalf since their last meeting. He had vetted her a good deal more thoroughly than he had vetted her flighty sister, Zara. 'According to my sources you're a loyal, devoted daughter and a gifted and committed teacher. I believe that you could offer those children exactly what they need—'

'Where did you get that information from?' Bee asked angrily.

'There are private investigation firms which can offer such details within hours for the right price,' Sergios fielded with colossal calm. 'Naturally I checked you out and I was impressed with what I learned about you.'

But I wasn't *seriously* offering to marry you, she almost snapped back at him before she thought better of that revealing admission and hastily swallowed it back. After all her father's threat still hung over her and his financial security was integral to her mother's support system. Take away that security and life as her mother knew it would be at an end. Suddenly Bee was looking down a long, dark, intimidating tunnel at a future she could no longer predict and accepting that if Sergios Demonides decided that he did want to marry her, she would be in no position to refuse him.

'If your cousin's children are disturbed, I have no experience with that sort of problem,' Bee warned him quietly. 'I have no experience of raising children either and I'm not a miracle worker.'

'I don't believe in miracles, so I'm not expecting one,' Sergios said very drily, resting sardonic golden eyes on her strained face. 'There would also be conditions which you would have to fulfil to meet my requirements.'

Bee said nothing. Still reeling in shock at the concept of marrying him, she did not trust herself to speak. As for his expectations, she was convinced they would be high and that he would have a very long list of them. Unhappily for her, Sergios Demonides was unaccustomed to settling for anything less than perfection and the very best in any field. She dug out her phone and rang her mother to warn her that she would be late home. By the time she finished the call the limousine was already filtering down a driveway adorned with silver birch trees just coming into leaf. They drew up outside a detached house large and grand enough to be described as a mansion.

'My London base.' Sergios shot her a rapier-eyed

glance from level dark eyes. 'One of your duties as my wife would be taking charge of my various homes and ensuring that the households run smoothly.'

The word 'wife', allied to that other word, 'duties', sounded horribly nineteenth century to Bee's ears. 'Are you a domestic tyrant?' she enquired.

Sergios sent her a frowning appraisal. 'Is that a joke?'

'No, but there is something very Victorian about mentioning the word wife in the same sentence as duties.'

His handsome mouth quirked. 'You first referred to the role as a job and I prefer to regard it in the same light.'

But Bee very much liked the job she already had and registered in some consternation that she was literally being asked to put her money where her mouth was. She had done what her father had asked her to do without thinking through the likely consequences of success. Now those consequences had well and truly come home to roost with her. As she accompanied Sergios into a sizeable foyer, he issued instructions to the manservant greeting him and escorted Bee into a massive drawing room.

'Unlike your sister, you're very quiet,' he remarked.

'You've taken me by surprise,' Bee admitted rue-fully.

'You look bewildered. Why?' Sergios breathed, his bronzed eyes impatient. 'I have no desire for the usual kind of wife. I don't want the emotional ties, the demands or the restrictions, but on a practical basis a

woman to fulfil that role would be a very useful addition to my life.'

'Perhaps I just don't see what's in it for me—apart
from you buying my father's hotels which would hopefully ensure my mother's security for the foreseeable
future,' Bee volunteered frankly.

'If I married you, *I* would ensure your mother's
security for the rest of her life,' Sergios extended with
quiet carrying emphasis, his dark deep drawl vibrating
in the big room. 'Even if we were to part at a later date
you would never have to worry about her care again,
nor would she have to look to your father for support. I
will personally ensure that your mother has everything
she requires, including the very best of medical treatment available to someone with her condition.'

His words engulfed her like a crashing burst of thun-
der heralding a brighter dawn. Instantly Bee thought of
the expensive extras that could improve Emilia Blake's
quality of life. In place of Bee's home-made efforts,
regular professional physiotherapy sessions might be
able to strengthen Emilia's wasted limbs and something might be found to ease the breathing difficulties
that sometimes afflicted her. Sergios, Bee appreciated
suddenly, was rich enough to make a huge difference
to her mother's life.

A young woman in a nanny uniform entered the
room with a baby about eighteen months old in her
arms and two small children trailing unenthusiastically
in their wake.

'Thank you. Leave the children with us,' Sergios instructed.

Set down on the carpet the youngest child instantly began to howl, tears streaming down her little screwed-up face, a toddler of about three years old grabbed hold of Sergios's trousered leg while the older boy came to a suspicious halt several feet away.

'It's all right, pet.' Bee scooped up the baby and the little girl stopped mid-howl, settling anxious blue eyes on her. 'What's her name?'

'Eleni…and this is Milo,' Sergios told her, detaching the clinging toddler from his leg with difficulty and giving him a little helpful prod in Bee's direction as if he was hoping that the child would embrace her instead.

'And you have to be Paris,' Bee said to the older boy as she crouched down to greet Milo. 'My sister Zara told me that you got a new bike for your birthday.'

Paris didn't smile but he moved closer as Bee sank down on the sofa with the baby girl in her arms. Milo, clearly desperate for attention, clambered up beside her and tried to get on her lap with his sister but there wasn't enough room. 'Hello, Milo.'

'Paris, remember your manners,' Sergios interposed sternly.

With a scared look, Paris extended a skinny arm to shake hands formally, his eyes slewing evasively away from hers. Bee invited him to sit down beside her and told him that she was a teacher. When she asked him about the school he attended he shot her a frightened look and hurriedly glanced away. It did not take a genius to guess that Paris could be having problems at school. Of the three children, Milo was the most normal, a bundle of toddler energy in need of attention and entertainment. Paris, however, was tense and troubled while the little girl was very quiet and worryingly unresponsive.

After half an hour Sergios had seen enough to convince him that Beatriz Blake was the woman he needed to smooth out the rough and troublesome places in his life. Her warmth and energy drew the children and she was completely relaxed with them where her sister had been nervous and, while friendly, over-anxious to please. Bee, on the other hand, emanated a calm authority that ensured respect. He called the nanny back to remove the children again.

'You mentioned conditions...' Bee reminded him, returning to their earlier conversation and striving to stick to necessary facts. Yet when she tried to accept that she was actually considering marrying the Greek billionaire the idea seemed so remote and unreal and impossible that her thoughts swam in a sea of bemusement.

'Yes.' Poised by the window with fading light gleaming over his luxuriant black hair and accenting the hard angles and hollows of his handsome features, Sergios commanded her full attention without even trying. His next words, however, took her very much by surprise.

'I have a mistress. Melita is not negotiable,' Sergios informed her coolly. 'Occasionally I have other interests as well. I am discreet. I do not envisage any headlines about that aspect of my life.'

The level of such candour when she had become accustomed to his cool reserve left Bee reeling in shock. He had a mistress called Melita? Was that a Greek name? Whatever, he was not faithful to his mistress and clearly not a one-woman man. Bee could feel her cheeks inflame as her imagination filled with the kind of colourful images she did not want to have in his vicinity. She lowered her lashes in embarrassment, her rebellious brain still engaged in serving up a creative picture of that lean bronzed body of his entangled with that of a sinuous sexy blonde.

'I do not expect intimacy with you,' Sergios spelt out. 'On the other hand if you decide that you want a child of your own it would be selfish of me to deny you that option—'

'Well, then, there's always IVF,' Bee broke in hurriedly.

'From what I've heard it's not that reliable.'

Bee was now studying her feet with fixed attention. He had a mistress. He didn't expect to share a bed with her. But where did that leave her? A wife who wasn't a wife except in name.

'What sort of a life am I supposed to lead?' Bee asked him abruptly, looking up, green eyes glinting like fresh leaves in rain.

'Meaning?' Sergios prompted, pleased that she had demonstrated neither annoyance nor interest on the subject of his mistress. But then why should she care what he did? That was exactly the attitude he wanted her to take.

'Are you expecting me to take lovers as well... discreetly?' Bee queried, studying him while her colour rose and burned like scalding hot irons on her cheeks and she fought her embarrassment with all her might. It was a fair question, a sensible question and she refused to let prudishness prevent her from asking it.

His dark eyes glittered gold with anger. 'Of course not.'

Bee was frowning. 'I'm trying to understand how you expect such a marriage to work. You surely can't be suggesting that a woman of my age should accept a future in which any form of physical intimacy is against the rules?' she quantified very stiffly, fighting her mortification every step of the way.

Put like that her objection sounded reasonable but Sergios could no more have accepted the prospect of an unfaithful wife than he could have cut off his right arm. Features taut and grim, his big powerful length rigid, he breathed with the clarity of strong feeling, 'I could not agree to you taking lovers.'

'That old hypocritical double standard,' Bee murmured, strangely amused by his appalled reaction and not even grasping why she should feel that way. So what was good for the goose was not, in this case, good for the gander? Yet she could barely believe that she was even having such a discussion with him. After all, she was a twenty-four-year-old virgin, a piece of information that would no doubt shock him almost as much as the idea of a wife with an independent sexual appetite.

In response to that scornful comment, Sergios shot her a seething appraisal, his dark eyes flaming like hot coals. 'Don't speak to me in that tone…'

Lesson one, Bee noted, he has a very volatile temper. She breathed in deep, quelling her wicked stab of amusement at his incredulous reaction to the idea of an adulterous wife. 'I asked you a reasonable question and you did not give me a reasonable answer. How long do you expect this marriage to last?'

'At least until the children grow up.'

'My youth,' Bee remarked without any emotion, but it was true. By the time the children acquired independence her years of youth would be long gone.

Sergios was studying her, recalling those lush violin curves in the evening gown she had worn at their first meeting. Full pouting breasts, generous womanly hips. He was startled when that mental picture provoked the heavy tightness of arousal at his groin.

'Then we make it a real marriage,' Sergios fielded with sardonic bite, blanking out his physical response with male impatience. 'That is the only other possible option on the table. If you want a man in your bed you will have me, no other.'

The flush in Bee's cheeks swept up to her brow and her dismayed eyes skimmed away from the intrusion of his. 'I don't really wish to continue this discussion but I should say that while you have other women in your life I would not be willing to enter an intimate relationship with you.'

'We're wasting time with this nonsense and we're adults. We will deal with such problems as and when they arise,' Sergios delivered curtly. 'There will be a pre-nuptial contract for you to sign—'

'You mentioned your homes and your, er…mistress. What other conditions are you planning to impose?'

'Nothing that I think need concern you. Our lawyers can deal with the contracts. If you choose to argue about terms you may do so through them,' Sergios completed in a crushing tone of finality. 'Now, if you will excuse me, I will have you driven home. I have business to take care of before I leave for New York.'

Bee, who had had a vague idea that he might invite her to stay to dinner, learned her mistake. She smoothed down her raincoat and rose slowly upright. 'I have a condition as well. You would have to agree to be polite, respectful and considerate of my happiness at all times.'

As that unanticipated demand hit him Sergios froze halfway to the door, wondering if she was criticising his manners. Since he had reached eighteen years of age before appreciating that certain courtesies even existed, he was unusually sensitive to the suggestion. He turned back, brooding black eyes glittering below the lush fan of his lashes. 'That would be a tall order. I'm selfish, quick-tempered and often curt. I expect my staff to adapt to my ways.'

'If I marry you I won't be a member of your staff. I'll be somewhere between a wife and an employee. You will have to make allowances and changes.' Bee studied him expectantly, for it would be disastrous if she allowed him to assume that he could have everything his way. She had no illusions about the fact that she was dealing with a very powerful personality, who would ride roughshod over her needs and wishes and ignore them altogether if it suited him to do so.

Sergios was taken aback at her nerve in challenging him, viewing him with those cool assessing green eyes as though he were an intellectual puzzle to be solved. His stubborn jaw line squared. 'I may make some allowances but I will call the shots. If we're going ahead with this arrangement, I want the wedding to take place soon so that you can move in here to be with the children.'

Consternation filled Bee's face. 'But I can't leave my mother—'

'You're a teacher, good at talking but not at listening,' Sergios chided with a curled lip. '*Listen* to what I tell you. Your mother will be taken care of in every possible way.'

'In every possible way that facilitates what *you* want!' Bee slammed back at him with angry emphasis.

He raised a brow, sardonic amusement in his intent dark gaze. 'Would you really expect anything different from me?'

CHAPTER THREE

LIFE as Bee knew it began to change very soon after that thought-provoking parting from Sergios.

Indeed Bee came home from school the very next day to find her mother troubled by the fact that her father had made an angry phone call to her that same afternoon.

'Monty told me that you're getting married,' Emilia Blake recounted with a look of frank disbelief. 'But I told him that you weren't even seeing anyone.'

Bee went pink. 'I didn't tell you but—'

Her mother stared at her with wide, startled eyes. 'My goodness, there is someone! But you only go out twice a week to your exercise classes—'

Bee grimaced and reached for her mother's frail hands. Not for anything would she have told the older woman any truth that might upset her. Indeed when it came to her mother's peace of mind, Bee was more than ready to lie. 'I'm sorry I wasn't more honest with you. I do want you to be happy for me.'

'So, obviously you weren't at classes all those evenings,' Emilia assumed in some amusement while she studied her blushing daughter with fond pride in her shadowed eyes. 'I'm so pleased. Your father and I haven't set you a very good example and I know you haven't had the same choices as other girls your age—'

'You still haven't told me what my father was angry about,' Bee cut in anxiously.

'Some business deal he's involved in with your future husband hasn't gone the way he hoped,' Emilia responded in a dismissive tone. 'What on earth does he expect you to do about it? Take my advice, don't get involved.'

Dismayed by her explanation, Bee had tensed. 'Exactly what did Dad say?'

'You know how moody he can be when things don't go his way. Tell me about Sergios—isn't he the man you met at that dinner your father invited you to a couple of months ago?'

'Yes.' So, although the marriage was going ahead, it seemed that her father was not to profit as richly as he had expected from the deal. Clearly that was why the older man was angry, but Bee thought there was a rare justice to the news that her sacrifice was unlikely to enrich her father: threats did not deserve a reward.

'My word, you've been having a genuine whirlwind romance,' Emilia gathered with a blossoming smile of approval. 'Are you sure that this Sergios is the man for you, Bee?'

Bee recalled Sergios Demonides's assurance that she would never again have to look to her father to support her mother. She remembered the fearless impact of those shrewd dark eyes and although she was apprehensive about the future she had signed up for she did believe that Sergios would stand by his word. 'Yes, Mum. Yes, I'm sure.'

Sergios phoned that evening to tell her that a member of his personal staff would be liaising with her over the wedding arrangements. He suggested that she hand in her notice immediately. His impatience came as a surprise when he had seemingly been content to wait several months before taking her sister Zara to the altar. He then followed that bombshell up with the news that he expected her to move to Greece after the wedding.

'But you have a house here,' Bee protested.

'I will visit London regularly but Greece is my home.'

'When you were planning to marry Zara—'

'Stop there—you and I will reach our own arrangements,' Sergios cut in deflatingly.

'I don't want to leave my mother alone in London.'

'Your mother will accompany us to Greece—but only after we have enjoyed a suitable newly married period of togetherness. I have already issued instructions to have appropriate accommodation organised for her. Have you heard from your father yet?'

In shock at the news that he was already making plans for her mother to accompany them to Greece, Bee was in a complete daze, her every expectation blown apart. On every issue he seemed to be one step ahead of her. 'I believe he was annoyed about something when he was talking to my mother today,' she admitted reluctantly.

'Your father did not get the deal he wanted,' Sergios

informed her bluntly. 'But that is nothing to do with you and so I told him on your behalf.'

'Did you indeed?' Bee questioned with a frown, her hackles rising at the increasingly authoritarian note in his explanations. Acting as chief spokesperson for the women in his life evidently came very naturally to Sergios. If she wasn't careful to keep his controlling streak within bounds, Bee thought darkly, he would soon have her behaving with all the self-will of a glove puppet.

'You are the woman I'm going to marry. It is not appropriate for your father to speak of either you or your mother with disrespect and I have warned him in that regard.'

Bee's blood ran cold in her veins, for she could picture the scene and the warning with Monty Blake raging recklessly and Sergios cold as ice and equally precise in his razor-sharp cutting edge. Her father was outspoken in temper but Sergios was altogether a more guarded and astute individual.

'How soon can you move into my London house?' Sergios pressed. 'It would please me if you could make that move this week.'

'*This* week?' Bee exclaimed in dismay.

'The wedding will be soon. I'm out of the country and the domestic staff are in charge of the children right now. If possible I would prefer you to be in the house while I'm away. If you're concerned about your mother being alone, you need not be—I've already requested a live-in companion for her from a vetted source.'

Bee came off the phone feeling unusually harassed

as she accepted that regardless of how she felt about it, her life was about to be turned upside down. Although she could not fault Sergios for his wish that she become involved with the children as soon as possible, she felt very much like an employee having her extensive duties listed and held over her head. As she had already told her mother about the three orphaned kids in Sergios's life, Emilia Blake was quick to understand her daughter's position.

'You really *must* put Sergios and those children first, Bee,' the older woman instructed worriedly. 'You mustn't make me more of a burden than I already am. I'll manage, I always have.'

Bee gently squeezed her parent's shoulder. 'You've never been a burden to me.'

'Sergios expects to come first and that's normal for a man who wants to marry you,' Emilia told her daughter. 'Don't let me become a bone of contention between you.'

Having drawn up innumerable lists and tendered her letter of resignation, for it was the last day of the spring term, Bee attended her evening pole exercise class and worked up a sweat while she tried not to fret about the many things that she still had to do. The list grew even longer after a visit from Annabel, the glossily efficient PA Sergios had put in charge of the wedding.

'I'm to have a consultation with a personal stylist and shopper?' Bee repeated weakly, staring down at the heavy schedule of appointments already set up for her over the Easter break that began that weekend. As well as a consultation with an upmarket legal firm concerning the pre-nuptial agreement, there was a day-long booking at a famous beauty salon. 'That's ridiculous. That's got nothing to do with the wedding.'

'Mr Demonides gave me my instructions,' Annabel told her in a steely tone.

Bee swallowed hard and compressed her lips. She would argue her case directly with Sergios. Possibly he thought a makeover was every woman's dream but Bee felt deeply insulted by the proposition. Her mother's new live-in companion/carer arrived that same evening and Bee chatted to her and helped her to settle in before she packed her own case ready for her move into Sergios's house the next morning.

When she arrived there she was shown upstairs into a palatial bedroom suite furnished with every possible necessity and luxury, right down to headed notepaper on a dainty feminine desk. The household seemed to operate just like an exclusive hotel. A maid came to the door to offer to unpack for her. Overcoming her discomfort at the prospect of being waited on by the staff, Bee smiled in determined agreement and went off to find the children instead.

Only Eleni, the youngest, however, was at home. Paris was at school and Milo was at a play group, the nanny explained. A rota of three nannies looked after the children round the clock. Bee found out what she needed to know about the children's basic routine and got down on her knees on the nursery carpet to play with Eleni. Initially when she was close by and utilised eye contact the little girl was more responsive but her attention was hard to hold. When the wind caught the door and it slammed shut Bee flinched from the loud noise but noted in surprise that Eleni did not react at all.

'Has her hearing been checked?' Bee asked with a frown.

The newly qualified nanny, who had replaced someone else and only recently, had no idea. During the preceding months the children had suffered several changes in that line and had enjoyed little continuity of care. Having tracked down the children's health record booklets and drawn another blank, Bee finally phoned the medical practice to enquire. She discovered that Eleni had missed out on a standard hearing check-up a couple of months earlier and she made a fresh appointment for the child. When she returned to the nursery the nanny was engaged in conducting her own basic tests and even to the untrained eye it did seem as though the little girl might have a problem with her hearing.

Milo, who was indiscriminately affectionate with almost everybody, greeted her as though they were long-lost friends. She was reading a picture book to the little boy as he dropped off for a nap when Paris appeared in the nursery doorway and frowned at the sight of her with his little brother.

'Are you looking after us now?' Paris asked thinly.

'For some of the time. You won't need so many nannies because I'll be living here from now on. Sergios and I will be getting married in a few weeks.' Bee explained, striving to sound much calmer than she actually felt about that event.

Paris shot her a resentful glance and walked past

into his own room, carefully shutting the door behind him to underline his desire for privacy. Resolving to respect his wishes until she had visited his school and met his teacher, Bee suppressed a rueful sigh. She was a stranger. What more could she expect? Establishing a relationship with children who had lost their parents, their home and everything familiar only months before would take time and a good deal of trust on their part and she had to hope that Sergios was prepared for the reality that only time would improve the situation.

Forty-eight hours later, it was a novelty for Sergios to return to a house with a woman in residence and not worry about what awaited him. He could still vividly remember when he had never known what might be in store for him when he entered his own home. That experience had left him with an unshakable need to conserve his own space. Bee didn't count, he told himself irritably, she was here for the kids, not for him personally and she would soon learn to respect his privacy. He was taken aback, however, when his housekeeper informed him that Bee had gone out. He was even less impressed when he rang her cell phone and she admitted that she was travelling back on public transport.

'I wasn't expecting you back this soon…I was visiting my mother,' she told him defensively.

When Bee finally walked back into the mansion, she was flushed and breathless from walking very fast from the bus stop and thoroughly resentful of the censorious tone Sergios had used with her on the phone. Didn't he think she had a right to go out? Was she supposed to ask for permission first? Was her life to be entirely consumed by his? Heavy dark brown hair flopping untidily round her face, she stepped into the echoing hall.

Sergios appeared in a doorway and she lost her breath at that first glimpse, his impact thrumming through her like a sudden collision with a brick wall. He was still dressed in a black business suit and striped shirt, his only hint of informality the loosening of his tie. He looked like an angry dark angel, lean strong features taut, stubborn jaw line squared and once again he needed a shave. Stubble suited him though, sending his raw masculine sex appeal right off the charts, she conceded numbly, reeling in shock from the sudden loud thump of her heartbeat in her ears and the dryness of her mouth.

Sergios subjected his flustered bride-to-be to a hard scrutiny. From her chaotic hair to her ill-fitting jeans she was a mess. He realised that he was eager for the makeover to commence. 'I gave orders that if you went out you were to use a car and driver,' he reminded her flatly.

Bee reacted with a pained look. 'A bit much for a girl used to travelling by bus and tube.'

'But you are no longer that girl. You are the woman who is to become my wife,' Sergios retorted crisply. 'And I expect you to adapt accordingly. I am a wealthy man and you could be targeted by a mugger or even a kidnapper. Personal security must now become an integral part of your lifestyle.'

The reference to kidnapping cooled the heated words on Bee's ready tongue and, although she had stiffened, she nodded her head. 'I'll remember that in future.'

Satisfied, Sergios spread wide the door behind him. 'I want to talk to you.'

'Yes, we do need to talk,' Bee allowed, although in truth she wanted to run upstairs to her bedroom and stay there until her adolescent hormonal reaction to him died a natural death and stopped embarrassing her. Her face felt hot as a fire. It had been such a long time since a man had had that effect on her. When it had happened in his office she had assumed it was simply the effect of nerves and mortification but this time around she was less naive and ready to be honest with herself. As a physical specimen, Sergios Demonides was without parallel. He was absolutely gorgeous and few women would be impervious to his powerful attraction. That was all it was, she told herself urgently as she walked past him, her head held high, into a room furnished like an upmarket office. He had buckets of lethal sex appeal and all her body was telling her was that she had a healthy set of hormones. It was that simple, that basic, nothing to fret about. It certainly did not mean that she was genuinely attracted to him.

Sergios asked Bee about the children and she relaxed a little, telling him that Eleni had performed very poorly at her hearing test and the doctor suspected that she was suffering from glue ear. The toddler was to be examined by a consultant with a view to receiving treatment. Bee went on to talk about the picture that Paris had drawn on his bedroom wall. She considered his depiction of his once-happy family complete with parents and home to be self-explanatory. He had no photos of his late parents and Bee asked Sergios if there was a reason for that.

'I thought it would be less upsetting that way—he has to move on.'

'I think Paris needs the time to grieve and that family photos would help,' Bee pronounced with care.

'I put his parents' personal effects into storage. I'll have them checked for photo albums,' Sergios proffered, surprising her by accepting her opinion.

'I think that all that is wrong is that the children have endured too many changes in a short space of time. They need a settled home life.'

Sergios expelled his breath with a slight hiss, his expression grim. 'I've done my best but clearly it wasn't good enough. I know nothing about children. I don't even know how to talk to them.'

'The same way you talk to anyone else—with interest and kindness.'

A grudging smile played at the corners of his sardonic mouth. 'Not my style. I'm more into barking orders, Beatriz.'

'Call me Bee…everyone does.'

'No, Bee makes you sound like a maiden aunt. Beatriz is pretty.'

Bee almost winced at that opinion. 'But I'm not.'

'Give the beauty professionals a chance,' Sergios advised without hesitation.

At that advice, Bee took an offended stance, her spine very straight, her chin lifting. 'Actually that's what I wanted to discuss with you.'

With veiled attention, Sergios watched the buttons pull on her shirt, struggling to contain the full globes of her breasts. He wanted to rip open the shirt and release that luscious flesh from captivity into his hands. More than a comfortable handful, he reckoned hungrily, his body hardening. Startled by the imagery, he decided that he had to be in dire need of sexual fulfilment. Clearly he had waited too long to release his desire. He did not want to look on his future wife in that light.

Lost in her own thoughts, Bee breathed in deep and spoke with the abruptness of discomfiture. 'I don't want a makeover. I'm happy as I am. Take me or leave me.'

Sergios was not amused by that invitation. His clever dark eyes rested on her uneasy face. 'You must appreciate that when it comes to your appearance a certain amount of effort is required. Right now, you're making no effort at all.'

Incensed by that critical and wounding statement, Bee threw her slim shoulders back. 'I'm not going to change myself to conform to some outdated sexist code.'

Sergios released an impatient groan. 'Leave the feminism out of it. What's the matter with you? Why don't you care about your appearance?'

'There's nothing the matter with me,' Bee answered with spirit. 'I'm just comfortable with myself as I am.'

'But I'm not. I expect you to smarten up as part of the job.'

'That's too personal a request…beyond your remit,' Bee spelt out in case he hadn't yet got the message. 'I have already given up my home, my job…surely how I choose to look is my business.'

His brilliant dark eyes flamed gold, dense black

lashes lowering over them to enhance the flash-fire effect. 'Not if you want to marry me, it's not.'

Bee flung her head back, glossy chestnut strands trailing across her shoulders, an angry flush across her cheekbones. 'That's ridiculous.'

'Is it? I find you unreasonable. It's normal for a woman to take pride in her appearance. What happened to you that made you lose all interest?' Sergios demanded starkly.

The silence hummed like a buzz saw against Bee's suddenly exposed nerves. She very nearly flinched, for that incisive question had cut deep and hit home hard. There had been a time when Bee had taken great interest in her personal appearance and had chosen her clothes with equal care. But it was not a period she cared to recall. 'I don't want to talk about this. It's absolutely none of your business.'

'The makeover is not negotiable. There will be public occasions when I expect you to appear by my side. There is no longer any excuse for you to go around in unflattering clothes with your hair in a mess,' Sergios asserted with derisive cool.

Rage surged up through Bee like lava seeking a vent. 'How dare you speak to me like that?'

'I'm being honest with you. Come over here,' Sergios urged, a firm hand at her elbow guiding her across to the mirror on the wall. 'And tell me what you see…'

Forced to acknowledge a reflection that displayed windblown hair, an old shirt and baggy jeans, Bee just wanted to slap him. Her teeth gritted. 'It doesn't matter what you say or what you want. I'm not having a makeover and that's that!'

'No makeover, no marriage,' Sergios traded without a second of hesitation. 'It's part of the job and I will not compromise on my expectations.'

Trembling though she was with the force of her emotions, Bee slung him a look of loathing and lifted and dropped her hands in a gesture of finality. 'Then there'll be no marriage because we need to get one thing straight right now, Sergios—'

Sergios lifted a sardonic black brow. 'Do we?'

'You are not going to rule over me like this! You are *not* going to tell me what I do with my hair or what I should wear,' Bee launched back furiously at him, green eyes pure and bright as emeralds in sunshine. 'You're a domineering guy but I won't stand for that.'

Her magnificent bosom was heaving. Was he, at heart, a breast man? he suddenly wondered, questioning his preoccupation with those swelling mounds and seeking an excuse for his strange behaviour. Her eyes were astonishingly vivid in colour. Indeed she looked more attractive in the grip of temper than he had ever seen her but he would not tolerate defiance. 'It is your choice, Beatriz,' Sergios intoned coldly. 'It has always been your choice. At this moment I am having second thoughts about marrying you because you are acting irrationally.'

Assailed by that charge, Bee quivered with sheer fury. '*I'm* being irrational?' she raked back at him incredulously. 'Explain that to me.'

His face set in forbidding lines, Sergios opened the door for her exit instead. 'This discussion is at an end.'

Bee stalked up the stairs in a tempestuous rage. She had never stalked before and she had definitely never been so mad with anger but Sergios Demonides had made her see red. Rot the man, rot him to hell, she thought wildly. How dared he criticise her like that? How dared he ask what had happened to make her lose interest in her appearance? How dared he have that much insight into her actions?

For something traumatic *had* happened to Bee way back when she was madly in love with a man who had ultimately dumped her. That man had replaced her with a little ditsy blonde whose looks and shallow personality had mocked what Bee had once foolishly believed was a good solid relationship. After that devastating wake-up call, the fussing with hair, nails and make-up, not to mention the continual agonising over which outfits were most becoming, had begun to seem utterly superficial, pathetic and a total waste of time. After all, given a free choice Jon had gone for a woman as physically and mentally different from Bee as he could find. For months afterwards, Bee had despised herself for having slavishly followed the girlie code that insisted that a woman's looks were of paramount importance to a man. That code had let her down badly for in spite of all her efforts she had still lost Jon and ever since then she had refused to fuss over her appearance and compete with the true beauties of the world.

And why should she turn herself inside out for Sergios Demonides? He was just like every other man she had met from her father to Jon. Sergios might have briefly flattered her by telling her that she was a loyal daughter and a gifted teacher, but regardless of those qualities he was still judging her by her looks and ready to dump her for failing to meet his standards of feminine beauty. Well, that didn't matter to her, did it?

No, *but* it would certainly matter to her mother, a little voice chimed up quellingly at the back of Bee's brain and she froze in consternation, recalled to reality with a vengeance by that acknowledgement. If Bee backed out of the marriage, Emilia Blake would most probably lose her home, for Bee was convinced that her angry father would try to punish Bee for his failure to get the price he wanted for the Royale hotel group. Monty Blake was that sort of a man. He always needed someone else to blame for his mistakes and losses and Bee and her mother would provide easy targets for his ire.

And if Bee didn't marry Sergios, Paris, Milo and Eleni would suffer yet another adult betrayal. Bee had encouraged the children to bond with her, had announced that she was marrying Sergios and had promised to stay with them. Paris had looked unimpressed but Bee had guessed that he wanted her to prove herself before he took the risk of trusting her. Her sister Zara had already let those children down by winning their acceptance and then vanishing from their lives when she realised that she couldn't go through with marrying their guardian because she had fallen for another man. Was Bee willing to behave in an equally self-centred fashion?

All over the prospect of a visit to a beauty salon and some shopping trips? Wasn't walking out on Sergios because of such trivial activities a case of overkill? He had too much insight though, she acknowledged unhappily. When he had asked her what had happened to her to make her so uninterested in her appearance he had unnerved her and hurt her pride. That was why she had lost her head. He had mortified her when he marched her over to that mirror and forced her to see herself through his eyes. And unhappily Bee had not liked what she saw either. She had seen that her hair needed a decent cut and her wardrobe required an urgent overhaul and that she was being thoroughly unreasonable when she expected a man of his sophistication and faultless grooming to accept her in her current au naturel state.

Bee tidied her hair before descending the stairs at a much more decorous pace than she had raced up them. A mutinous expression tensing her oval face, she lifted a hand as if she was about to knock on the door and then she thought better of the gesture and simply walked back unannounced into his home office.

Sergios was at his desk working on his laptop. His head lifted and glittering dark eyes lit on her, his expression hard and unwelcoming.

It took near physical force for Bee to rise above her hurt pride and part her lips to say, 'All right, I'll do it… the makeover thing.'

'What changed your mind?' Sergios pressed impassively, his expression not softening in the slightest at her capitulation.

'My mother's needs…the children's,' she admitted

truthfully. 'I can't walk out on my responsibilities like that.'

His hard cynical mouth twisted. 'People do it every day.'

Bee stood a little straighter. 'But I don't.'

Sergios pushed away his laptop and rose fluidly upright, astonishingly graceful for a man of his height and powerful build. 'Don't fight me,' he told her huskily. 'I don't like it.'

'But you don't always know best.'

'There are more subtle approaches.' He offered her a drink and she accepted, hovering awkwardly by his desk while she cradled a glass of wine that she didn't really want.

'I'm not sure I do subtle,' Bee confided.

He was suddenly as remote as the Andes. 'You'll learn. I won't be easy to live with.'

And for the first time as she tipped the glass to her lips and tasted an expensive wine as smooth and silky as satin, Bee wondered about Melita. Was he different with his mistress? Was she blonde or brunette? How long had she been in his life? Where did she live? How often did he see her? The torrent of questions blazing a mortifying trail through her head made her redden as she attempted to suppress that flood of unwelcome curiosity. It was none of her business and she didn't care what he did, she told herself squarely. She was to be his wife in name only, nothing more.

'We will drink to our wedding,' Sergios murmured lazily.

'And a better understanding?' Bee completed.

Sergios dealt her a dark appraisal. 'We don't need to understand each other. We won't need to spend that much time together. After a while we won't even have to occupy the same house at the same time...'

Chilled to the marrow by that prediction, Bee drank her wine and set the glass down on the desk. 'Goodnight, then,' she told him prosaically.

And as she climbed the stairs she wondered why she should feel lonelier than she had ever felt in her life before. After all, had she expected Sergios to offer her his company and support? Was he not even prepared to share parenting responsibilities with her? It seemed that in his head the parameters of their relationship were already set in stone: he didn't love her, didn't desire her and, in short, didn't need her except as a mother to the children. Being his wife really would be a job more than anything else...

CHAPTER FOUR

BEE stepped out of the spacious changing cubicle and up onto the dais to get the best possible view of her wedding dress in the mirrored walls of the showroom.

Although it galled her to admit it, Sergios had done astonishingly well. She had had a sharp exchange of words with him when he had startled her with the news that he had actually selected a gown for her.

'What on earth were you thinking of?' Bee had demanded on the phone. 'A woman looks forward to choosing her wedding dress.'

'I was at a fashion show in Milan and the model came down the catwalk in it and I knew immediately that it was *your* dress,' Sergios had drawled with immense assurance.

She had wanted to ask him whom he had accompanied to the fashion show, for she did not believe that he had attended one alone, but she had swallowed back the nosy question. Ignorance, she had decided, was safer than too much information in that department. What she didn't know couldn't hurt her, she told herself staunchly, and not that she was in any danger of being hurt. She could not afford to develop silly notions or possessive feelings towards a man who would not even share a bed with her. Although he had *offered*, she reminded herself darkly, preferring to sacrifice himself if she decided that she could not live without sex rather than allow her to engage in an extra-marital affair.

Now she posed in the wedding gown Sergios had chosen for her, noting how the style showcased her voluptuous cleavage while emphasising her small waist. The neckline was lower than she liked but the fitted bodice definitely flattered her fuller figure. Apparently, Sergios hadn't earned his notorious reputation with women without picking up some useful fashion tips along the way. Bee would have been the first to admit that her appearance had already undergone a major transformation. Her chestnut hair now curved in a sleek layered shoulder-length cut that framed her face, all the heaviness gone. Cosmetics had helped her rediscover her cheekbones and accentuate her best features while every inch of her from her manicured nails to her smooth skin had been waxed, polished and moisturised to as close to perfection as a mortal woman was capable of getting. The irony was that, far from feeling exploited or belittled by the beauty makeover, she was enjoying the energising feel of knowing she looked her very best.

In thirty-six hours it would be her wedding day, Bee acknowledged, breathing in deep and slow to steady her nerves. That afternoon she had a final appointment to sign the pre-nuptial agreement, which had already been explained to her in fine detail during her first visit to the upmarket legal firm employed by Sergios to protect her interests. Her mother's long-term care was comprehensively covered, but she had had to request the right of regular access to the children in the event of their marriage breaking down. Bee was more concerned that Sergios might refuse that demand than she was by the fact that divorce would leave her a wealthy woman. The more time she spent with Paris, Milo and Eleni the more they felt like *her* children.

As Bee left the showroom, elegant in a grey striped dress and light jacket, a bodyguard was by her side and within the space of a minute a limousine was purring up to the kerb to pick her up. She was getting used to being spoilt, she registered guiltily, as she emerged again directly outside the lawyer's plush offices. After only three weeks she was already forgetting what it was like to walk in the rain or queue for a bus.

She was seated in the reception area when she saw a familiar face and she was so shaken by the resulting jolt of recognition that she simply stared, her heartbeat thumping very loudly. It was her ex-boyfriend, Jon Townsend, and more than three years had passed since their last meeting. Now, without the smallest warning, there he was only ten feet away, smartly clad in a business suit and tie. He was slim, dark-haired and attractive, not particularly tall but still taller than she was. As she struggled to overcome her shock she wondered if perhaps he worked for the firm because he had just qualified in law when she first met him.

Jon turned his head and recognised her at almost the same moment as the receptionist invited her to go into Mr Smyth's office. Blue eyes full of surprise, Jon crossed the foyer with a frown. 'Bee?' he queried as though he couldn't quite believe that she was physically there in front of him.

'Jon…sorry, I have an appointment,' Bee responded, rising to her feet.

'You look terrific,' Jon told her warmly.

'Thanks.' Her smile was a mere stretch of her tense lips, for she had not forgotten the pain he had caused her and all her concentration was focused on retaining her dignity. 'Do you work here?'

'Yes, since last year. I'll see you after your appointment and we'll chat,' Jon declared.

Her fake smile dimmed at that disconcerting prospect and she hastened into Halston Smyth's office with a peculiar sense of both relief and anticipation. What could Jon possibly want to chat to her about? It might have happened three long years ago but he *had* ditched her, for goodness' sake. Did they even have any old times to catch up on? Having lost contact with mutual friends after they broke up, she did not think so. He was married now—or at least so she had heard—might even have children, although when she had known him he had not been sure he wanted any. Of course he had been equally unsure he was the marrying kind until he had met Jenna, Bee's little blonde bubbly replacement, the daughter of a high-court judge. A most useful connection for an ambitious young legal whiz-kid, her more cynical self had thought back then.

Mr Smyth ran through the pre-nup again while a more junior member of staff hovered attentively. On her first visit, Bee had realised that as the future wife of a billionaire she was considered big business and they were eager to please. As soon as she realised that her desire to retain contact with the children in the event of a divorce had been incorporated in the agreement, she relaxed. In spite of all the warnings to carefully consider what she was doing she signed on the dotted line while wondering how soon she could book physiotherapy sessions for her mother.

Mr Smyth escorted her all the way to the lift and at the last possible minute before the doors could close Jon stepped in to join her and her bodyguard.

'There's a wine bar round the corner,' Jon informed her casually.

Her brow furrowed. 'I'm not sure we have much to talk about.'

'Well, I can't physically persuade you to join me with a security man in tow,' he quipped with a familiar grin.

'Do you know this gentleman, Miss Blake?' her bodyguard, Tom, asked, treating Jon to an openly suspicious appraisal.

Meeting Jon's amused look, Bee almost giggled. 'Yes. Yes, I do,' she confirmed. 'I can't stay long, though.'

Curiosity had to be behind his request, Bee decided. After all, three years ago when Jon had been with her she had been a final-year student teacher from a fairly ordinary background. While her father might be wealthy, Bee had never enjoyed a personal allowance or, aside of the occasional family invite, an entrée into Monty Blake's exclusive world. Jon was most probably aware that she was on the brink of marrying one of the richest men in Europe and wondering how that had come about. She suppressed a rueful smile over the awareness that few people would believe the truth behind that particular development.

In the bar her bodyguard chose a seat nearby and talked on his phone. Jon ordered drinks and made light conversation. She remembered when his smile had made her tummy tighten and her heart beat a little faster and crushed the recollection.

'Jenna and I got a divorce a couple of months ago,' Jon volunteered wryly.

'I'm sorry to hear that,' Bee said uncomfortably.

'It was an infatuation.' Jon pulled a rueful face. 'I lived to regret leaving you.'

'Never mind about that now. I don't hold grudges,' Bee interposed, feeling a shade awkward beneath the earnest onslaught of his blue eyes.

'That's pretty decent of you. Now let me get to the point of my invite and you are, of course, welcome to tell me that I'm a calculating so-and-so!' Jon teased, extracting a leaflet from his pocket and passing it across the table to her. 'I would be very grateful if you would consider becoming a patron for this charity. It does a lot of good work and could do with the support.'

Bee was taken aback, for the Jon she recalled had been too intent on climbing the career ladder to spend time raising money for good causes. Maturity, it seemed, had made him a more well-rounded person and she was impressed. He was a trustee for a charity for disabled children, similar to one she had volunteered with when she was a student. 'I doubt that I could do much on a personal basis because I'll be based in Greece after the wedding.'

'As the wife of Sergios Demonides, your name alone would be sufficient to generate a higher profile for the organisation,' Jon assured her with enthusiasm. 'And if you were to decide to get more involved the occasional appearance at public events would be very welcome.'

Bee was relieved then that it appeared Jon's desire to see her was professional rather than personal. She very much appreciated the fact that he studiously avoided asking her anything about Sergios. They parted fifteen minutes later but before she could turn away, Jon reached for her hand.

'I meant what I said earlier,' he stressed in an undertone. 'I made a colossal mistake. I've always regretted losing you, Bee.'

Green eyes turning cool, Bee was quick to retrieve her hand. 'It's a little late in the day to tell me that, Jon.'

'I hope you'll be happy with Demonides.' But the look on his face told her that he didn't think she would be.

Unsettled by that exchange, Bee travelled back to Sergios's house to have tea with the children. Sergios had been jetting round the world on business for over two weeks and their only contact had been by phone. After their meal Bee supervised Paris's homework assignment and bathed Milo and Eleni before tucking them into bed. In a month's time, Eleni was scheduled for surgery to have grommets inserted in both ears to resolve her hearing problems. Having consulted Paris's teacher, Bee had learned that the boy was struggling to make friends at school and she had tried to improve the situation by inviting some of his classmates over to play after school. Paris was beginning to find his feet and as he did so he had become more receptive to Bee and less suspicious of her.

Just before Bee went to bed, Sergios called from Tokyo. 'Who was the man you accompanied to the wine bar?' he demanded.

Bee stiffened defensively. 'So, Tom's a spy, is he?'

'Beatriz…' Sergios growled impatiently, forceful as a lion roaring a warning to an unwary prey.

'He was just an old friend I hadn't seen since university.' Bee hesitated but decided to say nothing more, feeling she didn't owe Sergios any more of an explanation.

'You'll find that plenty of old friends will come scurrying out of the woodwork now that you're marrying me,' Sergios replied cynically.

'I find that offensive. This particular friend is asking me to get involved with a children's charity. You can scarcely find fault with that.'

'Is that why he was holding hands with you?'

Bee flushed scarlet. 'He grasped my hand—big deal!'

'In public places I expect you to be discreet.'

Her anger rose. 'You always have to have the last word, don't you?'

'And I'm always right, *latria mou*,' Sergios agreed equably, not one whit disturbed by the accusation.

That night Bee lay in her big luxurious bed and played the game of 'what if' with Jon in a starring role.

Well, she was only human and naturally she could not help wondering what might have happened had she met her charming ex when she was not on the brink of getting married to another man. Probably nothing would have happened, she decided ruefully, for had it not been for the pressure Sergios had put on her she would have looked like a real Plain Jane and Jon would have been less than impressed. In any case, Sergios was much better looking and had a great deal more personality...

Now where on earth had that thought come from? Bee wondered in confusion. There was no denying that Sergios was a very, very handsome guy but he was not *her* guy in the way Jon had once seemed to be and he never would be. Bee decided that she was far too sensible to indulge in 'what if' dreams. Besides she had long since worked out that if Jon had truly loved her he would never have dumped her because she had a mother who would always need her support. Jon's rejection had shattered the dream of family, which Bee valued most.

'That's a very romantic dress,' Tawny commented, studying her half-sister with frankly curious eyes, for the fitted lace gown with the flowing skirt was exceedingly feminine and not in Bee's usual conservative style. 'And a very thoughtful choice for a guy entering a very practical marriage of convenience.'

Bee went pink, wishing her other sister, Zara, had not been quite so frank with their youngest sister, who thoroughly disapproved of what Bee was doing in marrying a man she didn't love. She also wished Zara had not chosen to avoid what might have been an uncomfortable occasion for her by pleading her reluctance to travel while pregnant. 'Sergios isn't romantic and neither am I.'

'Granted the kids are cute,' Tawny conceded, her coppery head held at a considering angle, blue eyes troubled. 'And Sergios, on the outside he's sex on a stick, but only for an adventurous woman and you're as conventional as they come.'

'You never know,' Bee quipped, lifting her bouquet.

'If I was the suspicious type I would suspect that you're doing this for your mother's benefit,' Tawny commented with a frown, revealing a glimpse of wits that were sharp as a knife. 'You'd do anything for her and she's a lovely woman.'

'Yes, isn't she? My mother is also very happy for me today,' Bee slotted in with a pointed glance. 'Please don't spoil that for her by giving her the wrong idea about my marriage...'

'Or even the *right* idea,' Tawny muttered half under her breath, not being that easy to silence. 'Just promise me that if he's awful to live with you'll divorce him.'

Bee nodded instant agreement to soothe her half-sibling's concerns and descended the stairs with care in her high heels. She was in her mother's house for she had spent the last night of her single life there at the older woman's request. Tawny was not acting as a bridesmaid because Bee had drawn the line at taking the masquerade of her wedding that far.

'But I know you, you won't do it if it means leaving those cute kids behind.' Tawny sighed. 'You'll be like faithful Penelope, stuck with him for ever, and I bet he plays on it when he realises what a softy you are.'

Bee had no intention of being a pushover, convinced as she was that Sergios would happily tread a softy right into the ground and walk on without a backward glance. He was tough, so she had to be even tougher. She reminded herself of that fact when her scowling father extended his arm to her at the mouth of the church aisle and fixed a social smile to his face. Monty Blake had recently been trodden on by Sergios and his ego and his pockets were still stinging from the encounter. She thought it said even more about Sergios's intimidating influence that her father was still willing, however, to play his part at their wedding.

Full of impatience, Sergios wheeled round at the altar to watch his bride approach. His face unreadable, he studied her and started to frown. She had had her long hair cut back to her shoulders. Whose very stupid idea had that been? But aside from that, Beatriz looked… luscious, he finally selected after a long mental pause while he ran his brooding dark gaze from the sultry peach-tinted fullness of her mouth down to the generous curves he never failed to admire. He wondered absently if men developed a taste for larger breasts when they reached a certain age. He was thirty-two, not fifty-two though. But as he saw the burgeoning swell of those plump creamy mounds so beautifully displayed in that neckline there was no denying that he was spellbound. The model on the catwalk in Milan had had nothing to show off but an expanse of flat bony chest. In her place, however, Beatriz would have been a show-stopper. He frowned at that thought.

Determined not to be cowed by the fact her bridegroom was glowering at her, Bee lifted her chin. Even the most critical woman would have had to admit that Sergios did look spectacularly handsome in a beautifully cut morning suit. Encountering those hard eyes trained on her, she felt briefly dizzy and breathless. The minister of her church was inclined to ramble a little, but he soon controlled the tendency after Sergios urged him in an impatient undertone to 'speed it up'. Affronted by her bridegroom's intervention, Bee reddened to the roots of her hair. Had Sergios no idea how to behave in church? Well, it was never too late for a man to learn, although she suspected he would fight learning anything from her every step of the way. He thrust the wedding ring onto her finger with scant ceremony. She rubbed her hand as though he had hurt her, although he had not.

'You were rude to the minister,' she said on the way down the aisle again.

A brow lifted. 'I beg your pardon?'

'You heard me. There are some occasions when you just have to be patient for the sake of good manners and a wedding service is one of those occasions.'

In the thunderous silence that now enfolded the bridal couple, Milo wriggled like an eel off his nanny's lap and rushed to Bee's side to clutch her skirt. She patted his curly head to quieten him and took his hand in hers.

'He was repeating himself,' Sergios breathed harshly,

but, watching the toddler beam his big trusting smile up at Bee, he restrained the outrage her impertinence had sent hurtling through him. After little more than two weeks abroad he had returned to his London home and noticed a distinct change for the better in his cousin Timon's children. All the kids had calmed down. Milo had become less frantic in his need for attention, the little girl was smiling and even Paris was occasionally venturing into shy speech.

Sergios had never had a best friend but had he done so Timon would have come the closest, although on the surface serious, steady and quiet Timon would have appeared to have had little in common with Sergios's altogether more aggressive extrovert nature. But the bond had been there all the same and it was a matter of honour to Sergios to see Timon's children thrive in his care. Beatriz, it seemed, had the magic touch in that department.

A line of cameras greeted their emergence from the church. As Bee's eyes widened and she froze with the dismay of someone unaccustomed to media attention Sergios took immediate advantage of the moment. He swung her round into the circle of his arms and, with one hand braced to the shallow indentation of her spine to draw her close, he bent his head and kissed her, in-stinctively righting the status quo in the only way avail-able to him.

Shock crashed through Bee and made her knees shake at that first breath-taking instant of physical con-tact. She had never been less prepared for anything and impressions hit her in a flood of overwhelming sensuality: the exotic tang of his designer cologne, the uncompromising strength and power of that lean, muscular body crushing her softer curves, the hard, demanding pressure of his erotic mouth on hers. And while at the back of her mind a voice was shrieking no and urging her to pull back her body was singing entirely another song. There was a wildly addictive fire to the taste of him. She wanted more, she wanted *so* much more she trembled with the astonishing force of that wanting. His raw masculine passion sliced through her every defence and roused a surge of naked hunger within her. The plunge of his tongue into the sensitive interior of her mouth made her body tremble, while heat pooled between her thighs and her breasts swelled, pushing against the lace of her bra so that it felt too tight for comfort.

'You're not supposed to taste that good, *yineka mou*,' Sergios breathed in a roughened undertone, drawing back, his brilliant dark eyes cloaked and cool, his face taut.

Dragging her clinging hands from his broad shoulders, Bee was aghast and she turned blindly to pose for the cameras, her head swimming, her treacherous body torn by silent anguish as she struggled to suppress that monstrous hunger he had awakened. She had never felt like that in her life before, not even with Jon. It was as if Sergios had called up something she hadn't known existed within her and that treacherous loss of control had embarrassed the hell out of her. My goodness, she had *clung* to him, pushed her breasts into his chest like a wanton hussy and kissed him back with far too much gusto. She could not bring herself to look at him again and inside she was dying of mortification. Obviously he had planned to give her a social kiss for the benefit of the cameras but she had flung herself into it as though she were sex-starved.

Teeth gritted behind his determined smile, Sergios willed his arousal into subjugation and reminded himself forcefully that sleeping with his wife would curtail his freedom and deprive him of the choices that any intelligent man would value. One woman was much like another; all cats were grey in the dark. He repeated that oft-considered mantra to himself with rigorous determination: he had no plans to bed his bride, no need to do so either. To think otherwise was to invite chaos into his head and home. Breaking the rules of his marriage would cost him and why take that risk? Unless he was very much mistaken, and when the subject was women Sergios was rarely mistaken, his mistress would push out every sexual stop to impress him on his next visit. Satisfaction could be had without complications and wasn't that all that really mattered?

The reception was staged at an exclusive hotel where security staff vetted every arriving guest.

'Zara was such a fool,' Bee's stepmother, Ingrid Blake, remarked in her brittle voice. 'It could have been her standing here in your place today.'

Features austere, Sergios settled an arm to his bride's rigid spine. 'There can be no comparison. Beatriz is… special,' he murmured huskily.

Bee went pink at the unexpected compliment, although the apparent slur on Zara embarrassed her and as the older woman moved out of earshot Bee muttered, 'Ingrid has a wasp's tongue but I could have managed her on my own.'

'I will never stand in silence while my wife is being insulted,' Sergios asserted. 'But only the most foolish would risk incurring my wrath.'

'Ingrid is a sourpuss but she's my father's wife and a member of the family,' Bee reminded him gently.

Noting the anxious light in her gaze, Sergios laughed out loud. 'You can't protect everyone from me.'

His vital laugh, so full of his essential energy, ironically chilled her, reminding her how much ruthless power and influence he had in the world and how much he took it for granted. She thought of her father walking her down the aisle even though it would have been more in character for the older man to express his resentment by refusing to take part in the wedding. Monty Blake's submission to her husband's wishes had shaken Bee and shown her the meaning of true supremacy. She had no doubt that if she ever dared to cross Sergios he would become her most bitter enemy.

'I understood that your grandfather was planning to come today,' Bee admitted.

'He has bronchitis and his doctor advised him to stay at home. You'll meet him tomorrow when we arrive in Greece. I didn't want him to take the risk of travelling.'

It was not a particularly large wedding: Sergios equated small with the privacy and discretion with which he liked to separate his private life from his public one. Although there were only fifty guests everybody on Sergios's list was a *somebody* in the business world. He seemed to have very few actual relatives, explaining that his grandfather had had only two children, both of whom had died relatively young.

'Was he looking for an heir when he discovered you?'

'No. In those days he had Timon. Social services discovered my connection to Nectarios and informed him about me. He didn't know I even existed before that. He came to see me when I was seventeen. I needed a decent education, he offered the opportunity,' Sergios admitted tautly.

She wanted to ask him more about his parentage but his reluctance to discuss his background was obvious and it seemed neither the time nor the place to probe further. Tense at being so much the centre of attention, she ate a light meal. A celebrity group entertained them. Bee noticed a beautiful female guest casting lascivious eyes in Sergios's direction and felt her fingers flex like claws ready to scratch. She didn't like other women looking at him in that speculative sexual way as if trying to imagine what he would be like in bed. It was that wretched kiss, it had changed everything, even the way she thought about him, Bee conceded unhappily.

She had not known that a mere kiss could make her feel hot and hungry and frantic for another. In fact she had always believed that she wasn't that sexual, and even when she was in love with Jon keeping him at arm's length had not proved much of a challenge for her. She had longed for some sign of commitment from him before she slept with him, had wanted sexual intimacy to mean something beyond the physical. With hindsight she suspected that she had always sensed that

Jon was holding back as well and reluctant to get in too deep with her.

'This day seems endless,' Sergios breathed tersely as he checked his phone for the hundredth time, fingers tapping a restive tattoo on the table.

'It'll be over soon,' Bee said calmly, for she had guessed at the church that he found almost every aspect of their wedding day a demanding challenge. It made her wonder what his first wedding and his first wife had been like. Was he reliving disturbing memories? Had his first wedding been a day of love and joy for him? How could she not wonder? Yet Sergios didn't strike her as the kind of guy likely to have buried his heart with his dead wife and unborn child in the grave eight years earlier. He was too pragmatic and abrasive and far too fond of female company.

'Let's get the dancing over with,' Sergios breathed abruptly, springing upright and extending a hand to her.

'I love your enthusiasm,' Bee riposted, smiling brightly as her mother beamed at her. Emilia Blake was a happy woman and Sergios had not only visited her before the wedding but had also made the effort to sit down and talk that afternoon to her, which Bee appreciated. Emilia believed that her son-in-law was the sun, the moon and the stars and not for worlds would Bee have done or said anything to detract from that positive impression.

This marriage *had* to work, she reflected anxiously. If her mother came out to live in Greece their relationship would be on constant display, so she had to ensure from the start that the marriage worked for both of them. She would have to be practical, even-tempered and tolerant…for he was neither of the last two things. Sergios shifted his lean powerful length against her as he danced with a fine sense of rhythm and all those rational uplifting thoughts left her head in one bound for suddenly all she was conscious of were the tightening prominence of her nipples and the smouldering dark gold of his eyes as he gazed moodily down at her. Heat and butterflies rose and fluttered in the pit of her tummy. Desire, she recognised as the twisty sensation stirring up hunger in her pelvis, was digging talon claws of need into her.

'*Theos*…you move well,' Sergios husked, whirling her round and admiring both her energy and the pert stirring curve of her derriere as she wriggled it in time to the music.

'After years of dance classes, I ought to.'

From there the day seemed to speed up. Moving from table to table, group to group, they spoke to all their guests. Bee was impressed that Sergios put on such a good show. He did not strike her as a touchy-feely guy, but the whole time he was by her side he maintained physical contact with either an arm or a hand placed on her. The children got tired and the nannies took them back to the house. Within an hour of their departure Sergios decided they could leave as well and they climbed into a waiting limousine and were carried off. From below her feathery lashes, Bee glanced covertly at her new husband, recognising his relief that the occasion was over.

'Is it all weddings you don't like or just your own?'

'All of them,' he admitted, his handsome mouth hardening. 'I can't stand the starry eyes and the unrealistic expectations. It's not real life.'

'No, it's hope and there's nothing wrong with the fact that people long for a happy ending.'

Sergios shrugged a big broad shoulder in what struck her as the diplomatic silence of disagreement. He sprawled back into the corner of the leather seat, long powerful thighs splayed in relaxation. 'Do you long for a happy ending, Beatriz?'

'Why not?' Bee fielded lightly.

'It won't be with me,' he promised her grimly. 'I don't believe in them.'

Well, that was certainly telling her, she thought ruefully as the limo drew up outside the London house that had become her new home. They mounted the splendid staircase together and were traversing the landing to head off in different directions when Sergios turned to Bee, his face impassive. 'I'm getting changed and going out. I'll see you at the airport tomorrow.'

And with that concluding assurance delivered with the minimum of drama he strode down the corridor where his bedroom suite lay and vanished from view. A door thudded shut. Bee had fallen still and she was very pale. She felt as if he had punched her in the stomach, winding her so that she couldn't catch her breath. It was the first day of their marriage, their wedding night, and he was going out, leaving her at home on her own.

And why should he not? This was not a normal marriage, she reminded herself doggedly. It was not his duty to keep her company, was it? But was he going to see another woman? Why should that idea bite as if an arrow tipped with acid had been fired into her flesh? She didn't know why, she only knew it hurt and she felt horribly rejected. It felt humiliating to ask one of the maids for her assistance in getting out of her wedding finery. Yet, she knew that had he even been available she would not have approached Sergios for the same help. Still feeling gutted and furious with herself for a reaction she could not understand, Bee went for a shower to remove the last remnants of bridal sparkle from her body. Sergios wasn't her husband, not really her husband, so what was the matter with her?

Did Melita live in London or was she here visiting for a prearranged meeting? Or could it be that Sergios was rendezvousing with some other woman? Presumably he would be having sex with someone else tonight. Her tummy muscles tightened as if in self-defence and perspiration dampened her brow, leaving her skin clammy. There was no point being prudish or naive about the emptiness of her marriage, she told herself in exasperation. Right from the start Sergios had demanded the freedom to get naked and intimate with other women on a regular basis. According to the media and those ladies who, when he was younger, were anything but discreet about his habits in the bedroom, he was very highly sexed.

And what exactly did she have to complain about? Sergios was doing only what he had said he would do and by loathing what he was doing *she* was the one breaking the rules by getting too personally involved! It was time she was more honest with herself, she reasoned irritably. In the normal way a man of Sergios's dazzling good looks and wealth would never be attracted to a woman as ordinary as she was. She should not forget that his first wife, Krista, had been gorgeous, similar to Zara with her fragile blonde loveliness. Bee had won Sergios as a husband solely by agreeing to allow him to retain his freedom within the marriage and be a mother to his cousin's children. That was how it was and that was the reality that she had to learn to live with.

A knock sounded on the door and she called out. Paris, clad in his superhero pyjamas and slippers, peered in, a photo album tucked snugly beneath one arm. 'I saw Uncle Sergios going out. Do you want to see my photos?'

'Why not?' Bee said with resolute good cheer, for a regular appraisal of photos of his parents and his baby years had become quite a feature of the little boy's life in recent days. He would show Bee the pictures and explain who the people were and where and when he thought they were taken and she would *ooh* and *aah* with appreciation and ask questions while he worked through his sadness for a period of his life that was now gone.

'Would you like a hot drink to help you sleep?' she prompted, deciding that this was a wedding night that she would never forget.

And if Bee blinked back tears while she sat on the side of her bed with an arm anchored comfortingly round Paris's skinny little body and a mug of cocoa in her other hand, her companion was too intent on sharing his photo album to notice.

CHAPTER FIVE

Two nannies, Janey and Karen, were accompanying Bee and the children to Greece. Shown around Sergios's incredibly large and opulent private jet by an attentive stewardess late the next morning, Bee saw the entire party settled in the rear cabin, which was separate from the main saloon. Armed with enough toys, magazines and films to while away a much longer flight, the young women were thrilled by their deluxe surroundings.

In a lighter mood, Bee would have found it equally difficult not to be seduced by her newly luxurious mode of travel, but she had too much on her mind. She had slept badly and had been forced to out-act a Hollywood film star with her good cheer over the breakfast table, for she had been keen to soothe the boys' nervous tension. After all, Paris and Milo were apprehensive about making yet another move for they had already had to adjust to so much change in their short lives. Paris, however, was quick to address the steward in Greek and Milo's head tipped to one side and his brow furrowed as though he too was recalling the language of his very first words. Although they would not be returning to their former home in Athens, they were heading back to the country of their birth and they might well find Sergios's home on the island of Orestos familiar, for they had often visited it with their parents.

Having ensured that everyone was comfortable, Bee returned to the main saloon and took a seat to leaf through a magazine that she couldn't have cared less about. Having teamed a green silk top and cardigan with white linen trousers, she felt both smart and comfortable. Her hand shook a little when she heard voices outside and her fingers clenched tightly into the publication in her hand, her body tensing, her heartbeat literally racing as she heard steps on the metal stairs. Sergios was tearing her in two, she suddenly thought in frustration. One half of her could barely wait to lay eyes on him while the other half would have preferred to never see him again.

'*Kalimera*…good morning, Beatriz,' Sergios intoned, as tall, dark and gloriously handsome as an angel come to earth, perfect in form but exceedingly complex in nature.

And with her breath convulsing in her dry throat, she both looked at him and blanked him at one and the same time so that their eyes did not quite meet, a polite smile of acknowledgement on her lips combined with an almost inaudible greeting. Why was she embarrassed? Why the hell was she embarrassed? Enraged by her ridiculous oversensitivity, Bee glanced up at him unwarily and collided with golden eyes full of energy and wariness. She *knew* it, he was no fool, and indeed he was just waiting for her to say or do something she shouldn't, to react in some inappropriate way to his departure the night before. Keeping her smile firmly in place, Bee was determined to deny him that satisfaction and she dropped her attention resolutely back to her magazine.

And there her attention stayed…throughout takeoff, a visit to the children, lunch and the remainder of the flight. Sergios shot her composed profile a suspicious appraisal. She had said not one word out of place, not one word. He could not understand why he was not pleased by the fact, why indeed he felt almost affronted by her comprehensive show of disinterest and detachment. He did not like and had even less experience of being ignored by a woman. But Beatriz was very much a lady and he appreciated that trait. The acknowledgement sparked a recollection and he dug into his pocket to remove a jewel box.

'For you,' he murmured carelessly, tossing the little box down on the table between them.

Her teeth gritted. She lifted the box almost as though she were afraid it might soil her in some way, flipped up the lid, stared down at the fabulous diamond solitaire ring, closed the lid and set it aside again. 'Thank you,' she pronounced woodenly with anything but gratitude in her low-pitched voice.

Too clever not to work out that the denial of attention was some form of challenge and punishment, Sergios was becoming tenser because his brand-new bride was already revealing murky depths he had not known she possessed. Frustration filled him. Why did women *do* that? Why did they pretend to be straightforward and then welch on the deal with a vengeance? He knew she was strong-willed, stubborn and rather set in her conventional ways but he had not foreseen any greater problem and had by his own yardstick done what he could to cement their relationship.

'Aren't you going to put it on?' Sergios prompted flatly.

Bee opened the box again, removed the ring and rammed it roughly down over the third finger of her right hand with a lack of ceremony or appreciation that was even more challenging than her previous behaviour. She then returned to perusing her magazine with renewed concentration. She was so furious with him she could neither trust herself to speak to or look at him. If she did look, she would only end up picturing him cavorting in a messy tangle of bed sheets with some sinuous, sexy lover to whom she could never compare in looks or appeal. Yet until that very day looks or sex appeal had never seemed that important to Bee, who had been happier to put a higher value on her health and peace of mind. Unfortunately marrying Sergios appeared to have destroyed her peace of mind.

After a long moment of disbelief, for no woman had ever accepted a gift from him with such incivility before, dark temper stirred in Sergios. Simmering, he studied her, catching the jewelled glint of defiance in her green eyes as she sneaked a glance at him from below her curling lashes and bent her head. Shining chestnut hair fell against the flawless creamy skin of her cheek and her voluptuous pink mouth compressed. That fast he went taut and hard, sexual heat leaving him swallowing back a curse under his breath as he imagined what she might do with those full pouting lips if he got her in the right mood, and Sergios had never once doubted his ability to get a woman in the right mood.

'Excuse me,' Bee said without expression, breaking the tense silence. She was on her feet before he was even aware she was about to move. Seconds later she disappeared into the rear cabin and he heard Milo yell out her name in welcome.

Almost light-headed with relief at escaping the fraught atmosphere in the saloon, Bee sat down to amuse the children. The younger nanny, Janey, caught her hand and gasped at the huge diamond on her finger. 'That ring is out of this world, Mrs Demonides!' she exclaimed, impressed to death.

No, that ring is the price of lust, Bee could have told her. Bee was deeply insulted. He had had sex with another woman and it had meant so little to him that he had betrayed not a shred of discomfiture in Bee's presence. He was, as always, beautifully dressed and immaculate without even a hint of another woman's lipstick or perfume on him. That he was as cool as ice as well offended her sense of decency. She had wanted to throw that ring back at him and tell him to keep it. She had had to leave the saloon before she did or said something that she would live to regret.

Why couldn't she start thinking of him as a brother or a friend? Why was she burdened with this awful sense of possessiveness where Sergios was concerned? Why did she have to be so hatefully attracted to him? It was an appalling admission to make but she already knew that she couldn't bear the idea of Sergios with another woman in an intimate situation. Had she developed some kind of silly immature crush on him? She cringed at the suspicion but what else could be causing all these distressingly unsuitable feelings?

She had to reprogramme her brain to view him in the light of a brother, an asexual being, she instructed herself firmly. That was the only way forward in their relationship. That was the only way their marriage of convenience could possibly work for all of them. She had her mother's happiness to think about as well as that of Paris, Milo and Eleni. This marriage was not all about *her* and her very personal reactions to Sergios were a dangerous trap that she could not afford to fall into.

After all, Sergios was not all bad. He was tough, ruthless, arrogant and selfish, but while he might have the morals of an alley cat he had been remarkably kind to her mother. Without even being asked to do so, he had behaved as though theirs was a normal marriage for Emilia Blake's benefit. Although he appeared to have little interest in his cousin's kids or kids in general, he had still retained guardianship of the troubled trio and had married Bee on their behalf. Yet he could more easily have shirked the responsibility and retained his freedom by paying someone else to do the job of raising them for him.

The jet landed in Athens and the entire party transferred to a large helicopter to travel to the island of Orestos. Conscious of the cool gleam in Sergios's appraisal, Bee went pink and pretended not to notice while peering out of the windows to get a clear view of the island that was to be her future home. Orestos was craggy and green with a hilly interior. Pine forests backed white sand beaches that ran down to a violet blue shining sea and a sizeable small town surrounded the harbour.

'Gorgeous, just like a postcard!' one of the nannies commented admiringly.

'Has the island been in your family for long?' Bee asked Sergios.

'My great-grandfather accepted it in lieu of a bad debt in the nineteen twenties.'

'It looks like a wonderfully safe place for children to run about,' the other nanny remarked approvingly to her companion.

Bee thought of the far from safe and tough inner city streets where Sergios had grown up. Perhaps it was not that surprising that he was so hard and uncompromising in his attitude to the world and the people in it, she conceded reluctantly. The helicopter landed on a pad within yards of a big white house adorned with a tall round tower. Surrounded by the pine forest, it could not be seen except from the air. Sergios jumped out and spun round to help her leave the craft. Laughing uproariously in excitement, Milo jumped out too and would have run off had Sergios not clamped a restraining hand into the collar of his sweatshirt.

'There are dangers here with such easy access to the sea and the rocks,' he informed the hovering nannies. 'Don't let the boys leave the house alone.'

The warning killed the bubbly holiday atmosphere that had been brewing, Bee noted. Janey and Karen looked intimidated.

'The children are going to love it here but they'll have to learn new rules to keep them safe,' Bee forecast, stepping into the uneasy silence.

The housekeeper, Androula, a plump, good-natured woman with a beaming smile, came out to welcome them with a stream of Greek. Sergios came to a sudden halt as if something she had said had greatly surprised him.

'Nectarios is here,' he said in a sudden aside, his ebony brows drawing together in a frown.

'I assumed that your grandfather lived with you.'

'No, he has his own house across the bay. Androula tells me that his home suffered a flood during a rain storm, rendering it uninhabitable,' he said with the suggestion of gritted teeth. 'This changes everything.'

Bee had no idea what he was talking about. Androula swept them indoors and a tall, broad-shouldered and eagle-eyed elderly man came out to meet them. Paris rushed eagerly straight to his white-haired great-grandfather's side, Milo trailing trustingly in his brother's wake. Keen dark eyes set below beetling brows rested on Bee and she flushed, feeling hugely self-conscious.

'Introduce me to your bride, Sergios,' the old man encouraged. 'I'm sorry to invade your privacy at such a time.'

'You're family. You will always be a welcome guest here,' Bee declared warmly, some of the strain etched in her face dissipating. 'Look how pleased the boys are to see you.'

'Beauty and charm,' Nectarios remarked softly to his grandson. 'You've done well, Sergios.'

Bee did not think she was beautiful, but she thought it was very kind of the old man to pretend otherwise. At that very moment her make-up had worn off and she was wearing creased linen trousers stained by Milo's handprints. Eleni was whinging and stretching out her arms to her and she took the child and rested her against her shoulder, smoothing her little dark head to soothe her. The children were getting tired and cross and she took advantage of the fact to leave the men and follow Androula to the nursery. While the boys enthused over toys familiar from previous visits, Bee asked Androula to show her to her room. Her accommodation was in the tower and her eyes opened very wide when she entered the huge circular bedroom with full-height French windows opening out onto a stone balcony with the most fabulous view of the bay. It was a spectacular and comparatively new addition to the house and her eyes only opened wider when she was taken through the communicating door to inspect a luxurious en suite and matching dressing rooms. Purpose-built accommodation for two and her cheeks warmed. Naturally the household would be expecting Sergios and his bride to share this amazing suite of rooms.

Assured that she had time before dinner, Bee scooped up the wrap she glimpsed in one of her open cases and left the maids to unpack while she went for a bath. She was just in the mood to soak away her stress. Leaving her clothes in an unusually untidy heap and anchoring her hair to the top of her head to keep it dry, she tossed scented bath crystals into the water and climbed in, sinking down into the relaxing warmth with a sigh of appreciation.

A knock sounded on the door and she frowned, recalling that she had not locked it. She was in the act of sitting up when the door opened without further warning to frame Sergios.

Bee whipped her arms over her breasts and roared, 'Get out of here!'

'No, I will not,' Sergios responded with thunderous bite.

CHAPTER SIX

THE smouldering gold of anger in Sergios's stunning eyes dimmed solely because he was enjoying the view.

There Beatriz was, all pink and wet and bare among the bubbles. Her fair skin was all slippery and his hands tingled with the need to touch. Those breasts he had correctly calculated at more than a handful were topped by buds with the size and lushness of ripe cherries. Erect at that tempting vision within seconds, Sergios was deciding that the need to share facilities might not be quite the serious problem and invasion of privacy that he had gloomily envisaged. In fact it might well pay unexpected dividends of a physical nature.

Outraged green eyes seethed at him. 'Go!' Bee yelled at him.

Instead, Sergios stepped into the bathroom and closed the door to lean back against the wood with infuriating cool. 'Don't raise your voice to me. The maids are unpacking next door and we're supposed to be on our honeymoon,' he reminded her huskily. 'For someone so hung up on good manners you can be very rude. I knocked on the door—you chose not to answer!'

'You didn't give me the chance.' Bee said resentfully

before she reached for a towel, fed up with huddling like some cowed Victorian maiden in the water and all too well aware that her hands didn't cover a large enough expanse of flesh to conceal the more sensitive areas. As she got up on her knees she deftly used the towel as cover and slowly stood up, keen not to expose anything more.

Fully appreciating the rolling violin curve visible between her waist and hip, Sergios treated her to a wolfish grin of amusement. 'You need a bigger towel, Beatriz.'

And just like that Beatriz became instantly aware of the fact she was large and clumsy rather than little and dainty. Equally fast she was recalling her size zero sister, Zara, whom Sergios had initially planned to marry, not to mention his equally tiny first wife. That was the shape of woman that was the norm for her Greek husband. On his terms she *was* a big girl.

'Or you could just drop the towel altogether, *yineka mou*,' Sergios continued huskily, his dark deep drawl roughening round the edges at that prospect.

'If I wasn't so busy trying to knot this stupid towel I would slap you!' Beatriz countered, assuming that he was teasing her, for by no stretch of the imagination could she even picture circumstances in which she might deliberately stand naked in front of a man, even if he was the one whom she had married.

Sergios tossed her a much larger towel from the shelf on the wall and she wrapped it round her awkwardly. 'We have to share this suite,' he spelt out, suddenly serious.

Her brow indented. 'What are you talking about?'

'My grandfather is staying and I want him to believe that this is a normal marriage. He won't believe that if we occupy separate rooms and behave like brother and sister,' he said with a sardonic curl to his wide sensual mouth. 'We don't have a choice. We'll just have to tough it out and hope our acting skills are up to the challenge.'

'You're expecting me to share that bedroom with you...even *the bed*?' Bee gasped. 'I won't do it.'

'I didn't offer you a choice. We have an arrangement and it includes providing cover for each other.' Eyes dramatised by black spiky lashes raked her truculent face in an unashamed challenge. 'We do what we have to do. I don't want to upset Nectarios just as you didn't want to worry your mother. He needs to believe that this is a real marriage.'

'But I am not willing to agree to share a bed with you,' Bee repeated with clarity. 'And that's all I've got to say on the subject apart from the fact that if you sleep out there, I'll have to sleep somewhere else.'

His eyes glittered as bright as stars in the night sky. 'Not under my roof—'

Bee felt somewhat foolish and at a disadvantage swaddled in her unflattering towel for if she looked large without it how much larger must she look engulfed within its capacious folds? And had a towel the size of a blanket been a deliberate choice on his part or a coincidence?

'I'll get dressed for dinner,' Bee announced, waiting for him to step aside and let her out of the bathroom. *Not under my roof?* He could be as threatening as a sabre-toothed tiger but she was not about to change her mind: she was entitled to her own bed.

Eyes narrowed with brooding intensity, Sergios lounged back against the door frame like the lean, powerful predator that he was and the atmosphere was explosive. As she moved past he rested a hand on the bare curve of her shoulder and she came to a halt.

'I want you,' Sergios declared, using his other hand to ease her back against him and run his fingers lightly up from her waist to her ribcage.

In the space of a moment Bee froze and stopped breathing, panic gripping her. *I want you?* Since when?

'That's not part of our agreement,' she said prosaically, standing as still as a statue as if movement of any kind might encourage him.

Above her head, Sergios laughed, the sound full of vitality and amusement. 'Our agreement is between adults and whatever we choose to make of it—'

'Trust me,' Bee urged. 'We don't want to muddy the water with sex.'

'This is the real world. Desire is an energy, not something you can plan or pin down on paper,' he intoned, and his hands simply shifted position to cover her towel-clad breasts.

Even beneath that light pressure, her heartbeat went crazy. Boom-boom-boom it went in her ears as he boldly pushed the fabric down out of his path and closed his hands caressingly round the firm globes, teasing the stiffly prominent nipples between his fingers. A startled gasp escaped from Bee. She looked down at those long fingers stroking the swollen pink peaks, flushed crimson and then shut her eyes tight again, her legs trembling beneath her. She should push him away, she should push him away, tell him to stop, *insist* that he stop.

Sergios swept her up off her feet while she was still struggling to reclaim her poise and strode into the bedroom to lay her down on the big wide bed. He hit a button above the headboard and she heard the door lock and she sat up, wrenching the towel back up over her exposed flesh.

'You're not going anywhere...' Sergios husked with raw masculine assurance, coming down to the bed on his knees and reaching for her.

'This is not a good idea,' Bee protested in a voice that without the slightest warning emerged as downright squeaky.

'You sound like a frightened virgin!' Sergios quipped, using one hand to tip up her chin and kiss her with hard, hungry fervour, his teeth nipping at her full lower lip, his tongue plunging in an erotic raid on her tender mouth. With his other hand he stroked the straining sensitive buds on her breasts and it was as if he had jerked a leash to pull her in, for instead of pushing back from him she discovered that she only wanted to go one way and that was closer.

'Sergios...' she cried against the demanding onslaught of his sensual mouth.

'*Filise me*...kiss me,' he urged, his strong hands roaming. 'I love your breasts.'

As sweet tempting sensation executed its sway over her treacherous body, Bee felt her lack of fight travelling through her like a debilitating disease. In a sudden move of desperation she flung herself sideways off the bed. She fell with a crash that bruised her hip and jolted every bone in her body and Sergios sat up to regard her with a look of bewilderment. He reached down to help her up again. 'How did you do that?' he questioned. 'Are you hurt?'

'No, but I had to stop what we were doing,' Bee volunteered jerkily, hauling at the towel again and feeling remarkably foolish.

'Why?' Sergios countered in frank astonishment.

Bee veiled her eyes and shut her mouth like a steel trap. 'Because I don't want to have sex with you.'

'That's a lie.' Smouldering eyes came to a screeching halt on her. 'I can tell when a woman wants me.'

Sitting on the wooden floor on a rug that did not make the floor any more comfortable, Bee marvelled that she did not simply scream and launch herself at him like a Valkyrie. He was like a dog with a bone; he wasn't going to give it up without a fight. 'I forgot myself for a moment…a weak moment. It won't happen again. You said you didn't want intimacy—'

'I've changed my mind,' Sergios admitted without skipping a beat.

Bee very nearly did scream then in frustration. 'But I haven't—changed my mind, that is.'

An utterly unexpected grin slanted his beautiful shapely mouth, lending a dazzling charisma to his already handsome features that no woman could have remained impervious to. He lounged fluidly back on the bed and shifted a graceful hand. 'So, then we deal, *yineka mou*—'

'*Deal?*' Bee parroted in a tone of disbelief.

'You're so uptight, Beatriz. You need a man like me to loosen you up.'

Tousled chestnut hair tumbling round her wildly flushed oval face, Bee stood up still clutching the towel. 'I don't want to loosen up. I'm quite happy as I am.'

Sergios released his breath in an impatient hiss. 'You can get pregnant if you want,' he proffered with a wry roll of his stunning dark eyes as if he were inviting her to take two pints of his blood. 'We're already saddled with three kids—how much difference could another one make?'

Her eyes wide with consternation at that shockingly unemotional appraisal, Bee backed away several feet. 'I think you're crazy.'

Sergios shook his arrogant dark head. 'Think outside the box, Beatriz. I'm trying to make a deal with you. As you're not in business, I'll explain—I give you what you want so that you give me what I want. It's that simple.'

'Except when it's my body on the table,' Bee replied in a tone of gentle irony. 'My body is not going to figure as any part of a deal with you or anybody else. We agreed that there would be no sex and I want to stick to that.'

'That is not the message your body is giving me, *latria mou*,' Sergios drawled softly.

'You're reading the signals wrong—maybe it's your healthy ego misleading you,' Bee suggested thinly as she hit the button he had used to lock the door to unlock it again.

As Bee leant across him Sergios hooked his fingers into the edge of the towel above her breasts. Immobilised, she looked up at him and collided with his dazzling eyes enhanced by ridiculously long lush lashes. Her heart seemed to jump into her throat.

'It's *not* my ego that's talking,' Sergios purred like a prowling big cat of the jungle variety.

'Yes, it is. Even though you don't really want me and I'm not your type.'

'I don't go for a particular type.'

'Zara? Your first wife? Let me remind you—*slim, glamorous*?' Bee stabbed without hesitation, watching his face tauten and pale as though she had struck him. The hand threatening the closure of the towel fell back and Bee was quick to take advantage of his uncharacteristic retreat. 'That's your type. I'm not and never could be.'

Sergios dealt her a steely-eyed appraisal. 'You don't know what turns me on'

'Don't I? Something you've been told you can't have. A challenge—that's all it takes to turn you on!' Bee hissed at him, fighting to hide the depth of her outrage. 'And I accidentally made myself seem like a challenge this evening. You're so perverse. If I was throwing myself at you, you would hate it.'

'Not right at this moment, I wouldn't,' Sergios purred in silken contradiction, running a hand down over the extended stretch of one long powerful thigh and by doing so drawing her attention to the tented effect of his tailored trousers over his groin. 'As you can see, I'm not in any condition to say no to a reasonable offer.'

As he directed her gaze to the evidence of his arousal Bee could feel a tide of mortified heat rush up from her throat to her hairline and she did not know where to look even as a kernel of secret heat curled in her pelvis. 'You're disgusting,' she said curtly and knew even as she said it that she didn't mean it. The knowledge that lust for her had put him in that state was strangely stimulating and there was something even more satisfying in that unsought but graphic affirmation of her femininity.

'Over dinner, think about what you want most,' Sergios advised lazily. 'And remember that there's nothing I can't give you.'

Consternation in her eyes, Bee stepped back from the bed, her oval face stiff with angry condemnation. 'Are you offering me money to sleep with you?'

Sergios winced. 'You're so literal, so blunt—'

'You just can't accept the word no, can you?' Bee launched at him in a furious flood. 'You even sank low enough to try and use a baby as a bargaining chip!'

'Of course you want a baby—I've watched you with my cousin's kids. Nobody could be that way with them if they didn't want one of their own,' Sergios opined with assurance. 'I've had enough experience with women to know that at some point in our marriage you will decide that you want a child of your own.'

'Right at this very moment,' Bee told him shakily, 'I'm wondering how I can possibly stay married to such a conniving and unscrupulous man!'

'Your mother, the kids, the fact that you don't like to fail at anything? You're not a quitter, Beatriz. I admire that in a woman.' Straightening his tie and finger-combing his black hair back off his brow, Sergios sprang off the bed, his big powerful body suddenly towering over her. 'But I do have one small word of warning for you,' he murmured in a tone as cool as ice. 'I don't talk about my first wife, Krista...*ever*, so leave her out of our...discussions.'

Shell-shocked from that spirited encounter and that final chilling warning, Bee got back into her cooling bath and sat there blinking in a daze. When he had touched her, a tide of such longing had gripped her that she had almost surrendered. But she wasn't stupid, and even though she had never been so strongly affected before by a man she had always accepted that sex and the cravings it awakened could be very powerful and seductive. Why else did the lure of sex persuade so many people to succumb to temptation and get into trouble over it? It might be a sobering discovery but she had only learned that she was as weak as any other human being.

After Krista's death—she who must not be mentioned—Sergios had become a notorious playboy. He had to be a very experienced lover and he knew exactly how to pull her strings and extract ladies who ought to have known better from towels, she allowed in growing chagrin. Well, he hadn't got the towel the whole way off, she told herself soothingly. With a male as ferociously determined and untamed as Sergios even the smallest victory ought to be celebrated.

It was silly how it actually hurt her pride that Sergios didn't *really* desire her. He was annoyed that his grandfather's presence in his home would force them to live a lie to conceal the reality that their marriage was a fake. His ego was challenged by the prospect of having to share a bed with a woman he had agreed not to touch, so he was trying to tear up the terms of their agreement by whatever means were within his power. Even so, she reckoned it had to be a very rare event for a man to try to seduce a woman by offering to get her pregnant.

Sergios could certainly think on his feet. Indeed he was utterly shameless and callous in pursuit of anything he wanted. But he was also, Bee thought painfully, extremely clever and far too shrewd for comfort. He had sensed the softy hiding below her practical surface and made an educated guess that the prospect of having her own child would have more pulling power with her than the offer of money or diamonds. And he had guessed right, *so* right in fact that she wanted to scream in frustration and embarrassment.

How could he see inside her heart like that? How could he have worked out already what she had only recently learned about herself? Only since she had been in daily contact with Paris, Milo and Eleni had Bee appreciated just how much she enjoyed being a mother. Out on a shopping trip she had bought baby clothes for Eleni and found herself drawn to examining the even tinier garments and the prams, newly afflicted by a broodiness that she had heard friends discuss but until then had never experienced on her own behalf.

But common sense warned her that right now she had

to stand her ground with Sergios. If she allowed him to walk over her so early in their marriage she would be the equivalent of a cipher within a few years, enslaved by her master's voice. He had to respect the boundaries they had set together. After all, he had Melita and other women in his life and she had no wish to join that specific party. The reflection tightened her muscles and made her head begin to ache as she appreciated that she truly was caught between a rock and a hard place with a man who attracted her but whom she could not have. She stretched back against the padded headrest, desperate to shed her tension and troubled thoughts. Sergios was an absolute menace to her peace of mind. He kept on moving the goalposts to suit himself. He was like a pirate on the high seas, always in pursuit of an advantage or a profit. But when it came to fencing with Bee he was just as likely to run aground on the rocks hidden beneath her deceptively calm surface.

When Sergios strolled into the bedroom, Bee was putting the finishing touches to her appearance. Her full-length blue evening dress fitted her like a glove without showing a surplus inch of flesh. His brilliant eyes narrowing, she watched in the mirror as Sergios subjected her to a considering appraisal.

'Sexy,' he pronounced approvingly.

Bee stiffened defensively. 'It's high at the neck and it doesn't even show my legs,' she argued.

Her immediate protest at his comment made amusement curl the corners of his handsome mouth. He scanned the lush swell of breast and derriere so clearly defined by the clinging fabric and said nothing at all.

No skin might be on show but the dress hugged her every curve and those she had in abundance.

He touched the end of a straying strand of her dark hair where it lay on her shoulder. 'Grow your hair again. I liked it longer.'

'Are you used to women doing what *you* like with their appearance?' Bee prompted a tad sourly.

'Yes,' Sergios proclaimed without a shred of discomfiture.

'Any other orders, boss?' Bee could not resist the crack.

'Smile and relax,' he urged. 'Nectarios is already very taken with you. He sees a big improvement in his great-grandsons—'

'My goodness, it's not down to my influence. I've only been with the children a few weeks—'

'But they didn't see that much of their own mother, so your attention means a great deal to them.'

'Why didn't they see much of their mother?'

'She was a popular TV presenter and rarely at home. Timon adored her.'

Suddenly she wanted to know if Sergios had adored Krista but she found that she couldn't imagine him in thrall to a woman, eager to impress and please. There was a bone-deep toughness and a reserve to Sergios that suggested that nothing less than pole position in a relationship would satisfy him. Yet he had only been twenty-one when he wed Krista and to marry so young he must have been a good deal less cynical about the institution of marriage. Comparing that to his attitude at their wedding the day before, Bee could only assume that he had got badly burned by Krista in some way. Of course there was the alternative view that losing Krista and their unborn child had hurt him so much that he had resolved never to fall in love or marry again.

Suddenly irritated by her curiosity, she asked herself why she should care. He had married her purely for the sake of Timon's children and she needed to remember that. This afternoon he had wanted to bed her and the motivation for that staggering turnaround was not that hard to work out, Bee reflected ruefully. How many other sexual options could this little Greek island offer Sergios? He was supposed to be on his honeymoon and if he wanted his grandfather to believe that it was a normal marriage he could scarcely ditch his bride and rush off to seek satisfaction in some other woman's bed. So, for the present, Sergios was trapped in a masquerade and Bee had become miraculously desirable through a complete absence of competition. Right now she was the only option her sensual Greek husband had. It was an acknowledgement that would certainly ensure she didn't develop a swollen head about the precise nature of her attractions.

Dinner was served on a terrace outside the formal dining room. The sun was going down over the sea in fiery splendour and the food was delicious. Bee ate with relish while Nectarios entertained her with stories about the history of the island and family ownership. As the two men finally succumbed to catching up on business, it amused her to recognise how alike Sergios and his grandfather were in looks and mannerisms and she told them she would not be offended if they switched to talking in Greek. She would have to learn the language and quickly, she recognised, grateful that learning languages came relatively easily to her, for it was essential that she be able to communicate effectively with the staff and the children. She did not want to be shut out of half of the conversations going on around her.

She contemplated Sergios over her fresh fruit dessert. The low lights gleamed over his cropped black hair and cast shadows on his strong bronzed profile. He was extraordinarily handsome and even the way he moved was sensual, she thought abstractedly, her eyes following the elegant arc inscribed by an eloquent hand as he spoke. When she glanced up and realised that Nectarios was watching her watch Sergios she went pink. A few minutes later she said it was time she looked in on the children and she left the table.

Having checked on the kids and agreed to take Paris down to the beach in the morning, Bee walked past the door of the main bedroom and on up the final flight of stairs to the bedroom at the top of the tower. Earlier that evening she had found the room and had decided that it would do her nicely as a bolthole. Hadn't she read somewhere recently that it was fashionable for couples with sufficient space in their homes to pursue a better night's sleep by occupying different bedrooms? Separate beds need not mean that anyone's relationship was on the rocks and that was what she would tell Sergios if he tried to object.

She slid on a light cotton nightdress that was far from glamorous, for she had disdained the silk and satin lingerie the personal shopper had directed her towards in London. She climbed into her big comfortable bed and lay with her cooling limbs splayed in a starfish shape to let all her tension drain away. In time this house and the new life she was leading would feel familiar and comfortable, she told herself soothingly.

The door opened and she jerked in surprise, lifting her head several inches off the pillow to peer across the room. The light from the stairwell fell on Sergios's lean strong features and glimmered over his bare, hair-roughened chest and the towel that appeared to be all he was wearing. Bee's short-lived relaxation dive-bombed and her limbs scissored back together again as she sat up and switched on the light.

'What are you doing in here?'

'As you've deserted the marital bed so must I. Wherever we sleep, we stay together,' Sergios spelt out with hard dark eyes and an unyielding angle to his jaw line.

Bee was intimidated by the amount of naked masculine flesh on view. He was tall and broad and, stripped, his big strong shoulders, powerful torso and tight flat stomach were distinctly imposing. 'Don't you dare take off that towel!' she warned him thinly.

'Don't be such a prude,' Sergios told her impatiently. 'I sleep naked. I always have.'

'I can't treat you like a brother if I've seen you naked!' Bee snapped back in embarrassment.

Sergios, engaged in wondering why she would want to treat him like a brother when his own intentions had roamed so far from the platonic plane, threw up both hands in a sudden gesture of exasperation. 'You must've seen loads of guys naked!'

'Oh, is that a fact?' Bee hissed, insulted by that assumption. 'You think I've slept with a lot of men?'

'I've had quite a few women. I'm not a hypocrite,' Sergios said drily.

Bee was seething. 'FYI some of us are a little more particular.'

'Did they all wear pyjamas?' Sergios asked, unable to resist that crack as his wondering gaze took in the full horror of the nightdress she wore: a baggy cotton monstrosity edged with fussy lace.

Bee cringed inwardly. 'There hasn't actually been anyone yet,' she admitted, hoping dismay at her inexperience would persuade him that she really did need her privacy.

Sergios came to an abrupt halt about ten feet from the foot of the bed. A frown had drawn his brows together. 'You can't mean that you've never had a lover…'

Bee reddened but she lifted and dropped both shoulders in a dismissive shrug as though the subject did not bother her at all. 'I haven't.'

Momentarily, Sergios was transfixed by the concept. He had believed virgins had died out around the same time as efficient contraception was developed. He had certainly never expected to find one in his bed. He swung on his heel and strode back out of the room without another word. Released from stasis, Bee breathed in slow and deep and switched out the light. Well, that news had certainly cooled his jets, she conceded. She had fallen out of the challenge category into the sort of unknown territory he evidently had no desire to explore.

But in that conviction Bee was wrong for the bedroom door opened again, startling her, and she raised herself on her elbows with a frown. Sergios was back, minus the towel and clad in a pair of black boxers, which did spectacularly little to conceal the muscular strength and bronzed beauty of his powerfully masculine body.

Sergios got into the far side of the bed in silence. A *virgin*, he was thinking with unholy fascination, a novelty calculated to appeal to even the most jaded palate.

Bee's toes encountered a masculine leg and she pulled hurriedly away as if she had been burned by the contact. His persistence in doing exactly what he wanted to do, regardless of her objections, was beginning to wear down even her nerves of steel.

'I've never gone to bed with a virgin before…' Sergios informed her in his deep drawl. 'In today's world you're as rare as a dinosaur.'

And at that astonishing assurance a bubble of unquenchable mirth formed and swelled in Bee's chest and then floated up into her throat to almost choke her before she finally gave vent to her laughter.

Sergios snaked out an arm and hauled her close. 'I wasn't trying to be funny.'

'Try to picture yourself as a d-dinosaur!' Bee advised, shaking with a hilarity she could not restrain. 'I just hope you weren't thinking of a T-Rex.'

Her laughter was even more of a surprise to a man who took life very seriously and sex more seriously still. He held her while wave after wave of uncontrollable amusement rippled through her curvy body and rendered her helpless. Her breasts rubbed his chest, her thighs shifted against his and he breathed in the soapy scent of her, picturing her equally helpless from passion in his arms. Desire roared through him afresh with a savagery that took even him aback.

Knotting one hand into the fall of her hair to hold her steady, Sergios dipped his tongue between her parted lips with erotic heat. All lingering amusement left her in the space of a moment as he plundered her ready response, nibbling and suckling at her full lower lip, skating an exploration over the sensitive roof of her mouth until her toes were curling and she was stretching up to him helpless in the grip of her need for more.

'Sergios…' she framed in vague protest when he let her breathe again.

'You'll still be a virgin in the morning,' Sergios murmured. 'I promise, *yineka mou*.'

CHAPTER SEVEN

BEE was trembling, insanely conscious of every erogenous zone on her body, but that saying that curiosity had killed the cat was playing in the back of her mind as well. Sergios was playing a game with her and she didn't know the rules, was convinced that she would live to regret letting down her defences. But there was a tightening sense of pressure at the heart of her that pulled tighter with every insidious flick of his tongue against hers and she could not resist its sway.

He inched the nightdress down over her slim shoulders, trapping her arms at the same time as he exposed her generous breasts. In the moonlight pouring through the filmy drapes those high round swells were the most tempting he had ever seen. He kneaded them with firm hands, closed his mouth hungrily to a rigid pink nipple and teased with his lips and his teeth while her back arched and she whimpered beneath his attentions. He switched his focus to her other breast, treating her to one tantalising caress after another, steadily utilising more pressure and urgency on her increasingly sensitised flesh.

It was like being taken apart and put together again

in a different sequence, Bee acknowledged in an agony of uncertainty that did nothing to stop the raging hunger that controlled her. She might never be the same again yet she still could not summon the will power to pull back or insist that he stop touching her. Her clenching fingers delved into his luxuriant hair while he stroked deliciously at her pointed nipples and kissed and licked his passage across the creamy slopes of her breasts before possessing her mouth again, drinking deep from her. She was wildly, seethingly aware of the brimming heat and moisture between her thighs and the ache of longing that had her hips digging into the bed beneath her. Her hands shifted back and forth across his satin-smooth shoulders as the knot of tension at the heart of her built and built. She pushed up to him desperate for more powerful sensation and she couldn't stay still then, couldn't find her voice, couldn't stop the gasps emanating from her throat either. And then suddenly it was all coalescing into one explosive response and she was arching and jerking and crying out in ecstasy as her body took her soaring onto another plane and there was nothing she could do to control any of it.

Afterwards, Bee wanted to leap out of the bed and run but there was nowhere to run to. The thought of cowering behind the bathroom door was not appealing. Still in his arms, she lay like a stone that had been dropped from a height, insanely conscious of her ragged breathing and racing heartbeat, not to mention the feel of his potent arousal against her hip. Dear heaven, what had she done?

'That was interesting,' Sergios purred with dark amusement. 'Definitely an ice breaker.'

'Er…you…?' Bee mumbled unevenly, conscious that events had been distinctly one-sided.

'I'll have a cold shower,' Sergios said piously.

Her face burning, Bee was relieved by the get-out clause. She knew it was selfish to be relieved but she was out of her depth and feeling it. She hadn't known, hadn't even guessed that she could reach a climax that way and she was not pleased that he had put her on that path of sexual discovery.

'You're a very passionate woman, *moli mou*,' Sergios intoned as he vaulted out of bed. 'Obviously Townsend wasn't the right guy for you.'

Bee went rigid. 'What do you know about Jon?'

Sergios paused in the doorway of the bathroom and swung back. 'More than you were prepared to tell me,' he admitted unrepentantly. 'I had him checked out.'

'You did…what?' Bee was righting her nightdress and trying to get out of bed at one and the same time, the simultaneous actions resulting in a clumsy manoeuvre that only infuriated her more. 'Why on earth did you do that? I *told* you he was a friend of mine—'

'But he wasn't—he was your ex, which made the little get-together in the bar rather less innocent, *moli mou*,' Sergios intoned, studying her furious face with level dark eyes. 'But, as I see it, since you never slept with him he doesn't really count.'

'If you ever touch me again I'll scream.'

'No complaints on that score. I love the way you

scream in my arms,' Sergios traded with silky sardonic bite and shut the bathroom door.

Bee knotted her hands into furious fists and contemplated throwing something at that closed door. It would be childish and she was *not* childish. But she had let herself down a bucketful by succumbing to his sexual magnetism. A tide of irritation swept through her then. No wonder he had called her a prude. She might feel mortified but they had hardly done anything in terms of sex. She was taking it all far too seriously and it would be much cooler to behave as though nothing worthy of note had happened.

But, without a doubt, Sergios was lethal between the sheets. The minute he got in she should have got out because compared with him she was a total novice and certain to come off worse from any encounter. And why had he checked Jon Townsend out after her single trivial meeting with her former boyfriend? Didn't Sergios trust anybody? Obviously not. How often had he been betrayed to become that suspicious of other human beings? It was a sobering thought and, although he had not been in love with her sister, Zara had agreed to marry him and then let him down. Perhaps had Bee chosen to be more honest with him he might have had more faith in her.

Around that point of self-examination, Bee must have drifted off to sleep because she wakened when Sergios stowed her into a cold bed. 'Er….what… where…*Sergios*?'

'Go back to sleep, Beatriz,' he intoned.

Her eyes fluttered briefly open on a view of the circular main bedroom in the moonlight and she simply turned over and closed her eyes again, too exhausted to protest. She woke alone in the morning, only the indent on the pillow across from hers telling her that she had had company. After a quick shower she put on Bermuda shorts and a sapphire-blue tee for the trip to the beach she had promised the boys. Nectarios was reading a newspaper out on the terrace where Androula brought Beatriz tea and toast.

'Sergios is in the office working,' his grandfather told her helpfully, folding his paper and setting it aside. 'What are you planning to do today?'

'Take the boys to the beach,' Bee confided.

'Beatriz…this is your honeymoon,' the elderly Greek remarked thoughtfully. 'Let the children take a back seat for a while and drag my grandson out of his office.'

Her imagination baulked at the image of getting Sergios to do anything against his will, but she could see that Nectarios was already picking up flaws in their behaviour as a newly married couple. He asked her about her mother and said he was looking forward to meeting her. Having eaten, Bee went off to find Sergios, although after their intimate encounter the night before she would have preferred to avoid him.

Sergios was working on a laptop in a sunlit room while simultaneously talking on the phone. Her troubled gaze locked to his bold bronzed profile. No matter how angry he made her she could never deny that he was drop-dead beautiful to look at any time of day. Finishing the call, he turned his sleek dark head, brilliant eyes welding to her, and her colour fluctuated wildly while her mouth ran dry at the impact of his gaze. 'Beatriz…'

'I'm taking the children to the beach. You should come with us. Nectarios is surprised that you've already gone back to work.'

'I don't do kids and beaches,' Sergios replied with a suggestive wince at the prospect of such a family outing.

Bee threw back her slim shoulders and spoke her mind, 'Then it's time you learned. Those kids need you…they *need* a father as well as a mother.'

'I don't know how to be a father. I never had one of my own—'

'That doesn't mean you can't do better for your cousin's children,' Bee cut in, immediately dismissing his argument in a manner that made his stubborn jaw line clench. 'Even an occasional father is better than no father at all. My father wasn't interested in me and I've felt that lack all my life.'

Under attack for his views, Sergios had sprung upright. He shrugged a broad shoulder and raked an impatient hand through his hair. His wide sensual mouth had taken on a sardonic curve. 'Beatriz—'

'No, don't you dare try to shut me up because I'm saying things you don't want to hear!' Beatriz shot back at him in annoyance. 'Even if you can only bring yourself to give the kids an hour once a week it would be better than no time at all. One *hour*, Sergios, that's all I'm asking for and then you can forget about them again.'

Sergios studied her grimly. 'I've told you how I feel. I married you so that you could take care of them.'

'Was that our "deal"?' Bee queried in a tone of scorn. 'I was just wondering. As you've already changed the terms on my side of the fence, why do you have to be so inflexible when it comes to your own?'

Sergios raised a brow. 'If I come to the beach will you share a room without further argument?'

Bee sighed in frustration. 'Relationships don't work like deals.'

'Don't they? Are you saying that you don't believe in give and take?'

'Of course, I do but I don't want to give or take sex like it's some sort of service or currency,' Bee told him with vehement distaste.

'Sex and money make the world go round,' Sergios jibed.

'I'm better than that—I'm worth more than that and so should you be. We're not animals or sex workers.'

Her love of frankness was peppered with an unexpected penchant for drama that amused him and he marvelled that he could ever have considered her plain or willing to please. With those vivid green eyes, that perfect skin and ripe pink mouth she was the very striking image of natural beauty. He could still barely believe that she was the only woman he had ever met to have refused him. While rejection might gall him her unattainability was a huge turn-on for him as well and when she had admitted she was a virgin he had understood her reluctance a great deal better and valued her all the more.

Recognising the tension in the atmosphere, Bee stiffened. He gave a look, just a look from his smouldering dark golden eyes and her nipples tightened, her tummy flipped and moist heat surged between her thighs. Colouring, she hastily fixed her eyes elsewhere, outraged that she could have so little control over her own body.

'All right,' she said abruptly, spinning back to deal him a withering look that almost made him laugh. 'If you do the hour a week with the children without complaining, I won't argue about sharing a room any more. Over breakfast I realised that your grandfather doesn't miss a trick and he is suspicious.'

'I said a long time ago that I would never marry again and he knows me well. Naturally he's sceptical about our marriage.'

'See you down at the beach,' Bee responded a touch sourly, for she was not pleased that she had had to give way on the bedroom issue. Unfortunately her previous attempts to persuade Sergio to get involved with his cousin's children had proved fruitless and if there was anything she could do to improve that situation she felt she had to make the most of the opportunity.

Karen was on duty and the children were already dressed in their swimming togs while a beach bag packed with toys and drinks awaited her. Paris led the way down through the shady belt of pine forest to the crisp white sand. They were peering into a rock pool when Sergios arrived. Wearing denim cut-offs with an unbuttoned shirt and displaying a flat and corrugated muscular six-pack that took Bee's breath away, Sergios strode across the sand to join them. The boys made a beeline for him, touchingly eager for his attention. Paris chattered about boy things like dead crabs, sharks and fishing while Bee held Milo and Eleni's hands to prevent them from crowding Sergios. She paddled with the toddlers in the whispering surf to amuse them. When Paris began building a sandcastle, Milo and Eleni ran back to join their brother.

Sergios walked across to Bee.

'Thirty-two minutes and counting,' she warned him in case he was thinking of cutting his agreed hour short.

An appreciative grin slashed his handsome mouth. 'I haven't got a stopwatch on the time.'

'What happened to your father?' she asked in a rush before she could lose her nerve.

As he looked out to sea his eyes narrowed. 'He died at the age of twenty-two trying to qualify as a racing driver.'

'You never knew him?'

'No, but even if Petros had lived he wouldn't have taken anything to do with me.' Sergios volunteered that opinion with telling derision. 'My mother, Ariana, was a teenage receptionist he knocked up on one of the rare days that he showed up to work for Nectarios.'

'Did your mother ever tell him about you?' Bee prompted.

'He refused her calls and got her sacked when she tried to see him. She didn't know she had any rights and she had no family to back her up. Petros had no interest in being a father.'

'It must have been very tough for so young a girl to get by as a single parent.'

'She developed diabetes while she was pregnant. Her

health was never good after my birth. I stole to keep us,' he admitted succinctly. 'By the age of fourteen I was a veteran car thief.'

'From that to...*this*...' Her spread hands encompassed the big opulent house beyond the forest and the island owned by his grandfather. 'Must have been a huge step for you.'

'Nectarios was very patient. It must've been even harder for him. I was poorly educated, bitter about my mother's death and as feral as an animal when he first employed me. But he never gave up on me.'

'You were probably a more worthwhile investment of his time than the father you never met,' Bee offered.

Sergios surveyed her steadily, his stunning gaze reflecting the sunlight as he slowly shook his arrogant head in apparent wonderment at that view. 'Only you would think the best of me after what I've just told you about my juvenile crime record, *yineka mou*.'

Bee coloured, noticed that Milo was approaching the sea with a bucket and sped off to watch over the little boy. But it was Sergios who stepped from behind her and scooped up Milo as he teetered uncertainly ankle deep in the surging water, swinging the child up in the air so that he laughed uproariously before depositing him and, thanks to Bee's efforts, a filled bucket of water back beside the sandcastle.

Eleni her silent companion, Bee spread the rug and Sergios threw himself down beside her. As she knelt he closed a hand into her chestnut hair and lifted her head, searching her oval face with brooding eyes. She gazed back at him with a bemused frown. 'What do you want from me?' she questioned in frustration.

'Right now?' Sergios released a roughened laugh that danced along her taut spine like trailing fingertips. 'Anything you'll give me. Haven't you worked that out yet?'

He crushed her mouth under his, tasting her with an earthy eroticism that fired up every skin cell in her quivering body. Hunger rampaged through her like a fire burning out of control and the strength of that hunger scared her so much that she thrust him back from her, her attention shooting past him to check that the children were still all right. Paris had been watching them kiss and he turned away, embarrassed by the display but no more so than Bee was. Sergio rested back on an elbow, one raised thigh doing little to conceal the bold outline of his arousal below the denim. Suddenly as hot as though she were roasting in the fires of hell, Bee dragged her gaze from him and watched the children instead.

'You're trying to use me because I'm the only woman available to you right now,' she condemned half under her breath.

Sergios ran a fingertip down her arm and she turned her head reluctantly to collide with his glittering dark eyes. 'Do I really strike you as that desperate?'

Her full mouth compressed. 'I didn't say *desperate*.'

'I can leave the island any time I like to scratch an itch.'

'Not if you want to convince your grandfather that you're a happily married man.'

'I could easily manufacture a business crisis that demanded my presence,' Sergios countered lazily. 'You have a remarkably low opinion of your own attraction.'

'Merely a realistic one. Men have never beaten a path to my door,' Bee admitted without concern. 'Jon was special for a while but once he realised that my mother and I were a package he backed off.'

'And married a wealthy judge's daughter. He's ambitious, not a guy with a bleeding heart,' Sergios commented, letting her know how much he knew and making her body tense with resentment over the professional snooping that had delivered such facts. 'Doesn't it strike you as odd that he should now be approaching you as the representative of a children's charity?'

Bee ignored the hint that Jon was an opportunist because she did not intend to adopt Sergios's cynicism as her yardstick when it came to judging people's motives. 'No. As your wife I could be of real use to the charity.'

'And as my ex-wife you could be of even more use to Jon,' Sergios completed with sardonic bite. 'Be careful. You could be his passport to another world.'

'I'm not stupid.'

'Not stupid, but you are naive and trusting.' He studied her with amusement. 'After all, you ignored all the warnings and married me.'

'If you treat me with respect I will treat you the same,' Bee swore. 'I don't lie or cheat and I don't like being manipulated.'

Sergios laughed out loud. 'And I'm a very manipulative guy.'

'I know,' Bee said gravely. 'But now you've got me in the same bed that's as far as it goes.'

His curling black lashes semi-concealed his stunning eyes. 'That would be such a waste, Beatriz. We have the opportunity, the chemistry.'

'With all due respect, Sergios,' Beatriz murmured sweetly, cutting in, 'that's baloney. You only want to bed me because you believe it'll make us seem more intimate and therefore more of a couple for your grandfather's benefit. And while I think he's a lovely old man, I don't want to go that far to please.'

'I can make you want me,' Sergios reminded her smooth as silk but it was the tough guy talking, his dark eyes hard as ebony, his strong bone structure taut with controlled aggression.

'But only in the line of temporary insanity. It doesn't last,' Bee traded, longing for the smile and the laughter that had been there only minutes earlier and suddenly recognising another danger.

It would be so easy to fall for this man she had married, she grasped with a sudden stab of apprehension. He wasn't just gorgeous to look at, he was an intensely charismatic man. Unfortunately he had very few scruples. If she let him, he would use her and discard her again without thought or regret. Where would she be then? Hopelessly in love with a guy who didn't love her back and who betrayed her with other women? She suppressed a shudder at that daunting image, and her heart, which he had made beat a little faster, steadied again.

A ball suddenly thumped into her side and the breath

she was holding in escaped in a startled huff. Instantly Sergios was vaulting upright and telling Paris off, but Bee was relieved by the interruption and quick to intervene. She threw the ball back to the boys, retrieved Eleni from the shells she was collecting and joined in their game.

Unappreciative of the fact that she was using the children as a convenient shield, Sergios was equally challenged by the idea that she could so easily discard the idea of becoming a proper wife. He thought of the countless women who had gone to extraordinary lengths to get him to the altar and failed and then he looked at Beatriz, distinctly unimpressed by what he had to offer in bed or out of it. He was out of his element with a woman who put a value on things without a price. He didn't do feelings, fidelity or…virgins. Basically he operated on the belief that women were all the same, money greased the wheels of his affairs and he had few preferences. That ideology had carried him along a safe smooth path after his first marriage right up to the present day. But nothing in that credo fitted Beatriz Blake. In her own quiet way she was a total maverick.

A manservant came down to the beach to tell Sergios about an important call. He departed and Bee tried not to care that he had gone, leaving behind a space that absolutely nothing else could fill. It was impossible to be unaware of a personality and a temperament as larger than life as Sergios Demonides. When Bee trekked up from the beach late afternoon with two tired little boys and an equally tired and cross little girl, she was damp and sandy and pink from the sun in spite of her high factor sun cream.

Having fed Eleni and spent some time cuddling the little girl while chatting with the nannies about the child's upcoming surgery that would hopefully improve her hearing, Bee left the nursery and went for a shower before changing for dinner. In the bedroom she found several boxes of exclusive designer nightwear on the bed in her size, items fashioned to show off the female body for a man's benefit and not at all the sort of thing that Bee wore for comfort and cosiness. She could barely believe Sergios's nerve in ordering such items for her but it was certainly beginning to sink in on her that he was a very determined man. When she returned to the bedroom, clad in her own light robe, Sergios was there and she stiffened, unaccustomed to the lack of privacy entailed in sharing a bedroom. Engaged in tying the sash on the robe to prevent it from falling open, she hovered uncomfortably.

'Did you order those nightgowns for me?' she pressed.

'Yes. Why not?'

'They're not the sort of thing I would wear.'

Sergios shrugged off the assurance. 'My grandfather has decided to return to his home.'

'I thought it was uninhabitable.'

'Two rooms are but it's a substantial property. I think that was an excuse to allow him to check us out,' Sergios confided wryly. 'He's taking the children and their nannies back with him.'

Her head flew up, green eyes wide with surprise and

bewilderment 'Why on earth would he take the kids with him?'

'Because it's a rare newly married couple who want three children around on their honeymoon,' Sergios drawled, his face impassive. 'Don't make a fuss about this. It's a well-meant offer and he is their grandfather—'

'Yes, I know he is *but*—'

'Objecting isn't an option,' Sergios sliced in with sudden impatience. 'It's a done deal and it would look strange if we turned him down.'

Bee could not hide her consternation at the arrangement that had been agreed behind her back. He had married her to act as a mother to those children but it seemed that she was not entitled to the rights or feelings of a mother if they conflicted with his wishes. 'Yes, but the children are just getting used to me. It's unsettling for them to be passed around like that.'

'You can go over and see them every day if you like.' His beautiful wilful mouth took on a sardonic slant. 'First and foremost you are my wife, Beatriz. Start acting like one.'

Bee reddened as though she had been disciplined for wrongdoing, her temper flaring inside her. 'Is that an order, sir?'

'*Ne*…yes, it is,' Sergios confirmed without hesitation or any hint of amusement. 'Let's keep it simple. I tell you what I want, you do it.'

Those candid words still echoing in her ears, Bee vanished back into her bathroom to do her make-up. Being ordered around when she was naked below a wrap didn't feel right or comfortable. But then she never had liked being told what to do. In addition she was very angry with him. He had encouraged her to act like a mother, only to snatch the privilege back again when it no longer suited him. *Act like a wife?* If she did that he wouldn't like it at all…for a wife would make demands.

CHAPTER EIGHT

CLEARLY in no mood to make the effort required to convince the staff that he was an attentive new husband, Sergios did not join Bee at the dinner table until she was halfway through her meal and the silence while they ate together screamed in her ears like chalk scraping down a blackboard.

'I didn't think you'd be the type to sulk.'

'Am I allowed to shout at you, sir?'

'Enough already with the sir,' Sergios advised impatiently.

Her appetite dying, Bee pushed her plate away.

'I'll take you out sailing tomorrow morning,' he announced with the air of a man expecting a round of applause for his thoughtfulness.

'Lucky me,' Bee droned in a long-suffering voice.

'Later this week, I'll take you over to Corfu to shop.'

'I hate shopping—do we have to?'

The silence moved in again.

'When I married you I believed you were a reasonable, rational woman,' Sergios volunteered curtly over the dessert course.

'I believed you when you said you wanted a platonic

marriage,' Bee confided. 'Just goes to show how wrong you can be about someone.'

'Do you think your own mother will be fooled by the way we're behaving into believing that this is a happy marriage?'

Hit on her weakest flank by that question, Bee paled.

'Don't wait up for me,' Sergios told her as he too pushed away his plate, the food barely touched. 'Last month I took over my grandfather's seat on the island council and it meets tonight. I'll stay for a drink afterwards.'

Frustrated by his departure when nothing between them had been resolved, Bee phoned her mother and lied through her teeth about how very happy she was. She then tried very hard to settle down with a book but her nerves continued to zing about like jumping beans and at well after ten that evening she decided that, as she wasn't the slightest bit tired, vigorous exercise might at least dispel her tension. At her request a pole had been fitted in the house gym and she had politely ignored Sergios's mocking enquiry as to what she intended to do with it. Like all too many people Sergios evidently assumed that pole dancing was a lewd activity best reserved for exotic dancers in sleazy clubs. Clad in stretchy shorts and a crop top, Bee did her warm-up exercises to loosen up before putting on her music.

Sergios was resolutely counting his blessings as he drove back along the single-track road to his home. Unhappily a couple of drinks and all the jokes with his colleagues on the island council that had recognised his status as a newly married man hadn't taken the edge off his mood. In fact he was engaged in reminding himself that being married was by its very nature tough. Learning how to live with another person was difficult. Nobody knew that better than him, which was why he had cherished his freedom for so long. Indeed the lesson of having once lost his freedom was engraved on his soul in scorching letters, for Sergios never forgot or forgave his own mistakes. He knew he should be grateful that Beatriz was so very attached to children who were not her own. She was a good woman with a warm heart and strong moral values. He knew he should be appreciative of the fact that if he came home unexpectedly he was highly unlikely to walk into a wild party...

When he walked into the lounge, however, he was vaguely irritated to find that Beatriz had not waited up for him, thereby demonstrating her concern for his state of mind and their marriage. He was hugely taken aback to recognise that he actually *wanted* her to do wifely things of that nature. That she had just taken herself off to bed was definitely not a compliment. It was hardly surprising, he acknowledged in sudden exasperation, that Beatriz should be confused about what he wanted from her when he no longer knew himself.

The bedroom, though, was also empty and Androula, plump and disapproving in her dressing gown, answered his call and informed him that Beatriz was in the gym. Having dispensed with his tie and his jacket, Sergios followed the sound of the music but what he saw when he glanced through the glass doors of the gymnasium brought him to a sudden stunned halt.

Beatriz was hanging upside down on a pole. By the

time he got through the door she was doing a handstand and swirling round the pole, legs splaying in a distinctly graphic movement that he would not have liked her to do in public. He was astonished by how fit she was as she went through an acrobatic series of moves. That stirring display was so unexpected from such a quiet conservative woman that it made it seem all the more exciting and illicit. He watched her kick, toes pointed, slender muscles flexing in a shapely leg and in a rounded, deliciously plump derriere. Around that point he decided simply to enjoy the show. As she undulated sexily against the pole, full breasts thrust out, hips shifting as though on wires, he was hard as a rock and her sinuous roll on the floor at the foot of the pole was frankly overkill.

'Beatriz?' Sergios husked.

In consternation at the sound of his voice, Bee flipped straight back upright, wondering anxiously for how long she had had an audience. Brilliant dark eyes welded to her, Sergios was by the door, tall, darkly handsome and overwhelmingly masculine. Lifting her towel to dry the perspiration from her face, she paused only to switch off the music.

'When did you get back?'

'Ten minutes ago. How long have you been doing that for?'

'About three years,' she answered a little breathlessly, drawing level with him. 'It was more fun than the other exercise classes.'

His gaze smouldering, he bent his dark head and crushed her parted lips hotly beneath his, ravishing her mouth with the staggering impact of a long, drugging kiss. A shiver of sensual shock ran through her as his arms came round her and she felt the hard urgency of his erection against her stomach.

'*Se thelo*…I want you,' he breathed raggedly. 'Let's make this a real marriage.'

Taken aback by that proposition, Bee tried to step back but Sergios had a strong arm braced to her spine as he walked her down the corridor. 'We need to think about this,' she reasoned, struggling to emerge from that potent kiss, which had made her head swim.

'No, I believe in gut instinct. We've been thinking far too much about things,' Sergios fired back with strong masculine conviction. 'You're not supposed to agonise over everything you do in life and look for all the pitfalls, Beatriz. Some things just happen naturally.'

He thrust open their bedroom door, whirled her round and devoured her mouth hungrily beneath his again, his tongue darting into the tender interior of her mouth, setting up a chain reaction of high voltage response inside her. This, she registered, was the sort of thing he believed should happen naturally, but from Bee's point of view there was nothing natural about the fact that she was trembling and unable to think straight. The force of his passion knocked her off balance while a raging fire leapt up inside her to answer it. Locked together, they stumbled across the room and down on the bed, his hands smoothing over her Lycra-clad curves with an appreciative sound deep in his throat.

'I don't want anyone else seeing you dance like that,' Sergios spelt out. 'It's too sexy—'

'But that's how I keep fit—it's only exercise.'

'It's incredibly erotic,' Sergios contradicted, wrenching off the shorts with impatient hands.

'We really ought to be discussing this,' she told him anxiously.

A heart-breaking smile slashed his beautiful mouth. 'I don't want to talk about it…we've talked it to death.'

That smile made her stretch up to kiss him again, her fingertips smoothing over a hard cheekbone and delving into his silky black hair with a licence she had never allowed herself before. If they made love he would be hers as no other man had ever been and she wanted that with every fibre of her being and a strength of longing she had not known she was capable of feeling. Unbuttoning his shirt, she pulled it off his shoulders and he cast it off, laughing at her impatience. Standing up, he dispensed with the rest of his clothing at efficient speed and a tingling hum of arousal thrummed through her as she looked at his powerfully aroused body. He was ready for her.

Sergios pulled her up and peeled her free of the crop top and the sports bra she wore beneath. With a groan of sensual satisfaction he cupped the creamy swell of her breasts and licked and stroked the swollen pink tips until she shivered. 'Perfect,' he husked.

Liquid heat pooled between her legs as he located the damp stretch of fabric between her legs and eased a finger beneath it to trace her delicate centre. She twisted beneath his touch and lifted her hips as he took off her knickers. He kissed a trail down over her writhing length until he found the most truly sensitive spot of all. As he lingered there to subject her to the erotic torment of his skilled mouth and hand, she had to fight her innate shyness with all her might.

Had she been in control it would have been wrenched from her by the power of her response. As it was, she was free to abandon herself to sensation and she did, her head moving restively back and forth on the pillow, shallow gasps escaping her throat as her hips rose and fell on the bed. She was at the very height of excitement before he came over her and entered her in one effortless stroke. Even so there was still a stark moment of pain and she cried out as he completed his possession, driving home to the very core of her. The discomfort swiftly ebbed even as his invasive hard male heat awakened and stimulated her need again.

'Sorry,' he sighed with intense male pleasure. 'I was as gentle as I could be.'

'You're forgiven,' she murmured, very much preoccupied as she arched her spine and lifted her hips to accept more of him, desire driving her to obey her own needs.

'You're so tight,' he breathed with earthy satisfaction, rising up on his elbows and withdrawing only to thrust back deeper into her receptive body in a movement that was almost unbearably exhilarating.

Her breath catching in her throat, her heart thundering with growing fervour she shut her eyes, revelling in the feel of him inside her. She writhed beneath him as he drove deeper with every compelling thrust and his fluid rhythm increased, plunging her into an intoxicating world of erotic and timeless delight. The excitement took over until all she was aware of was him and the hot, sweet pleasure gathering stormily at the heart of her. She reached an explosive climax and plunged over the edge into ecstasy, gasping and writhing in voluptuous abandon.

Shuddering over her, Sergios cried out with uninhibited fulfilment gripped by the longest, hottest climax of his life. As her arms came round him to hold him he pulled back, however, releasing her from his weight. He threw himself back against the pillows next to her, enforcing a separation she was not prepared for at that most intimate of moments.

'That was unbelievably good, *yineka mou*,' Sergios savoured, breathing in a lungful of much-needed air. 'Thank you.'

Thank you? Bee blinked in bewilderment at that polite salutation and reached for his hand, closing her fingers round his and turning over to snuggle into his big powerful body, spreading her fingers across a stretch of his warm muscular torso. He stiffened at the contact.

'I don't do the cuddling thing, *glikia mou*.'

'You're not too old to learn,' Bee told him dreamily, dazed by what they had just shared but also happy at the greater closeness she sensed between them. 'You just persuaded me to do something spontaneous and that's not usually my style.'

Recognising the truth that Beatriz almost always had a smart answer for everything, Sergios made no comment. Instead he settled curious dark golden eyes on her flushed face. 'I hurt you. Are you sore?'

Bee gave a little experimental shift of her hips and winced. 'A little.'

'Shame,' he pronounced with regret, a sensual curve to his firm mouth. 'Right now, I would love to do it all over again but I'll wait until tomorrow.'

'You didn't use a condom,' Bee remarked, her surprise at that oversight patent.

'I'm clean. I have regular health checks. Hopefully we'll get away with it this once on the contraception front. I don't keep condoms here,' he admitted bluntly. 'I don't bring women to my home. I never have done.'

There were so many questions brimming on her lips but she wouldn't let herself ask them. She liked the fact that the room and bed had not been used by other women. But she did want to know about his first wife—there was not even a photo of Krista on display in the house. Then there was his mistress, and where Bee and Sergios were to go from here, but that thorny question would be a case of too much too soon for a guy who had fought so hard to retain his freedom and keep his secrets. He wasn't going to change overnight, she told herself ruefully.

Let's make this a real marriage, he had said in the gym. Had he truly meant it? Or had a desire for sex momentarily clouded his judgement when her dancing awakened his libido? Could he simply have told her what he thought she wanted to hear? Uneasy at that suspicion, Bee tensed but refused to lower herself to the level of asking him if he was genuinely committed to their marriage. Expressing doubt, after all, might just as easily encourage what she most feared to come about.

'We'll put a pole up in the bedroom so that you can exercise in here where nobody else can see you,' Sergios informed her lazily.

Bee could not believe her ears. His persistence on that subject was a revelation. He had not been joking in the gym when he said he didn't want anyone else to see her dancing. 'I didn't think you would be such a prude.'

'You're my wife,' Sergios reminded her, but his face was taut, as if giving her that label pained him.

Looking up into those darkly handsome features, Bee could already see the wheels of intellect turning as he questioned their new intimacy. How did he really feel about that? She lowered her lashes, refusing to agonise over something she had no control over. Living with Sergios would be a roller-coaster ride and as he did not suffer anything in silence she had no doubt that she would soon know exactly how he felt.

'I'll be late back tonight,' Sergios told her, sinking down on the side of the bed. He hesitated for a split second before he grasped the hand that she had instinctively extended to stop him leaving the room.

Still half asleep, for it was very early, Bee studied him drowsily, noting the brooding tension etched into his face while loving the warmth of his hand in hers and the golden intensity of his gaze. 'Why?'

'It's the anniversary of Krista's death today. I usually attend a memorial service with her parents and dine with them afterwards,' Sergios explained, his intonation cool and unemotional.

Taken aback, for although they had been married for

six weeks he still never ever mentioned his first wife, Bee nodded and belatedly noticed the sombre black suit that he wore.

'It's an annual event,' he said with an uneasy shrug. 'Not something I look forward to.'

She bit back the comment that some people regarded a memorial service as an opportunity to celebrate the life of the departed. 'Would you like me to go with you?' she asked uncertainly.

'That's a generous offer but I don't think Krista's parents would appreciate it. She was their only child. I get the impression that they don't want to be reminded that my life has moved on,' Sergios commented, compressing his handsome mouth with the stubborn self-discipline that was so much a part of his character.

Her ignorance of what he was feeling troubled Bee for the rest of the day. But then she was madly, hopelessly in love with Sergios and prone to worrying about what was on his mind. Although the sexual chemistry they shared was indisputably fantastic, that wasn't what had awakened more tender feelings in her heart. It was while Bee was busily working out what made Sergios tick that she had fallen head over heels in love with him.

When he was away on business she felt as though she were only half alive. Deprived of his powerful and often unsettling charismatic presence, she would watch her phone like a lovesick adolescent desperate for his call, count the hours until he came home and then lavish attention on him in bed until he purred like a big jungle cat. He was in her heart as though he had always been there, strong and stubborn and infuriatingly unpredictable.

In learning to love him she had also recognised his vulnerabilities. He was unsure how to behave with the children because his mother's ill health had deprived him of a carefree childhood. Although Bee had come from a similar background the burden of caring had been lightened in her case by her mother's deep affection. Sergios's mother, however, had been very young and immature and might possibly have resented the adverse impact of a child on her life and health. For whatever reasons, Sergios had not received the love and support he had needed to thrive during his formative years.

Within days of being removed to their grandfather's home on the other side of the bay Paris, Milo and Eleni had made it clear how much they were missing Bee and Sergios had swiftly accepted the inevitable and agreed to their return. With Bee's support since then Sergios had gradually spent more time with his cousin's kids, getting to know them so that he no longer froze when Milo hurled himself at him or looked uneasily away when Eleni opened her arms to him. Bridges were being built. Paris turned to Sergios for advice, Milo brought his ball and Eleni smiled at him when he risked getting close. Sergios was slowly learning how to accept affection and how to respond to it.

Bee had been relieved when she received the proof that their unprotected lovemaking on the first night they had spent together had not led to her conceiving a child. In her opinion an unplanned pregnancy would have been a disaster for their marriage. Sergios was very much a man who needed to make the decision that he wanted to be a father for himself. Yet when she had told him that he need not worry on that score, he had shrugged.

'I wasn't worrying about that,' he had insisted. 'If you had conceived we would have coped.'

But Bee would not have been happy while he merely 'coped'. She only wanted to have a baby with a man who was actively *keen* for her to have his baby. She did not want Sergios to make the best of an accidental conception or to offer her the option of a pregnancy because she was broody: she wanted him to make a choice that he wanted a child with her, a child of his own.

The weeks they had shared on the island had not been only about the children. Bee had stopped fretting about the future and had lived for the moment and Sergios had made many of those moments surprisingly special. He had proudly given her a tour of the wheelchair-friendly cottage in the grounds where her mother was to live. A carer whom Emilia would choose for herself from a list that had already been drawn up would come in every day to help her cope. Bee could hardly wait to see the older woman's face when she enjoyed her first cup of tea on the sunny terrace with its beautiful view of the bay.

Sergios had also flown Bee to Corfu for a week. The busy streets lined with elegant Italianate buildings, sophisticated shops and art studios had delighted her and one afternoon when Sergios had briefly lost her in the crowds he had anchored his hand to hers and kept it there for the rest of the day. He had bought her a beautiful silver icon she admired and they had had drinks on The Liston, an arcaded building modelled on the Rue de Rivoli in Paris. By the time they had returned to their designer hotel she was giggly and tipsy and he had made passionate love to her until dawn when she fell asleep in his arms. Opening her eyes again on his handsome features in profile as he worked at his laptop, getting some work out of the way before the day began, she had seen into her own heart and had known in the magic of that moment that she loved him. Loved him the way she had never thought she would ever love any man, with tenderness and appreciation of both his flaws and his strengths.

They had enjoyed numerous trips out and about on Orestos. He had shown her all over the island, had taken her swimming and sailing and snorkelling, letting the children join in whenever possible. He had enjoyed the fact that she was energetic enough to share the more physical pursuits with him. She also now knew that he was very competitive when it came to building sandcastles or fishing and that he was crazy about ice cream. He also loved it when she and the children were there to greet him when he came home from a trip. There was an abyss of loneliness deep inside Sergios that she longed to assuage.

With such uneasy thoughts dominating her mind about Krista's memorial service and what those memories might mean to her husband, Bee could not settle that afternoon. She received another text from Jon Townsend, who had stayed in surprisingly regular contact with her since her arrival in Greece, and suppressed a sigh. Her ex-boyfriend had sent her reams of information about the charity he was involved with and was keen to set up a meeting with her during her approaching visit to the UK.

On such a beautiful day it had seemed a good idea to collect Milo from his playgroup in town on foot rather than drive there as she usually did. The summer heat, however, was intense and by the time she picked up Milo Bee was questioning the wisdom of having trudged all the way along the coast road, particularly when she had no alternative other than to walk back again. Milo, in comparison, hopped, jumped and skipped along by her side with the unvarnished energy that was his trademark.

She was walking through the town square with Eleni dozing below a parasol in her pushchair when Nectarios waved at them from a table outside the taverna. He wore his faded peaked cap, and only a local would have recognised him as the powerful business tycoon that he still was even in semi-retirement. She guessed by his clothing that he had been out sailing in the small yacht he kept at the harbour and she crossed to that side of the street.

'What are you doing here on foot?' he asked with a frown, spinning out a chair for her and snapping his fingers for the proprietor's attention.

'Milo was at his playgroup. It didn't seem quite so warm when I left the house.'

'My lift will be here in ten minutes. You can all ride back with me.' The old man ordered drinks for Bee and the children while calmly allowing Milo to clamber onto his lap and steal his cap to try it on and then treat it like a frisbee.

While they sat there enjoying the welcome shade of the plane tree beside the terrace various passers-by came over to chat to Nectarios. Bee was daily picking up more Greek words and she understood odd snatches of the conversations about fishing trips, weddings and christenings. Tomorrow she was returning to London, where Eleni would have surgery on her ears, and when they came back to the island her mother would be travelling with her. She was helping Eleni with her feeding cup when she became aware of a flutter of whispers around her. Glancing up, Bee noticed the statuesque blonde walking through the square. She wore a simple figure-hugging white dress and she had that swaying walk and brash confidence that men almost always seemed to find irresistible. Certainly every man in the vicinity was staring in admiration.

'Who's that?' she asked the man beside her, who had faltered into a sudden silence. 'Is she a tourist?'

The woman looked directly at them with big brown eyes and a sultry smile on her red-tinted lips, her attention lingering with perceptible curiosity on Bee.

Nectarios gave the blonde a faint nod of acknowledgement. 'That's Melita Thiarkis.'

That familiar first name struck Bee like a slap but she would have thought nothing of it if Nectarios had not looked distinctly ill at ease.

'And she's...*who*?' she pressed, hating herself for her persistence in the face of his discomfiture.

'A fashion designer in Athens, but she was born on the island and maintains a property here.'

That fast Bee's stomach threatened to heave and she struggled to control her nausea with perspiration beading her brow and her skin turning unpleasantly clammy. The blonde *had* to be Sergios's mistress, Melita. There could not be such a coincidence. Indeed Nectarios's embarrassment at her appearance had confirmed the fact. But Bee was in shock at the news that Melita was actually staying on the island. That possibility had not even occurred to her and she had naively assumed that Orestos offered Sergios no opportunity to stray. But how many evenings had he left her alone for several hours while he attended island council meetings? Or to visit his grandfather's home? Lately there had been several such occasions and she had thought nothing of them at the time. Had she been ridiculously naive?

'May I offer you some advice?' Nectarios enquired as the four-wheel drive that had picked them up raised a trail of dust on the winding, little-used road back to the big white house with the tower on the headland.

Bee shot him a glance from troubled eyes. 'Of course.'

'Don't put pressure on my grandson. Give him the time to recognise what you have together. His first marriage was very unhappy and it left deep scars.'

The old man was the product of another generation in which men and women were not equal and women expected and even excused male infidelity. Bee had no such guiding principle to fall back on and she could not excuse what she could not live with. And she knew that she would never be able to live in silence with the suspicion that Sergios might have laid lustful hands on another woman while he was sharing a bed with Bee.

Oh, how the mighty had fallen, Bee conceded wretchedly. Now she had to face up to the reality that she had allowed Sergios to run their marriage *his* way rather than hers. They had not renegotiated the terms of their original marriage plan. There had been no earnest discussions, no agreements and no promises made on either side. For almost two months they had coasted along without the rules and boundaries that she had feared might make Sergios feel trapped. Take things slowly, Bee had thought in her innocence, eager to pin her husband down, but too sensible not to foresee the probable risks of demanding too much from him upfront.

Now she was paying the price of not frankly telling him that he could not have her *and* a mistress. Strange how she had no doubt that he would angle for that option if he thought he could get away with it. Bee was well aware of how ruthless Sergios could be. In any confrontation he was hardwired to seek the best outcome that he could. Sometimes he manoeuvred people into doing what he wanted purely as a means of amusement. She had stood on the sidelines of his life watching him, learning how he operated and monitoring her own behaviour accordingly. Although she loved him she didn't tell him that and she certainly didn't cling to him or cuddle him or flatter him or do or say any of the things that would have given her true feelings away. She had decided that she was happy to give him time to come to terms with their new relationship…as long as he was faithful.

The thought that he might not have been, that he might already have betrayed her trust in another woman's arms, threatened to tear Bee apart. In the circumstances he might even try to persuade her that he had assumed that their original agreement that he could have other women still held good. After all, Sergios thought fast on his feet and was, she reckoned ruefully, liable to fight dirty if she pushed him hard enough.

But Melita Thiarkis was a different kettle of fish. She was an islander, a local born and bred on Orestos, so Sergios had probably known her for a very long time. A fashion designer as well—no wonder he was so hung up on even his wife being stylish. There would be ties between Melita and Sergios stronger than Bee had ever wanted to consider. Melita was strikingly attractive rather than beautiful but very much the hot, sexy type likely to appeal to Sergios's high-voltage libido. The blonde was also confident of her place in Sergios's life, Bee recognised worriedly, recalling the way the other woman had looked her over without a shade of discomfort or concern. Melita, Bee reflected wretchedly, did not seem the slightest bit threatened by the fact that Sergios had recently got married. And what did that highly visible confidence signify? Had Sergios slept with his mistress since he had become Bee's husband?

As for the confirmation from Nectarios that Sergios's first marriage had been unhappy, Bee had long since worked that out for herself. The fact that there were no photos of Krista and her name was never mentioned had always suggested that that had been anything but a happy marriage. But Sergios, even though given every opportunity to do so, had still not chosen to confide that truth in Bee.

On the other hand, Bee reminded herself doggedly, she *had* been really happy and contented until she laid eyes on Melita Thiarkis and realised that temptation lived less than a mile from their door. Sergios, after all, had been remarkably attentive since they had first made love, but how could Bee possibly know what he got from his relationship with Melita? That he had insisted Melita was a non-negotiable feature of his life even *before* their marriage suggested the blonde had very good reason to be confident.

He did have a thing for blondes even though he wouldn't admit it, Bee thought bitterly as she peered at her dark brown locks in the bedroom mirror and tried to imagine herself transformed into a blonde. It would be sad to dye her hair just for his benefit, wouldn't it? Just at that moment of pain and stark fear she discovered that she didn't care if it was sad or not and she decided that she might well return from London with a mane of pretty blonde hair.

CHAPTER NINE

'I THOUGHT you would be in bed,' Sergio admitted when he landed in a helicopter after eleven that evening and strolled into the house. His tie was loosened and he was unshaven, his stunning eyes shadowed with tiredness. His sense of relief at being home again was intense and it startled him. 'It's been a long day and we have an early flight to London tomorrow morning.'

Bee glanced at him in surprise. 'You're coming with us?'

'Eleni's having surgery,' he reminded her with a frown. 'Of course I'm coming. Didn't you realise that?'

'No, I didn't.'

Delighted by his readiness to be supportive, Bee resisted the urge to immediately dredge up Melita's presence on the island. After all, if the blonde had a home and relatives on Orestos, she had a perfect right to visit and it might have nothing to do with Sergios. Was that simply wishful thinking? Bee asked herself as she put together a light supper in the big professional kitchen. She saw no need to disturb the staff so late when she was perfectly capable of feeding Sergios with her own fair hands.

He came out of his bathroom with a towel wrapped round his hips and sat down at the small table she had set up for his use. With his black hair flopping damply above his face and clean shaven, he looked less weary.

'Was it a difficult day?' Bee prompted uncertainly.

'It's always difficult.' Sergios grimaced and suddenly shrugged, acknowledging that it no longer felt reasonable to continue to keep Beatriz in the dark when it came to the touchy subject of his first marriage. 'Krista's parents remember a young woman I never knew, or maybe the young woman they talk about is the imaginary daughter they would have *liked* to have had—she certainly bears no resemblance to the woman I was married to for three years.'

Bee was confused. 'I don't understand…'

'Krista was a manic depressive and she loathed taking medication, didn't like what the prescribed tablets did to her. I didn't know about that when I married her. To be fair I hardly knew her when I asked her to marry me,' Sergios confided with a harsh edge to his dark deep drawl. 'I was young and stupid.'

'Oh.' Bee was so shattered about what his silence on the subject of his first wife had concealed that she could think of nothing else to say. A manic depressive? That was a serious condition but treatable with the right medical attention and support.

'I fell in love and rushed Krista to the altar, barely able to believe that the girl of my dreams was mine. Unfortunately the dream turned sour for us both,' he volunteered grittily, his face grim. 'As she refused medication there was no treatment that made an appreciable difference to her moods. For most of our marriage she was out of control. She took drugs and threw wild parties before crashing drunk at the wheel of one of my cars. She died instantly.'

'I am so sorry, Sergios,' Bee whispered with rich sympathy, her heart truly hurting for him. 'So very sorry you had to go through that and lose your child into the bargain.'

'The baby wasn't mine. I don't know who fathered the baby she was carrying at the time of her death.' His handsome mouth twisted. 'By then we hadn't shared a bed for a long time.'

'I wish you'd shared this with me sooner.' Bee was still struggling to accept his wounding admission of how much he had loved Krista, for she had convinced herself that Sergios didn't know *how* to love a woman. Now she was finding out different and it hurt her pride.

'I've always felt guilty that Krista died. I should've been able to do more to help her.'

'How could you when she wouldn't accept that her condition needed treatment?' Bee prompted quietly as she got into bed and rested back against the pillows. 'Didn't her parents have any influence over her?'

'She was an adored only child. They were incapable of telling her no and they refused to recognise the gravity of her problems. Ultimately they blamed me for her unhappiness.'

Striding restively about the room, his stunning eyes bleak with distressing memories and his strong jaw line clenched, he finally told her what his life had been like with Krista. When he came home to the apartment he had shared with his late wife in Athens back then he had never known what would greet him there. Violent disputes and upsetting scenes were a daily occurrence, as were his wife's periods of deep depression. Krista had done everything from shopping to partying to excess. On various occasions he had found her in bed with other men and high as a kite on the illegal drugs that she was convinced relieved her condition better than the proper medication. Staff walked out, friends were offended, the apartment was trashed and valuable objects were stolen. For three long years as he struggled to care for his deeply troubled wife Sergios had lived a life totally out of his own control and the love he had started out with had died. Bee finally understood why he had been so determined to have a businesslike marriage, which demanded nothing from him but financial input. He had put everything he had into his first marriage and it had still failed miserably. Krista had betrayed him and hurt him and taught him to avoid getting too deeply attached to anyone.

'Now you know why I never mention her,' Sergios murmured ruefully, sliding into bed beside her. 'I let her down so badly.'

'Krista was ill. You should forgive her and yourself for everything that went wrong,' Bee reasoned. 'You did your best and that's the most that anyone can do.'

Eyes level, Sergios lifted a hand and traced the full curve of her lower lip with a considering fingertip. 'You always say the right thing to make people feel better.'

Insanely conscious of his touch as she was, her heart

was galloping and her mouth had run dry. 'Do I?' she asked gruffly.

'When Paris asked you if his mother was in heaven you said yes even though you know she was an atheist, *moli mou*.'

'She still could have made it there in the end,' Bee reasoned without hesitation. 'Paris was worrying about it. I wanted him to have peace of mind.'

'I should've told you about Krista a long time ago but I hate talking about her—it feels wrong.'

'I understand why now and naturally you want to be loyal to her memory.' Melita's name was on the tip of her tongue but she could not bring herself to destroy that moment of closeness with suspicion and potential conflict. That conversation about Krista was quite enough for one evening.

'So sweet, so tactful…' Sergios leant closer, his breath fanning her cheek, and pried her lips apart with the tip of his tongue. With one kiss he could make her ache unbearably for the heat and hardness of his body.

'Someone round here has to be,' she teased, her breath rasping in her throat.

His tongue explored her tender mouth in an erotic foray and her nipples tingled into prominence. Desire slivered through her then, sharp as a blade. He freed her of the silk nightdress, cupping her breasts with firm hands, stroking the prominent pink crests with ravishing skill. She gasped beneath his mouth as he found the heated core of her and he made a sound of deep masculine satisfaction when he discovered how ready she was.

He turned her round and rearranged her, firm hands

cupping her hips as he plunged into her velvety depths with irresistible force and potency. He growled with pleasure above her head and pulled her back hard against him as he slowly rotated his hips to engulf her in an exquisite wash of sensation. While he pumped in and out of her he teased her clitoris with expert fingers. A soul-shattering climax gripped Bee as the tightening knot of heat inside her expanded and then exploded like a blazing star. Shaking and sobbing with pleasure, she fell back against him, weak as a kitten and drained of every thought and feeling.

'Go to sleep,' Sergios urged then, both arms still wrapped round her damp, trembling body. 'You'll exhaust yourself fretting about Eleni tomorrow.'

That he should know her so well almost made her laugh but she was too tired to find amusement in anything. Worry about Melita and Eleni and the passion had exhausted her and she fell heavily asleep.

Her first night back in London, Bee spent with her mother, who was both excited and apprehensive about her approaching move to Greece. Eleni was admitted to hospital the next morning. Both a nurse and the surgeon had talked Bee through every step of the entire procedure, which was likely to take less than an hour to complete, but Bee remained as nervous as a cat on hot bricks on Eleni's behalf, particularly because the little girl was too young to be prepared for the discomfort that might follow the surgery.

'We've already discussed all this,' Sergios reminded Bee firmly, very much a rock in the storm of her concern and anxiety. 'There is very little risk attached to this procedure and she will recover quickly from it. It may not improve her hearing but she is falling so far behind with her speech that it is worth a try.'

Cradling Eleni's solid little body in her lap with protective arms, Bee blinked back tears that embarrassed her for she had long since decided that surgery was currently the best treatment available. 'She's just so little and trusting.'

'Like you were when you married me,' Sergios quipped with a rueful grin, startling her with that light-hearted sally. 'You really didn't have a clue what you were signing up for but it hasn't turned out too bad for you, has it?'

'Ask me that in a year's time,' Bee advised, in no mood to stroke his ego.

'What a very begrudging response when I'm trying so hard to be the perfect husband!' he mocked.

Bee looked up at his handsome face and felt her heart leap like a dizzy teenager's. The perfect husband? Since when? And why? She had made no complaints, so it could not be her he was trying to influence. Most probably he was trying to please his grandfather, who was openly keen to see his only surviving grandson settling down with a family. But she didn't want Sergios putting on an act purely to impress Nectarios. Anything of that nature was almost certain to make Sergios feel deprived of free choice and she did not want their marriage to feel like an albatross hanging round his neck.

Bee accompanied Eleni to the very doors of the operating theatre and then waited outside with Sergios. He had taken the whole day off, which really surprised her. It was true that he stepped out several times to make and receive phone calls and that a PA brought documents for his signature, but it was so unusual for him to put work second that she was very appreciative of his continuing support.

The surgery was completed quickly and successfully and Bee took a seat by Eleni's bed. By that stage the little girl was already regaining consciousness. While she was groggy she was not, it seemed, in pain and, reassured by Bee's presence at her bedside, she soon drifted off to sleep. One of the nannies arrived to sit with the child while Sergios took Bee out for a meal and a much-needed break.

'You're exhausted. Why do I employ a team of nannies only to find you in this state? Come home with me,' Sergios urged when Bee's head began to nod towards the latter stages of their meal.

Her eyes widened and she studied him ruefully. 'I should be there if Eleni wakes up again and there is a bed in the room for me to use,' she reminded him. 'I won't have an entirely sleepless night.'

'Sometimes you should put yourself first,' Sergios reasoned levelly.

Bee tensed at that declaration and lost colour. Would he tell himself that when he felt the need for something a little more exotic than the marital bed could offer him? Would boredom or lust be his excuse? Would he even need an excuse or was sex with Melita already so familiar that it would not feel like a betrayal of his marital vows? She studied his features: the level line of his brows, the stunning dark golden eyes above those blade-straight cheekbones and the wide carnal mouth that could transport her to paradise. Her cheeks burned as she tore her attention from him. She should challenge him about Melita. Why wasn't she doing that? When would there ever be a *right* moment for such a distressing confrontation?

When Eleni was lying in a hospital bed was definitely not the right time, she decided unhappily. That conversation was not something she wanted to plunge blindly into either. She needed to know exactly what she planned to say and right at that instant it felt like too emotive a subject for her to maintain a level head. She didn't want to shout or cry. She was determined to retain her dignity. After all she was in love with him and at the end of day dignity might be all she had left to embrace, along with the empty shell of her marriage as they both retired behind their respective barriers. Would they ever share a bed again after that conversation?

'What's wrong?' Sergios demanded abruptly. 'You look haunted. Eleni's going to be fine. Stop doing this to yourself. It was a straightforward procedure and it went perfectly.'

'I know...I'm sorry. I think I'm just tired,' Bee muttered evasively, embarrassed that he could read her well enough to know that she was currently existing in a sort of mental hell. Melita was a sexy stunner; there was no getting round that hard fact. Every man in the taverna between fifteen and eighty-odd years had been staring appreciatively at the racy blonde. Just at that instant Bee could not forget, humiliatingly, that she had had to get half naked and swing provocatively round a pole to tempt her highly sexed and sophisticated husband into making their marriage a real one.

'You worry far too much about stuff.' Sergios shook his handsome dark head in emphasis. 'It's like you're always on the lookout for trouble.'

Bee was back by Eleni's bed when her cell phone vibrated silently in receipt of a text and she took it out of her jacket pocket, wondering wearily if it would be Jon Townsend again. Once he knew she would be over in London he had asked her to lunch with key charity personnel. Too concerned about Eleni's needs to spare the time for such an occasion, Bee had hedged. But it was not Jon texting her this time…

I'm in London. I would like to meet you in private*. Melita.*

Aghast at the idea while noting that the word private was emphasised, Bee looked at her phone as though it had jumped up and bitten her. Her husband's mistress was actually texting her? Was it for real? But for what possible reason would anyone try to set Bee up with a fake text purporting to be from Melita? Assuming the text was genuine, how on earth had Melita Thiarkis got Bee's phone number? Had she taken it from Sergios's phone? It was the most likely explanation and as such hit Bee's spirits hard because it was not long since she had got a new number and if Melita was in possession of it, it suggested very recent contact between Sergios and the other woman.

Bee got little sleep that night although Eleni slept like a little snoring log. Sergios put in an appearance on his way into his London office. Bee was in the corridor and noticed the ripple of interest that her extraordinarily good-looking husband excited among the nursing staff. With his tall, wide-shouldered, long-legged frame encased in a charcoal-grey designer suit, Sergios looked spectacular. Eleni was equally impressed and whooped with glee when he came through the door and held out her arms.

An odd little smile softened the hard line of Sergios's mouth as he set down the package in his hand. Bending down, he scooped the little girl gently out of her bed, addressing her in Greek as he did so.

And for the very first time Eleni answered, looking up at him with big dark eyes. The words were indistinct and the sentence structure non-existent, but it was a response she would not have attempted before the surgery.

'I noticed she was more attentive to what I was saying from the minute she woke up this morning,' Bee told him with forced brightness. 'She's definitely able to hear more. Her eyes don't wander the same way when you're speaking to her either.'

Bee helped Eleni unwrap the wooden puzzle that Sergios had brought and pulled up the bed table for the little girl's use. A ward maid popped her head round the door and offered them a cup of coffee.

'Not for me, thanks,' Sergios responded. 'I have an early meeting.'

'If her consultant thinks everything is in order, Eleni will be released later this afternoon,' Bee revealed.

'Good. The boys missed you last night,' Sergios told her.

If he had told her that *he* had missed her she would have thrown herself into his arms like a homing pigeon, but no such encouraging declaration passed his lips. Nor would it, Bee reflected wretchedly. Sergios didn't say sentimental stuff like that or make emotional statements. She loved a guy who would never ever tell her he loved her back. And why would he settle solely for Bee's charms when he already had a woman like Melita and countless other discreet lovers eternally on offer to him? He was an immensely wealthy tycoon and, when it came to women and sex, spoilt for choice and it would always be that way. Somehow, she didn't know yet *how*, she would have to come to terms with the reality of their marriage. Possibly meeting Melita Thiarkis in the flesh would be a sensible first step in that much-needed process.

That decision made, Sergios had barely left the building before Bee texted the other woman to set up the requested meeting. After all, what did she have to lose? Sergios wouldn't like the idea of them meeting at all but why should that bother her? He would never find out, would he? Had he chosen to be more frank about the relationship, however, Bee would probably have ignored the text from his mistress. Melita replied immediately and asked Bee to meet her in the bar of her Chelsea hotel mid-morning. Wary of staging such a delicate encounter in a public place, Bee suggested she come to her room instead.

Bee would very much have liked her entire designer wardrobe on hand to choose from before she met up with Melita. But, travelling direct from the hospital, that was not possible and Bee, not only had very little choice about what to wear, but despised the vain streak of insecurity that had prompted such a superficial thought. She could hardly hope to top a fashion designer in the style stakes, she told herself wryly as she freshened up her make-up and left Eleni with her nanny for company. Pausing only to tell her security team of two that she did not require them, she walked out of the hospital.

The receptionist sent her straight up to Melita's room on the first floor. She knocked only once on the door before it opened to frame the strikingly attractive woman, who even at that point impressed Bee as being vastly overdressed for morning coffee in her low-cut glittering jacket, narrow skirt and very high heels.

'Beatriz...' Melita murmured smoothly. 'I'm so grateful that you agreed to come, but let's not tell Sergios about this. Men hate it when we go behind their backs.'

CHAPTER TEN

BEE took due note of the fact that her husband's mistress, Melita, was more scared of consequences than she was. As Bee had no intention of keeping their meeting a secret unless it suited her to do so, she did not reply.

Melita already had a pot of coffee waiting in her opulent hotel room with its black and white designer chic decor. She sat down opposite Bee, a process that took a good deal of cautious lowering and wriggling in six-inch heels and a black skirt so tight it would split if put under too much pressure. Melita walked a thin line between sexy and tarty.

'I didn't think that Sergios would ever marry again,' the Greek woman said plaintively. 'But we're adults. There's no reason why we can't be, er…distant friends.'

Only one, Bee completed inwardly. *If you sleep with my husband I might try to murder you.*

'Sergios and I have been very close for a great many years,' Melita informed her with a self-satisfied smile.

Not a muscle moving on her taut face, Bee compressed her lips and pretended to sip at the too-hot coffee that Melita had poured for her. 'I guessed that.'

'I have no intention of poaching on your territory,'

Melita declared importantly. 'I've never wanted to be a wife or a mother, so I don't covet what you have.'

'But you do covet Sergios,' Bee heard herself say helplessly.

'*Any* woman would covet him,' the other woman fielded, her sultry eyes widening in amused emphasis. 'But there's no reason why we can't share him.'

'Just one,' Bee murmured flatly. 'I *don't* share.'

Melita's pencilled brows drew together in surprise at that bold statement. 'Is that a declaration of war?'

'It's whatever you choose to make of it. Why did you invite me here?' Bee enquired drily.

'I wanted to reassure you that I have no desire to damage your marriage. Sergios really does need a wife to do wifely things like looking after his houses and his children. Naturally I'm aware that it is a marriage of… shall we say…' Melita looked unconvincingly coy for a moment '…mutual convenience?'

'Oh, dear…is that what Sergios told you?' Bee asked, wincing with an acting ability she had not known she possessed, for she refused to cringe at the apparent level of Melita's knowledge about Sergios's reasons for marrying her. 'Men can be so reluctant to break bad news. I'm afraid our marriage is rather more than one of convenience.'

'If by that you mean that Sergios shares your bed, I expected that. After all you're there when I can't be and he's a man, very much a man,' Melita purred with glinting eyes of sensual recollection.

For a split second Bee felt so sick that she almost ran into the en suite and lost her sparse hospital breakfast.

She could not bear to think of Melita naked and intimately wound round Sergios. That *hurt*, that hurt like a punch in the stomach. Nor could she bear to consider herself a sexual substitute, a sort of cheap and available fast-food option instead of the grand banquet of thrilling sensuality that she imagined Melita might offer.

'You do realise, I hope, that your husband is still shagging me every chance he gets!' Dropping the civilised front with a resounding crash, Melita surveyed Bee with angry, resentful dark eyes. 'He was with me on your wedding night and I have no intention of giving him up.'

'Whatever,' Bee framed woodenly, setting down the cup with precise care and rising to her feet again with all the dignity she could muster. 'I think we've shared a little too much for comfort. If you contact me again I'll tell Sergios.'

'Don't you dare threaten me!' Melita ranted furiously.

Bee walked out and she didn't look back or breathe until she was safe inside the lift again. Sergios was still sleeping with his mistress and had been from the first night of their marriage. Why was she so shocked? What else had she expected? That a man with a notoriously active libido would suddenly turn over a new leaf on entering a platonic marriage? That had never been a possibility. Before their marriage she had agreed to him maintaining his relationship with Melita. He had said upfront that Melita was not a negotiable facet of his life. Having received that warning, she had chosen to ignore it by allowing their marriage to become much more real than either of them had ever envisaged.

Leaving the hotel, Bee was blank-eyed, her mind in chaos and emotions raging through her in horribly distressing waves. She didn't know where she was going but she knew she couldn't return to the hospital in such a state, nor would she involve her mother when she was so upset. Her cell phone was ringing and she checked it. It was Jon Townsend. Heaving a sigh, but in a strange way grateful for the distraction, Bee answered his call. He invited her to join him at his apartment for lunch with the charity's PR woman. It was somewhere to go, something to do in a world rocking on its foundations, and she agreed and boarded a bus, too wrapped in her own unhappy thoughts to notice that she was being followed.

Sergios had already cancelled appointments and left his office, planning to meet with Beatriz at the hospital. The news that she had met up with Melita had hit him like a torpedo and almost blown him out of the water. Where had that come from? How had that happened? What had he done to deserve that outcome? Nourishing a strong sense of injustice along with the suspicion that he was being royally stitched up, Sergios was in no mood to receive the bodyguard's second piece of news: Beatriz had entered an apartment owned by Jon Townsend?

'Beatriz…' From the minute Bee stepped through the door, she began regretting having agreed to lunch. Jon was alone, the PR lady apparently having been held up in traffic. Unfortunately her host's effusive welcome made Bee feel even more awkward.

Bee toyed with the salad on her plate and for the third time attempted to steer their conversation back to the subject of the charity and away from the past times that Jon seemed much more eager to discuss.

'We were so close back then.' Jon sighed fondly.

'Not as close as I thought at the time. We *were* still very young,' Bee pointed out lightly.

'I didn't realise how much you meant to me until it was too late and I'd lost you,' Jon said baldly.

'It happens.' Her attempted smile of acknowledgement was a mere twist of her lips, for she was in no frame of mind to deal tactfully with Jon's evident determination to resurrect their shared past. 'If you had been happy with me you wouldn't have strayed.'

Jon brought a hand down on top of hers and she was so irritated with him that she very nearly lifted her other hand to stab him with the fork. 'Jenna—'

Bee lifted a hand to silence him. 'Stop right there. I really don't want to hear about your marriage, Jon. It's none of my business.'

'Perhaps I want to make it your business.'

'More probably you're barking up the wrong tree— I'm in love with my husband,' Bee responded impatiently. 'And now I think it's time I went. I want to get back to the hospital.'

As she got up Jon leapt up as well and the doorbell went in one long shrill shriek as if the caller's finger had accidentally got stuck to the button.

'A shame your PR lady is arriving so late,' Bee remarked.

'That was just a ruse, Bee,' Jon snapped, his fair features twisting with bad temper and momentarily giving him the aspect of a disgruntled little boy.

'Evidently, Sergios was right to tell me that I'm too trusting,' Bee was saying as Jon angrily yanked open the front door, annoyed by the timely interruption.

Bee was totally shattered to see Sergios poised on the doorstep. 'What are you doing here?' she asked in astonishment. 'How did you find out where I was?'

His eyes had a smouldering glitter and were welded to Jon's discomfited face. 'Why did my wife say that I was right to call her too trusting?'

Bee really couldn't be bothered with Jon at that moment. The whole silly lunch set-up had thoroughly irritated her, but she didn't want Sergios to thump him. And that, she sensed, very much aware of the powerfully angry aggression Sergios exuded, was quite likely if she didn't act to defuse the tension.

'I was just joking. We were discussing a charity dinner—'

Sergios closed a hand round her wrist and drew her out of the apartment as if he couldn't wait to remove her from a source of dangerous contagion. His face hard as iron, he studied Jon, who was pale and taut. 'Leave my wife alone,' he instructed with chilling bite. 'What's mine stays mine. Try not to forget that.'

What's mine stays mine. Bee could have been very sarcastic about that assurance had she not been outraged by Sergios's intervention and sexist turn of phrase.

'Sometimes you're very dramatic,' she commented lamely, recognising that quality in him for the first time and surprised by the discovery.

'What were you doing in Townsend's apartment alone with him?' Sergios shot at her, visibly unrepentant.

'None of your business.'

As the lift doors opened on the ground floor Sergios shot Bee an arrested look. 'Explain yourself.'

'Are we going to pick up Eleni?' Bee enquired coldly instead, picturing Melita with her smug cat-got-the-cream smile. Nausea pooled in her tummy again and turned her skin clammy.

'Eleni was released an hour ago. Karen phoned me and I told her to take Eleni home.'

'Oh.' Bee made no further comment, stabbed by guilt that she had forgotten the little girl was due to leave hospital that afternoon. She felt drained by the emotional storm of the past couple of hours. The man she loved had a mistress whom he regularly slept with and would not give up. Where did she go from there? Did she really want to lower herself to the level of arguing about Melita? Did she want to run the risk of exposing how deep her own feelings went for him?

Or did she do the sensible thing? Take it on the chin and move on? Obviously no more sharing of marital beds. That kind of intimacy was out of the question with Melita in the picture. But she had signed up to a long-term relationship for the sake of her mother and for the children. Every fibre of her being might be urging her to make some sort of grand gesture like walking out on her marriage, but too many innocent people would be hurt and damaged by her doing that. Even Sergios had said that she wasn't a quitter and he had been right on that score. She gave her word and, my goodness, she stuck to it through thick and thin.

Even through Melita? Could she still stick to her word in such circumstances? Pain slivered through Bee and cut deep like a knife. They had roamed so far from their original agreement. Far too many tender feelings had got involved. Stepping back from that intimacy, learning to be detached again would be a huge challenge, she acknowledged wretchedly. Had she really once believed that she could treat Sergios like a rather demanding employer? Looking at Sergios's beloved face now, she was no longer sure that she had the strength to stand by her promise and survive the sacrifices that that would demand.

How could she bear to turn her back on what she had believed they had and know that Melita was replacing her in every way that mattered? From now on it would be Melita he kissed awake in the morning, Melita he took to dine in cosy little restaurants where nobody recognised him, Melita he bought whopping big diamonds for. How could Bee live with knowing that he had only made love to her because she was there when more tempting sexual prospects were not? What had meant so much to her had evidently meant very little to him. A cry of anguish was building up inside Bee. She felt as though she were being ripped apart.

The limo came to a halt. White-faced, she got out without even looking to see where she was going and came to a sudden bemused halt once she realised that they had not alighted at the mansion that was their London home but outside an apartment building she had never seen before. 'Where are we?'

'I own an apartment here.'

'Oh…do you?' she queried drily, wondering if this was where he had come on their wedding night to make love with his Greek blonde. She was ready to bet that he had not had to nudge Melita towards the sexy lingerie. Gut instinct warned her that Melita already had that kind of angle covered, or uncovered, as regarded his preference, she thought bitterly. Had she seriously considered dying her hair blonde? Had she really been that pathetic? Where had her pride and her independence gone?

Love had decimated those traits, she decided painfully, standing, lost and sick to the soul, in the lift on the way up to the apartment she had not known he possessed. Love had made her hollow and weak inside. Love had made her want to cling and dye her hair and wear the fancy lingerie if that was what it took to hold him. But her brain told her that that was nonsense and that those were only superficial frills, not up to the challenge of keeping a doomed relationship afloat. And a relationship between plain, ordinary, sensible Bee Blake and rich and gorgeous Sergios Demonides had always been doomed, hadn't it? A union between two such different people was unlikely to be a marriage that ran and ran against all the odds…unless you believed in miracles and wild dreams coming true. And

Bee had so *badly* wanted to believe that she could have the miracle, the dream.

Virtually blind to her surroundings while that ferocity of emotion remained in control of her, Bee preceded Sergios into a spacious lounge that had that slightly bare, unlived in quality of a property not in daily use. 'So this is where you and Melita—'

Sergios froze in front of her as though she had said a very bad word, his face clenching hard, sensual mouth compressing. 'No, not here. My grandfather uses this place when he visits London—he likes his independence. It's a company property.'

Bee nodded and her spine relaxed just a jot. She had conceived a loathing for Melita Thiarkis, everywhere the other woman had ever been with Sergios and everything to do with her that was excessive to say the least.

'She's never been here—she has her own apartment,' Sergios breathed abruptly as if he were attuned to Bee's every thought.

Never having had quite so many mean, malicious thoughts all at once, Bee seriously hoped that he was not that attuned. Her disconcerted face was hot, her complexion flushed to the hairline with embarrassment and the distress she was fighting to conceal. Suddenly unable to bear looking at him, she spun away and faked an interest in the view.

'Whatever it takes I want to keep you,' Sergios breathed with startling harshness. 'I hope you appreciate the fact that I didn't knock Townsend's teeth down his throat the way I would've liked to have done.'

'You can be such a caveman.' In a twisty way that

appealed to the dark side of her temperament, she was painfully amused that despite his own extra-marital interests he could still be so possessive of *her*. The logic of his attitude escaped her. But, of course, he wanted to keep her as a wife: he needed her for the children. They loved her and she loved them. Now there had to be a compromise found that she and Sergios could both live with. Some magical solution that would provide a path through the messy swell of emotion currently blurring her view of the world.

'Look at me…' Sergios urged.

'I don't want to,' Bee said truthfully, but she turned round all the same.

She wondered why it was that she could now see that Jon sulked and pouted like a spoilt little boy when he didn't get his own way, but that in spite of what she had learned about Sergios she still could not see a visible flaw in him. He remained defiantly gorgeous from his stunning dark golden eyes to his slightly stubbled and shadowed chin.

'That's better,' he murmured, scrutinising her with an intensity that made her uncomfortable.

'Why did you bring me here?'

'If we're going to argue, if there's going to be dissension between us, I didn't want the children as an audience,' Sergios admitted flatly, features grave.

'My word, you think of everything!' Bee was all too wretchedly aware that she would not have considered that danger until it was too late.

'They deserve better from us—'

'Is that you reminding me of my duty?' Bee prompted tightly, her throat suddenly thickening with tears.

'Whatever it takes I want to hold onto you.'

'You already said that.'

'It's more than I've ever said to a woman,' Sergios breathed roughly, challenge in the stance of his big powerful body. He stood tall with broad shoulders thrown back and strong legs braced as though he were expecting a blow.

He wanted everything, he wanted too much, she reflected unhappily. He wanted his mistress and he wanted his wife, a combination he evidently believed necessary to his comfort and happiness. Emotion didn't come into it for him. If only it didn't come into it for her either! Her eyes prickled hotly and she kept them very wide, terrified that the tears threatening her would spill over in front of him.

'If we're staying here I could do with lying down for a while,' she said abruptly, desperate for some privacy.

'Of course.' He crossed the room and pressed open a door that led into a corridor. He showed her into the bedroom and startled her by yanking the bedspread off the bed and pulling back the duvet for her. He looked across at her, a dark uncertainty in his eyes that she had never seen before, and for the first time it occurred to her that he was upset as well.

'Thanks,' she said dully, taking off her jacket and kicking off her shoes.

'Would you like a drink?' he enquired without warning.

'A brandy,' she responded, dimly recalling that

being recommended for shock in a book she had read. Probably not at all the right remedy for shock in today's world, she thought ruefully. In fact, couldn't alcohol act as a depressant? In the mood she was in, she didn't need that, did she?

Seemingly glad, however, of something to do, Sergios strode out of the room and she sat down on the bed. Time seemed to move on without her noticing, for he reappeared very quickly and handed her a tumbler half full of brandy. 'Are you trying to get me drunk?' she asked in disbelief.

'You look like a ghost, all white and drawn. Drink up,' Sergios urged.

'I can't live like this with you…' she framed, the admission leaping off her tongue before she could stop it.

Sergios came down on his knees at her feet and pushed the tumbler towards her mouth. 'Drink,' he urged again.

'It might make me sick.'

'I don't think so.'

All of a sudden she noticed that the hand he had on the glass was trembling almost infinitesimally. He was behaving as though the drink might be a lifesaver, rather than a pick-me-up. She sipped, shuddering as the alcohol ran like a flame down her throat, making her cough and splutter. She collided with strained dark eyes.

'What the heck is the matter with you?' Bee demanded in sudden frustration. 'You're behaving very oddly.'

Sergios vaulted upright. 'What do you expect? You go and see my former mistress—then you run straight off to stage a private meeting with your ex, who's clearly desperate to get you back!' he exclaimed wrathfully. 'I mean, it's not exactly been my dream day and I still don't know what the hell is going on!'

Former mistress? Her ears were practically out on stalks. Was he planning to try and lie his way out of the tight corner he was in? Pretend that his relationship with Melita was over? While pondering that salient point, Bee drank deep of the brandy, grateful for the heat spreading and somehow soothing her cold, empty tummy.

'Why did you go and see Melita?' he demanded heavily. 'What the hell made you do such a thing?'

Her brow indented. 'She asked me to come and see her.'

His lean powerful face set granite hard at that claim. '*She* asked…*you*?'

Bee lifted her chin. 'Yes and I was curious. Of course I was. I saw her on the island last week.'

His gaze narrowed. 'Nectarios mentioned it but I hoped you didn't realise who she was.'

Bee rolled her eyes. 'I'm not stupid, Sergios.'

'Not obviously so,' he conceded. 'But if you believed I've been with her since we got married, you are being stupid.'

'According to Melita you've been shagging her every chance you got—that's a direct quote from her,' Bee told him.

Sergios looked astonished. 'I thought better of her. We parted—as I thought—on good terms.'

'When did you last see her?'

'About six weeks ago in Athens. We did not have sex,' Sergios added sardonically. 'I have not slept with her since we got married.'

Bee vented a scornful laugh. 'How am I supposed to believe that about the woman you insisted you had to keep in your life in spite of our marriage?'

'It's the truth. Melita was part of my routine.'

'Routine?' Bee repeated with distaste.

'It wasn't a romantic relationship. I financed her fashion house, she shared my bed. She travelled all round the world to meet up with me. It was easier keeping her as a mistress than having to adapt to different women,' Sergios admitted, his discomfort with the topic obvious. 'I've known her for a long time. I backed her first fashion collection because she was an islander. We ended up in bed after Krista died and I found Melita's casual approach to sex attractive at a time when I didn't want anything heavy.'

'If it was over why did she lie?'

'Presumably because she thought that if she could cause trouble between us I might come back to her,' Sergios suggested grimly. 'I'm furious that she approached you and lied to you. I made a generous settlement on her at the end of our affair and she should've been satisfied with that.'

'She said you were with her on our wedding night.'

Sergios swore only half below his breath, anger burning in his keen gaze. 'I was supposed to see her but I cancelled.'

'You went out.'

'I went to a casino, played the tables and drank.

Going to her didn't feel right. I know our marriage was supposed to be a fake but making a point of being with her that particular night...' Sergios shrugged uncomfortably. 'It would've felt disrespectful, so I didn't do it.'

'Disrespectful,' Bee echoed weakly, her attention nailed to his face, recognising the combination of discomfiture and sincerity she saw there.

'I swear I have not been with Melita,' Sergios growled, his patience taxed almost beyond its limits. 'And if I have to drag her here and make her admit that to your face, I will not shrink from the challenge.'

'She wouldn't come.'

'She would if I threatened to withdraw the settlement I made on her. She signed a legal agreement, promising to be discreet about our past relationship and approaching my wife and lying to her is not, by any stretch of the imagination, discreet!' he bit out thunderously, his anger at what he had learned unconcealed.

Bee recalled how very keen Melita had been to ensure that Sergios did not know about their meeting, hardly surprising if the money he had given her was dependent on her remaining tactfully silent about their affair. Was it possible that she had simply wanted to cause trouble? Naturally she would blame Bee for Sergios having broken off their relationship.

'I'm starting to believe you,' Bee confided with a frown, worried that she was being ridiculously credulous while at the same time recalling that she had yet to find out that Sergios had ever lied to her about anything. He was much more given to lethal candour than dishonesty.

'Thank God,' he breathed in Greek.

'But I still don't get why you were so determined to retain Melita that you even told me about her before the wedding…only to get rid of her a few weeks later.'

Sergios groaned like a man in torment. 'Obviously because I had you and didn't need her any longer.'

'Oh…' was all Bee could think to say to that. Was it really that simple for him? Instead of sex with Melita he had discovered sex with his wife and found it a perfectly adequate substitute? Seemingly it *was* that simple on his terms. It was a huge relief to appreciate that he had not betrayed her with Melita. Her head was swimming a little and she thought that perhaps she had had a little too much brandy.

'You're fantastic in bed, *yineka mou.*'

'Am I?' Bee settled big green eyes on him, wide with wonderment at that assurance.

'I haven't even looked at another woman since I married you,' Sergios spelt out forcefully. 'Nor will I in the future. That's a promise. Will you come home with me now?'

A huge smile was tugging the last of the stress from round her ripe mouth. 'You still haven't explained how you knew where I was this afternoon.'

'Your security team know not to listen to you if you try to go anywhere without them in tow. They followed you. What did Townsend want?'

'Me apparently, but after all this time I'm really not interested. I told him that I…er…' Bee hesitated at what she had almost revealed. 'I told Jon that I had become quite attached to you.'

'Attached? Is that a fact?' Sergios prompted softly, sitting down on the bed beside her and tucking her hair back behind one small ear with a gentle hand. 'I'm quite attached to you as well.'

'Sexually speaking,' Bee qualified, a glutton for accuracy.

'Well, I have to admit that you have the most fabulous breasts and I'm ashamed to admit that they are the first thing I noticed about you the night we met,' Sergios confessed with the beginnings of a wicked grin. 'But you've contrived to build whole layers on that initial impression. You're a great listener, marvellous company, very loyal, intelligent and affectionate. When I'm angry or stressed you make me feel calm. When I'm unkind you make me see another viewpoint. I'm not even mentioning how wonderful you are with the children because that's not what you and I are about any more—'

Bee went from hanging on his every flattering word to cutting in with a quick question. 'It's...*not*?'

'Of course, it's not. We started out with a practical marriage.'

'You told Melita that too, didn't you?' Bee recalled unhappily, her brow indenting with a remembered sense of humiliation.

His forefinger smoothed away the tension that had tightened her mouth. 'I'm afraid it slipped out but I really did believe we were going to have a marriage that was like a business deal.'

'And how do you feel now?' she whispered.

'Like I made the killing of a lifetime when I got you to the altar,' Sergios declared, his eyes warmer than she had ever seen them as he studied her intently. 'You've got to know how crazy I am about you. You taught me to love again. You taught me how to trust and you transformed my life.'

Bee stared at him wide-eyed. 'You're crazy about me?'

'I'm hopelessly in love with you.'

Bee wrapped both arms round him as though he were a very large teddy bear and dragged him down to her. 'I was trying to save face when I said I was attached to you.'

'I rather hoped that that was what you were doing, *agape mou*.'

'I love you too but I still don't know why.'

'Don't question it too closely in case you change your mind,' Sergios warned.

'It's just you weren't the most loveable guy around when we got married.'

'But I'm really working at it now,' he pointed out. 'And I won't stop.'

Bee studied him with bemused green eyes. 'You promise?'

'I promise. I love you. All I want is to make you happy.'

The sincerity in his liquid dark gaze went straight to her impressionable heart and tears stung the backs of her eyes. Finally, she believed him. Their marriage was safe. Even better, he was hers in exactly the way she had dreamed. He loved her and love was, she sensed, the only chain that would hold him.

'I should've known I was in trouble when I bought that wedding dress,' Sergios confided with a rueful laugh.

'What were you doing at a fashion show?' As he winced she guessed the answer. 'You were there because of Melita and yet you picked a dress for me?' she prompted in amazement.

'I saw the dress and I couldn't help picturing you wearing it and I know it was high-handed of me but I was determined that you should have it,' Sergios revealed.

She was touched by the admission that even before their wedding he had been attracted to her to that extent. 'Yet we both thought that I was going to be more of an employee than a real wife.'

'Even I can be stupid.'

Bee grinned with appreciation. 'Hold on while I get a microphone and record that statement.'

'Well, I was stupid about you. I was fighting what I felt for you right from the start.'

'Your marriage to Krista hurt you a great deal,' Bee commented softly, understanding that and willing to forgive the time it had taken for him to recognise his feelings for her.

'I thought I would be happier living without a serious relationship in my life. You rewrote everything I thought I knew about myself. I wanted you. I wanted you in my bed, my home, involved in every aspect of my day.' Sergios circled her mouth slowly, gently, with his. 'I know I didn't tell you that I'd finished with Melita but I didn't see the need.'

'I thought that maybe you thought you could still have both of us.'

Unexpectedly, Sergios laughed. 'No, I was never that stupid. I knew that wasn't an option but possibly I felt a little foolish about changing my mind so quickly and wanting the kind of marriage I said I definitely didn't want.'

Bee brushed a high cheekbone with gentle fingertips, loving the new confidence powering her. 'That aspect never occurred to me.'

'It should've done. I thought I had our marriage all worked out and it blew up in my face because I couldn't keep my hands off you.'

'When I saw Melita I decided you only liked blondes…and for just a little while I actually considered getting my hair dyed. It was my lowest moment,' Bee confided with a wince of shame.

Sergios groaned out loud, his long fingers feathering through her glossy dark hair. 'I'm very grateful you didn't do it. I love your hair the way it is—'

'I might grow it longer for you,' Bee proffered, feeling unusually generous.

Sergios pressed her back against the pillows and extracted a kiss that was full of hungry urgency. 'Now that we're here, we might as well take advantage.'

'Oh, yes,' Bee agreed, full pink lips swollen, eyes wide with desire as the tug of arousal pinched low in her tummy.

And the kissing shifted into a fairly wild bout of lovemaking. Afterwards, Bee lay in her husband's arms, feeling loved and secure and boundlessly happy and grateful for what she had.

On the drive back to their London home that evening, Sergios dealt her a slightly embarrassed appraisal and said abruptly, 'I thought that possibly in a few months' time we might consider having a baby.'

'On the grounds that we've got so many children we might as well have another?' Bee prompted very drily.

Sergios grimaced. 'I suppose I deserve that reminder but I've changed. I would like to have a child with you some day in the future.'

'I can agree to that now you've got the right attitude,' Bee told him chirpily and she flung herself into his arms with abandon and snuggled close. 'And now I know that you love me, you had better get used to me doing stuff like this.'

His strong arms enfolded her and dark golden eyes rested on her animated face with tender appreciation. 'And maybe I've even learned to like it, *yineka mou*.'

Bee relaxed and knew she could hug him to her heart's content. From here on in there would be no more boundaries she feared to cross.

EPILOGUE

'How do you feel?' Sergios asked, his anxiety obvious.

'Absolutely fine!' Bee exclaimed, widening her bright eyes in reproach. 'Stop fussing!'

But Bee was less than pleased with her reflection in the mirror. It was Nectarios's eighty-third birthday and they were throwing a big party for the older man at their home on the island. She was wearing a beautiful evening gown in one of her favourite colours but, it had to be said, nothing, not even the fabulous diamonds glittering in her ears and at her throat, could make her elegant in her own eyes while she was heavily pregnant. At almost eight months pregnant with their first child, she felt like a ship in full sail.

Sergios drew her back against him, his hands splaying gently across her swollen abdomen, his fascination palpable as he felt the slight ripple of movement as their daughter kicked. A little girl, that was what they were having according to the most recent sonogram. Eleni was four years old and she was very excited about the baby sister who would soon be born. Bee had enjoyed furnishing a nursery and had frittered away many a happy hour choosing baby equipment and clothing.

Bee, however, could hardly believe that she and Sergios had been married for going on for three years. They had waited a little longer than they had originally planned to try for a baby but she had conceived quickly. There was not a single cloud in Bee's sky. The previous year, Melita Thiarkis had sold her island property and set up permanent home in Milan with an Italian millionaire. Bee had never got involved with the charity Jon Townsend had worked with because he made her uncomfortable, but she had picked another charity, one that concentrated on disabled adults like her mother. When she was not running round after the children or travelling with Sergios, for they did not like to be kept apart for more than a couple of nights, she put in sterling work seeking out sponsors for the organisation and raising funds.

Bee's mother, Emilia was firmly settled now in her cottage on Orestos. Happier and healthier than she had been for several years, the older woman was fully integrated into island life and a good deal less lonely and bored. She loved living close to her daughter and took great pleasure in Paris, Milo and Eleni running in and out of her house and treating her as an honorary grandmother. Nectarios was a regular visitor to his grandson's home and a very welcome one. He was thrilled that his fourth great-grandchild was on the way.

'You've made so many arrangements for this party. I don't want you to tire yourself out,' Sergios admitted.

The house was full of guests and there was a distant hum, which probably signified the approach of another helicopter ready to drop off more guests.

'I'll be fine.' Bee was wryly amused by the level of his concern, for she had enjoyed a healthy pregnancy that had impinged very little on her usual routine. He was so supportive though, having rigorously attended every medical appointment with her.

Sergios studied the woman he loved and once again worked to suppress his secret fear of the idea of anything ever happening to her. The more he loved her, the more central she became to his world, and the more he worried but the bottom line, the payoff, he had learned, was a level of love and contentment he had never known until she entered his life.

'I love you, *agape mou*,' he murmured gently at the top of the sweeping staircase.

Bee met his stunning dark golden eyes and felt the leap of every sense with happy acceptance. The world they had made together was a safe cocoon for both them and the children. 'I love you more than I could ever say.'

* * * * *

MARRIED FOR THE GREEK'S CONVENIENCE

MICHELLE SMART

CHAPTER ONE

IF XANDER TRAKAS had thought his week couldn't get any worse, this was the nail in the coffin to finish him off.

His American lawyer, a thorough man if ever there was one, had confirmed that Xander's marriage to Elizabeth Young was indeed registered with all the relevant jurisdictions and authorities. However, there was no evidence of their annulment.

They were still married.

He grabbed the back of his neck and rubbed it hard, breathing deeply.

The whole *Celebrity Spy!* scandal was the mess that just kept giving. What had started as a relatively small teaser promising to reveal the 'juiciest and most scandalous details' about the world's most eligible and debauched bachelors had grown into the scandal of the decade. And to think he had dismissed that initial teaser... Yes, he was considered one of the world's most eligible bachelors, but debauched? He'd heard plenty of lewd stories about his new brothers in arms over the years. Compared to them he was practically a virgin.

Okay, that might be a notion too far, but a few monogamous affairs throughout the years had nothing on the legendary exploits of Dante Mancini, Benjamin Carter or Sheikh Zayn Al-Ghamdi.

The subsequent articles, not just in *Celebrity Spy!* but in its rival tabloids and websites the world over, had painted a picture of himself he simply did not recognise. Three of his ex-lovers had sold him out, embellishing and sensationalising what, to him, had been perfectly normal healthy affairs. Half a dozen women he struggled to remember even meeting had sold tales of their nights together. It was complete rubbish.

Strangely enough, the only woman from his past he hadn't worried about selling her soul for a piece of gold was the woman he'd made the mistake of marrying a decade ago.

All it needed was for one tenacious reporter to go digging through the court records and his marriage would be there for the world to see. It wouldn't take them long to put two and two together and see that while his jilted Greek fiancée had been falling apart at the seams, he'd been romancing and marrying an American beauty, oblivious to the destruction he'd left behind.

He'd never spoken of his marriage to Elizabeth. Not to anyone. Not his parents. Not his friends.

They'd never lived as man and wife. They'd met, married and gone their separate ways in a mad two-week period on the honeymooner's paradise of St Francis.

But their separate ways did not include the annulment Elizabeth had sworn—with an uncouth curse thrown at him for good measure—she would obtain.

The last time he'd seen her had been in their hotel villa. She'd had tears streaming down her shell-shocked face.

Did she know their annulment had been denied? Did the billionaire matchmaker know she was the legal wife of a billionaire herself? It beggared belief that she didn't know, but in all their years apart she'd never reached out to him, not once.

And he'd never reached out to her. He'd pushed her face from his mind almost completely.

He would have to tread carefully.

The report he'd had compiled on her had revealed a different woman from the one he'd known then. She was no longer a carefree nineteen-year-old who lived for nothing more than to feel the wind in her hair and the sun on her face. In the decade since they'd gone their separate ways she'd built a new and successful life for herself.

His phone vibrated, breaking through his thoughts. Hoping it would be his lawyer, who he'd ordered to find out exactly *why* their annulment had failed, he only just stopped himself pressing the accept button in time. The caller was his father, someone he was not in the mood to speak to.

Xander couldn't face another argument. The daily calls from Greece were becoming increasingly fractious, from both sides. Late last night, his sister-in-law had been admitted into hospital with alcohol poisoning. Liver failure had been diagnosed. Unless Xander's brother stopped shovelling drugs into his system, his body would be the next to break down.

All of this would have been difficult enough to cope with without having to deal with the major press intrusion the *Celebrity Spy!* scandal had unleashed.

Tonight he needed to keep himself together and his head straight. He would return home first thing in the morning but for now he had the annual gala for the Hope Foundation, the main charity he supported, to attend. The press would be out in force. All four of the men in the eye of the scandal would be under the same roof for the first time. They all supported this charity, and evidence was growing that it was now suffering because of its association with them.

Although their businesses lay in different fields, they'd been rivals for years. All four of them were strong, ultra-wealthy men with hard noses for business. There had been nothing friendly about their interactions. Tonight, he suspected they would have to find a way to breach their usual silent antagonism.

All four of them were feeling the pressure. They were in the eye of the storm and the sooner they found their way out of it, the better.

Two weeks later

Elizabeth Young stepped into her West Village apartment with a very real sense of relief. After a week away in Rome, she welcomed the return to the space she called home.

She loved her apartment, set in the heart of New York's oldest district. While it wasn't the largest piece of real estate around—she earned excellent money but not *that* excellent—she had never lived with such contentment anywhere else.

For perhaps the dozenth time since she'd landed at JFK, she checked her cell phone, telling herself it was concern for Piper that had her looking and not the looming possibility of her ex-husband getting in touch.

It was hearing Piper vocalise his name that had her so on edge. The beautiful Australian had been openly prying her with questions. Elizabeth didn't blame her. In Piper's shoes she would have been curious too. Three of the men implicated in the *Celebrity Spy!* scandal had called on her services so it was only natural the fourth would require her assistance too.

Dante did say Xander must call you too.

Were those Piper's words? They had definitely been something along those lines and had forced Elizabeth to confront what she had spent almost a fortnight in denial about.

Benjamin, Zayn and Dante had all said they'd been recommended to her by Xander. He'd passed her details to them.

She had no idea how her ex-husband knew what she did for a living or how he'd got her details. Leviathan Solutions was run in utter secrecy on a strict word-of-mouth basis.

She assured herself that just because he'd recommended her to the other men it didn't mean he required her services for himself. His situation was different from the others. Timos SE had been solely owned by the Trakas family for generations.

As a company, it owned countless beauty and clothing lines that were sold around the world. Their customer base couldn't care less about the scandal. They had no shareholders to pacify or stock markets to tumble from. Xander didn't need to marry to preserve a family image...

In those first few raw days after he'd dumped her, she'd lived in a cold uncomprehending fog. She would wake hoping it had all been a bad dream and stretch her fingers out, hoping to find him there.

On the fourth day she'd checked her cell phone for the hundredth time, praying for word from him. At that exact same moment her mother had walked into her room. Elizabeth had looked from the cell in her hand to the woman who'd raised her, and the rose-coloured glasses she'd worn all her life had slipped off.

Romance and everlasting love were myths. Her parents were prime examples of this truth and she'd been a naïve idiot to think she would be any different.

From that moment her life changed. Everything.

Over the subsequent years she'd *refused* to think of the man who'd broken her heart. As far as she'd been concerned, he didn't exist, which worked for three years until she stumbled on a profile article about the newly appointed head of Timos SE, Xander Trakas. Xander had managed the seemingly impossible and broken into the American market.

Reading it, she'd learned exactly how wealthy he and the Trakas family were, and how powerful; on a par with the Onassis family. It was through this article she'd learned about Ana Soukis. His childhood sweetheart. Xander and Ana had been going to marry but Ana had tragically died in a car accident before they could exchange their vows.

Xander had been twenty when Ana died. The same age he'd been when he'd married *her*, the lying, cheating dirtbag.

Either he'd married Elizabeth when he was engaged to another woman or he'd married her when he should have been grieving the love of his life.

She'd burnt the article and thanked her lucky stars the lying, cheating scumbag had dumped her before it had been too late to get an annulment. She didn't think she would have been able to handle a divorce.

As much as she'd hated herself for doing it, she'd kept an eye out for his name over the years. Xander had never remarried. And why should he? He had women falling off his arm; even more women than she had thought possible if one believed *Celebrity Spy!*

Of all the men in the eye of the scandal's storm, Xander was the least affected. He had no need to find a wife.

She shouldn't be thinking of him, she told herself crossly, slipping into her bathroom and putting the plug in the tub.

After a fourteen-hour flight she felt grubby and completely out of sorts.

If Piper hadn't said what she had, Elizabeth wouldn't even be thinking of him.

Determined to shove him from her mind, she thought of Piper instead and wished with all her heart she could warn her away from Dante. Elizabeth hadn't matched them together. Their marriage was being born from a one-night stand that had resulted in a pregnancy. Elizabeth's services had been required only to make the poor woman over and turn her into a shining, sparkly wife who would look good on Dante's arm.

If she'd been asked to match Dante with anyone, Piper would have been the last woman on the list. She was much too sweet and naïve for the world she was being thrust into.

Just as she, Elizabeth, had once been too sweet and naïve.

She stripped naked and stepped into the steaming, frothy water, then lay back and closed her eyes.

Her cell rang.

Every atom in her body froze. Including her brain.

Then her heart kick-started, hammering against her ribs as if demanding attention.

Breathing deeply and keeping her eyes squeezed shut, Elizabeth did something she had never done before and ignored it.

Eventually it rang off to voicemail.

A short vibration a moment later told her the caller had left a message.

She opened her eyes and gazed up at the white ceiling she had painted herself, and willed her body into calm.

It didn't have to be him. It could have been anyone. Her clients were the richest of the rich and not used to waiting for anyone. Most had no concept of personal space or personal time, not when it came to anyone but themselves. To them, she was employed to do a job and if they wanted to call her at ten p.m. on a Friday evening then she should damn well be available to take the call.

She would check the message when she got out and call whoever it was back. Her business was her baby and the one thing in her life she was proud of. She'd built it up from scratch and…

The cell rang out again.

This time her heart flew up her throat. She turned her head to stare at it. She'd placed it on the small ledge where she always put it, within arm's reach. The screen was flashing in time to the ring.

Before she could galvanise herself to do anything, it went through to voicemail again.

Within ten seconds it started ringing again.

A surge of adrenaline propelled her up. She wiped her hand on the towel on the sink then snatched the phone. It wasn't a number she recognised.

Her heart now gearing itself to fly out of her mouth, she put the cell to her ear.

'Hello?' she said tremulously.

'Elizabeth?'

Hearing Xander's deep voice in her ear was as shocking as if she'd plunged herself into a bucket of ice. Her body reacted as if she had, the phone slipping from her rigid fingers and landing with a splash in the water between her legs.

Twenty minutes later, her blood pressure almost back to normal, her body dry and cocooned in a thick towelling robe, Elizabeth unplugged her hairdryer, which she'd blasted at the SIM card she'd yanked out of her sopping phone. Still cursing herself for her stupidity and hoping the damage was minimal, she inserted the SIM card into her old phone, which she'd dug out of a drawer.

It took three nail-biting minutes before she could confirm the switchover had been successful and that all her contacts had been saved. Unfortunately there was no way to track Xander's number on the old cell, but intuition told her it wouldn't be long before she heard from him again, and this time she would be prepared.

Her intuition was correct.

Her old cell still had everything set up on it, including emails. A message pinged into her inbox.

Elizabeth, it's Xander. I assume you're having issues with your phone. Here's my number. Call me as soon as possible.

Her first impulse was to burst into tears but, before they could be unleashed, anger so strong it burned flushed through her and dried the unshed tears in an instant.

So he *was* going to follow in the footsteps of his fellow Casanovas and employ her.

The *nerve* of him. The crassness. The complete lack of sensitivity.

What did *he* need a wife for?

As tempting as it was to fire an angry email back and tell him in graphic detail what he could do with his order to call him back *as soon as possible*, she held herself back.

Xander had left her ten years ago. If she were rude or ignored him it would imply that she was still angry with him, which in turn would imply she had never gotten over him, which in itself was ridiculous. She was simply tired and overwrought after a busy few weeks.

She would *prove* she didn't have any residual feelings for him.

She stood in front of her bedroom mirror and counted to thirty, then keyed in the number. It was answered on the first ring.

'Thanks for calling me back.'

His businesslike tone echoed into her ear.

Keeping her focus on her reflection, Elizabeth fixed a smile to her face so her complete lack of residual feelings for him echoed down the line. 'No problem. My apologies for earlier. I dropped my cell phone in Rome and it's been playing up since.' The lie fell smoothly from her tongue. Her voice sounded as friendly as she wanted it to be.

'Is it liable to cut out again?'

'No. I'm back home and have switched to my old one.'

'Good.' Without any pause he added, 'I need to see you.'

'Okay.' She dragged the word out to stop herself from screaming at him and then hurtling the cell down the toilet. Still smiling, she said, 'Do you have a particular date in mind?' If she could get out of this she would but her company—her very reputation—was built on her personal touch. She brought her own unique take to matchmaking and it was hugely successful. The staff she employed were for technical and clerical support only.

'I'm flying to your part of the world shortly. Are you available to meet tomorrow?'

Xander lived on a Greek island. Elizabeth made some swift calculations. It had to be almost six a.m. there. What time did the man get up?

Then she remembered the news stories. He probably hadn't gone to bed yet.

Or was he speaking to her *from* his bed? Did he have a woman asleep beside him at that very moment?

'Elizabeth?'

Swallowing back the sick feeling roiling in her stomach, she thought of her upcoming schedule. 'When you say tomorrow…?'

'Saturday. I should land around three p.m. Eastern time.'

'I have a lunch appointment tomorrow.'

'So you can do the afternoon.' It was a statement not a question and it set panic clawing through her.

'I'm free for the whole of Sunday,' she said, jumping at the chance to delay the meeting, even if only by a day. 'Do you know where my office is?'

'We won't be meeting there. I need you to fly out to meet me.'

Prickles made a slow crawl up her spine but she kept her tone breezy. 'Meet you where?'

'St Francis.'

All the air seemed to knock itself out of her lungs and the smile fell from her face.

'There won't be time to get my jet to New York to collect you, so I'll charter one to fly you over when your appointment's finished,' he continued. 'Pack an overnight bag and keep Sunday clear for me.'

She couldn't speak. Her brain had gone cold, her knees weakening enough that she shuffled back and sank onto the edge of her bed.

'Is there a problem, Elizabeth?' There was a hint of challenge in his businesslike tone.

She covered her mouth to hide the sound of herself clearing her throat, then said, 'There's no problem at all. I'll meet wherever it's most convenient for you.'

'St Francis is where it's convenient for me.'

'Are you aware I require a down payment of a quarter of my fee for overseas trips?' She strove to keep her voice composed and her breathing even.

'Message me your banking details and the amount, and I'll get it paid.'

Before she could think let alone voice any objection, he said, 'That's everything settled, then. I'll see you tomorrow.'

And then the line went dead.

She pulled the phone away from her ear and gazed at it as if it might suddenly bite.

Had that really just happened?

Billionaires throwing their weight around was nothing new. She was used to acting on their whims and fancies, had once conducted an interview with a client in a luxury Saharan Bedouin tent less than twelve hours after his initial call. To reach billionaire status required a ruthlessness mere mortals struggled to achieve. They weren't all bad people by any means but they were used to getting their own way and working to their own agenda, and she was used to complying with their whims. It was one of the reasons she'd become such a hit in their world.

Her conversation with Xander was a variety of one she'd held dozens of times with other clients. It hadn't been anything special. They were strangers who happened to have been married once and spent a grand total of fourteen days together. He clearly had no residual feelings for her, just as she had none for him.

It was the destination of St Francis that had thrown her into a funk.

Of all the places in the world, why there? *Why?*

It couldn't be coincidence that her ex-husband had chosen the very island where they'd met, married and separated to employ her services in finding him a new wife.

* * *

Xander disconnected the call and sighed heavily. He walked to his window and looked out over the Aegean, where the sun's first rays bounced on the horizon between the lightening sky and the still dark sea.

That was a call he'd hoped to not have to make. After the furious row with his parents that had gone on into the early hours, he'd come to the conclusion he had no other choice.

For his nephew's sake he needed a wife and he needed one now. It was sheer chance that he already had one.

All he had to do was convince Elizabeth to go along with it. After the way he'd ended things between them all those years ago, he knew he had a fight on his hands to get it. He could handle it. He was used to battles. Every day of his life was one.

He'd heard her sharp inhalation when he'd mentioned their destination. He'd deliberately kept their conversation short and to the point so she wouldn't have time to object. He would not give her the time or place to reject his proposal.

Elizabeth wasn't the girl he'd fallen for all those years ago who wore her heart on her sleeve and her emotions on her face. She'd matured into a discreet, professional woman with a cool analytical head.

She would need that cool head if she were to make the correct decision and agree to be his wife again.

CHAPTER TWO

THE PRIVATE JET Xander had chartered for her circled St Francis's small airport. Elizabeth gripped the hand rest. It wasn't fear of landing that made her knuckles whiten but fear of what the evening would bring.

She'd had one night to dream up something inventive to get out of it; family emergency, car accident, diabetic coma... She'd rejected every one of them.

When all was said and done, this was her job. Her services were discreet and known only to a select few, but those select few inhabited their own world. All it would take was one whisper of unprofessionalism or unreliability and the reputation she'd spent eight years building up would be smashed down.

The Xander she'd known didn't exist. All she knew of the real Xander was his reputation, and that was of a man who didn't suffer fools. If he had any affection left for her he wouldn't have insisted they meet at St Francis.

She'd loved him once, with the whole of her heart. The morning she'd packed her suitcase full of excitement at the thought of flying to Diadonus, the island he lived on, to meet his family and begin their new life together, he'd pulled the rug out from under her. He'd told her that he'd made a mistake; that he didn't love her, his family would hate her and he'd be returning to Diadonus alone.

Her lungs and stomach contracted into balls as the pain of that moment hit her afresh. But she would give anything to live it again, so she could keep her composure and not have his last memory of her being one where she could hardly breathe through the tears.

In their short time together on this island she would show nothing but her professional face. She would be polite and friendly. She would treat him exactly as she would any other client. She would smile and pretend he wasn't a lying cheat who'd broken her heart.

The jet landed smoothly but that didn't stop the nausea increasing. She hadn't been this nervous since she'd walked out of her home and into the big wide world alone and unsupported.

The early evening sun still blazed over the pristine airport, casting the ground and small white terminal in a golden haze. She stepped off the jet, holding tightly to her carry-on case, purse and laptop bag. After the freezing New York temperatures, the warmth was welcome.

Before she'd travelled to St Francis, Elizabeth had never left the States, had hardly left New York. Then her granny had died and left some money for her only grandchild, her will stipulating clearly that she wanted Elizabeth to use some of it 'to get out of this darn country and see something of the world'.

Her granny would be delighted to know Elizabeth's work took her all over the world. And of all the places she'd been, this exclusive Caribbean island remained in her mind as the most beautiful place on earth…but the memory was tainted. It was as if the fine white sand had become tiny shards of glass and the clear blue Caribbean Sea, so enticing and welcoming, filled with poison.

An official in a golf buggy greeted her, gave her passport a cursory glance and whisked her off to the car park.

A rugged black four-by-four gleamed beside the terminal wall. At their approach, the driver got out, the setting sun enveloping him in the same haze as the surroundings.

Her heart leapt and her throat closed. It was Xander.

He strode towards her, his long legs covered by a pair of tan chinos, a short-sleeved pale blue shirt stretched across his honed torso, the brown hair she remembered as rumpled now cropped with a slight quiff at the front.

Her grip on her case tightened. He reached them, nodded at the driver and then fixed the sparkling blue eyes she'd once gazed into without blinking for what had seemed like hours on her...

Her insides turned to jelly. From deep in her chest a swell erupted; that awful need to burst into tears and sob. Where it came from she didn't know, but she controlled it. She'd known this wouldn't be easy and, she told herself, this would be the worst of it. That first time seeing and speaking to him again. That was always going to be the worst part and no amount of preparation could mitigate it.

'Elizabeth,' he said by way of greeting, stretching out a hand.

She'd always loved how he pronounced her name. Her mother always affected an English accent when she said it. Her father always addressed her as Lizzy but she suspected that had always been to needle her mother. From Xander's wide, generous mouth, her name rolled like a caress.

There was nothing wide or generous about his mouth now, fixed as it was in a tight line.

Plastering the brightest, most toothsome smile she could muster to her face, she released her hold on the case and accepted his hand. 'It's great to see you again.'

His lips curved into a taut smile. 'You're looking well.'

'Thank you.' Still holding his hand, she used it for

support to climb out of the golf buggy, pretending that every inch of her skin hadn't started dancing at his touch.

He was as tall as she remembered but the years had given an added hardness to his physique and he'd gained an overall edginess she didn't remember from before. The sparkle that had always been in his eyes was muted and faint lines had appeared on his face, yet somehow he was even better looking than he'd been a decade ago.

So gorgeous had he been that when he'd approached her on her arrival at La Maison Blanc Hotel and insisted on helping her with her luggage, she'd assumed he worked for the hotel. In hindsight, that he'd been wearing a pair of swim shorts and had had a towel slung over his shoulder should have been a giveaway that he was a guest rather than a hotel porter. That, and the fact the other porters had been wearing navy blue uniforms, right down to the silly hats they were forced to wear. Xander's brown hair had been damp from a swim in the sea.

It had taken her a good ten minutes—enough time to check in and find her room—before she'd realised the drop-dead gorgeous young man with the infectious smile, sparkling blue eyes and a deep rich accent to die for wasn't an employee but a fellow guest, and that he was helping her because he was interested in her. In *her*!

They'd arranged to meet at the pool bar an hour later. By the time she'd unpacked and changed she'd convinced herself she'd dreamt him up. But there he had been, exactly where he'd promised. Two cocktails later and she'd learned he was Greek, twenty years old, and a single traveller like herself. Dreamer that she was, she'd been *convinced* fate had brought them together.

'Is this everything you've brought with you?' Xander asked, taking in the physical changes time had brought on his wife. He'd known she would have changed over the years but he hadn't expected it to be quite so profound.

Ten years ago she'd had the rounded features of a young woman. Now she was leaner, her cheekbones more defined. Large dark glasses stopped him seeing her eyes but she had a polish to her, a sophistication far removed from the wide-eyed ingénue who had captured his attention from the very first glance. That Elizabeth had been a fresh-faced open book.

This Elizabeth, the rampant curls he remembered straightened and glossed into long, tumbling waves, was professional and collected. She was dressed in slim-fitting dark grey jeans with studs across the pockets, and a fitted white shirt, which together emphasised her litheness. She could be anywhere, at a semiformal business meeting or out with friends for lunch. She was the perfect chameleon. Her looks were too striking for people not to look twice at her but she would fit in perfectly wherever she happened to be.

He carried her case to his Jeep. Elizabeth easily kept pace with him. He'd forgotten how long her legs were, and lengthened further by a pair of simple yet sexy black heels.

She was sexy. The way she carried herself. Her confidence. She was dazzling.

He pulled the passenger door open and waited until she'd taken her seat before closing it. Through the slight breeze he caught her delicate scent, which put the frangipani and butterfly jasmine St Francis was famed for to shame.

'I've booked us a table at a restaurant on LuLu Beach,' he said as he drove them out of the small airport, which mostly consisted of a landing strip and a pristine white hut. St Francis was one of the smaller Caribbean islands and had a colourful beauty that was world renowned. Not for nothing was it known as a honeymooner's paradise.

He'd chosen St Francis for a myriad reasons. It hadn't occurred to him that being on the island again would unsettle him so much. Sitting next to Elizabeth only unsettled him further, something he should have anticipated.

'Sounds good,' she said in the same easy tone she'd greeted him with. Yet, despite her friendliness, he detected a frost around her.

He could be imagining it, he supposed, but he doubted it. Meeting an ex wasn't normally a big deal but what he and Elizabeth had shared had been different from all his other relationships.

His honesty when he'd left her had verged on brutal but he'd known it was necessary. If he'd strung it out it would have hurt her a lot more.

Had she kept quiet about their annulment's failure as a means of punishing him; to make a bigamist of him if he'd married again? Had she spent a decade quietly biding her time for revenge?

Or did she genuinely not know they were still married?

He would learn the truth soon enough. Either way, a clean break had been the right thing to do and he had no regrets on that front. He'd disconnected the call from his mother and looked at the woman he'd married five days before and understood what a terrible mistake he'd made. His world was cut-throat and ruthless. If a woman raised in it like Ana couldn't cope, what chance would a dreamer like Elizabeth have? She would never have been accepted or fitted into it.

It wasn't long before they arrived at the LuLu Beach restaurant.

A waitress led them out to the terrace and to a table overlooking the beach. They sat opposite each other, both getting a good view of the tranquil surf lapping at the fine white sand like a loving puppy.

'Water for me,' Elizabeth said when asked what she wanted to drink.

'Water?' Xander queried.

'Water.'

He shrugged and turned to the waitress. 'One water and one bottle of beer.'

Once they were alone again he openly studied Elizabeth. The setting sun made the honey of her hair look like spun gold. 'You look as though life has treated you well.'

He wished she would take those damned sunglasses off so he could see her eyes and gauge what she was really thinking. The sun was now set so low its glare reflected directly off them.

'Thanks.' Elizabeth resisted the urge to say she knew life had been treating *him* well. After all, Xander's life had been all over the news and Internet for weeks.

She took a breath to calm the unexpected rage shooting through her.

Xander was her client and her clients' private lives were none of her concern. The salacious stories about the other three men hadn't bothered her in the slightest and she would not allow the burn that ravaged her brain whenever she imagined Xander acting out some of the described racier acts to cloud her judgement or control her emotions.

She'd thought she was prepared for this and for seeing him again but the racing of her heart and the dampness of her palms proved it to be a lie. She could have had a month to prepare and she still wouldn't have been ready.

The waitress returned with their drinks then pulled her notepad out to take their food order. Elizabeth ordered the Yellowfin Tuna Tartare appetiser. She wasn't hungry but it would be good to have something to nibble on, a distraction. Like most of the restaurants on the island, LuLu's menu was a mixture of French and Creole. She'd adored the fusion when she'd been here before. She'd actively avoided both since. She'd avoided anything that would bring the memories back.

'Why did you want to meet here?' she asked, glad the sun was still strong enough to warrant keeping her shades on. She'd read once the eyes were the gateway to one's true emotions. She couldn't bear to think of Xander looking into hers and seeing the pain all the bittersweet memories were evoking.

'It bothers you?'

'It bothers my pride. I have no issue finding a life partner for you but I do think you could have shown some sensitivity and chosen somewhere neutral for us to meet.'

'I don't require a life partner. I require a wife.'

'Is that not the same thing?'

'A life partner suggests permanency. I only need a temporary wife.'

Removing her professional notebook from her bag, Elizabeth wrote 'temporary marriage' in it and circled it so heavily the nib of her pen bent.

Determined as she was to keep things on a professional footing, she couldn't help but say, 'Using your ex-wife to find you a new wife is one thing, but conducting the preliminary interview on the very island we met and married screams insensitive jerk to me. You have the money and resources to travel anywhere your heart desires so why here? Was it to rub my nose in it?'

When she finally looked at him, he was staring at her with a look she couldn't interpret.

'I had a number of reasons.'

She forced herself to remain poised. If he wanted to play mind games he could play them on his own. She was here to do a job and nothing else. 'Tell me what kind of woman you have in mind to marry. Are there any turn-offs I need to avoid, like smokers or bearded ladies?'

Or five-foot-eight blondes with a pedigree your mother wouldn't approve of.

She wished she had a chain-smoker with the world's worst halitosis on her books to fix him up with.

Elizabeth waited for him to answer but his gaze remained on her, the same unfathomable expression on his gorgeous face.

Uncertainty crept up her spine. The way he was looking at her...

He took a swig of his beer then set the bottle steadily on the table.

'I don't need you to find me a wife, Elizabeth. I already have one.' He leaned forward and lowered his voice. 'There is no easy way for me to say this but you're still my wife. Our marriage was never annulled. We're still married.'

Xander watched the blood drain from Elizabeth's face.

Long moments passed before she gave a quick shake of her head and finally removed her shades.

The dazzling amber eyes Xander had never forgotten finally met his, flecks of gold and red firing at him, disbelief resonating. Not even a professional actress could fake shock that well. It put the last of his doubts to rest. She hadn't known.

Although the compression in his chest loosened a little at this, it made no difference to how things needed to proceed.

'Elizabeth?'

Her throat moved. Her words came out in a croak. 'Our marriage was annulled.'

'Our annulment was rejected by the judge at the last hurdle.'

Blinking rapidly, she put her sunglasses back on and pushed them up to sit atop her head. 'You're not joking, are you?'

He shook his head and watched her slump in her chair.

She inhaled heavily. 'I don't get it.'

Xander had a two-week heads up on it and he still didn't understand. 'Did you ever receive official confirmation?'

Her eyes were wide and bewildered before she put her elbows on the table and rubbed at her forehead. 'I received confirmation of the paperwork. I remember that. I remember it saying it would be rubber-stamped within a month, or whatever the time frame was.' She looked back at him. 'It was ten years ago. I don't remember all the details.'

'But you don't remember receiving the official annulment?'

'I...' She slumped some more. 'I moved out.'

'Moved out from where?'

'My mother's. I left home soon after I received the confirmation letter. Mom was supposed to forward all my mail to me but she didn't. I ended up having to redirect it myself.' She straightened and let out a forced shaky laugh, muttering, 'I can't believe her.'

Their marriage had been too short-lived to get to the 'meet the parent' stage. They'd both been so wrapped up in each other they'd hardly spoken of their families. All he'd known of hers was that her parents were divorced and she was an only child. She'd taken a vacation to St Francis on the back of an inheritance she'd received from her paternal grandmother.

Elizabeth shook her head, trying to clear it of all the noise crowding in it. She felt as if she could explode. She shoved her chair back and got to her feet. 'I need to walk.'

He stayed seated, a set look on his handsome face, his blue eyes turning to steel as they held hers. 'You can walk later. Right now we need to talk.'

Her stomach clenched and there was a moment she feared she would bring up the morsel of food she'd managed to eat since their phone call the evening before.

Being with Xander again was a thousand times harder than she'd imagined and learning they were still married...

It wasn't possible. It wasn't.

Yet somehow it was.

Swallowing a ragged breath, she sat back down heavily.

The sun had almost set, its orange crescent gleaming over the horizon, the sky a deep blue shining with stars peeking out and waving at them. Such a beautiful sight and one that felt sacrilegious with all the turmoil Xander had just thrown her into.

Their food was brought to them. Xander had ordered monkfish fillets. The delicious scent from it turned her stomach.

Elizabeth looked at her tuna tartare, beautifully presented with an avocado salad, and knew she wouldn't be able to manage even a bite of it.

'Why was the annulment denied?' she asked, trying frantically to get a grip on herself.

'The judge determined there were *"no unknown facts from either party"* and that *"no law had been broken"* so there was nothing to justify it.'

'But we were only married for five days.'

He sighed. 'Another judge would probably have rubber-stamped it without any issue. We were unlucky that ours landed on the desk of a judge who took issue with it. We'll never know his real reasons why—he passed away four years ago. How did you not *know* the annulment was declined?'

'I never received the letter.' Her mother had probably thrown it away unopened in a fit of pique.

'You've already said that, but why didn't you chase it? It seems strange that you didn't call or do something to find out where the confirmation was.'

'The same could be said for you,' she retorted, removing her gaze from the sunset to look at him. 'Didn't you think you would receive something too?'

'Hardly. I live on the other side of the world. You said you would handle it. As I recall, you insisted.'

'How long have you known?' she asked tightly.

'Just over two weeks.'

She clenched her fists to stop herself from lashing out at him. 'You've waited that long to tell me?'

'I was trying to work out the best way forward. I only looked into it because I was hoping to bury the annulment so the press wouldn't find out.'

'Why would you do that?'

'The press are digging into every aspect of my life. I knew it would only be a matter of time before they stumbled onto it. I thought it best to bury it completely before they found it and used it as additional ammunition to hit me with. My family don't know about us...'

'You never got round to telling them? What a surprise.' She didn't bother hiding her sarcasm. *My family will never approve of or accept you.*

She hadn't told her own family either but that had been for entirely different reasons. She hadn't been ashamed of Xander. She'd just been too humiliated and heartbroken to speak of it. She couldn't have endured hearing her mother's condemnation and her father's fake concern on top, then the fights as they tried to find ways to blame the other for it. Because it was always about them, never about her.

'Things are hard for us at the moment without having to deal with all the press intrusion,' he said.

'Am I supposed to feel sorry for you?' He'd been engaged to another woman. He'd used her and lied to her and then dumped her in the cruellest way possible.

'You're not supposed to feel anything. I'm just telling you how it is.'

'But you had to fly me all this way to tell me? You could have told me in New York—you could have told me *anywhere*. It seems particularly cruel to bring me to the island we were married on just to discuss our divorce. Well, you have nothing to worry about. I have more to lose than you if our marriage comes out and I want it buried just as much as you...'

'If I wanted a divorce I would have been in touch two weeks ago.'

Shaking off the fresh dread crawling up her spine at his words, Elizabeth said tightly, 'You went through the court records specifically to bury our marriage.'

'That was my original intention,' he agreed easily although his eyes remained hard. 'Learning we were still married changed things.'

The dread had lodged into her throat, suffocating her vocal cords so all she could do was plead with her eyes. *Don't say it. Whatever you do, don't say it.*

'I need us to rekindle our marriage.'

CHAPTER THREE

HIS MEANING HIT Elizabeth immediately, no initial instant of uncomprehending shock, no moment of bewilderment. 'Not in a million years.'

'You're a matchmaker, Elizabeth,' he said calmly. 'You arrange marriages…'

'For other people,' she interjected.

'I want to employ you to rekindle ours. It won't be for ever, a few months at the most.'

A passing waiter noticed they hadn't touched their food. 'Is everything all right? Can I get you anything?'

'I'd like a cab to the airport,' Elizabeth said.

Bemusement spread over the waiter's face. 'The airport's closed now.'

She'd completely forgotten flights were forbidden on or off the island after sundown.

'We'll have two coffees,' Xander cut in smoothly while she eyed him furiously.

'Cappuccino, latte…?'

'Two filter coffees will be fine.'

As the waiter drifted back inside, Elizabeth leaned forward and glared at Xander. 'Is that why you brought me here? So I couldn't escape?'

'Partly. I had a number of reasons.'

'Well, guess what? I don't care what your reasons

are. Keeping me here overnight isn't going to change my mind so you've lucked out there. I'm not doing it. Period.'

If he was perturbed by her vehemence, he didn't show it. Xander was treating the bombshell he'd just thrown at her as dispassionately as if he were conducting a business deal. She could be anyone to him, whereas for Elizabeth…

He had once been her world. Being with him again brought everything back. All of it. The delirious happiness followed by pain so sharp she had never allowed herself to get close to feeling either emotion again. They went hand in glove. If she hadn't known the joy she would never have suffered so much in the aftermath.

But it hadn't killed her. It had made her stronger and she would hold on to that strength.

'You don't even need a wife,' she said in a much calmer tone than the explosion her tongue wanted to fire. 'Your business has been completely unaffected by the *Celebrity Spy!* scandal…'

'It has nothing to do with my business.'

The waiter wandered back to them with their coffees, eyeing their still untouched plates with obvious confusion.

Once alone again, Xander stirred a spoonful of brown sugar into his cup and then fixed his eyes on her. 'My sister-in-law is an alcoholic. She's recently been diagnosed with cirrhosis of the liver. If she doesn't stop drinking she will be dead within five years.'

'You're talking about Katerina?' Elizabeth asked, shocked at this revelation.

His brow furrowed. 'You remember her name?'

Feeling her body heat under his narrow-eyed scrutiny, she took a hasty sip of her coffee.

How embarrassing to remember the name of a woman

she'd never met who had probably been mentioned only the once, and in passing at that. But she remembered every conversation between them, had committed to memory the names of his family members. She'd looked forward to meeting them and being a part of their lives.

'Yes. I'm talking about Katerina,' Xander continued when Elizabeth didn't bother to answer his question. 'I don't know what will happen to her or if she will be able to stop drinking. I just don't know. But what happened to her has acted as a wake-up call to my brother. I have been begging him for years to get help for his addictions.' He gave a small tight smile. 'Yanis's poison of choice is cocaine, but he's not fussy. If it comes in white powder form he'll snort it. If it comes in liquid form he'll inject it.'

Now he reached for his coffee and cradled the cup in the same manner Elizabeth was cradling hers.

'Yanis admitted himself into a specialist lockdown facility in America ten days ago.'

The facility in Arizona was supposed to be one of the best in the world. Xander hoped with all his heart it could help his brother. If not...

He didn't want to witness his brother's coffin being lowered into the cold ground. He'd watched Ana's body be lowered and the grief and guilt had almost sliced him in two. He couldn't go through the same with his own flesh and blood, the only adult in his family he felt any affection for.

'That's good,' Elizabeth said in a softer tone. The stoniness of her eyes had softened a little too.

'It is. Very much so. He'll be in rehab for around two months. As Katerina is unlikely to leave hospital any time soon and will not be in a position to look after their son, Yanis left Loukas in my care.'

'Loukas is your nephew?'

Xander nodded. 'He's eight. Despite all the crap he's had to put up with, he's a great kid.' And now he'd come to the real reason he needed her. 'My parents have hired a lawyer to go for custody of him.'

Elizabeth's brows drew together. 'Custody of Loukas?'

'Yes. Full custody. They're saying Yanis and Katerina are unfit parents.'

He could see her brain whirling before she tentatively said, 'Is giving them custody really a bad thing? What, with the way your brother and Katerina are...?'

'It is the worst thing,' he stated flatly. 'My brother, when he's not high, is a good father. He's doing everything he can to straighten himself out so he can care properly for his son. My parents have made this move knowing full well that neither Yanis nor Katerina are in a position to fight it, so I must fight on their behalf.'

'But...'

'Elizabeth, I will not allow my parents to take custody of him. I wouldn't allow it even on a temporary basis.'

'Where's Loukas now?'

'At my home. I have a court order granting me temporary custody for two more weeks and then there will be another hearing. Now they know they're fighting me, my parents will go for the jugular. They will paint me as an unfit guardian too.'

'Why?'

'To stop me from winning. This scandal couldn't have come at a worse time. It's painting me as someone debauched and without any morals. The only way I'll be able to convince the court to let me keep guardianship of Loukas and fight Yanis's corner is if I can prove I have a stable home for him, and that's why I need us to rekindle our marriage. Having you as my wife will prove I'm a stable influence and kill my parents' plans.'

'It's that simple?'

'Sure.' He took a sip of his coffee. 'My country is still inherently conservative with a bias towards female carers. With you as my wife, they will see two people able to care for Loukas until his parents are well enough to take him back. If my parents get custody, they will never give him back.'

Her eyes clouded. 'Are they really likely to do that?'

'Without doubt. My family has been at war for years and my parents think they finally have a chance of winning a battle.'

Elizabeth removed her shades from the top of her head and folded the bows, her eyes distant, not looking at him, clearly weighing up everything he'd just shared.

'It really is quite simple,' he said. 'You and I announce our marriage to the world and stay together long enough for Yanis to get straight. With any luck, Katerina will make the road to recovery too.'

'And what if Yanis gets straight but then relapses?' she challenged. 'Will I be expected to act as your wife again?'

He shook his head. 'As soon as he's released from his facility, I'll get the steps put in place that I am to be Loukas's legal guardian in the absence of his parents. You and I will stay married until this has been done. Yanis will agree. If we'd known our parents would take this action we would have done it before but neither of us imagined even they would stoop so low. They hardly know Loukas.'

They *should* have imagined it, Xander thought grimly. His parents were a law unto themselves. They treated family life as they treated business: as a sport in which there could only be one winner.

'As I said, it's a simple matter of us rekindling our marriage. I appreciate it's asking a lot of you…'

'A lot?' she exclaimed, blinking furiously. 'My business will be finished. Everything I've worked for...gone. It works on discretion, remember? And what about the rest of my life?'

'What life, Elizabeth? All you do is work.'

At the darkening of her features, he figured he might as well get everything out in the open and deal with it all in one go. 'I had you investigated. There's no significant other in your life. You have some friends you socialise with occasionally and you take yoga classes when time allows, but there is nothing else. So tell me, what will you be giving up to help me?'

Now her face was ablaze with outraged colour. 'You went digging into my life? Well, that explains how you discovered Leviathan Solutions.'

He was unrepentant. 'I learned about your business when searching for our annulment. I had a deeper search made to be sure you had nothing in your past that could be used to paint you as an unsuitable guardian for Loukas.'

As it was, his investigations hadn't revealed anything. If she had skeletons in her closet, they were tucked too far out of reach for discovery. If she'd dated anyone unsavoury, that was hidden away too. Indeed, he hadn't found evidence of a link with *anyone*, not even a fling, never mind anything approaching a committed relationship. Whatever relationships she'd had in the past decade, they'd been conducted discreetly and that was all that mattered.

'I don't care what excuses you make, that's a gross invasion of my privacy,' she raged. 'It's inexcusable.'

'If you were in my position you would have done the same.'

'If I were in your position I wouldn't need to—your

private life is splattered on the front page of every red top for the whole world to see.'

'I can assure you the vast majority of it is highly exaggerated, the rest of it lies,' he said icily.

'Of course it is.' Her sarcasm was delivered with extra bitterness.

His temper rising, Xander finished his coffee and carefully set the cup on the table before pointing to the beach. 'Do you see the man with the camera round his neck?'

She followed his gaze.

'That man is a paparazzo, tipped off by my assistant that we're here.'

Her face contorted into such anger she looked ready to explode.

'He has your name. He knows about Leviathan Solutions and the service you provide. He knows we're married. What the story that accompanies his pictures tells is for you to decide.'

Elizabeth listened to Xander's words and knew her world was crumbling around her.

He'd set her up.

Whatever happened between them, pictures of one of the Casanovas from the *Celebrity Spy!* scandal pictured in a Caribbean paradise with a woman purported to be his wife would beam around the world. It would be headline news.

'I can't believe you would do this.' She was so angry she could hardly breathe. 'You say your parents have stooped low…you are exactly like them.'

He was unrepentant. 'I regret I've had to take these steps but everything I'm doing is for my nephew. If you say no to my proposal I have nothing left to play. I have nothing left to lose. My reputation can't be damaged any more than it already has been. Say yes and you'll be financially set for life. Thirty million dollars for you, and I'll pay off your staff too.'

Elizabeth listened with the feeling of talons being dragged over her skin and her head swimming in cold sludge.

Her business was finished. Her life—everything she'd built for herself—was over.

Once the world learned she was married to this Casanova and her face graced the front pages of all the glossies and all the major Internet search engines, no one would be able to risk using her discreet services any more.

As if on cue, the photographer put the camera to his eye and fired off a ream of shots of them.

She took a long breath and rose from the table, pulling herself to her full height. 'I would have agreed to do it without the threats and blackmail.'

'I couldn't take the risk you would say no. I haven't seen you in ten years. For all I knew you were holding a grudge against me. I had to consider if you'd deliberately withheld the failure of our annulment as a weapon to use against me when a time came that suited you.'

'*What?* How could you *think* such a thing?' She shook her head, trying to comprehend it. Ten years ago she'd laid herself bare to him, in all senses, and he thought her capable of something like *that*?

'Manipulation is a common thing in my world. I can count the number of people I trust on two fingers.'

'Well, you've certainly mastered the art of manipulation yourself,' she said bitterly. Where was the man she'd married? That man had been *nothing* like this.

A pulse throbbed in his jaw. 'I am trying to protect my nephew.'

'When adults go to war it's always the child who

suffers the most.' She knew that better than anyone. 'I would never stand by and let it happen if there was something I could do about it. You didn't need to go to such grotesque lengths for my help. You didn't need to make me hate you more than I already do.'

'I'm sure the thirty million I'm offering will sweeten the pill.'

'No amount of money will recompense for the loss of my business and the invasion of my privacy.'

'You want more money?'

She caught the sneer on his lips, which only fuelled her fury further. 'Don't try and make me out to be a money-grabber,' she snapped. 'If you hadn't given *Celebrity Spy!* so much gossip to shout about, you wouldn't be in this mess and you wouldn't need me to get you out of it—your moral fibre wouldn't even be a matter of discussion. Your parents wouldn't be able to paint you as an unfit guardian.'

Another flash of anger resonated from his eyes but his lips formed into a taut smile. 'Your opinion of my character means nothing to me. All I want is your agreement. Do I have it?'

'I don't have any damn choice.'

'I'm pleased you can see that.'

'But let's get one thing straight. Our marriage will be as short as possible and strictly platonic.'

The pulse in his jawline throbbed harder. 'Married couples in my family share adjoining rooms. It's an arrangement that will suit us.'

'Good. And any adjoining door will have a lock.'

'Yes.' His eyes glinted through the darkness, impossible to read. He got to his feet and pulled some notes from his wallet. 'It's time to go—we have a hotel to check into.'

'*We?*'

'Yes, *kardia mou*,' he said with a mocking smile. 'We are setting the seeds for the rekindling of our marriage. We have been pictured dining together. That photographer has been given the name of our hotel. I guarantee you he has a scooter in easy reach for him to rush there and meet us. Come the morning, the world will know we have spent the night together. All that will be left for us to do is make a statement, which I have already prepared.'

'My God, you've planned *everything*.'

'You don't get to my position without forward thinking.'

'Really? I could have sworn you'd got to your position through a fate of birth.'

It gave fleeting satisfaction to see his face darken at that comment.

'But really, Xander, is this necessary? Do you really think your parents are going to be fooled by us getting back together when they didn't even know I existed? Don't you think they'll find it convenient?'

When he replied his voice was tightly controlled. 'It's not my parents we need to convince, it's the judge, and, unless you want to forfeit the money, I suggest you make it *very* convincing.'

'You have got to be kidding me.' Elizabeth's voice was flat but her amber eyes blasted incredulity and fury right at him.

Xander brought the car to a stop at the front of La Maison Blanc Hotel. 'Is there a problem?'

'Why here?'

'Because it's fitting. This is where we married and now it's where we're rekindling our marriage.'

'And to hell with my feelings, eh?' She shook her head

with loathing. 'Just when I didn't think it was possible to hate you more...'

'Hate me as much as you want in private, but in public...' He nodded at the scooter that had come to a screech at the hotel's entrance.

She sucked in her cheeks and contemplated the photographer, whose camera was still around his neck. 'This is pointless. No one's going to believe we're for real, especially not a judge. I *hate* you. And you never even mentioned me to your family or...'

'I never mentioned you to anyone because the topic was too painful,' he cut in smoothly. 'We never wanted to part but we were too young at the time and we knew it would never work. You called me when the scandal first erupted to offer your support. My world was falling apart around me and you were there for me.'

He stretched out a hand to touch her face. The soft, almost translucent skin still felt like satin to his touch. Before she could flinch away he wound his fingers round the back of her head and gathered a large mass of her thick hair into his fist. He wondered what had happened to her curls. He'd adored the shaggy mop of hair she'd sported a decade ago.

'It was in the course of one of our discussions that we realised our annulment had never gone through and we were still married.' He leaned closer and studied the soft kissable lips that were pressed tightly together sucking in the rounded cheekbones.

Did those lips still taste the same? Would they still fit to his as if they'd been moulded specially?

She'd stopped breathing. Her eyes had widened, her face a frozen mask.

Still gazing at her mouth, resisting the urge to run a finger over it, he continued, 'It was also through the course of our talks on the phone that I remembered how special you were to me and all my old feelings for you came back. I convinced you to meet me here because I wanted to see if the old magic was still alive. We realised how much we still loved each other and decided that we'd both matured enough to make our marriage work.'

He released his hold on her hair and let his fingers drift down the slender neck he had once kissed every part of, and felt the tiniest of shivers under his fingers.

Her eyes were wide and stark on his.

A long-forgotten memory sluiced him; their first time together, her dreamy pleasure, her soft moans...

The flash of the photographer's camera cut through the moment and pulled him back to the present.

He removed his hand from her neck.

Elizabeth might have an allure that sang to his senses but this was one relationship he had no intention of taking to the bedroom. Things were going to be difficult enough between them without throwing sex into the mix.

It gave him no pleasure to threaten and blackmail her but he couldn't afford to give her a way out. Loukas was all he cared about and he would do whatever it took to keep his nephew out of his parents' clutches, even if it meant destroying the woman he had once thought himself in love with.

CHAPTER FOUR

'OH, THAT IS very clever,' Elizabeth whispered after a long pause during which her breathing deepened. 'Machiavelli would be proud.'

Xander didn't say a word. What *could* he say?

It wasn't for ever, he told himself in mitigation. A few months of her life at the most, and he would pay her handsomely for it.

'Just tell me how you plan to explain Ana.'

His stomach lurched. 'You know about her?'

Throughout the years, whenever an unguarded moment found him thinking of Elizabeth, he would wonder if she'd learned of Ana. He'd never spoken of Ana to the press but occasionally an article would appear that mentioned his tragic fiancée.

When Xander had ended his engagement, he hadn't hung around to deal with the fallout. He'd been sick of everything: his family, her family... He'd needed a break from it all. And so he'd found himself in St Francis, where he'd met Elizabeth.

She'd been a ray of light that had beamed straight into his heart, a loving innocent when he'd only known indifference and manipulation. In the greedy haze of lust he'd been certain he was in love with her. He'd been unaware that his and Ana's families had postponed the statement about the end of the engagement, both families *convinced* he was suffering from nothing more than cold feet and would realise the error of his ways on his return and marry Ana after all.

Ana had known he would never change his mind.

The call from his mother notifying him of Ana's death had brought him crashing down to earth and he'd seen the truth right there in front of him: Elizabeth wouldn't have lasted a week with his family. All the joy and sunshine she brought into a room would have been snuffed out with the poison his parents and those they mixed with breathed.

'I know you were engaged to her,' Elizabeth said in a whisper. 'You were childhood sweethearts. And I know you never mentioned her to me. You told me...' She swallowed. 'You said you'd never been in love before. That was a lie.' Then she shook her head, her voice regaining a brisk tone. 'So how are you going to explain marrying me when you were engaged to someone else? How is that going to paint you in a respectable fashion?'

He didn't blink. 'I'd ended my engagement to Ana before I met you. She died while I was here with you. I didn't cheat on anyone. When I met you I was single. I couldn't have predicted what would happen to her.'

Xander knew he sounded cold. Thinking of Ana and what happened to her always made him *feel* cold. He would never know what had been going through her head the night she died but knew he would carry the guilt for ever.

For a long time Elizabeth did nothing but stare at him. And as he stared back, a pain settled in his chest as he recalled her devastation when he'd walked away.

'Is that the truth or another clever statement you've concocted?' she asked coldly.

'It's the truth. Ana and I were over when I met you.'

She inhaled deeply, then gave a sharp nod and, without uttering another word, opened her door. She took hold of her belongings, and got out of the car, handing her stuff to the porter who had rushed to meet them.

Alone in the car, Xander closed his eyes.

Elizabeth really *had* changed.

Ten years ago she'd been easy to read. Everything she thought or felt was there in those amber eyes. He couldn't read them now. She'd built a wall around herself, a guard he suspected she rarely let anyone see beneath.

This wall would stand her in good stead. But it wasn't just the wall she'd built; she'd developed a tough core.

The old sweet Elizabeth would have been destroyed to have his mother's venom turned on her. This Elizabeth wouldn't take crap from anyone. She would survive their short rekindling intact.

Filled with resolve that he was doing the right thing, he got out and threw the keys at the valet. With a camera flashing frantically in his face, he strode into the grand foyer.

It was time to play their romance to a wider audience.

Elizabeth was waiting at the reception desk. Reaching her side, he slipped an arm around her waist and gave his name to the receptionist, who wasn't quick enough to hide the widening of her eyes.

Even the inhabitants of tiny St Francis had heard of his so-called debauchery.

He signed the forms, and the key cards were handed over to them.

Elizabeth looked at hers, read the name of the villa they were staying in, and nearly dropped it.

'Enjoy your stay,' the receptionist said with a coo.

All she could give was a rigid smile in return.

Xander took her hand and tugged at it to get her moving.

Just about ready to kill him but determined to affect nonchalance with an audience watching, she let him lead her to the far door that would take her to the same private villa he'd upgraded them to after they'd married. The honeymoon suite.

They followed the same narrow rocky path they'd taken a decade ago, passed the same open-air restaurant with the same jazz music playing, the same sweet-smelling flowers as the path took them further from the main hotel, the same herbaceous borders, the same distant noise of crickets calling to each other…everything the same. Even her husband.

But Xander was no longer the irrepressible young hunk she'd fallen in love with. He was a hard-nosed, wildly successful businessman with a ruthlessness that made her mother look like an amateur.

And he'd never been in love with her. The most she'd been to him was a rebound fling that went too far.

The sights, scents and sounds opened up so many memories her head flooded with them. This first step to their villa was the place Xander had scooped her into his arms and carried her to their door. This villa door where he now swiped the key card was where he had put her down, pressed her against this very wall and kissed her so hard her lips had bruised. This threshold she now crossed was the same one he'd picked her back up to carry her over.

And this villa was the very same one they'd made love in so many times it had been impossible to keep count, right until he'd received one phone call and dropped her quicker than an outfielder letting an easy catch slip through his fingers.

She hadn't known it then but that call had been the one telling him his fiancée had died.

Was he telling the truth that he'd ended the engagement before he'd met her? Or was it just another strategy to accompany their charade?

What did it matter anyway? It had all happened a decade ago. It meant nothing to her now. She only felt so raw and unhinged because…well, because her life had just been devastated all over again by the same man who'd almost broken her before.

Holding her breath, she walked into the villa. Her stuff had been placed on the floor of the spacious living area next to a suitcase she assumed was Xander's, although she hadn't seen any sight of it until then.

'Where are the staff?' she asked stiffly. The villa came with its own butler, maid and chef.

'I've told them we want privacy. They won't come unless we call them.'

He'd done the same when they'd married, ensuring the utmost privacy for them. Back then she had rejoiced in it.

The villa had a large kitchen in the corner of the main living area.

Xander peered into the huge American fridge and pulled out a bottle of white wine. 'Drink?'

'No.' She nearly followed it with a thank you but stopped herself in time. She didn't owe him anything, least of all good manners. 'I'm going to bed. You're welcome to the master bedroom.'

She would rather swim with piranhas than sleep in that room. The second bedroom was every bit as nice and came with the added bonus of not being seeped in memories of them being together.

'We've only just got here.'

'The sooner I get to sleep, the sooner I'll wake up and can go back to New York.' She didn't want to think any more. Her head hurt too much to handle anything else. All she wanted now was a few hours of oblivion.

'We'll be flying directly to Athens.'

'You can. I need to go home. I have work.'

'Elizabeth, your home is with me now.' As he spoke he put the wine back in the fridge and took out a bottle of beer as replacement.

'I can't come with you yet. I have things to do, arrangements to make…'

'You'll have to do it remotely.' He opened a drawer.

'That's impossible.'

He rooted through another drawer and pulled out a bottle opener. 'I need to get back to Loukas. I promised him I wouldn't be longer than two days.' He fixed her with a stare. 'Or do you think I should break a promise to an eight-year-old boy?'

'That's not fair,' she protested. 'I didn't know you'd promised him that. Of course you must keep it, but your promise doesn't involve me. You go ahead and I'll fly over when my affairs are straight.'

'You will fly with me in the morning. The rekindling of our marriage starts immediately. The longer we're together before the court hearing, the more established and stronger we will look as a couple.'

'My staff deserve better than to be laid off by email.'

'The money I'll transfer into their bank accounts will make up for it. Give me their details and I'll do it now. I'll also transfer a quarter of a million dollars into your account—call it a retainer. You'll get the balance when we go our separate ways.'

'And if we fail?' Was there a chance she could walk out of this nightmare and *still* lose everything?

His eyes narrowed.

'What happens to me if the judge gives your parents custody?' she persisted.

Xander's voice was like ice as he said, 'It will only come to that over my cold dead body.'

Elizabeth sat in the lotus position on the floor of her locked bedroom, eyes closed, willing her mind to clear and for tranquillity to seep into her consciousness.

It wasn't happening.

How could she find any peace of mind with Xander situated on the other side of the wall?

God, that was all that separated them. After ten years apart they now had nothing but a wall of bricks dividing them.

An hour after she'd left him swigging moodily from his beer bottle, she'd heard the faint sound of a shower running from the next room.

She hadn't heard anything from him since. That didn't stop her ears straining for any movement.

It was a struggle to take in everything that had happened over the past few hours. How could she not have realised the annulment was never finalised and they were still married? It defied credulity. But back then she'd had so many other things to deal with and she had never dreamt their annulment would be denied. How could any judge fail to give an annulment with the facts before them?

Turned out a judge could, and if she'd only taken the effort to make one phone call she wouldn't be in the mess she was in now.

Her life as she knew it was over, at least for the foreseeable future.

This time tomorrow, her business would be over permanently.

She'd dealt with major upheaval before. She'd left the path she'd originally chosen and taken a completely different route and not only survived but thrived. She could thrive again. When all this was over she would pick herself up and start again, just as she had before.

All she had to do to get out of this mess without being left flat broke was convince a Greek judge that she and Xander were a stable couple in love.

It would be easier to feign love with a rattlesnake and, she suspected, safer.

Her thighs aching and her brain still refusing to switch off, Elizabeth gave up her attempts at meditation and took a shower.

Just as wired after her shower as she'd been before, she accepted she could kiss any sleep goodbye. The walls of the room seemed to be compressing in on her, squeezing the air from her lungs. She needed to get out. She wished she could take a long walk.

Throwing on the robe provided by the hotel, she went to the door and turned the handle. She strained her ears but the only sound to be heard was her own heart pumping.

She took a deep breath and stepped out onto the ceramic tiles, cautiously checking Xander's door. It was shut.

Ghostly moonlight poured in through the high windows and patio doors where the shutters hadn't been closed.

After a moment's indecision she crossed to the patio doors and stared out.

Cut into the mountains, the villa had the perfect view of St Francis Bay, which rippled gently in the near distance, matchstick figures walking hand in hand along the shore. She swallowed back the ache that formed to remember her and Xander doing that same moonlit walk.

Sliding the patio door open, she stepped outside and was immediately enveloped in the rich, balmy Caribbean night. The moon loomed huge in the sky, bathing everything in light.

The heady sweet scent of butterfly jasmine, always at its strongest in the midnight hours, filled the air. As she breathed it in, a lancing pain shot through her, so strong she flattened a hand against her stomach to counteract it. It was the scent that had sat the strongest in her memories of her time at St Francis and a scent she had actively avoided since because it always carried her back to the time before he'd rejected her, when she'd thought she'd found her soulmate.

Elizabeth had never felt as if she belonged to anyone as anything other than a possession to be fought over, but for two glorious weeks with Xander she had felt as precious and invaluable as any jewel.

And then he'd dumped her as if she were worthless and broken her heart as easily as if it had been made from glass.

Hearing movement behind her, she sighed and swallowed back a lump in her throat.

'Beautiful night, isn't it?' he said quietly, coming to stand beside her at the balustrade. He sounded different from earlier. Less edgy.

'It was.'

He laughed, a low rumbly sound that carried through the still air. It was the first sign of the old humour she had adored. 'Don't hate me, Elizabeth.'

She turned her head a fraction to look at him and immediately wished she hadn't. Xander was wearing nothing but a pair of low-slung black shorts. She could smell the citrusy scent of his shower gel. She could smell *him*, and closed her eyes tightly along with her breath.

In their time apart it wasn't just his shoulders that had filled out, it was all of him. The fit, lithe young man who could have been mistaken for a surfer dude was now a toned, muscular thirty-year-old. The years had hardened him but they'd also added a whole new testosterone-filled dimension.

An ache formed low in her belly, a liquid tightness that turned into a throb...

She turned her attention back to the beach. 'You could have just told me about Loukas from the start. It didn't have to be like this.'

'To guarantee your agreement, it did. I wasn't prepared to hear you say no and I didn't have the time to sweet-talk you into it.'

'I don't want your sweet talk.'

'I've figured that out for myself,' he said drily.

'Then you're smart enough to figure out that it's impossible for me not to hate you.'

'That is regrettable.' He rested his hands on the balustrade next to hers.

She looked down at them, so close to her own, and experienced another pang. His muscular arms were tanned and covered in sun-bleached fine hair that stopped at the wrists. The long, strong hands...how could she have remembered them in such detail, right down to the silvery scar on the left one? Was there not a single thing she'd forgotten even though she'd spent the last decade determinedly not thinking of him except in the most unguarded of moments?

At least her private thoughts weren't something his spies could have discovered.

Her body heated with the rise of humiliation at what they would have learned and relayed to Xander. While he was busy enjoying life to the full, bedding as many beautiful women as he could get his greedy hands on, she'd spent the intervening years alone. Not even a brief fling or two to even things out between them and stop her feeling like an English spinster in an old-fashioned novel.

God, she'd never even thought this way before. She'd been *happy* in her solitary life. She'd had her business. She'd employed some great people who were fun to be around and had some great friends. She had enough money not to worry about starving and was able to splash out on the odd pair of her favourite designer's shoes whenever the mood took her.

But prying eyes wouldn't see this. All prying eyes would see was her retiring to bed alone every night.

She took a step back and jutted her chin. 'The only regrettable thing is that I ever met you in the first place.'

Without wishing him a good night—for she absolutely did not wish him anything other than a sleep full of bad dreams—Elizabeth went back into the villa and locked her bedroom door behind her.

CHAPTER FIVE

THE NEXT DAY Xander sipped at his strong coffee, watching Elizabeth work. As soon as his plane had taken off, she'd taken herself to the furthest point away from him, to the large oak desk in his study area. There she had spent the past three hours making calls and working on her laptop.

She'd dressed in a short black skirt topped with an oversized monochrome top, her long hair sleek and glossy and falling over her shoulders. Last night, when he'd found her on the balcony, her hair had been wet. When she'd stormed away from him he'd noticed little curls springing up where it was starting to dry.

He remembered her curls so clearly and his heart throbbed to know they were still there even if they were straightened to within an inch of their life. She must have risen before the sun to get ready.

As polished as she appeared, carefully applied make-up could not disguise the dark rings under her eyes.

Done with her call, she put her cell phone on the desk.

He rose and walked over to her. 'You should take a break.'

She didn't look at him, turning her attention back to the screen in front of her and tapping out a few words on the keyboard. 'When I'm finished.'

'Lunch will be served soon.' She hadn't eaten anything since she'd landed in St Francis, her tuna tartare from the night before left untouched.

'I'll eat while I work.'

Her cell phone rang out. She snatched it up and put it to her ear.

'Hey,' she said in a much softer tone than she used with him.

Seating himself on the rounded sofa, nonchalantly hooking an ankle on his thigh, Xander listened to her one-sided conversation.

'I'll get it finished within the next hour,' she was saying. Then she smiled. 'Really? That's great. I'd be lost without you.' More silence, then, 'I'll call you later, when I'm settled.'

'Who was that?' he asked when she'd ended the call.

'My PA.'

'How's she taking things?' He thought of the large wedge of money he'd transferred into her four members of staff's bank accounts.

'*He's* taking things fine.'

'You have a male assistant?'

'Yes. I call him my PA but, really, he's my right-hand man. Not only is he an excellent organiser but he's a whizz with technical stuff and can fix any of the gremlins our computer systems get with his eyes closed. Not that any of that matters any more.' She sighed.

'You work closely with him?'

'More than anyone else, yes. Steve's been with me pretty much from the beginning. He keeps the office running smoothly, which is just what I need as I travel so much. I couldn't have done it without him.'

'And is your relationship strictly professional?' Her tone with 'Steve' had been tender. Now he knew it was a male she'd directed that tone at he felt an inexplicable urge to crush something.

Her face darkened. 'Not that it's any of your business but that's a totally crass thing to ask.'

'It is my business and it's a natural thing to wonder about. You sounded very cosy speaking to him.' Had their relationship been so obvious, so right there in front of them that his investigators had missed it?

'Do not put me on the same level as you—not everything's about sex. Steve's my friend. I care about him. I care about all my employees. They're all waking up to find they've lost their jobs but, rather than taking the money and running, they're doing their best to help me wind the company up seeing as I'm going to be stuck in Greece for the foreseeable future and unable to do it myself, *and* they're fielding calls from panicking clients who are all suddenly terrified their relationships are about to be exposed. So don't even think of questioning my relationship with any of them. They're the best bunch of people I know.'

As Xander had promised, pictures of the pair of them together had flooded the Internet, every gossip blog headlining with them. The photographer had got a good one of them in the car outside the hotel, when Xander's hand had been buried in her hair. They were gazing into each other's eyes.

Elizabeth had to admit, this picture would go a long way into making people believe they were in love. There was an intensity to their gazes that made her stomach do a funny turn.

It looked as if they were about to kiss.

She'd studied that picture for far too long, holding her breath as warmth spread through her veins until she'd clicked away from it with the tap of a shaking finger.

Two members of the cabin staff bustled through carrying trays of food.

'I'll eat here, thanks.' Elizabeth pushed her laptop to one side to make room for hers. Xander indicated for his to be placed there too and sat himself on the leather seat opposite her.

She didn't say anything, diving a fork into her salad and turning her attention back to her screen, determined to tune him out. It proved impossible.

Not wanting him to think he was affecting her appetite, she forced herself to eat. She was quite sure her Niçoise salad was the best salad she'd ever eaten but she couldn't taste any of it.

Another message hit her inbox. She read it with a sigh.

'A problem?'

She looked at the man responsible for this entire mess. 'Nearly all my clients have terminated their contracts with me.'

Thanks to Xander tipping the paparazzo off, the whole world now knew about Leviathan Solutions. A member of his staff had released a statement that was practically word for word as he'd recited it in the car.

'You knew that would happen,' he reminded her.

'Yes, but I wanted to tell my current clients personally. They deserve that much.'

At least the other Casanovas from the *Celebrity Spy!* scandal were matched already. She was confident Benjamin and Julianna would work out. They might have been playing cat and mouse with each other but, along with all the other things that made them perfectly suited to each other, there was real chemistry between them.

As for Zayn…the ladies she'd matched him with had turned out to be surplus to requirements as the beautiful Amalia, a PA, had unexpectedly been given the role.

From the whispers Elizabeth had heard, blackmail was involved in this marriage. Whatever the truth, having seen Zayn and Amalia together she'd decided that, unlike Dante and Piper, they were a couple she *would* have matched.

She closed her eyes and fought back bitter tears.

She'd known yesterday that agreeing to rekindle their marriage would mean the end of her business. She hadn't realised how swift its destruction would be.

'Have you transferred the quarter-million you promised me?' She didn't have her pass key to access her bank via the Internet; Steve had promised to get it couriered to her in Diadonus.

She hated how Xander's eyes narrowed at her question.

'My current clients have paid for a service I can no longer provide,' she explained hotly. 'I have to refund them. There's not enough in my account to pay it without that money.'

'It's been transferred.'

She sighed her relief and almost said thank you.

'What will you do with the rest of the money I give you?' he asked.

'I'll be earning that money. It won't be a gift.' By the time this was done, she would have earned every cent.

He quelled her with a stare. 'Thirty million dollars is more than you've earned in your career. I'd say it's a handsome pay-off for a few months' work.'

'Money isn't everything.'

'Tell that to the person who has nothing.'

Which was what *she* would have if they didn't pull this off.

'And if money means nothing to you, you would have turned it down.'

'Just because I'm not that materialistic doesn't mean

I'm a fool. Once this is over I'll still have to eat. I'll still have a mortgage to pay.' She just wouldn't have her business. Her baby.

They'd talked of having babies, she remembered. They'd even chosen names. Imogen and Rebecca for the girls, Samuel and Giannis for the boys.

Leviathan Solutions was the closest thing to a baby she would have.

'You'll be able to pay your mortgage off.'

She shrugged. She wouldn't allow herself to think of what she'd do with the money until this was over and the money was sitting pretty in her bank account.

'How did you get into matchmaking?' he asked. 'You were going to be a writer.'

She forked a tomato and strove not to react. She hadn't imagined he would remember anything important about her.

What harm could it do to tell him? It didn't matter any more. The mystique she'd created around Leviathan no longer applied.

'Chance. I had a college friend from my Brown days whose family would only agree to him joining the family firm if he married. Mike loathed the idea but not enough to forego his place in the firm. Phoebe was a friend from my junior high days, working as a legal secretary and hating everything about her life—she came from old money but her family had frittered most of it away. All she wanted was to marry someone with enough money for her to quit work, and raise kids and sit on charity boards. Shallow, I know, but she's a really fun person to be around. Anyway, instinct told me they would be perfect for each other, and they were.'

'How did that translate into providing a matchmaking service for the elite?'

'Mike's part of the Garcia family.'

Comprehension dawned in his eyes. Garcia's was one of the largest privately owned investment banks in the US. 'I see. And you went to college with Michael Garcia?'

'Yes. I stayed in touch with a lot of my friends from Brown when I transferred to New York State.'

'Why did you transfer?' When Xander had received his investigator's report on Elizabeth he'd been stunned to discover she'd transferred from the prestigious Ivy League Brown University to New York State. From the timings, it had happened soon after their time together on St Francis, right before she'd started her second year.

'Lots of reasons, none of which I want to discuss with you.'

Shutters had come down on her amber eyes.

Whenever he'd unwittingly thought of her over the years he'd imagined her sitting at a desk, surrounded by novels and notebooks, scribbling away. Yet, instead of majoring in English Literature as she'd planned and becoming a scriptwriter, she'd majored in business and set up a matchmaking company.

'Do you ever match people for love?' She'd been an incurable romantic when he'd known her, a believer in destiny and the alignment of stars.

Her honey hair swung around her shoulders as she shook her head. 'That's not what my company's about. What it *was* about. I brought together people who had specific needs in a partner which had nothing to do with love.' Her eyes met his. 'Both parties knew exactly what they were getting into. No lies. No deceit. No unrealistic expectations. No broken hearts.'

Her words were loaded with meaning, all of it singing loud and clear.

'Doesn't love come into it?' he asked, refusing to believe the dreamer he'd met so long ago was completely gone.

She shook her head even more vigorously. 'If people are stupid enough to want to be matched for love then they can go elsewhere for help in finding it. It doesn't exist and I want no part in the destruction of their dreams.'

He contemplated her a little longer. Their thoughts on marriage aligned. Romantic happy ever afters were a nonsense. Hearing it from her lips though…it proved like nothing else that Elizabeth really had changed.

She was as cynical as he was.

Fourteen hours after leaving St Francis, they landed in Athens.

After years of travelling the world's time zones, Elizabeth still struggled to adjust to the major differences. Her exhausted body thought it was midnight and time to sleep. The early Greek sunshine begged to differ.

Adjusting her watch to seven a.m., she followed Xander through the airport where they were whisked through the official bits, and out into a car. A short drive took them to a smaller airport, where they climbed the steps into a much smaller plane for the short flight to Diadonus.

Small but perfectly formed, Diadonus was part of the densely packed Cyclades and unmistakably Greek. The clear blue skies brought a chill to the morning but the rising sun promised warmer weather ahead.

Another car met them on the landing strip and soon they were on their way to Xander's home.

'Will your parents be there?' she asked, voicing the fear in her belly that had been gnawing at her since they'd landed in Athens.

'No. They rarely come to Diadonus. It's unlikely you'll meet them before the court hearing.'

'Won't they come and visit Loukas?'

The smile he gave her was bitter. 'I can count on one hand the number of times they've visited him. Neither of them like it here. It's too quiet for their tastes.'

'But I thought you'd always lived here?'

'The Trakas family has always had a home here but my parents prefer Athens. When I took over the running of Timos they moved there full-time.'

'Do you live in the family home?'

'Yanis and Katerina have it. I had a new home built for me five years ago.'

The new home turned out to be a palatial white Mykonian-style villa set above a horseshoe-shaped beach. Elizabeth had visited many palatial homes during the course of her career, none of which failed to evoke her admiration. This was the first that properly took her breath away. It had such simplicity and cleanliness yet such beauty, and the *views*... Breathtaking.

The Aegean rippled close by, its white surf skimming the sandy beach, clusters of white homes nestled close to the shoreline in all directions but far enough away to ensure absolute privacy. Squinting when she got out of the car, she could make out another island in the far distance.

Her throat closing, she followed Xander up white concrete steps to the front entrance. Her few possessions were taken in by a member of his household staff who materialised from nowhere with a friendly smile.

They had barely stepped inside before a squeal sounded out and a small, skinny figure in rumpled navy pyjamas hurtled into the reception room to throw his arms around Xander.

Loukas.

Xander lifted him high into the air and planted kisses all over his nephew's face, to further squeals of delight.

It was only when he'd been placed back on his feet that Loukas noticed Elizabeth, hanging back a little, feeling decidedly like an intruder.

The happiness resonating from the blue eyes so like his uncle's turned to wariness and he visibly shrank into himself.

Xander noticed the change and crouched down. 'Loukas, this lady is my friend Elizabeth,' he said slowly in English. Like generations of Trakas children, Loukas had an English nanny to ensure he grew up bilingual, but in recent months his learning had taken a backwards turn. His teachers at the local school he attended—a break from the Trakas tradition of educating privately in Athens—had reported him becoming ambivalent about his lessons and withdrawing more into himself. 'She has come to stay with us.'

Loukas didn't answer, just stared at Xander with his big blue eyes.

'Will you say hello to her?'

Loukas shook his head, his thick mop of blond hair falling into his eyes. It needed cutting, Xander thought, his heart aching to see the emptiness in his nephew's eyes.

It was at moments like this he wanted to grab his brother by the throat and shake him for all the crap he'd put his son through.

He knew Yanis and Katerina couldn't help their addictions. He'd read all the literature and spoken to all the specialists; they all said the same thing. And in fairness to his brother and sister-in-law, they'd done their best to protect Loukas from it all. In their pitiful marriage they had at least tried to do the right thing by him, but they hadn't accounted for their son being like a sponge and taking it all in: the regular hospitalisations, the frequent disappearing acts, the rows when the pain of their marriage broke through the alcohol and drug-inflicted stupors.

The best thing would be for them to divorce. They should never have married in the first place.

He did his best to understand them. The greatest emotion he felt towards them was pity but he could gladly shout himself hoarse to tell them that their best wasn't good enough and that their son deserved better. But they already knew that.

Taking Loukas's hand in his, Xander smiled. 'Elizabeth is a nice lady. I promise. Maybe you can talk to her later. Would you like that?'

Loukas shook his head.

He could sense Elizabeth flinching behind him.

'Can we have breakfast? I've been waiting for you,' Loukas whispered in Greek. 'We've set the table in the infinity room.'

'Nai.' Yes.

'Not you.' Loukas's eyes suddenly fixed on Elizabeth. He'd rediscovered his English. 'You go away.'

Elizabeth felt as if she'd been struck.

The little boy's intense gaze didn't leave her face, as if he thought he could make her disappear with the force of his will.

'Loukas, that isn't a polite thing to say to our guest, is it?' Xander said in a low tone. 'You must say sorry to her.'

To her horror, a tear appeared in Loukas's left eye and fell down his face. His little shoulders heaved and this time a torrent of tears fell. Xander gathered him into his arms and carefully stood, Loukas clinging to him, his face buried in his neck.

Murmuring soothing words in Greek to his nephew,

Xander threw an apologetic look at Elizabeth before indicating that she should follow them.

She walked behind them through an enormous living area, then through to a second cavernous room with a rounded ceiling. A dining table had been laid by a far wall. Xander set Loukas down and brushed away the last of his tears with his thumb, then took the seat next to him.

Feeling as awkward as she'd ever done in her life, Elizabeth sat herself opposite Loukas, Xander sitting between them at the head of the table. She barely registered the infinity pool just feet from them pouring out into a wall-less expanse that looked out over the Aegean, too overwhelmed at the situation to be overawed by anything like such an ostentatious display of wealth.

More staff appeared, carrying trays of yogurt and honey, fresh fruit, pastries and coffee.

Loukas shuffled his chair as close to his uncle as he could get, clearly thrilled to have him back. More than thrilled, she came to think later. Enthralled.

As she watched uncle and nephew interact, she understood why Xander had been so resolute in keeping his promise in returning to him. Xander was clearly Loukas's hero.

When they'd finished eating and the plates had been cleared, a woman who was introduced as Loukas's English nanny came in.

'It's time to get dressed,' she told her charge. 'We're meeting Alekos soon to make dens.'

He pulled a mutinous face. 'I don't want to go.'

'You wanted to the other day. Come on.'

Loukas looked hopefully at his uncle. 'Can you come with me?'

Xander ruffled his hair. 'We've had a long flight and

need to rest. We'll do something fun when you get back. Does that sound good?'

His chin wobbling, his nephew nodded and got down from the table.

Throughout their breakfast he hadn't looked at Elizabeth once.

CHAPTER SIX

XANDER POURED HIMSELF another cup of coffee then moved to fill Elizabeth's. She put a hand over her cup.

'I think my brain might explode if I have any more caffeine.'

He knew the feeling. He was struggling to keep his eyes open himself.

'I apologise for Loukas's behaviour,' he said.

She gave a rueful smile. 'He's protective of you, that's all. He's vulnerable. With his parents both absent, you're his security.' She paused before asking, 'Is he used to seeing you with women?'

'God, no.' He'd always been comfortable entertaining women in Athens but Diadonus was his home, a place to live and entertain family and close friends, not the socialites who littered his world. If he brought a lover here they might start getting ideas that he wanted to make the affair permanent.

Xander conducted his relationships in the same way Elizabeth matched her clients, without lies or deceit. Straight down the line. He didn't want marriage and he made damned sure any lover knew it.

He'd done marriage once with Elizabeth but that had been a whole combination of elements thinking for him, mostly his libido, most definitely not his brain.

In those dark awful days of dealing with Ana's death, Elizabeth's tears still fresh in his mind, he'd known he would never marry again. He didn't need it or want it, or the misery and contempt that accompanied every marriage he knew.

He didn't know a single couple who'd found lasting happiness together. Quite the opposite.

Strangely, his parents had the most content marriage he knew, if *content* was the right word, but they were incredibly well-suited, narcissists the pair of them.

Elizabeth's cheeks coloured and she looked away, tucking a strand of honey-blonde hair behind her ear. 'He's probably scared I'm going to take you away from him. Does he know where his parents are?'

'He knows his mother's in hospital. He thinks Yanis is away on business.'

'Has he seen Katerina since she was hospitalised?'

'A couple of times.' Noticing how wiped out Elizabeth looked, he finished his coffee and got to his feet. 'I'll show you around.'

Elizabeth followed him out of the cave-like living area she'd been told was known as the infinity room, and into the proper living area that was fully protected from the elements. From there she was shown the main dining room, study, playroom with a full-sized snooker table, and kitchen. The sense of space was everywhere and, despite all the futuristic gizmos and gadgets, the design of the villa itself was sympatic to the island's heritage.

'Did you design this yourself?' she asked.

'I worked closely with the architect on the blueprints but I can't take credit for it.'

Then he took her down a flight of extraordinarily wide stairs to the ground floor. There were seven bedrooms in all, each with their own bathroom. They passed a room with the door open. It was a young boy's bedroom. Muffled voices came from it.

'Does Loukas have his own bedroom here?' she whispered.

Xander nodded grimly and matched her low tone. 'He's stayed with me regularly since he was born but in recent years it's become a lot more frequent. When I had the house built I let him choose his own furnishings and decoration for his room. He knows he'll always have a home here.'

'Does he have a bedroom at your parents' place too?'

'He's never spent a night with them and he never will,' he answered with such venom that Elizabeth took a wary step back.

'If you hate your parents so much, how can you work with them? Or have I got that wrong?'

'I wouldn't go as far as to say I hate them,' he said.

'But you do still work together?'

'Of course.'

'How does that work with you being at war over Loukas?'

'That's personal. Work is business. We're very adept at separating the two.'

And she thought *her* family was dysfunctional.

'So you don't have *any* issue working with them? You've never been tempted to sack them? I read that right; you *are* the boss?'

'Yes, I'm the boss, but why would I? They're both excellent in their respective roles within the company. It's only as human beings that they're useless.'

This was too much for Elizabeth to get her head around. She'd surrounded herself with a workforce of warm, decent people. She'd never even contemplated employing someone she didn't like, once passing over a multilingual secretary who would've been able to translate contracts into six different languages. She'd preferred the one who could only translate three because she'd been a warmer person.

She'd had her fill of cold people growing up.

'I need to get some sleep before I do any more work,' she said, wanting nothing more than to be alone. So much had happened in the past twenty-four hours she felt dizzy. 'Which one's my room?'

'We're at the end of the floor.' He set off towards it.

'Adjoining rooms?' she clarified, only following him when he nodded. 'And there's a lock?'

'Correct. Worry not, *kardia mou*, your virtue is safe with me.' But as he spoke a flash of heat pulsed from his eyes, quickly gone but there long enough to make her heart ripple.

He looked away to put his hand on the handle of her door. 'Spend the day resting. Tomorrow we'll go to Athens.'

'What for?'

'You need clothes, don't you?'

'Doesn't Diadonus have shops?'

'Not the sort of clothes a wife of mine should wear. I don't care what style of clothing you buy but I do care about the label on the back.'

She nodded, understanding. Image was important in this world. To some people, image was everything. If she was to be Xander's wife, she had to look the part and that meant couture clothing.

What did she mean, *if she was to be* his wife? She already *was* his wife.

The thought sent a little jolt through her and, for the first time, it really hit her. Xander was her husband. Her legally married husband.

And, for the first time, she allowed herself to see the memory she had shoved in a tight box in the furthest recess of her mind. What it had been like to make love to him as his wife. How it had felt to have him inside her, a part of her...

Long-forgotten heat coiled through her loins at the memories, burning into her brain...

A long, long silence stretched out between them, the atmosphere thickening until Xander's jaw clenched and he shoved the door open. He spoke brusquely. 'This is your room. Make yourself at home. If you need anything you'll find a member of staff in the kitchen.'

She practically dived into it, shutting the door firmly behind her without exchanging another word, desperate to be away from him.

Alone in the pretty room that would put the world's finest hotels to shame, she clutched at her cheeks.

It was the lack of sleep causing her thoughts and emotions to veer so wildly, she assured herself. It was no wonder old memories were being dredged up. A good night's sleep and some distance from Xander would put her back on an even keel.

She tried the internal doors. She opened three before she found the one adjoining Xander's room. It was already locked on the other side.

'Have you been to Athens before?' Xander asked her the next day, shortly before they were due to land. 'Other than just the airport?'

'A handful of times, but that was work. I don't know the city at all.' She was dressed in the clothing she'd worn out to St Francis, his staff having laundered it for her overnight. Her honey-blonde hair was loose and glossy around her shoulders, all signs of exhaustion from the day before eradicated.

They'd managed to avoid each other for the rest of the day, Elizabeth staying in her room, only emerging at dinner. She'd eaten quickly, making only the blandest of conversation before excusing herself, her goodnight to Loukas going unacknowledged.

They'd breakfasted early and dropped Loukas at school on their way to the airstrip. He had refused to look at Elizabeth. He hadn't spoken to her since he'd told her to go away. Xander knew the best thing he could do was give his nephew time to get used to her being there.

He handed her a credit card.

'What's this for?'

'To pay for your clothes and other stuff. There's no limit on it so spend whatever you like.'

She looked momentarily disconcerted but then nodded and slipped it into her purse.

'You don't feel comfortable taking it?'

'I've paid my own way for ten years. It's a little strange, that's all, but I know it's necessary. I can't afford to buy a new expensive wardrobe with what's in my bank account. The money you've paid me won't last long once I've refunded all my clients.'

'Give me a list of the refunds and I'll reimburse you.' He should have thought about that before.

'Okay.' She shrugged. 'And I'll give you my shopping receipts later so you can deduct it from the final amount you pay me when this is all over.'

'There will be no deductions. While you're acting as my wife I'll pick up all your tabs. The money I'm giving you is recompense for the loss of your business.'

But they weren't acting, he reminded himself. Elizabeth really *was* his wife. And as he thought this, she met his gaze. A look passed between them, one that sent heat to his loins and the faintest hint of colour to her cheeks.

Xander gritted his teeth and turned away to look out of the window.

When he'd first learned their annulment hadn't gone through, the thought of her being his wife had been an abstract concept. It hadn't seemed in the slightest bit real. Their marriage was a piece of paper, nothing more.

Two days together, back with the one woman in the world who'd been able to turn his head as well as his loins, and that piece of paper was starting to feel a lot different.

He didn't deny that he'd once had real feelings for Elizabeth but that had been the result of the chemistry neither had felt restrained from acting upon. So strong had it been that it was hardly surprising remnants of it still simmered between them.

How would she react if he grabbed her to him and kissed her?

Locking his jaw, he wiped the pointless question from his mind.

Whatever desire Elizabeth might feel for him now, she'd made it clear she wouldn't entertain acting upon it. And neither would he. She might not be the dreamer from before but he'd given his word and intended to keep it.

The adjoining door separating their two bedrooms would remain locked for the duration of their marriage.

Elizabeth's few visits to Athens had left an impression in her head of a bustling city brimming with noisy, exuberant people. Those impressions turned out to be correct. Athens was an *amazing* city.

Xander got his driver to drop her in the Kolonaki district where, he assured her, she would have no trouble finding suitable shops to buy a new closet of clothes in.

Being an enthusiastic shopper, she welcomed the opportunity to forget her troubles for a few hours of retail therapy. That she didn't have to consider price tags made for a welcome bonus.

Living in New York was expensive. Her mortgage payments took a huge chunk of her income so she normally selected her clothing carefully, knowing she had to choose items that made her look professional but not threatening. She had to fit into whoever's company she might find herself and, most of all, she had to not stand out. She had to be unobtrusive. Most of all, what she selected had to be affordable.

Suddenly, she could dress for herself again, something she hadn't felt able to do since she'd left college and formed Leviathan.

About to hand her new credit card over to an assistant in a boutique that sold the most gorgeous clothes, she felt her cell vibrate through her purse and pulled it out. It was a message from Xander telling her to make sure to buy herself some evening wear.

Her cheeks heated at the words. Evening wear…? Then she realised he meant cocktail dresses and gowns, not lingerie.

Turning her mind away from wearing anything racy in front of Xander, she paid for her goods, which were boxed up for her and put aside for Xander's driver to collect later, and walked to an upmarket department store further up the street. She might have no intention of buying anything racy but she did need to buy underwear.

After five hours she'd spent an absolute fortune and wandered to Kolonaki Square to find the café she'd agreed to meet Xander at.

Her heart skipped to find him already there, chatting on his phone. He'd removed his tie and undone the top button of his shirt.

When he spotted her, he ended his call and stood to greet her.

'Are you done?' he asked, putting his hands on her hips and pressing a kiss to her lips.

The gesture was so unexpected that she froze.

Xander had *kissed* her.

He gave a half-smile and traced a thumb across her jawline. 'Married couples usually kiss, *kardia mou.*'

Totally flustered, she groped for the nearest chair to sit on. 'Can't we just settle on air kisses?'

His eyes held hers. 'Not in public. Take a seat. I've ordered us coffee.'

She put her purse on the table and opened the menu. 'I'm starving. Have we got time for me to grab a salad?'

'We've plenty of time.'

She scanned the menu, anything but to have to look at him. Looking at Xander made her stomach do funny things. It made her entire body do funny things.

When a waitress arrived with their coffee she ordered a slice of chocolate baklava tart.

Xander pulled a bemused face at her choice. 'I thought you were going to have a salad?'

'So did I until I saw the word chocolate.'

He grinned and there, right before her eyes, he turned into the young man with the irresistible smile she'd fallen in love with all those years ago.

Her heart, already pounding erratically, seemed to bloom within her chest and an ache spread low in her belly. She had to fight to stop herself staring at the exposed strong throat and the sensuous lips she had so loved to kiss.

'Is something the matter?' he asked, staring at her closely.

She grabbed her coffee, but as she shook her head to deny anything was wrong a sense of dread raced through her to realise that, as incomprehensible as it was, she wanted him to do far more than kiss her.

Xander checked his watch as he waited for Elizabeth to appear. He'd had to leave early that morning for a breakfast meeting in Athens and only just made it back in time to say goodnight to Loukas.

He hadn't seen her all day. That hadn't stopped him from constantly thinking about her, which was damned frustrating as he was supposed to be concentrating on spreadsheets for the company's year end.

He took satisfaction from the fact that their profits for the year were up seven per cent, but with his head in Diadonus and the woman living under his roof that satisfaction was muted.

His thoughts were broken when a figure stepped into the infinity room.

The effect was like being struck by a bat. 'Elizabeth?'

'You sound surprised,' she said tartly. 'You summoned me and here I am.'

He'd messaged her earlier to say they would be eating out that night.

'Your hair…'

Unlike the glossy sleek hair he'd become accustomed to, she'd gone for the natural look, drying it into a mass of thick, tight blonde curls.

'What's wrong with it?' she demanded.

'Nothing. It's beautiful.' He'd forgotten how curly her hair truly was. The difference was astounding.

Looking at her…

It was like staring at a portrait of the past and he had to swallow a lump in his throat that accompanied the sudden strong hammer of his heart.

The insolence that had been set on her face when she entered the room softened and colour stained her cheeks as she looked away from him and murmured, 'It takes for ever to straighten.'

'Why do it, then?'

A shrug. 'It made me feel more professional. And now I don't need to look professional, so...' Another shrug.

She was wearing a pretty baby-pink dress that fell below her knees and had the thinnest of straps, falling in a V to skim her golden cleavage.

He remembered the first time he'd taken one of her breasts into his mouth. He'd thought nature must have made them especially for him. Small but beautifully formed, enough to fit into his mouth and cover with the palm of his hand. He remembered making love to her, how she would arch her back and grab his hair, how her legs would tighten around him as she came with loud moans.

Suddenly he ached to have her, to thrust deep inside her and experience that heady pleasure again.

He'd never found that compatibility or connection with anyone else. He'd had relationships throughout the years but had always been careful in his selection of lovers. No wide-eyed dreamers with a zest for life. No one with the potential to charm him with one beaming smile or a ringing laugh. Not that there was anyone remotely like her in his world.

A decade ago she'd been a virgin. He'd been old enough to have experience but young enough to still be discovering women's bodies. By the end of their fortnight together he knew more about the workings of Elizabeth's body than he knew of his own.

Making love to her now would be different from how it had been ten years ago. They both had an adulthood of experience to add into what was already proving to be a combustible mix.

'Let's make a move,' he said abruptly. *Theos*, he couldn't be alone in a room with her for a minute without thinking of sex.

She wrapped a creamy shawl around her shoulders. 'Where are we going?'

'Diadonus Town.'

Her relief was obvious.

'What?'

'I thought you were going to take me to Athens.'

'You don't like Athens?'

'Sure, but it's a bit of a pain to get to if we're only going for a meal.'

That those were his exact thoughts was something he kept to himself.

'Just so you're prepared, there's a few members of the press on the island itching to get another picture of us together, so remember to smile.'

'I shall turn my frown upside down.'

With a tug in his groin, he was taken by the urge to wipe the frown off her face with something stronger than words.

Jamming his hands in his pockets, he led the way out.

The restaurant Xander took her to was a short drive away, an old-fashioned *taverna* perched above a beach. There were only six other diners.

'Is it always this quiet?' Elizabeth asked while they waited for the main courses to be served.

'It's winter,' he answered with a shrug. 'Come the spring and the whole of Diadonus will be filled with tourists.'

'I read it's a party island.'

'We attract a young crowd but it's not like Mykonos or Santorini. We get a lot of family vacationers.'

'Do the tourists bother you?'

'Not at all. Tourists are what keeps our economy floating.'

She sipped her glass of rosé and was relieved when the owner returned to their table with their next course. If they were eating she could pretend the atmosphere between them didn't shimmer with a strange electricity and that every time she met his gaze her lower belly didn't clench with longing.

CHAPTER SEVEN

FOR THE FIRST TIME in days, Elizabeth finished a meal. A couple Xander knew had joined them for a few minutes to say hello, which had given her time to regroup mentally. They hadn't spoken English so the only requirement on Elizabeth's part had been to smile and not flinch when Xander took possessive control of her hand. Having his warm skin against hers...

She could still feel the tingles in her bloodstream.

Now they were alone again, she pushed her empty plate to one side and gazed out across the sandy beach, drinking the view in. Diadonus was more beautiful than she had imagined. 'Why did you go to St Francis for a vacation when you live in your own paradise?'

Xander took so long to answer that she thought he was ignoring her.

'Going to St Francis, it wasn't a vacation, it was an escape,' he eventually said.

'Why?'

His eyes met hers. 'I didn't want to stick around for the fallout when I ended my engagement to Ana.'

'You ran away?'

'That's one way of looking at it,' he conceded.

Looking back, Xander could see he had taken the coward's way out. It hadn't seemed like that at the time of course. To his twenty-year-old self it had seemed perfectly logical. If he took himself off, there would be no one in his ear demanding he change his mind. He'd determined to go back when the dust had settled but in the interim take some time out and see something of the world that wasn't business related. Have some fun like others of his age.

In his arrogance it hadn't crossed his mind that Ana would have to suffer the price of his absence.

'How long after you ended your engagement did you leave?'

'Two days.'

'You didn't even give me two hours.' She shook her head, her long curls bobbing with the motion.

'There was no point in prolonging it for either of us.'

'For either of us?' There was a catch in her voice. 'That makes it sound like you cared for me.'

'I *did* care for you, Elizabeth.'

Her eyes flashed. 'Did you care for Ana too? Did you tell her you loved her and that you couldn't live without her like you told me?'

He took a long drink of his beer, studying the tight-set face before him. He remembered saying those words to Elizabeth. He remembered meaning them.

'My relationship with Ana was nothing like the one between you and me.'

'Of course it wasn't. She was your childhood sweetheart.'

'We were *never* childhood sweethearts. We mixed in the same circles, we were casual friends, but that was the extent of it. We got engaged when I turned twenty because it was expected of us and our parents made it very clear it was what they wanted. It's traditional in my family to marry young and with someone who can bring wealth and contacts to the family business. My father married my mother because she was an heiress. Their marriage was arranged by their own parents. My brother married Katerina for the same reason. Ana came from an extremely rich family from Mykonos. We were engaged for less than a month.'

'If you were so well-suited, why did you end it?'

'Because it wasn't what I wanted and I should never have gone along with it.' He should have trusted his gut instincts from the start. Instead, he'd let his misgivings fester until they'd become bugs hatching in his skin.

Elizabeth's expression remained stony.

'I wasn't in love with her. I didn't want to be trapped in a marriage I couldn't get out of like Yanis was. Divorce is unheard of in my family. It's too risky for the business. From what Yanis tells me, they haven't had sex since they conceived Loukas. Even before that it was a volatile relationship.' He drained his beer. 'I decided that no marriage was better than living with one like theirs.'

'Yanis wanted out even then?'

'They both did. I'm certain it's why they turned to drugs and alcohol. It numbed it for them.' He paused before adding, 'They were both in love with other people.'

Her eyebrows drew together. 'So why did they go along with the marriage in the first place?'

'The alternative meant being cut off.'

'Weren't you worried that would happen to you when you dumped Ana?'

He grimaced at her bluntly delivered words. 'For sure, but I've always been more independently minded than Yanis. I took an educated risk. Yanis has never had much input in the business but I'd already proven myself to be an asset. I knew my decision would enrage my parents but they're clever people and clever people do not cast off assets making them money.'

But they hadn't been so clever when Xander had made the deal that resulted in Timos SE being signed under his control, taking the power and control away from them for ever.

Elizabeth was silent before asking, 'How did Ana take it?'

Xander signalled for another beer. 'Better than I thought she would. I thought she was okay with it. For sure, I knew she would be a little hurt; everyone's got their pride, but she understood. She was a nice girl. Better than most of the socialites I grew up with who were so vapid they made a plastic doll seem like a Nobel laureate.'

Ana really *had* been nice. She'd been sweet and warm, a woman any right-thinking man in his position would have been proud to call his wife. It hadn't been her fault he'd felt zero desire towards her.

His parents had both openly taken lovers through the years but that hadn't been something he could entertain. To Xander, marriage meant fidelity and commitment otherwise why do it? If he'd had to marry anyone it would be someone he desired and who held his intellectual interest too. He'd been selfish. He'd wanted it all. And so he'd ended it with Ana, determined that he *would* have it all.

Then he'd met Elizabeth and had known for certain he'd made the right choice. In his continued arrogance he'd married her without taking into account how utterly unsuited she was to a life as his wife.

His fresh beer was brought over. He took it straight from the waiter's hand and took a large swig of it.

Talking about Ana, thinking about Ana, was *hard*,

talking about her to Elizabeth, who he'd also hurt, doubly so. It brought it all back: all the rancid guilt that lived inside him. Ana would never marry. She would never have children.

He forced the rest of the story out. 'Two weeks after I ended it she crashed her car into a tree. She wasn't much of a drinker but she'd drunk heavily that night. I have no idea if she intended to kill herself or not.'

Elizabeth didn't say anything, just stared at him with a stunned expression on her face. He searched for the condemnation he knew he deserved but couldn't interpret what came from her eyes.

'Her family…even though I told *everyone* that she was blameless, they blamed her for not doing enough to keep me. I didn't know it at the time. Yanis filled me in when I got home. They put pressure on her. My parents got in on the act too. They all told her I would come to my senses and that she would have to change to keep me. But she knew I wouldn't change my mind. She knew the situation was hopeless but I was oblivious to it all, thousands of miles away in a Caribbean paradise, all my problems forgotten about because I was with you.'

'You don't blame yourself, surely?' she asked with sudden animation.

'If I hadn't abandoned her to deal with the fallout of the break-up alone, she would be alive today, of that I am certain.' He shook his head, self-loathing filling him. Talking of Ana's death made his guts feel they were being eaten without anaesthetic.

Elizabeth's eyes held his for the longest time, the gold and red flecks shining. 'If anyone's to blame it's her family and your parents for treating her like a commodity.'

He'd known that ever since Yanis told him of the pressure they'd all put her under, but that didn't change his own responsibility.

He'd left Ana to deal with the fallout on her own, in his arrogance assuming that because he was all right then she would be too. It hadn't occurred to him that their families would turn on her. He should have protected her.

At least he'd been able to protect Elizabeth from his family, however badly it had hurt her at the time.

'And, Xander, you can't know what was going through her head or what other influences might have been in play when she got behind the wheel.'

'Whatever was going on in her head wasn't good.'

'The outcome might have been the same even if you hadn't broken the engagement.'

What a tragic waste of a life, Elizabeth thought, her heart aching for the young Greek woman. A tiny part of her heart also ached for Xander bearing the weight of such guilt. She could see it in his eyes.

He held her gaze for an age before his eyes snapped back into focus and he said in a measured voice, 'So there it is. You know it all. My world is a beautiful place to live in but a cruel place to be. Think yourself lucky that in a few months you'll be able to leave it.'

She finished her wine and gazed back out at the foamy surf, a deep ache spreading out from her chest.

'Do you want dessert?' he asked.

'No, thank you.'

He reached for his phone. 'I'll get my driver to collect us.'

She stared with more longing at the sandy shore. 'If we walked along the beach, would it take us to your villa?'

'Yes but it's a couple of miles.'

'I think I'll do that. I need to walk.' Walking was good. It always cleared her head and made sense of whatever madness she was living in. Right then, she had so many thoughts racing through her it would take a marathon to clear it.

She could sense his surprise. 'Okay. Give me a minute to settle the bill and we'll get going.'

To reach the beach from the restaurant involved descending a steep incline with only the moonlight to guide them. Inhaling the air that reminded her so heavily of St Francis it made her heart clench and twist. Biting the swirling emotions back, Elizabeth removed her heels and navigated her way carefully down the incline until she felt cool sand between her toes.

The night sea was making its familiar lapping noise. She remembered how soothing she'd found the sound on her first trip to St Francis, her first trip to any beach. *Everything* on St Francis had been soothing. Except it had all been an illusion. The serenity had created an ambiance that had lulled her into believing things that weren't real. Here, on Diadonus, there were different scents, equally beautiful, but without the muscle memory reactions.

Would she one day inhale a scent and be taken back to this moment in time?

At least if that happened the memories wouldn't lance her.

There was a gentle breeze coming from the sea and she wrapped her shawl around her shoulders and walked right to the water's edge. She prodded a toe into it but the surf was too cold and she stepped back, right in time for a gentle wave to cover her foot.

Needing to move, she set off, treading footprints into the wet sand that were eradicated almost immediately by the waves. Just as their marriage had been eradicated almost immediately after exchanging their vows.

'If divorce is too risky for your business, how can you risk divorcing me?' she asked quietly.

'You haven't brought any assets into the marriage. There's no contract between us. I can pay you off and that's it. Over with.'

'And when we finally are over with? Will you ever marry again?'

'No.' The word was blunt. 'I know of no marriages that last without turning to hell. I would be left with the choice of living with someone I dislike or risk destroying my company with a bitter divorce.'

Elizabeth knew exactly how vicious divorces could be. And while he wasn't saying anything she didn't agree with, it still made her heart twinge.

'What about children?' she forced herself to ask, glad she didn't have to see his expression when he gave his answer. He was walking beside her, his hands deep in his pockets, a foot apart but close enough that her senses danced with awareness.

It had always been like this. She'd only needed to catch a glimpse of him to feel every atom of her body vibrate.

'Don't you want to produce the next generation of Trakases?'

'Loukas is the next generation.'

'But don't you want your own?' she persisted. He had once. Or had that been a lie too?

'Children need two parents. I'm never going to marry again so for me it's not a consideration.'

'What if Loukas doesn't want to join the business?'

'That's for him to decide when he's old enough. While I'm alive and kicking I shall run it the best way I can and put the structures in place for it to thrive when I'm gone.'

There was nothing she could say to that. And what did it matter to her in any case? They would go their separate ways soon enough and then she'd never have to see him again.

They were approaching a harbour. A row of yachts of varying sizes lay before them, pearlescent under the moonlight.

She remembered the day Xander had chartered a yacht for them. It was the first time she'd really considered that he must come from money, his familiarity with sailing and the unwritten protocols…

It should have been a warning sign. Instead it had delighted her. In her head she'd already moved to Diadonus to be with him. They wouldn't starve while she completed her degree, learnt his language and found a job.

Her blood burned and her heart ached to remember her innocence. Voices called out in her head, happy memories that had turned into scars.

'I seem to remember you never liked walking,' he said, breaking the rolling silence that had formed between them.

She tried not to flinch. It was hard to hold on to her loathing of him when he so casually dropped in things she'd expected him to have forgotten.

She was finding it hard to hold on to her loathing period.

'I learned to like walking when I enrolled at New York State. After rent and tuition were paid I was stony broke. To save money I walked everywhere. I still do.'

'Why did you quit Brown?'

After the confidences he'd shared over their meal it seemed petty not to answer him. 'My mother withdrew her funding so I had no choice.'

'Why did she do that?'

'I told her I didn't want to major in English any more.'

She could feel his eyes burning into her.

'Why on earth would you do that? You'd only ever wanted to be a writer.'

'I did,' she agreed, wishing her heart didn't twist to remember the person she'd been then. 'I wanted to write scripts for films about modern-day love; stories with hints of the classics running through them, but when I returned home to New York the idea of writing *anything* about love was laughable. There was no way I could write about something I didn't believe in any more, and script writing? Every girl in my class and her cat wanted to do that. I decided to go into business instead. I had no idea at the time what kind of business I wanted, but I knew I would be my own boss. My mother had other ideas, so I decided to go it alone.'

'Why would she not want you to go into business?'

'The only thing my mom has ever taken pride in about me were my achievements in English. I was winning literature prizes when I was eight and a career in writing was a foregone conclusion. When I told her I wanted to major in business…' She took a deep breath, hating the memories. It felt like a different life. 'The long and short of it was that if I refused to major in English, she would stop supporting me.'

'So you moved out and transferred colleges off your own back?'

She wrapped her shawl tighter around her. The breeze had picked up, the chill now setting goosebumps off on her flesh. 'I was legally an adult. She couldn't force me to do anything. No one could. I still had some of the money granny had left me. It wasn't enough to support me at Brown but was enough to pay for the first year's tuition and rent at New York State, which was my home college. So I moved out of my mom's and transferred there.'

'Your father couldn't help you?'

'Nope. He'd just remarried a woman equally as manipulative as my mother. After a decade of war with my mom he was tired of arguing with women—that's what he told me, anyway.' She speared him with a look. 'So you don't have the monopoly on dysfunctional, emotionally abusive parents.'

'I'm beginning to see that,' he said after a long pause.

Somehow during their walk, their pace had slowed and the distance between them closed. Xander's arm brushed lightly against hers.

The heat that rushed through her…

Her lungs seemed to close in on themselves.

'No wonder you forgot to chase our annulment with all that going on,' he murmured.

She forced herself to concentrate on the conversation at hand, not on the warm body brushing against her own, and moved out of his way so they were no longer touching.

The chill felt starker without his heat warming her.

'The annulment was the last thing on my mind,' she croaked. 'I never even thought there might be a problem with it.'

Xander's villa appeared shortly ahead of them. As they got closer, they drifted together again, close enough that if she flexed her fingers she'd be able to touch him.

In silence they passed the barrier onto his private section of beach, security lights bathing them the moment they stepped onto his land.

Her heart rate increasing so much she no longer felt the individual beats, Elizabeth hurried up the steps to enter the villa from the kitchen. She didn't know the entry code.

She moved back down to allow him to get to it but the

steps were narrow and it turned into an awkward kind of dance as they tried to step around each other.

And then, without knowing how, she found herself trapped between the railing and Xander.

Her breath caught in a throat that had filled with moisture. Unable to help herself, she tilted her head to gaze into eyes that trapped her more effectively than any chain could. The few senses not already on high alert sprang to life, lips tingling, every cell in her body straining towards him.

The look in his eyes…it was as if he wanted to eat her whole.

His mouth drifted slowly to hers, his eyes open and holding hers in their hypnotic gaze until the lids closed and she felt his warm breath brush against her skin in the moment before his mouth found hers.

For the longest time they didn't move, their lips only whispering against the other's.

He pulled back a little to stare at her again, and the hunger in his eyes darkened and he wrapped his arms around her to crush her to him.

Their lips fused together in a kiss full of such passion that her bones melted and then *she* melted, right into him, her hands grasping round to hold onto his back, crushing herself to *him*.

As their tongues danced together and the heat of his mouth consumed her, she clung even tighter, dizzy with the familiarity of his taste and the terrifying yet exhilarating familiarity of her own responses.

His hands burrowed into her hair and she wanted to cry as she remembered how he had done the exact same thing the first time he'd kissed her all those years ago.

If the kitchen door hadn't burst open at that moment,

there was every chance she would have lost herself completely.

'So this is what you get up to when you're supposed to be caring for my grandson.'

Elizabeth let go of Xander as sharply as if she'd had ice tipped over her.

Standing in the doorway, as tall and menacing as Morticia Adams with all her hair chopped off, stood a woman she could only presume was Xander's mother.

CHAPTER EIGHT

XANDER REGAINED HIS composure before she did. He straightened and shook his head, and brushed past his mother.

'How did you get in?'

'I knocked and the door was answered. Your house-keeper told me you were out. I said I would wait.'

Listening to her, Elizabeth revised her opinion of Morticia Adams to one of Marlene Dietrich but with less of an accent. Her English was, like her son's, impeccable. As was her timing.

Hastily straightening her dress, Elizabeth grabbed her shawl that had fallen to the ground and, her head reeling, her legs weakened, her body vibrating from the effect of his kiss, she followed them inside.

She didn't know what she was most mortified about: that she'd fallen into Xander's arms so easily or that his mother's first impression of her would be her kissing her son so passionately.

She could get down on her knees in gratitude that she'd interrupted them before it had gone any further.

As skinny as a pencil, Mirela Trakas had cropped jet-black hair and the surprised face of someone on first-name terms with her plastic surgeon. Wearing a black pantsuit with full make-up and a dozen solid gold bangles hanging on her wrists, she strongly resembled a glamourous undertaker.

'If you'd called first I would have told you not to bother,' Xander said.

'That's why I didn't call first. I'll have a gin and tonic.'

A grim smile on his handsome face, he strode through the kitchen and dining room and into the infinity room, where he kept a wall-length bar. 'I thought you were in Milan.'

'We wrapped up early, so I thought I'd call in on my favourite son.'

The look Xander gave her perfectly conveyed his feelings. Nostrils flaring, he said, 'Dad not with you?'

'He's gone to Monte Carlo for the evening to gamble your inheritance at the roulette table.'

Xander rolled his eyes. 'I assume Elizabeth's the reason you're here?'

'Elizabeth? Is that her name?'

'You know perfectly well it is. Elizabeth, meet my mother. Mirela, meet your new daughter-in-law.'

Mirela didn't even glance in Elizabeth's direction. 'It would have been nice to learn my son had married from the son in question rather than hear about it third-hand. My phone has been ringing off the hook. All my friends know about it. The whole world knows about it. Even nuns in Outer Mongolia know about it but you couldn't take the time to tell me.'

'We've been busy.'

'So I see.' Her nostrils flared in an exact replica of her son's. 'You tell the judge you want guardianship of my grandson yet leave him with strangers to take your fake wife out. I'm sure the judge will be thrilled when I share it with him next week.'

He poured himself a large Scotch and downed it in

one. Feeling as if she needed something strong too, Elizabeth stood beside him and poured herself one, downing it the same as he'd done.

Oh, wow. Her throat *burned*. And Mirela noticed, wicked pleasure alive in her cold eyes.

Thrusting a gin and tonic into his mother's hand, Xander contemplated her coolly before saying, 'Loukas is in bed asleep. He's being watched by people he's known his entire life, and who love him. Rather like you and Dad would leave Yanis and I alone while you two went out which, if I'm remembering correctly, was every night. You also left us alone for weeks at a time...'

'That was always business, darling.'

'That week in the Maldives was not business. Nor the frequent skiing trips to Canada. I could drink this whole bottle of single malt and I'd still be listing the times you and Dad took off without us that had nothing to do with business.'

Mirela waved her hand. 'The Maldives would have bored you.'

'Yes, you told us that when you got back after not bothering to tell us you were going in the first place. We had to find out from the staff.'

'We couldn't have been expected to report our every movement to our *children*. We had a multimillion-euro business to run and the staff were perfectly well placed to look after you.' She laughed and took a good sip of her drink.

'You could have done and you should have done. That multimillion-euro business has turned into a multibillion business since I've been at the helm and I'm still able to eat breakfast every day with Loukas when he's in my care. His future is all that matters and that future does not include you being his guardian, so finish your drink and get out.'

She pouted. Elizabeth would have laughed if she weren't so appalled. Mirela had actually *pouted*.

'You're kicking me out when I still haven't spoken properly to my new daughter-in-law?' Mirela's beady eyes finally fixed upon her. 'Or should that be *old* daughter-in-law?'

Was that a dig at her age or that they'd been unwittingly married for a decade?

'You're not pregnant already, are you, darling? Or do you just like your food?'

'When I get pregnant you'll be the first to know,' Elizabeth said, ignoring the barb. She held out a hand. 'It's been a pleasure meeting you... Do I call you Mother?'

Mirela looked at the extended hand and then surprised Elizabeth by shaking it. Before she released it, she studied it a moment then said, 'I know a good manicurist in Athens. I'll get the number passed on to you. And I know just the place you can get a chemical peel for your acne scars.'

If Elizabeth had acne scars she might have been offended. As she didn't, she did the only thing she could think of. She laughed. 'I can see exactly why Xander and Yanis don't want you anywhere near Loukas.'

'And I can see exactly why Xander kept you a secret for ten years,' Mirela shot back. She opened her mouth again, most likely to spew another sweet insult, when Xander took her arm.

'Time to go. Don't bother coming back until you can show some civility to my wife.'

'I can walk. You don't need to manhandle me.' She tugged her arm free, finished her drink and handed the empty glass back to him. 'I'll see you in the morning, darling. Don't forget your father's flying to Germany for the Munich Conference so he won't be at the board meeting.' Then she looked at Elizabeth one last time. 'I'll see *you* in court. Goodbye, darlings.'

Only when she was sure Mirela had truly gone, looking through the window as the chauffeured car sped off to make doubly sure, did Elizabeth dare look at Xander.

'My *God*. Your mother is something else.'

He'd poured them both another Scotch and sat himself in one of the rounded pods by the infinity pool, gazing out into the distance with a grim expression on his face.

'I can only apologise.'

'You weren't to know she was coming.'

His head dropped forward and he rubbed the back of his neck. 'For what she said to you.'

'You don't control her mouth.'

'I'm glad you didn't let her intimidate you. I would have cut in sooner but I thought I should see how you handled her.' He lifted his head, his eyes suddenly lightening. 'You handled her beautifully.'

'Better than I would have ten years ago,' she admitted. Ten years ago his mother would have cut her down in flames.

Ironically, it was Xander's dumping of her to supposedly protect her from Mirela that had toughened her up to deal with the witch.

'And don't forget I've had practice with my own mom. I would love to get them in a room together. I have no idea who'd come out as top dog but it would be fun to watch.'

'It sounds like my idea of hell,' he commented drily.

Then the look between them changed, all the amusement dissolving. Her lips began tingling again as she recalled their kiss…

A mistake that wouldn't be repeated.

She crossed her arms tightly across her chest before

giving a decisive nod. 'I totally understand why you wouldn't want her to have custody of Loukas. I will do everything in my power to make sure the judge sees us as a loving, stable couple.'

Xander didn't say anything, simply stared at her in the way that made her veins heat and her belly turn to mush.

The kiss they'd shared loomed like a spectre between them and it was all she could do not to gaze at those firm lips that had covered hers so deliciously.

She edged away to the door with a pounding heart, and cleared her throat. 'What happened before your mother turned up...' She cleared her throat.

He didn't fill the silence.

She shuffled further back. 'It was a mistake.'

His jaw clenched. 'It won't happen again,' he stated flatly, then took another large drink of his Scotch, eyes like steel as they bore into her.

Unable to say another word, she jerked a nod and left.

Her heart was still thumping madly when she reached the safety of her room.

A noise woke her from the light doze she had finally fallen into hours later.

She lifted her head from the pillow but only silence rang out. Just as she'd convinced herself she'd imagined it, she heard it again. A cry.

Throwing the covers off, she jumped out of bed and hurried to unlock her door, then sped down the wide hallway to Loukas's room.

Cautiously, she put her ear to his door at the same moment he cried out again.

Heart pounding, she pushed it open and entered his room.

He was on his bed, his covers kicked off and half on

the floor, his little body twisting and turning, whimpers coming from his mouth.

Should she wake him? Or was it only sleepwalkers you weren't supposed to rouse?

Another cry came from him and she quickly placed the covers back on him, then sat beside him and tentatively put a hand on his head.

Maybe she could just soothe him back to a happy dream, she figured, holding her breath as she gently stroked his hair.

It seemed to work. After a while he stopped thrashing and the whimpers lessened until they'd gone entirely.

Her heart almost stopped when his eyes opened.

He stared at her wide-eyed, hardly blinking, his mouth forming a tight miserable line.

Wanting to weep for him, Elizabeth continued to stroke his hair. She didn't speak, hoping he'd be able to see in her eyes that she meant him no harm and only wanted to help.

She remembered so clearly the nightmares she'd suffered as a child, the dreams of finding herself lost and alone. Even as a small child she'd known her parents didn't love her. The one person who had shown her love had been her granny but their time together had been infrequent and fleeting. Elizabeth's mother had despised her mother-in-law and her father had feared her. For Elizabeth her granny had been sent from heaven; a security blanket to love and care for her.

It was in that silent moment that she fully understood why Xander had forced her back into his life. He might be incapable of loving her—or any other woman—but he did love this defenceless little boy. And Loukas loved him. Xander was *his* security blanket in a world where his parents were often incapable of caring for him themselves.

Loukas had learned that adults, Xander excepted, could not be trusted to always be there when he needed them. And, as much as she tried to keep her distance from the little boy, reluctant to form an attachment when she knew her time here was limited and she didn't want him to have to deal with the abandonment of yet another adult—because that was how Loukas would see it; as an abandonment—all she wanted was to wrap her arms tightly around him and smother him in love.

Loukas's eyelids became heavier. She stayed where she was until his rigid frame relaxed, his eyes closed a final time and he turned on his side and burrowed back under his covers.

Placing a gentle kiss on the top of his head, she carefully got back to her feet. Only when she turned to tiptoe out of the room did she see Xander standing in the doorway, wearing nothing but a pair of black boxers.

Xander didn't think his heart had ever felt so full or his chest so tight. For hours he'd lain in his bed, reliving their kiss, castigating himself for starting it, fighting the urge to kick the adjoining door down and get into her bed.

Interspersed with all this had been anger he couldn't rid himself of over his mother's surprise visit.

It shouldn't have been a surprise. His mother was a law unto herself. Both his parents were.

He must have fallen asleep as it had taken him a few moments of disorientation to hear Loukas's cries. Before he could go to him, he'd heard Elizabeth's door open and her soft footsteps treading away. He'd arrived at Loukas's room in time to see her place a hand to his nephew's head.

There had been such tenderness in her touch, such compassion for the child who had shown her nothing but animosity, that all he could do was watch with the most enormous lump in his throat.

Now, as she padded to the door, he stepped back to let her pass and captured the delicate floral scent she carried everywhere.

His blood thickening, he pulled the door to so it was slightly ajar and faced her.

Only soft night lights gave any colour to the hallway, a glow that gave Elizabeth an ethereal quality, highlighting the beauty of her oval face. All she wore was a T-shirt that fell to her knees, which, with her mass of curls springing in every direction, stripped back the years to a time when she'd briefly been the centre point of his world.

It had been her beauty that had first captured his attention but there was nothing unique about beautiful women, especially in his world where imperfections were dealt with in a permanent manner from the minimum legal age, turning all the socialites he'd mixed with into one homogenous face.

Elizabeth's beauty had been matched by her smile, which he'd seen her bestow on everyone she made eye contact with. She'd been kind too, another rarity in his world, opening doors for a chambermaid struggling with an enormous cleaning trolley when it seemed as if no one else had even seen her though she was right there before them. *He* wouldn't have seen her if he hadn't been watching Elizabeth.

She might have matured into a cynical sassy bombshell over the years but the Elizabeth from old was in there too, the warm, generous woman he'd been crazy about, still there, ready to spring out and soothe a defenceless child from a nightmare.

'Thank you,' he said quietly, struggling to speak through the raggedness of his chest.

She sucked her lips in and swallowed. 'He's sleeping now.'

Theos, he ached to touch her again. Her small breasts were like little juts straining through her T-shirt and he so badly wanted to taste them again. He wanted to taste all of her again.

But he'd given his word that it wouldn't happen and he intended to keep it. Unless Elizabeth threw herself at him and demanded he take her, he would keep his hands to himself, no matter how many cold showers he had to take.

Elizabeth waited for Xander to say something else and break this strange chemical cocktail weaving around them. She couldn't tear her eyes from him.

Her heart hammered and she struggled to breathe. The generous proportions of the hallway shrank around them as she gazed into eyes that swam with unashamed desire and made her lungs close up. A pulse set off low within her, her skin heated...

She wanted him so much. Too much. So much that she was in danger of losing her grip on reality, of turning the clock back to a time when she had believed that love was out there and that the desire she had felt for him *must* translate into love.

These were things she didn't want to feel. Not ever again. She couldn't trust her own heart to do the right thing so she must trust her head and let it keep her grounded in reality.

'We should get some sleep.'

He nodded and put a hand to her cheek, rubbing his thumb gently over her cheekbone.

She closed her eyes, her skin burning under his touch, certain he must be able to see her thundering heart beneath her T-shirt.

There was the lightest brush of lips against hers before she heard a deep inhalation. 'Goodnight, Elizabeth.'

When she opened her eyes, all she could see were the muscles across his back rippling as he walked to his bedroom and shut the door firmly behind him.

Xander ruffled his nephew's hair. 'Sleep tight. I'll see you in the morning.'

Loukas sat up and hooked his arms around Xander's waist. 'Can I see Mummy again tomorrow?'

'If she's well enough.' He wouldn't make any false promises. Katerina needed a liver transplant. To get this, she would have to be sober for six months. For Katerina to recover and have anything like a normal life, she had to quit drinking. This was an issue in itself as she refused, despite all the evidence including her once glowing complexion now an almost fluorescent yellow, to admit she was an alcoholic. She'd been transferred to a different private hospital, one that was more like a convalescence home. There she was watched twenty-four hours a day and given all manner of counselling. Getting a drink was impossible. For the time being she was safe, even if in denial.

She'd been happy to see Loukas though. Xander had wanted to grab her shoulders and force her to look in her son's face.

If you won't admit your problem and fight to save yourself, do it for him, he'd longed to shout. But shouting wouldn't have changed anything. The change could only come from Katerina herself, a woman who had spent her life controlled by others and who had found her only freedom in the bottom of a bottle of spirits.

He thought of Elizabeth—hell, when *didn't* he think of Elizabeth?

She'd been back in his life for a week. Since their kiss three nights ago they'd hardly seen anything of each other except during the evening meals they shared with Loukas, during which they were studiously polite to each other.

Elizabeth had taken control of her life in an entirely different way from Katerina. She'd formed her own successful business from nothing after putting herself through college, never giving up even when it meant having to walk miles every day as she didn't have the money to pay a bus fare. He felt intense admiration for that, for driving herself to succeed when it would have been far easier to fail.

Once he'd extricated himself from Loukas's hold, he turned off the bedside light and left the room. It was time for a shower.

Tonight, he and Elizabeth were going to a fundraising gala at the Athens Museum so the three of them and Loukas's nanny were staying the night in Xander's Athens home.

It was the perfect opportunity for them to be photographed together and the gala was for a good cause.

After showering, he shaved, then set about dressing, donning a dark blue suit with a white shirt and striped silver tie. He spent half a minute styling his hair, fastened his cufflinks, dabbed some cologne on, checked his shoes for scuffs and declared himself good to go.

Impulse made him knock on the adjoining door. 'Are you nearly ready?'

'Two minutes. I'll meet you in the living room.'

The two minutes turned into twenty. Just as he was starting to get annoyed, footsteps sounded down the stairs.

Rising to meet her, he stepped through the living room door and all the air sucked itself from his lungs.

She came to a stop two steps from the bottom of the wide stairs, consternation on her face. 'Well? Am I presentable for Greek society?'

He swallowed to dislodge a boulder jammed in his throat. 'You look...' he shook his head '...ravishing.'

Her full-length couture dress fitted snuggly against her lean body, high-necked with a frill at the cuff of the long sleeves. Dark grey in colour, it was overlaid with a mesh of tiny white metallic roses that glimmered under the light. A thin black belt with a large crystal buckle and a matching purse completed the outfit. She'd swept her mass of hair to one side in a knot at the base of her ear with a crystal fastener, a couple of stray curls left free to soften her oval face. Her eyes were subtly made up while her lips matched the blood red of her fingernails. The whole effect was dramatic and classy and hit him in the groin more effectively than if she'd worn something revealing.

It was only when she took the last remaining steps that he noticed the slit running the entire length of her right leg, right up to mid-thigh, showcasing a pair of sparkling silver heels, and the ache in his groin became altogether harder.

Gritting his teeth, determined not to show his arousal—for God's sake, he was thirty years old, far too old to be getting inappropriate erections—he held out an arm to her.

The slightest of curves tugged on her lips, and she slipped a hand into it.

It was time to face the cameras.

CHAPTER NINE

THE ATHENS MUSEUM was in the Monastiraki neighbourhood, a short distance from Xander's home.

'We could've walked,' Elizabeth said when they came to a stop outside an impressive neoclassical building.

He arched a brow. 'You want to walk in those shoes?'

'Maybe not,' she agreed demurely.

All day she'd had butterflies playing in her belly. Throughout her career she'd acted as a stylist for many of her clients, mostly her female ones. Some were new to a particular section of the wealthy world their date inhabited. Others, unwilling to confide in anyone what they were doing, simply wanted the company. What Elizabeth rarely did was doll herself up and attend a function such as this. When she did it was always with one eye on her watch, looking for the earliest polite time to leave.

Tonight she'd deliberately left her wrist bare and her cell in her room. Like in Diadonus, Xander had put her in the adjoining room to his.

The car door opened and Xander got out. He turned to her and held out a hand.

Meeting his eye, she took it, swinging her legs out in what she hoped was a graceful manner, and was thrown back to a week ago on St Francis when he'd helped her out of the golf buggy at the airport.

It was crazy to think only a week had passed since that evening. She'd gone to bed that night hating him, certain she would never forgive him for his threats and blackmail when a simple explanation of the situation would have been enough to get her agreement.

She felt differently now. Having met Loukas and lived under the same roof as him for almost a week, she understood why Xander had been so determined to bring her here. Having met Mirela, she doubly understood.

It was to protect Loukas from that narcissist woman that she'd determined to be the best wife a man could want. In public in any case. In the privacy of Xander's home it was safer to hide away when he was around.

Tonight though, they were on display to the public and she would play her part to perfection.

It was with this thought in mind that she kept her hand in Xander's, even when she was upright. And it was with this thought in mind that she laced her fingers through his.

The butterflies ratcheted up a notch.

Their evening meal in Diadonus Town had felt like a punishment.

Tonight…

This felt like a date.

She had to remind herself it wasn't a date in the true sense of the term.

And she had to remind herself that she didn't *want* a date with him in any real sense of the word.

But when he let go of her hand and placed his arm around her back to clasp her hip and bring her closer to his side, her frantically beating heart begged to differ.

'You look like you're enjoying yourself,' Xander said when they'd finally been left alone for a few minutes.

It seemed every guest there wanted to say hello to the newly-weds who'd actually been married ten years. Their rehearsed story fascinated them. Elizabeth had repeated it so many times she was starting to believe it herself.

'I do? Great. My acting skills are paying off.'

'You're *not* having a good time?'

She considered it, raising her champagne glass to her lips and letting the bubbles play on her tongue. 'I'm not sure. I've been so busy trying to look like I'm having a good time that I haven't had time to wonder if I actually am.'

He laughed. 'You're going to a lot of effort.'

'I don't want your mother hearing that her new old daughter-in-law had a sourpuss look on her face when we're supposed to be showing devotion and happiness.'

'Happiness was never on the list of requirements.'

'It should have been. What couple in love *doesn't* look happy?'

'Look around you,' he said. 'Is there anyone here who looks anything less than happy?'

'That's smugness. It's a different kind of happiness from the happiness that radiates when someone's fool enough to think they're in love.' Ten years ago *she* had radiated in it.

Xander looked so darn gorgeous in that suit. Its colour matched his eyes so well she could believe it had been commissioned specially for it. There was just something about the way he filled a suit and the command in which he wore it... It was incredibly sexy.

He was sexy.

It occurred to her that she should stop drinking.

Silver trays of canapés were brought out. Elizabeth selected a square of pizza with a smile of thanks, and then there was a loud call for silence and they turned to see the museum director climb a podium to begin his talk.

'Are you going to sponsor one of the pieces?' Elizabeth asked, after it had been explained how individuals who donated above a certain—extortionate—amount could select which artefact they wanted their name to appear under when the renovations were complete.

'That's why we're here.'

'Which one do you fancy having your name under?'

He shrugged. 'We're a country with a rich heritage that brings pride to our nation and attracts tourists from all over the world. Preserving that heritage is important and I'm in a position where I can help. It doesn't matter where my name is.'

'Good for you.' From the corner of her eye she spotted a face that made her look twice. Tugging at the sleeve of his suit jacket, she whispered, 'Do you see that couple standing by the chocolate fountain? *Don't* make it obvious.'

Rubbing his head and turning casually, Xander looked. A tiny snicker escaped his throat. 'Little and large?'

'That's the one. I matched them together.'

Morgan Adie was a tech genius from Silicon Valley who barely topped five feet with a stomach almost as wide as his height. His wife, Miranda, was a good foot taller than him with her heels on and rake thin.

'How did you match *them*?'

'Morgan likes tall women with more than one brain cell to rub together. Miranda has a degree in mathematics and likes billionaires. Her only requirement other than money was someone without a hairy back. They've been married for five years now.'

Amusement was evident all over his face. 'Shall we go and say hello?'

'I think they're avoiding us—they're the only guests who haven't introduced themselves.' At his furrowed brow she explained, 'Now the whole world knows what I did for a living, they're worried people will think they know me, put two and two together and come up with four.'

The hours passed, more canapés were eaten, more champagne drunk. But it didn't drag. Not in the slightest. She hadn't seen Xander so relaxed since he'd forced her back into his life and it felt the most natural thing in the world to mingle with their hands clasped together and the warmth of his body pressed close enough to heat her skin.

Elizabeth had to constantly remind herself that this was all for show, but when they got back in the car at the end of the night, the dividing partition up, blacked-out windows that didn't allow anyone to see in, he made no effort to let go of her hand.

Conversation that had come easily in the museum dried up. The silence was so absolute she could hear his breaths. She could hear the roar of blood pumping through her.

Suddenly she was afraid to move.

She should move her hand from his. But she couldn't. Her hand refused to obey.

The short drive back took for ever, every second feeling like a minute.

When they pulled up outside Xander's four-storey house her heart went into overdrive.

No sex. That's what you both said.

She unlaced her fingers from his. Her hands had clammed up.

The driver opened the door on her side so she got out first. Xander followed and, as they walked up the steps to his front door, placed a hand in the small of her back.

The house was in silence, the only light the soft glow of a lamp in the reception hall, left on by a member of the staff for them.

Elizabeth removed her shoes and as she straightened she met Xander's gaze and all the oxygen left her body.

The look in his eyes...

She waited breathlessly for him to make his move but he stood quite still, the only movement the pulsing in his eyes.

He was waiting for a signal from her.

He wouldn't make a move without her explicit blessing even if they had to stand there the whole night doing nothing but gazing at each other.

This was her moment to run away and lock herself in her room but her body fought back, the longing careering through her trumping anything like rationality.

But desire had never been based on rationality. And desire didn't have to mean anything unless she chose to make it so and hadn't she decided long ago that love didn't mean anything? And if that was the case then what was she so frightened of?

She wasn't a naïve nineteen-year-old any more. She'd stopped believing in true love when Xander had broken her heart. It was a lesson she should've learned from her parents' experience. She'd been a fool to believe that she would be different.

Some people found love but they were a rarity. For everyone else, lust was the driving force, confused and twisted into believing it was love. When the desire was gone there was nothing left apart from bitter recrimination. Only the lucky ones were left feeling empty.

She would not make that mistake again. Being with Xander again had unleashed a huge box of desire within her but she would not fool herself into believing it was love.

She was older, wiser and had learned how to protect her heart. But that didn't mean she couldn't experience the desire so long as she accepted it for what it was and so long as she accepted it would never go anywhere.

It had been so long…

Her hand trembling, she reached out to touch his face. His eyes *blazed*…

'Say it,' he commanded.

She exhaled a ragged breath and met his gaze head-on.

'Please, Xander, kiss me.' Her words were barely above a whisper but it was enough. His pupils pulsed and he stepped to her.

Large hands cupped her cheeks, sliding back to loosen the crystal fastener holding her hair in place and letting it fall to the floor while his fingers speared her tumbling hair.

He lowered his head…

Her stomach melted and when his mouth covered hers, heat fired through her veins. Her lips parted and his tongue swept into her mouth; he was kissing her with such passion her knees weakened.

Dear heaven, this was what she needed, what she craved. Xander, and the all-consuming pleasure he gave.

And everything he gave she returned.

His hands slid down the nape of her neck and she moaned to feel his skin on hers. But not enough. Never enough. Her sensitised flesh wanted to be touched everywhere.

He pulled at her arms and laced his fingers through hers, then raised her hands above her head and pressed them to the wall.

Then he broke the kiss. For a moment he didn't say or do anything, just stared intently at her with eyes that swirled, before saying roughly, 'Not here.'

More than a little dazed, Elizabeth realised they were still in the reception room and that they could be walked in on at any moment.

'Bed?' she whispered.

His chest rose and he kissed her hard. 'Come.'

Feeling as if she were floating, Elizabeth hurried up the stairs holding tightly to his hand. Neither made a sound until he'd shut his bedroom door behind them, thrown his suit jacket and tie onto the floor—she hadn't even noticed him take them off—and pulled her back into his arms with a groan.

'*Theos*, Elizabeth. You're driving me mad.'

'In a good or bad way?'

'Both.' And then he twisted her round so her back was to him. He gathered all her hair together and lifted it high and pressed a kiss beneath her ear.

She shivered with pleasure. Little moans flew from her throat as he undid the top button of her dress and found the hidden zipper. He pulled it down all the way to her bottom, trailing his tongue down her spine to follow before kissing back up to her neck.

Exquisite sensation flooded her, her body responding to his caresses with unbound delight.

His breath hot in her hair, he took each arm in turn and gently manipulated them out of the sleeves while she unbuckled the skinny belt around her waist. Nipping at her ear, he took hold of the material at her waist and tugged her dress past her hips and let it fall to the floor.

Now all she had on were her bra and panties. Even that felt like too much.

Xander pressed himself flush against her. His arousal was thick through the fabric of his clothes, his erection pushing into the small of her back. His hands bit into her flesh and swept up her thighs and over her belly, cupping her aching breasts for the briefest of moments then sweeping up to her shoulders and bunching her hair together again.

He stilled for a moment and she closed her eyes. Her senses were in overload, the need to touch and taste him…

She twisted round to face him and slid her arms over his shoulders, finding his mouth to devour it with kisses.

He held her tightly, muttering incomprehensible words into her mouth while she worked frantically, pulling at his shirt to loosen it from his trousers. Fumbling with his buttons until she could yank it apart, with a breath of relief she pressed herself against him, chest against chest, skin against skin, the lace of her bra the only barrier between their top halves. She could feel his heart beating and grabbed at his head, catching her breath as she stared into the dark blue eyes that contained as much desire in them as she knew echoed from hers.

It had always been like this; one kiss enough to ignite the fire that burned for him and only him. And now she didn't want to fight it. She wanted to exalt in it. She wanted to let it burn.

He felt so solid in her arms, his skin smoother than she remembered. But his kisses were every bit as greedy as they'd been before, plundering her mouth as she plundered his in turn.

Heaven had come into her life ten years ago in the form of Xander Trakas and now, for one night, she would experience it again and she would revel in every minute of it. How could she fight something that grew so strongly within her, a physical connection she had never found or wanted with anyone else?

But she didn't want to think. All she wanted was to feel. And in Xander's arms, pleasure was the only feeling to be had.

Impatient sensations hurtled through her skin from her head to her toes, every part straining closer to him, desperate to lose the last barrier between them.

Xander must have felt it too for he released his hold on her to put his hands at the belt of his trousers as hers went to her bra and panties. His lips brushed reverently across her cheeks and nuzzled into her neck, then he unbuckled his belt and tugged his pants and boxers off, freeing himself.

A breathless sigh escaped her mouth as their lips found each other again and now, when they came together, every part of her that could touched him. His erection pressed right above her pubis, teasingly out of reach to where she really wanted it to be, and she ground against him, silently pleading.

And then she was swept up in his arms and he carried her to his bed.

Flat on her back, Elizabeth reached out her arms for him but he gave the smallest of smiles and sat beside her. His eyes glistening, his chest rising and falling in a tight rhythm, he placed his fingers on her belly and gently traced a circle around her navel.

Shivers raced down her spine and spread out, and she closed her eyes as he slowly traced his hands over her, stroking her breasts before dipping his head to take one in his mouth.

Sharp, acute pleasure speared her. The heat within her liquefied and she gasped. Then he moved his attention to her other aching breast, his wandering hands making circular motions over her shoulders and then down to her belly.

His lips moved from her breasts and up her neck, fire spreading through her flesh. He reached her mouth and nipped her bottom lip.

'You're even more beautiful than I remember,' he murmured into her mouth, his breath merging with hers. His eyes held hers with an intensity that made the need inside her deepen, and he lowered his hand down onto her pubis and then lower still.

He slid a finger into her heat. She gasped again and clasped her thighs together to hold him there, in the place she most ached.

His eyes swirled, a thousand desires gleaming from that one look, and then his mouth was on hers and he was moving on top of her.

When he covered her completely, he kissed her again, a lingering yet gentle brush of the lips that filled her heart in the same way he filled the rest of her.

With one hand burrowed in her hair, he ran the other down her stomach and to her thigh, gently parting it before nudging the other aside too.

His erection was now pressed against the top of her thigh. It was so close to where she wanted it to be yet so far away. She grabbed his buttocks, kneading her fingers into the tight flesh, and writhed beneath him, urging him on.

He groaned and half pulled away. 'We need protection.'

Elizabeth's head reeled. If he hadn't mentioned it, protection would never have crossed her mind.

What was *happening* to her?

He yanked his bedside drawer open and groped in it, removing a silver square, which he ripped open. He made deft work of putting it on, then his mouth found hers again and he shifted enough for his erection to be right there, where she needed. Raising her thighs a touch, she pushed forward at the same moment he thrust inside her.

Her last conscious thoughts evaporated.

The feel of him inside her...

It felt like heaven.

She didn't think she had ever wanted him so much, not even in their heady lust-driven weeks of old. This was something else, the pleasure so intense that all she wanted was to hold on to it for ever.

Bound as tightly as two lovers could be, they moved in a slow, sensuous rhythm, lips locked together, the only sounds muffled gasps and tiny moans.

Not even heaven could feel this good.

His groin meshed against her pubis, intensifying the sensations happening inside her. One hand clasping his buttock to drive him in ever deeper, her other hand raced up and down the back she had never imagined she would scratch again and she embraced the growing pulsations within her until she was driven over the edge and into the blissful land of heightened pleasure that overcame her senses and drowned out everything else, locking her to him completely.

Xander's groans deepened. His movements gained in fever, carrying her climax with him until he shuddered in her arms and thrust one long last time, so tightly inside her she felt every moment of it, and then he slumped down, his face buried in the crook of her neck.

His strong heartbeat echoed through her skin to her own skittering heart, and she drifted a lazy hand across his back, marvelling at the strength she found there, awed at the strength of her climax, at her feelings...everything.

'I must be squashing you,' he murmured into her neck a short while later.

'Only a little bit.' Quite a bit in truth but at that moment she felt so blissed out she didn't care. She wasn't yet ready to break the bond.

His muffled laugh played across her skin. He raised

his head and kissed her before climbing off and heading to his bathroom.

Elizabeth sighed and closed her eyes.

The euphoria of their lovemaking was already seeping away, memories of the black days after he'd ended it between them, when she would wake praying it had all been a bad dream, flooding her in its wake.

Those were days she would never go back to. Her feelings for him were already dangerous and she couldn't afford to let them deepen further. Spending the night entangled in his arms was a danger too far.

By the time Xander returned, she'd gathered her clothes together.

He came to an abrupt halt to see her standing there.

Affecting nonchalance, she attempted a breezy smile. 'I need to go back to my room. Loukas will be upset if he finds me in here.'

Xander, still trying to get a handle on what had just occurred between them, stared at her and tried to dissect what was going on in her head. When they'd been making love her eyes had been full of passion. Now the familiar shutters had come back down.

What they'd just shared had been better than anything he could have imagined. Better than he remembered it being and it had been damned spectacular then.

He'd felt as if he were a part of her.

And now she stood at the adjoining door acting as cool as if what they'd shared had been nothing but a pleasant interlude in a busy day.

And then he saw it. A flash of vulnerability.

For a spark of time he saw the old Elizabeth.

Yes. She should leave. Right now.

He ran a hand through his hair and gave a curt nod.

She hesitated only a moment, then gave a tight, awkward nod and slipped through the adjoining door.

She disappeared so quickly he could almost believe he'd imagined everything that had just happened.

CHAPTER TEN

XANDER ROLLED OVER, looked at his watch and gave a start. It was ten a.m.

He hadn't slept in so late for years.

All those nights of patchy sleep had finally caught up with him.

Taking a quick shower, he dried, brushed his teeth and threw on a pair of jeans and an old T-shirt.

He found Elizabeth in the dining room sipping from a mug of coffee and reading something on her cell. Opposite her, drinking a glass of milk and playing on his tablet, was Loukas.

They both looked up when he entered the room. Loukas's smile was wide, displaying his mouth of gappy teeth. Elizabeth's smile was polite but wary.

His chest tightened to see her and he was immediately assailed with images of their lovemaking.

She'd clearly been up for hours, her drying curls springing in whatever direction they fancied. All he could see of what she wore was a long-sleeved black top. He wondered if she had anything on her feet and if she'd kept the blood-red varnish on her toenails.

With great effort, he slid onto the chair beside Loukas. 'Have you two had breakfast?'

Loukas nodded, then said in Greek, 'I wanted to come and see you but she said I wasn't to wake you.'

He didn't look at Elizabeth when he said *she* but for once Xander didn't detect any animosity. If anything, the atmosphere between them when he'd walked in had been, if not comfortable, not *un*comfortable.

'Speak in English,' Xander chided gently before asking where Loukas's nanny, Rachael, was.

'She's popped out for an hour,' Elizabeth said, not looking up from her screen. 'I said I'd sit with Loukas.'

'Are we going to see Mummy?' Loukas asked.

'I'll give the clinic a ring and see how she is.'

'Can you call them now?'

'Okay.'

Xander made the call, his gaze drifting to Elizabeth as he spoke to the duty manager.

Theos, he could look at her for hours and never tire of the view.

He pushed thoughts of her naked breasts from his mind and put his attention to the call in hand.

'We can visit,' he confirmed when he'd finished.

Loukas beamed and excused himself. Xander knew his nephew was going to his room to select an outfit that would please Katerina. He'd done the same thing with his own mother when he'd been Loukas's age. Starved for her company, he would make a huge effort when he knew he would be seeing her, always hopeful of an approving smile if not physical affection. A pat on the head was the most he or Yanis could have hoped for.

By the time Xander hit adolescence, he'd stopped hoping for any parent-son interaction and learned that to get attention from them all he needed to do was show interest in the family business.

As far as his parents were concerned, it went without saying that their sons would join the company. It was what generations of Trakases had done, future spouses selected on what they could bring to it. Mirela, Xander's mother, had been the heiress of a luxury cosmetics company that had been gobbled up to sit alongside the rest of the Timos SE lines.

Unlike other Trakas spouses, Mirela had never been content to sit at home and play the dutiful wife and mother. An only child, she had been taught by her father everything there was to know about the cosmetics industry and she'd married Dragan Trakas with a determination to be an asset in the boardroom rather than the bedroom. Xander would admire her refusal to be pigeonholed as a wealthy adornment if she hadn't been so inherently selfish.

Dragan and Mirela had formed a powerful union and taken Timos from strength to strength while severely neglecting their sons in the process. Until, that was, their sons were old enough to be taught the mechanisms of business.

Yanis had gone along with it half-heartedly. Business didn't interest him. He'd wanted to be a musician but that had never been an option for him.

Xander had grabbed the opportunity with both hands. He'd been determined to outshine both his parents. He'd soaked up every crumb of information they threw at him, spent hours going through the accounts of the varying divisions, learnt the name of every employee in their Athens head office then progressed to the names of those in their European branches. If they'd had an American division he would have learnt those employee names too, but the US had proved to be a market his parents were unable to crack. Critics said their products were *'too European'*, whatever that meant.

When he'd returned from St Francis it had been with a renewed determination to not only live his life under his own terms but to be master of his own destiny and in the process wreak revenge on his parents for their part in Ana's death and the steady ruin of Yanis's life.

He'd made a deal with them. He would launch their products in North America and turn a hundred-million-dollar operating profit within three years. If he succeeded, they were to step down as joint bosses and pass the mantle to him. They'd been so dismissive of him succeeding where they had failed that they'd agreed. Indeed, they'd laughed at him. If *they* couldn't succeed in the American market then he certainly couldn't.

They hadn't reckoned on his stubbornness or the anger that fuelled him. He had no doubt he could make a success of himself elsewhere but that wouldn't give the same satisfaction as wresting control of his parents' own company and shifting the balance of power into his own hands.

Three years to the day after they'd made their deal, Xander became the official boss of Timos SE. His parents' had never forgiven him, even though he'd kept them on, valuing their business acumen and talents. In that one regard he was like his parents—why cut off an asset that was making you money?

Now, alone with Elizabeth, who was still studying her phone, he was awash with memories of how he'd constantly needed to touch her all those years ago. He hadn't been able to keep his hands off her, and not just because he'd wanted to be inside her all the time. She'd been the same with him. They couldn't even eat a simple meal without locking their ankles together. It was a relationship like nothing he'd experienced before, as intense as the descent of the steepest roller coaster.

If there wasn't a steady flow of staff busy around the villa he would be tempted to take her in his arms right then.

'Would you like to visit Katerina with us?'

She put her phone down. 'I don't think that's a good idea.'

'She's curious to meet you.'

'Loukas is just starting to get used to me. I don't want to ruin it by barging in on his time with his mother. He won't see her for another week and doesn't need me intruding on their time together.'

He gazed at her through narrowed eyes. 'Or is it that you don't want to spend time with him?'

He'd seen the affection she had for Loukas the other night during his nephew's nightmare but it concerned him that she seemed unwilling to draw him out of the shell he formed when she was around.

To her credit she didn't pretend not to understand what he was talking about. She sighed and scrunched her hair in her hands. 'I don't want to push him, Xander. He's a scared little boy and any friendship has to come from him. I do want him to be comfortable with me—that's why I was happy to amuse myself on my phone while he played with his tablet, so he could just *be* while with me, but I'm wary of getting too close. If he gets too used to me it'll be even harder on him when I go back to New York.'

Needles dragged up his spine at the mention of her going back.

He rubbed his forehead with a knuckle and gave a stiff nod.

A member of his household staff came into the dining room with his breakfast and a fresh pot of coffee.

Elizabeth watched Xander cut into his poached egg on toast and her heart beat a little faster. There was something about the way his throat moved when he ate that made her belly tighten and her heart want to weep.

She cradled her coffee with both hands and gazed at the priceless paintings that lined the walls of this great room. Xander's Athens home was as grand as his Diadonus one but had a darker, more oppressive feel to it.

She longed to return to Diadonus and the lightness she found there.

She could feel his gaze on her, and closed her eyes as fresh memories of Xander being deep inside her rushed through her, turning her insides into liquid...

'How do you understand Loukas so well?'

Her head was so filled with their lovemaking that it took a moment to understand what he was asking.

'I was like him at that age,' she said simply when she'd gathered her thoughts together. 'Lost.'

'Is that when your parents divorced?'

'It's when they decided their marriage was over. Loukas's mom's and dad's addictions are very public so he'll be dealing with school friends asking questions about it and telling him the "facts" they've picked up when listening to their own parents discuss it.'

His brows drew together. 'You've dealt with something similar?'

'My parents' divorce got so vicious it made the New York dailies.'

He gave a slow shake of his head.

'They spent so much on legal fees fighting each other over the silliest things that the judge basically hauled them into court and gave them a public dressing down.' She gathered all her hair together in a big bunch at the nape of her neck and sighed. 'They're both attorneys so you'd think they'd know better.'

'What started it all? Did one of them have an affair?'

'The one thing they both agree on is that there was nothing specific. It was an accumulation of things. I can't remember a time when they weren't at loggerheads. I was seven when Dad filed for divorce but they lived under the same roof for five more years because neither of them was prepared to give any ground. They both wanted the house and all the contents. They were like a pair of big cats marking their territory in it.'

'Who got the house?'

'Neither of them. They were ordered to sell it and split the proceeds.' She dropped her hold on her hair and swallowed back the nausea thinking of this period always induced. 'I was so relieved when they finally got their own homes. I honestly thought things would get better if they weren't in each other's faces every day but, jeez, it got worse. Both of them were determined to believe the other had diddled them and sneaked out stuff belonging to the other. Can you believe my mom reported my dad to the police over a photo frame?'

Xander's breathing had become heavy. When she dared look at him she saw his features had darkened.

'Who got custody of you?' he asked tightly.

'They had to share me, which pleased neither of them. One week with Mom, the next with Dad. No deviations apart from Thanksgiving and Christmas, which I was court-mandated to alternate between them. They both fought it. Dad became vegetarian just to spite her and tried to get a court order to force her to only feed me vegetarian food too. Mom retaliated by trying to pay a doctor to falsely diagnose me with anaemia, which she could blame on the vegetarianism and so declare him a bad father.'

She'd been like a toy to be played with. A weapon to

be used against the other. They hadn't loved her. They just hadn't wanted the other to have her.

Xander's stomach churned violently, cold fury sweeping through him at such despicable behaviour from the people who'd been supposed to love and protect her. 'Some people don't deserve to have children.'

'Agreed,' she replied softly, looking away from him and blinking rapidly. 'They only married because she got pregnant. They were united in their belief the other was at fault for that too.'

A sudden burst of mirthless laughter escaped from her. 'If I were to write a book about them everyone would think it was fiction. No one would believe two fully grown people could behave so childishly.'

Xander couldn't even bring himself to smile. His fury remained, coiling like a snake in his chest.

There were many words to describe her parents' behaviour. Childish was the mildest of them, by far.

He thought of how Elizabeth had been all those years ago: open-hearted, warm and optimistic. He'd taken her at face value, never dreaming that she'd lived through such hell.

How could someone so loving come from a union mired in such bitterness?

Their conversation was interrupted when Loukas's nanny came in, back from her short trip out and looking for her charge.

Elizabeth jumped to her feet, thankful for the interruption. Remembering those horrible years was never easy but worse was remembering how desperately she'd clung to the belief that her life would be different. She would marry the right person for her and it would be true love that lasted for ever. The children they had would be so loved they would never doubt their own worth for a second.

She must—*must*—remember her old romantic ideals were nothing but a myth.

A myth she'd contributed to, she acknowledged ruefully. She'd gone to St Francis full of romantic dreams but also, she now realised, grieving for her grandmother. Her granny had been the only person in the world to love her, and, though their time together had been limited, Elizabeth had adored everything about her. Her death had devastated her.

When she'd arrived in St Francis she'd been that deadly combination of vulnerable and idealistic. She'd been desperate for love, and so willing to throw caution to the wind when love finally presented itself in the form of Xander.

'I've got some stuff I need to catch up on,' she said, already heading for the door.

'I thought you'd wrapped the business up.'

'I've a few loose ends to sort.'

He nodded. 'I'll take Loukas to visit Katerina and then we can get something to eat before we return to Diadonus.'

She smiled her agreement and left, thankful to make her escape without discussing the one thing that had echoed between them. The night they'd spent together.

She knew that when they next found themselves alone again, things would be different.

While Xander took Loukas to visit Katerina, Elizabeth took a cab to Monastiraki, wanting to explore the area that had captured her attention through the car's window the previous evening. As it was Sunday, most shops were closed, but there was a flea market to wander around before she found a small art museum to while away more time. None of the art particularly grabbed her attention but it had an excellent gift shop and she spent an age browsing the goods.

She trailed her fingers over the notebooks, remembering her obsession with stationery when she'd been young. When she'd moved out of her mother's house, she'd binned almost one hundred notebooks filled with childish scribblings, a childhood where she'd created her own worlds on paper, worlds where parents loved their children and there was someone for everyone to love.

She hadn't written anything creative in ten years. The notebooks she'd used for her business had always been plain and professional-looking.

On impulse, she snatched a notebook up. Its cover was a reprint of a gorgeous nude painting of a woman sleeping. Helping herself to another and a couple of pretty pens, she paid for her purchases with a thumping heart.

For the first time in a decade she felt the compulsion to write. To create.

Back out in the cool sun, she fished for her shades and found a café to wait for Xander at, firing off a message to him with her location.

While she waited, she sipped on a coffee and, a slight tremor in her hands, removed one of the notebooks' clear wrappings.

Xander's driver dropped them off round the corner from the café Elizabeth was waiting at for him.

Holding Loukas's hand, he passed through the throngs of people meandering through the streets.

He spotted her immediately, alone at a table, shades atop her curly hair, her head bent forward. As they got closer, he saw she was writing. It was a sight that inexplicably made his heart clench.

'You look busy,' he said when they reached her.

She dropped the pen and looked up, colour suffusing her cheeks as she sat her forearm over her notebook.

He liked that she blushed to see him. He very much liked that her eyes took on a glazed look when he held them with his.

He could hardly wait to get her alone.

'Just passing the time.' She shoved the book in her bag, then pulled out a different notebook with a reprint of a painting depicting Zeus on its cover and handed it, along with a pen, to Loukas. 'A present for you,' she said with a smile.

After a moment's hesitation, Loukas took them and studied the notebook carefully.

'Thank you,' he whispered in English.

Startled amber eyes met his. As far as Xander was aware, they were the first words his nephew had spoken to Elizabeth since he'd told her to go away.

His chest swelled but he took pains not to show it. 'Shall we eat here?'

Loukas took a seat. It was as far from Elizabeth as he could get but at least he didn't curl his body away from her.

As Elizabeth studied her menu, and Loukas unwrapped his notebook, Xander studied Elizabeth and was consumed with the urge to unwrap *her*.

'Have a drink with me,' Xander said, pouring himself a Scotch.

Loukas's nanny had just whisked him away from the dining table for a bath and Elizabeth had stood too, looking ready to bolt.

She hesitated.

'I'm requesting a drink, not to rip your clothes off. Unless,' he added when her eyes found his, 'you want me to rip them off.'

'Look, Xander...' She perched her bottom on the edge of the table and dragged her teeth over her bottom lip. 'Last night was great.'

'It was,' he agreed. A twinge pulled at his groin as he recalled for the hundredth time that day just how great it had been.

Pouring a liberal dose of gin in a glass for her, he added two cubes of ice, a slice of lemon, and topped it up with tonic water.

He took it over and held it out to her.

'I didn't say I wanted one,' she said softly, accepting it nonetheless.

He deliberately brushed his fingers against hers. 'You didn't say no.'

A curl had fallen onto her face. He pushed it away then dove his hand into her thick mass of hair.

Her breath hitched. 'Xander...'

'I've been fantasising about you all day.' He pressed his cheek against hers so his words flowed into her ear. Her beautiful scent played into his senses, heating him. 'Have you been thinking of me?'

'I've been with you for most of the day,' she protested, but made no attempt to escape his hold or move her soft cheek from his.

He moved his mouth over hers and nipped her bottom lip. 'All I've wanted today is to get you alone.'

He took the glass from her hand and set it on the table, then used his thighs to nudge her legs apart so he stood between them. Her eyes gleamed and he knew she could feel his arousal through the thick denim of the jeans they both wore.

'You're here. I'm here,' he murmured, brushing his lips across her skin as he spoke. 'We both want each other. We both know how good the sex is between us. The genie's out of the bottle and it's not going back in.'

He trailed his fingers down her spine, delighting in the little shivers she gave at his touch. He kissed her then looked deep into her bright eyes. 'We both know where we stand. No false hopes. No one gets hurt.'

She gazed at him for an almost insufferable length of time before she sighed and wound her arms around his neck.

'No one gets hurt,' she agreed with a whisper. Then her lips parted and she was kissing him, her hold around his neck tightening as she pressed her chest to his.

The ache in his groin worse than ever, Xander devoured her mouth, plundering it as he leaned her back so she was almost flat on the table.

How badly he wanted to be inside her.

A discreet cough shattered the moment.

Loukas's nanny stood in the doorway, bright red with embarrassment. 'Loukas left his new notebook in here.'

Xander pulled away from a clearly mortified Elizabeth. The notebook was on the table next to her delectable bottom.

Once Rachael had disappeared he took a drink of his Scotch. Elizabeth was still cringing from her perch on the table.

'Sometimes I think I employ too many staff,' he said drily, adjusting his jeans, which had become painfully constricting.

Given the opportunity he would lock her in a secluded

retreat, just the two of them, and make love to her until they were both so sated neither could walk.

She took a sip of her gin with a trembling hand but her voice was steady and her gaze unwavering as she said, 'And I think an early night is called for.'

He raised his glass in a salute and adjusted his jeans again with a wince. 'I'll drink to that.'

Five hours later, Xander watched Elizabeth collect her strewn clothing from the mess on floor. By the time they'd got to his bedroom they'd been so desperate for each other they hadn't even made it into the bed. He'd taken her against the door with only a fraction of their clothing removed.

Afterwards, they'd taken a shower together then got into bed and taken each other all over again.

She noticed him watching her and smiled. 'Next time you can do the walk of shame.'

'Through an adjoining door?'

She laughed softly and blew him a kiss.

Resisting the urge to ask her to stay, he said only, 'You know where my bed is if you want another repeat.'

'Goodnight, Xander.'

The last sound he heard from her room was the adjoining door being locked.

CHAPTER ELEVEN

NOW THEY WERE officially lovers again, the antipathy Elizabeth had been holding on to seeped from her like a slowly deflating balloon.

Their lives over the next few days took on a routine. Xander would fly to Athens early each morning after they'd breakfasted with Loukas, while she would take a long walk along the beach. Once back in his villa, she would set herself up in the infinity room with her notebook. Within a couple of days she'd filled it. When she asked Xander if she could hitch a lift with him to Athens he readily agreed, suggesting they meet for an early lunch.

Alone there, she found an excellent stationery shop, made her purchases, then decided to take a wander around the vibrant city. As she passed a news stand, the front cover of a paper caught her eye. It had a photo of her and Xander on it, taken at the museum fundraiser four days ago.

It was a vivid reminder of why she was there.

The court case was only two days away.

Studying the picture some more, she could see it had been taken when they'd first arrived at the museum, mere hours before they'd become lovers again, when she'd still been determined to fight her attraction to him.

The nights they shared were wonderful but, no matter how deeply sated she was or how badly she longed to sleep in his arms, she wouldn't spend the night with him. It was safer that way.

As wary as she was of Loukas forming an attachment to her, she was doubly wary of allowing herself to form an attachment to Xander.

She would not leave herself open to heartbreak again. It had been hard enough to get over him the first time.

But you never really got over him, did you? If you had you wouldn't have spent the rest of your life alone.

It was a thought she kept shoving away, scared to even dwell on it.

She found the restaurant she'd agreed to meet Xander at and, the sun shining down, decided to take an outside table. While she waited, her cell rang.

She pressed the accept button at the moment she spotted Xander heading towards her and raised her hand in greeting.

When he reached her, she rose to kiss him then carried on with her conversation.

'Who was that?' he asked when she'd finished the call.

'Steve.'

Was she imagining it or did Xander's jaw clench?

'I thought you'd got everything wrapped up about Leviathan Solutions?'

No, she wasn't imagining it. There was a definite edge to his voice.

'He was calling to catch up.'

'Catch up? Friends catch up.'

'And Steve's a friend. He wanted to tell me about the temp work he's found and how awful his new colleagues are.'

His fingers drummed on the table. 'Are you lovers?'

She reared back a little. 'Are you insane? How many times do I have to tell you we're just friends?'

'You never answered the question properly before. Friends are capable of being lovers. It happens all the time.'

Her cheeks now scarlet, Elizabeth leaned over the table and said, 'What does it matter? I don't drill you on your sex life.'

'That's it though. I don't know anything about who you've been involved with.' Xander dragged a hand through his hair. 'You know everything about my past relationships—including the ones that never happened,' he added with a grin that belied the undercurrents racing through his veins. Whenever he heard the name Steve he wanted to thump something.

That she'd been his wife all these years was neither of their faults and he accepted he had no right to feel possessive towards her. It didn't change the fact that he *did* feel possessive.

It was a level of possessiveness he hadn't felt for many years. Ten of them.

'That's your own fault.' She showed no sign of softening.

'Those stories about me were bull and you know it. I was barely on first-name terms with half the women who said they'd shared my bed.'

Her eyes flashed. 'Bull or not, it doesn't give you the right to know every aspect of my life and your petty jealousy isn't going to make me tell you anything.'

'I'm not jealous.'

'Then don't act like you are.'

Xander had never been jealous in his life. The idea was ridiculous.

And yet...

The thought of another man touching her made him want to do more than thump things.

He rolled his neck and forced a deep breath. 'Let's change the subject to something neutral.'

After all, with Loukas's custody case only two days away, the last thing they needed was to have a public argument. The restaurant was busy and, judging by the side-eye they were getting from most of the other diners and passers-by, they'd been recognised.

'Can you ask your pilot to take me home?' Elizabeth asked when she'd had enough. 'I don't want to hang around here for the rest of the day.'

Now that she had her new notebooks, she was itching to get back to the script idea slowly unfolding in her head.

Also, watching Xander spear his chicken pieces as if they'd personally offended him had affected her appetite. If they'd been in the privacy of his home she would have had it out with him but being in public she'd held her tongue and contented herself with throwing daggers at him with her eyes.

Was he really jealous of Steve? And if he was, what did that mean? That he was developing feelings for her?

He raised a shoulder and pulled his phone out. 'Sure.'

He made the call and then looked at her. His lips, which had been pressed in a thin line, softened. 'Do I get a kiss goodbye?'

'Are you going to say sorry for being a butthead?'

'A what...?' His eyes narrowed but then he grinned and shook his head. 'I'm sorry for being a butthead.'

'Apology accepted.'

'Now do I get a kiss goodbye?'

'For the sake of the cameras?' There were no lurking photographers that she could see.

His eyes gleamed. 'Why else?'

* * *

Xander had arranged for a cab to meet her at the Diadonus airstrip. When Elizabeth walked into the villa she understood why he hadn't got a member of staff to collect her. It was market day in Diadonus Town and all the staff had gone there.

Wandering into the kitchen to make herself a coffee, she was searching for cups when her cell rang.

'Are you home?' Xander asked without preamble.

'I've just walked in. What's up?'

'I've had a call from the school. Loukas has fallen out of a tree—he's okay but they think he might have fractured his arm. I'm on my way to the airport but it's going to be a good hour until I get there. It's Rachael's day off so I need you to collect him for me and take him to the medical centre.'

'Me?'

'The school's expecting you. Take one of my cars. The keys are in the top drawer of my desk in my study. I'll meet you at the medical centre.'

Before she could protest that she hadn't driven a car in over a decade, the line went dead.

Oh, well, she'd explain about her lack of driving experience when she got into an accident or something.

Oh, God, she had to drive Loukas in it too. As if the poor kid hadn't suffered enough.

Mentally trying to remember the mechanics of driving, she sped to Xander's study and found his collection of keys where he'd said they would be and took the first set that came to hand.

Entering the enormous garage, which was more like a hangar and filled with dozens of the world's most famous and expensive cars in a neat row, she clicked the key until she spotted a car's lights flashing.

It was the black Porsche Spyder.

She hit the button to open the main garage doors then scratched her head trying to figure how to get into the car. Once she'd managed that she stared at the spectacular array of gizmos and gadgets feeling rather dizzy and wondering how on earth she started the thing.

She'd learned to drive when she was sixteen but had never owned a car and hadn't got behind the wheel since she quit Brown. She much preferred walking and, besides, New York was a nightmare for traffic.

She put the Porsche into gear and, sending a prayer to the God of Not Pranging Xander's Car, inched forward and stalled it. After many starts, stalls and splutters she finally drove out of the garage and onto the open road.

Terrified of what she would find at the school, she parked badly at the front of the building and hurried into the reception.

The headmistress was waiting for her and looked at her with much suspicion. In her hand was a newspaper. It took Elizabeth a moment to realise it was the paper she'd seen in Athens earlier with her and Xander on the front. The head was satisfying herself Elizabeth really was Xander's wife and therefore a person she could admit into her school.

'He fell from tree,' the headmistress said. 'He was hiding.'

'Is it only his arm that's hurt?'

'*Nai.*'

'Where else is he injured?' she asked in alarm before remembering *nai* was the Greek word for yes.

She was taken to a small room where a white-faced Loukas sat on a sofa, a young serious-faced woman beside him. Someone had made a sling for his damaged arm.

When he saw her his little face crumpled.

Kneeling before him, Elizabeth said gently, 'How are you feeling?'

Loukas didn't answer but tears started to fall.

'Your arm hurts?'

He nodded.

'Your uncle's on his way home. He's asked me to take you to the medical centre to get it looked at.'

Now he shook his head violently.

'The doctor will be able to give you medicine to make you feel better,' she cajoled.

More head shaking.

'Don't you want your arm to be better?'

A slight hesitation then a nod.

'So why don't you want to come with me? Your uncle will meet us there.'

So used to her every question being met with muteness, Elizabeth thought she was hearing things when his lips parted and he whispered something.

'What did you say, honey?'

She leaned closer and tucked her hair behind her ear so he could speak into it, half expecting him to say he'd rather suffer his broken arm than go anywhere with her.

'The doctor will keep me there.'

'No…' As she immediately repudiated his words, she thought of his mother and understood where his fears were coming from.

His mother had gone to hospital a month ago and there was no sign of her coming home any time soon.

'Loukas,' she tried again, 'I promise you, they won't keep you there. If your arm is broken they might have to keep you in overnight—I'm not a doctor so I don't know, but I promise, cross my heart, that you will come home very soon.'

'I don't want to be on my own.'

She could cry for him.

'Your uncle won't let that happen and neither will I. One of us will stay with you the whole time.'

'You promise?'

She made a solemn sign of the cross over her chest. 'I promise.'

Loukas seemed to think about it before giving a tentative nod.

Elizabeth held out a hand to him. 'Shall we get your arm fixed now?'

The arm that wasn't in a sling reached out. A little hand slipped into hers.

That one simple, trusting gesture melted her heart completely.

Xander made the journey to the medical centre ready to ram cars and people for not moving fast enough.

When he finally pulled up in the car park, he spotted his Porsche Spyder, sticking out like a sore thumb parked as it was almost diagonally over two spaces.

Despite the worry gnawing at him it was a sight that brought a wry smile to his face.

He knew he'd been unfair passing the responsibility for Loukas onto Elizabeth's shoulders but he hadn't been able to think of another option. It wasn't that he thought her incapable of caring for his nephew; quite the opposite, but he was worried about Loukas's reaction to her. His nephew seemed no closer to accepting her as a presence in his life and Xander had to keep reminding himself that Elizabeth was doing the right thing in not forcing it seeing as she wasn't going to be a part of it for ever.

The medical centre had opened in Diadonus only four years ago and was like a miniature hospital with first-class medical staff, state-of-the-art scanners and even an operating theatre.

The lady working behind the reception desk recognised him and sent him off with a smile to the paediatric ward. There, he found them in a private room. They were both sitting on the bed, Elizabeth reading him a story.

They both smiled widely to see him.

To Xander's amazement, Loukas was holding her hand.

Elizabeth saw the direction of his gaze and gave him a look that clearly said, 'Do not say *anything*.'

Pulling up a chair to sit beside them, Xander made the usual small talk such circumstances necessitated, doing his best to be nonchalant about Loukas's arm and the fact he seemed to have finally accepted Elizabeth.

He never had a chance to dissect it as the doctor came into the room.

'I have good and bad news,' he said in Greek, addressing Xander. 'The arm is broken but it's a clean fracture.'

'Will I need an operation?' Loukas asked.

'Yes, young man.'

'But I want to go home.'

'If we get the operation done today there's no reason you can't go home tomorrow.'

Elizabeth was watching this exchange intently, a puzzled look on her face.

'The doctor says I need an operation,' Loukas told her forlornly in English.

'Cool! You'll get your arm put in plaster and everyone will draw silly pictures on it.'

To Xander's complete amazement—as if the past ten minutes hadn't provided enough of it—Loukas cheered up.

The doctor raised his clipboard. 'The anaesthetist's

on her way. The rest of the team's ready. We'll do the operation in around an hour, so shall we get the paperwork signed?'

Sitting in the family room while Loukas was being operated on was tantamount to torture. All Xander could see was his nephew's brave little face as the mask that would put him to sleep was placed over him.

He knew it was only a routine operation but Loukas had looked so vulnerable and pale on that theatre bed.

He'd wanted both Xander and Elizabeth there and had made them both promise to be there when he woke up.

It had been Elizabeth's breeziness about the whole thing that, he was certain, had stopped Loukas's nerves. Judging by her wan complexion now, it had all been an act put on to stop a little boy's fears. She was just as worried as he was.

'Did Loukas tell you what happened?' he asked quietly.

'He was hiding.'

'Who? Loukas?'

'Yes. His classmates were all playing tag. He didn't want to play so he hid in the tree.'

'Why didn't he just say he didn't want to play?'

'He thought they would laugh at him.'

'He told you this?'

She nodded.

A nurse came in with another coffee for them.

'Did you have anything to do with this medical centre?' Elizabeth asked after more slowly turning time had passed.

'What makes you ask?'

She smiled. 'The main general ward is called the

Trakas Ward, plus in the waiting room there's a plaque on the wall with your name on it.'

He laughed with as much humour as he could muster. 'The islanders raised the bulk of the money for the building. I just paid the remainder and gave the cash for the equipment.'

Her eyes widened. 'All of it?'

He shrugged. 'Diadonus is my home. My family are fortunate enough to be able to afford any medical intervention we need. The rest of the islanders aren't so lucky.'

'Did the rest of your family contribute?' Elizabeth was awed at his generosity.

'Yanis and Katerina made a donation.'

'Your parents?'

He raised a brow that quite clearly said she'd asked a stupid question. 'My family have lived here for generations but have never contributed to life here. Yanis and I wanted to do things differently. Loukas is the first Trakas child to attend the local school and not to go private. His parents wanted him to have friends on his doorstep and not have to fly hundreds of miles for a play date. We have enormous wealth and it's time we started putting something back into the place we call home.'

'How did your parents take the decision to educate him here?'

'Badly.'

That one word was enough. She'd only met Mirela the once but Elizabeth could well imagine her disdain at her only grandchild being educated with 'normal' children. It would have been a huge black mark against Yanis and Katerina's names.

But it was a welcome reminder that, despite their addictions, Yanis and Katerina loved their son and had done their best for him. She just hoped they both recovered enough to do their best for him in the future too.

If they didn't...

Well, Xander would always be there for him, loving him as fiercely as if he were his own.

But all this was speculation. They had the court case to get through first. Mirela and Dragan *couldn't* win. They couldn't. If she had to pledge her whole life to stop that happening she would give it gladly.

Elizabeth was so lost in her thoughts that at first she didn't notice the nurse come back in the room.

She was smiling as she spoke to them.

Xander got to his feet, relief all over his face. 'The operation's done and Loukas is in the recovery ward. He's expected to start waking any moment.'

'It was a success?'

He nodded. 'They're confident.'

She smiled and expelled air she hadn't realised she'd been holding.

Xander wished Loukas a good night and closed the bedroom door behind him. The nanny had moved into the next room so she could keep an eye on him throughout the night.

Elizabeth was waiting for him in the corridor.

'I have a confession to make,' she blurted.

He studied her exhausted face, wondering what could cause her to look and sound so tense. They'd both spent the night at the hospital with Loukas and the majority of the day there waiting for him to be discharged. He doubted either of them had got more than a couple of hours' sleep in all. 'What's wrong?'

'I pranged your car.' She sounded so miserable he had to bite back a laugh.

'Is that all? I thought you were going to tell me something really bad. Are you hurt?' She didn't look hurt, only tired. Her gorgeous curls were starting to frizz.

'It happened when I was driving it back from the hospital.'

He'd driven himself there in his Lotus, doing the return journey with Loukas beside him and Elizabeth following them. Now he thought about it, he remembered losing her and getting back a good ten minutes before her. He'd been so concerned with making sure his nephew was comfortable he'd forgotten all about it.

'Did you hit another car?'

'No. But there's a barrier along the coastline with a fresh dent in it.' She stared at the ground. 'The road was really narrow and there was a truck coming towards me. I didn't think there was enough room for the two of us so I pulled over to let him pass and scraped the barrier.'

'As long as you're not hurt, I couldn't care less.' Thinking of her hurt or injured...

'But it was your Porsche.'

He wrapped his arms around her and drew her to him, swallowing back the constriction in his throat. 'It's a car and I'm sure it's repairable. If not, it's replaceable. You're not.'

She never had been...

She rested her head against his chest. 'Will your parents know about Loukas's arm?'

'Probably. They seem to know most things. It doesn't matter. It was an accident.'

'If they try and twist it I'll put them straight.' She said it with such venom he was taken aback.

The events of the past two days had opened up an understanding between his wife and nephew. A bond. Loukas had put aside his fears and opened his heart to her, something Xander knew had taken an enormous amount of courage from the little boy.

And Elizabeth had opened her heart to Loukas, something that had taken an enormous amount of courage from *her*.

Thinking of his investigator's report on her, he now considered it with a fresh perspective.

The life she'd lived had, on the surface, been glamorous and filled with friends if not lovers. But all her friends predated their first time on St Francis. Apart from her employees, for whom she clearly retained a deep affection, she hadn't made a single new true friend in a decade.

Was it possible she hadn't dated in that time too?

He didn't know how he felt about that possibility. The reasoning for it led to too many different avenues, none of which sat comfortably with him.

If she didn't date, how could she ever be a mother?

They'd spoken of having kids together. Hell, they'd even chosen names for them: Samuel, Giannis, Imogen and Rebecca.

Where had *that* memory come from? And why did his heart twist with it?

He was comfortable with the idea of never being a father. He had Loukas in his life. That was enough.

'Do you want to get something to eat?' he asked, more to break the darkness of his thoughts than out of hunger.

Her chest jerked against his. 'I'm so tired I'd probably fall asleep in it.'

He drew back to take her face in his hands. 'What do you say we take a shower together and go to bed? Stay the night with me.'

Xander knew he was being selfish asking this of her but, after the stress of the past two days and the additional stress of the coming day, he didn't want to be alone with his own thoughts. Elizabeth had a way of soothing the stress so it was more a dull ache than a thudding beat.

Besides, he was sick of them sneaking between the two rooms. They weren't furtive teenagers. They both knew where they stood with each other. Neither of them would mistake comforting the other through the night with anything more meaningful.

Her amber eyes held his as if she was searching for something. Then a small smile curled her lips and she nodded.

They slept in a tangle of limbs until his alarm clock woke them.

It was time to go to court.

CHAPTER TWELVE

Xander's knuckles were white.

When Elizabeth met his gaze, she realised it wasn't nerves causing it but contained anger.

This was a court battle he had no intention of losing.

It was a battle she was determined to help him win.

In the courthouse they were taken to a private hearing room with Xander's team of lawyers.

His parents were already there with their own team of lawyers.

It was the first time she'd met Dragan, his father. First glances did not inspire optimism.

Like his wife and son, Dragan was impeccably groomed. A little shorter than his wife, he kept himself in good shape and a thick mop of dark hair on his head made him appear younger than his years. It occurred to her that it was too dark and thick to be natural, and she had to bite her cheek not to laugh. It was the only thing she could find to laugh about.

They'd left Loukas behind, a day of watching movies and eating ice cream with Rachael on his agenda, oblivious that his future would be determined that day. If his grandparents won, he would be uprooted from his home and everyone he loved and forced to live, probably permanently, with people he barely knew.

If Xander won, he would soon be able to return to his own home with his father, if not his mother. If Xander won, Loukas would always be able to call his uncle's home *his* home too.

Xander's love for his nephew was not in doubt. It saddened her that he wouldn't have a child of his own. He would be a brilliant father but he had no intention of making a proper marriage and so had discounted having a child. Just as she had done...

But now was not the time to think of this.

Mirela and Dragan had written a statement. As Xander had predicted when they'd discussed the case, they were portraying themselves as innocent victims who'd been deliberately pushed out of their only grandson's life by his addicted parents. Their second son, Xander, was an enabler. If he cared about his nephew he would have insisted his brother go into rehab much sooner and it was a sign of his short-sightedness due to his inherently selfish nature that this had only happened when he'd realised his parents weren't prepared to be bystanders in their grandson's life any more.

Elizabeth watched Xander's reaction as this statement was read out. She was quite certain that if she put a pin in him he would explode with rage.

She wanted to explode with rage too. How dared his parents tell such lies?

Then it was time for Xander's statement. He'd spent hours drafting it and a copy was handed to the judge. Instead of one of his lawyers reading from it, Xander rose to speak for himself, without notes.

He laid the facts out in chronological detail, starting with his and Yanis's own wretched childhood at the hand of their parents and explaining that it was for this reason Yanis and Katerina had been determined to protect their only child from the influence of two people incapable of showing a child affection. The statement ended with a request for common sense to prevail and a copy of the report from the facility where Yanis was being treated— successfully—was produced for all to read. All being well, Yanis would be home in a month.

His parents had no legal or moral basis to take away a loved child from the people who had cared for him since his birth. If Yanis and Katerina felt they were unable to care for their own child any more, then they should be given the chance to determine who could do so in their absence, just as they'd done in this circumstance when they'd left Loukas in Xander's care.

'That only goes to show how the drugs and alcohol have affected their judgement,' Mirela said. 'Our youngest son is an exceptional businessman, we concede that, but he doesn't know the first thing about raising a child. He's a pleasure seeker, a sex addict who has brought shame and scandal on the Trakas name, just as his brother has with his substance addiction. Children need two parents. My daughter-in-law is very ill; Yanis is not fit to care for Loukas on his own. The wife Xander has produced is a stooge, brought here so you forget he's not fit to raise a child—if you allow Xander to continue his guardianship, she will disappear as soon as the paperwork is signed.'

The lawyer to Elizabeth's left, who was translating for her, explained what she'd said.

She clenched her hands into fists, her brain burning.

If she weren't in a courthouse she might very well launch herself at Mirela and scratch her face.

'Am I allowed to say something?' she asked.

The lawyer asked the judge, who nodded her consent.

Speaking slowly so her words could be translated,

Elizabeth said, 'Forgive me my lack of preparation but I didn't expect to speak today.'

The judge nodded her understanding.

'My husband is not the man the papers have portrayed him to be. Even if he was, it doesn't affect his relationship with his nephew. Loukas adores him and respects his authority over him. Xander is his one constant. He's comfortable and happy with him, but he doesn't know his grandparents. They're strangers to him…'

'Strangers because Yanis has never let us be in his life!' Dragan interjected heatedly.

'And that's because Yanis doesn't want his son under your influence.' She focused on staying calm, knowing if she were to raise her voice any valid points the judge might think she was making would be nullified. 'Yanis has addictions, there's no disputing that, but it's hardly surprising when you consider he never felt you, his parents, loved him and that to receive your approval he had to marry a woman he didn't love when he was twenty.

'The only reason Xander hasn't turned out the same is because he watched his brother go through it first and determined not to be like him. To do that he had to defy you and all the plans you'd made for him, and you have never forgiven him for that, and you've never forgiven him for taking control of the business from you, and you've never forgiven Yanis for raising his son differently from how you think he should be raised. Because that's what this is about, surely? Revenge on your sons. If it was about what's best for Loukas we wouldn't be sitting here.'

Now she looked directly at the judge. 'I don't know if Yanis will stay clean from his addictions and I don't know if Katerina will recover, but I do know that Xander will be there for them both and, most importantly, he will love and care for Loukas as if he were his own.'

Although there were thousands more words she wanted to say, Elizabeth figured she'd gone far enough. She could feel Xander's eyes boring into her but didn't dare look at him. Would he be angry with her for speaking out? She couldn't have kept her mouth shut a moment longer if she'd tried.

The rest of the hearing flew by until they were excused by the judge and filed out while she contemplated her judgement.

'Let's get something to eat,' Xander said in an undertone that, she was relieved to note, didn't sound angry. If anything he sounded pleased.

As soon as they were outside the courthouse, he grabbed hold of her and kissed her, a huge passionate kiss that took her by such surprise she clung to the lapels of his jacket to stay upright.

'You are brilliant,' he said when he finally unlocked his mouth from hers.

'You're not angry with me?'

He shook his head, incredulity in his eyes. 'Elizabeth... What you said...'

'All I said was the truth, as I see it.'

He kissed her again then led her to a cramped restaurant around the corner from the courthouse. No sooner had they been shown to a table when his parents strolled in. They took one look at him and Elizabeth and walked straight back out.

'I think you were right that this is all about revenge,' he said after they'd ordered.

'Having met your mother, it was the only thing that made sense to me. You refused to do as they wanted when you reached adulthood *and* wrested control of their own company from them.'

He'd told her the story of the deal he'd made with them

for control of the business while Loukas had been sleeping in the hospital.

'They taught me too well.'

'When this is over, you should make your peace with them,' she said softly.

That killed his good mood. 'To find peace one has to acquire forgiveness. They don't deserve that.'

Her gaze was steady on his. 'Maybe not, but hasn't there been enough revenge and punishment within your family?'

His parents had neglected their sons, forced Yanis into a loveless marriage and played a part in Ana's state of mind before her death. Who could forgive that?

In return, Xander had taken control of their company and put himself in a position of power over them. As far as revenge and punishment went, he'd hit them where it hurt the most.

And then they'd gone for custody of Loukas. A never-ending circle of revenge.

He evaded the question. 'Have you forgiven your parents for the way they treated you?'

She pursed her lips thoughtfully before answering. 'I've lost my anger towards them. I don't see them all that much but the time I do spend with them isn't filled with resentment. I've let that go. If that's forgiveness then I guess I have forgiven them.' Her amber eyes looked up at him, shining. 'And I've forgiven you for how you treated me all those years ago.'

Everything constricted in him. 'I really am sorry for how I ended things. I thought I was doing the right thing.'

Walking away from Elizabeth had been one of the only selfless things he'd ever done in his life.

'You had the best of intentions,' she conceded. 'It's how you carried it out that left much to be desired.'

He sighed. 'Everything was so intense between us, like a hundred holiday romances rolled into one. When I knew I had to end it I knew it would be kinder to sever it in one stroke rather than string you along.'

'Just answer me one thing: if Ana hadn't died, would you have taken me home?'

'I don't know. Probably. But her death was the wake-up call I needed. You were a different woman then. If you'd come home with me we would never have lasted. My parents—my mother especially—would have crushed you. We've both changed since then.'

'We didn't have a chance, did we?' she said sadly.

He grimaced, thinking how right she was. 'You forgive me for then but what about now? Can you forgive me for blackmailing you?'

'And forcing me to lose my business?' she added drily.

'For that too.'

Her eyes melted before him and then she gave a smile of such beauty, light seemed to radiate from her. 'I'm getting there.'

He took her hand in his and brought it to his lips.

He'd never asked for or sought Elizabeth's forgiveness before but now he had it, it felt as if a weight he hadn't known was there had been lifted from him.

It was to their immense relief that the judge threw out Mirela and Dragan's custody claim. Xander insisted on taking Elizabeth out to celebrate.

After kissing Loukas goodnight, the little boy blissfully unaware how close his life had come to being ruined, she went to her room to change while Xander put him to bed.

As the evening was a touch chilly, she settled on a pair of skinny jeans and a sweeping blush top with sequins around the neckline and hem. Ready before Xander, she turned her laptop on. The first thing that flashed up when it had loaded was the gossip site she used as her home page, mostly so she could keep a watchful eye on her matches. Its main headline picture was of Dante and Piper, dressed to the nines, gazing into each other's eyes with complete adoration. There was no way it could be faked.

This was the last thing she'd expected. Dante Mancini in love?

She smiled as she imagined how Piper must be feeling and was glad she'd held back the warnings she'd wanted to give the sweet Australian about protecting her heart.

When this was all over between her and Xander, she would give Piper a call and hear for herself how she was getting on.

When this was all over...?

Blinking the thought away, she wondered how the other two Casanovas were faring with their matches. Although she hadn't actually matched Zayn with Amalia she had seen enough to think there was a big enough spark between them to see them through. Benjamin and Julianna, she was convinced, were the real deal.

It occurred to her that only a week ago she would have been silently furious at how things had turned out for them. *You fools,* she would have wanted to yell, *don't you realise you're going to get your hearts broken?*

But it was with her own heart thundering that she realised she no longer felt like that. Love didn't have to end with heartbreak and misery.

When this was all over...

Her heart ready to explode through her ribcage, the enormous truth she'd been hiding from herself smacked her round the face.

She wasn't ready for this to be over. She didn't want to say goodbye to Xander. Not yet. Not ever…

By his own admission they'd both changed. *Could* there be a proper future for them?

There was a light rap on the adjoining door and then Xander appeared through it. 'Ready to go…?' His brow furrowed. 'Are you okay?'

She nodded and closed the lid of her laptop, trying to get a handle on her thoughts. 'Yes and yes. Is Loukas asleep?'

'Out like a light.'

Hand in hand, they strolled out of the back of the villa and down to Xander's private beach where his yacht was waiting on the jetty. From there they sailed to Mykonos where, Xander insisted, the best fish restaurant in Greece was located. And he was right. They shared a seafood platter filled with the most delicious jumbo prawns, whitebait, calamari, octopus and mussels, served with salad, dips and pitta. They also drank their way through a carafe of white wine and two shots each of ouzo.

It was the best evening Elizabeth could remember, certainly the best since the day she'd pledged to spend the rest of her life with Xander.

Would things have been different if they'd first met as adults? she wondered for the tenth time that evening, as he regaled her with an old story of his mother getting the better of an Italian cosmetics company. They'd been competing for prime floor space in a Europe-wide department store chain. Mirela had won the space, despite offering less than the Italians.

Listening to him speak about his parents, she quite understood why he would continue working with them. Between them and with Xander at the helm they were a formidable team.

It was, as he'd said a few weeks ago, only as human beings that his parents were useless.

And listening to him, seeing him unwind and relax… it was like being with the Xander of old.

Watching him via press cuttings over the years, when he was always presented in an impeccable business suit, never a hair out of place, his shoes never less than shiny, his expression never less than inscrutable, she'd forgotten how fun he could be. But he'd liked having things his own way then too, she remembered. If he'd wanted something to happen he'd made it happen, including the fast track of their marriage. When he'd proposed to her she'd been convinced it would take weeks to get everything in place, not days as Xander had ensured.

He'd been formidable even then but she'd been so in love that this side of him had never really registered on her radar. She'd only cared about his fun and passionate sides.

Now she knew the whole man, the good, the bad and the ugly. The real Xander, not the idealised image he'd portrayed to her on their sunny Caribbean paradise. Not the idealised image *she'd* formed him into being to fill the massive gap in her heart.

And as she drained the last of her wine, she realised she loved him even more now than she had then.

Yes. She could admit it. She loved him. And as he gazed at her, the expression in his eyes the same as when he'd looked at her a decade ago, her hopeful heart couldn't stop her thinking that he might feel the same about her.

Nothing was said about their future. Life carried on as before but with a lightness of heart that made Elizabeth feel she was walking on air.

Her days were spent scribbling in her notebook—she

was on her sixth one now—either on the beach or, if it was too cold, in the infinity room. The sound of the infinity pool was almost as soothing as the sea but the underfloor heating kept her warm. Now that she'd admitted to herself that she loved him, it was as if her heart had bloomed and the storyline for her script came pouring out of her, so fast she struggled to keep up with it. Once she had the whole thing plotted she would get the actual script written on her laptop.

Should she find an agent? she wondered.

Get it written first and then think about the next step.

Yet no matter how deeply into her storyline she sank, she still spent the hours Xander worked with a watchful eye on the time for when he returned.

Such was the bubble of bliss she'd cocooned herself in that it came as something of a shock when Xander returned home a month after the court case with the news that Yanis was coming home.

Leaving Loukas, whose arm was mending beautifully, in her care, Xander flew to America to collect him.

As she'd successfully pushed this event to the back of her mind, Elizabeth was suddenly terrified of the implications of Yanis's return. To get through it she had to keep herself busy. Luckily it was the weekend so she and Loukas spent most of it together building sandcastles, watching movies and playing hide and seek. He was a gorgeous child and, now he'd accepted her, she'd discovered his funny, mischievous side. She would miss him when it was time for her to leave…

But she didn't want to think about leaving. It was taking everything to hold back the tears as it was.

This was what she wanted. She wanted to be here, with Xander, creating their own family.

There were times when he made love to her or when

she caught him looking at her in an unguarded moment when she thought he *had* to feel the same but just because she'd forgiven him for the past didn't mean she could forget. She'd thought he loved her a decade ago and she'd been wrong then. She could easily be wrong now.

It was thus with a certain amount of trepidation mingling with the excitement of him being home that she saw Xander's car appear on the driveway late on the Sunday afternoon.

Loukas spotted it too and went tearing out to meet them while she hung back sedately, practising her calm face, trying to forget that as soon as Xander and Yanis came up with a legally binding agreement for Xander to be guardian in Yanis's absence, her agreement with Xander would be over. She'd be free to go home.

But would he want her to stay? That was the million-dollar question.

It was somewhat of a shock to actually meet Yanis. Like Xander he was tall but that was the only similarity. His handsome face was gaunt, his hair, a darker shade than his brother's, receding. He looked exactly like what he was: a recovering drug addict.

He came straight to her and gave her a tight hug. 'It is a pleasure to meet you,' he said in a raspy voice. 'Xander has told me what you've done. I thank you for everything.'

'It's lovely to meet you too,' she murmured, pleasurably taken aback at such a warm welcome.

They kissed on both cheeks then chaos ensued. All the household staff appeared wanting to welcome Yanis home. Some, like Rachael the nanny, normally worked for Yanis directly in his home, Xander having seconded them in his brother's absence. Loukas ran around like a hyperactive bee, so much so that Xander had to warn him that he was in danger of breaking his arm again, which slowed him down for all of half a minute.

It was a happy day that culminated in a celebratory dinner. When it was time for Loukas to go to bed, Elizabeth excused herself.

'You're going to bed already?' Xander asked in surprise.

'I've got a headache,' she lied. She sensed Yanis had found the day overwhelming and needed some space. Alone with his brother he could relax and not put on a happy front for her benefit.

Xander had the feeling she wasn't being truthful but let it go. He and Yanis had discussed many things on the flight back from America and during the detour they'd taken in Athens, but there were still things to talk about in more depth. He would deal with that and then he would deal with his wife.

'I'll see you soon,' he said, tugging her down for a kiss.

She brushed her hand over his hair with a smile and disappeared.

'She's lovely,' Yanis said when they were alone.

'She is,' he agreed. He'd told Yanis everything. His brother hadn't been able to show a modicum of shock at their parents' actions but his eyes had blazed with glee when Xander relayed how Elizabeth had decimated them in front of the judge.

She had been magnificent.

'Loukas seems very taken with her.'

'They understand each other. She's very protective of him.'

'She's protective of you too.'

'Is she?'

Yanis stared at him as if he were an idiot.

But it got him thinking. Elizabeth was not the woman

he'd married a decade ago. The sweet, loving woman he'd met was still there but with added spine. And what a spine it was! Whenever he thought of the off-the-cuff speech she'd made to the judge, his heart would swell with pride.

Now his brother was back and everything was being sorted, he knew their arrangement was at an end. He'd imagined at the beginning that when this moment came he would help her pack her bags but now…he felt different.

CHAPTER THIRTEEN

A FEW HOURS LATER Xander found Elizabeth reading in his bed.

She welcomed him with a lazy smile.

'How's your head?' He climbed onto the bed beside her.

She turned to face him and planted a kiss on his lips. 'Fine. How's Yanis? He was looking a little overwhelmed with everything.'

'He's getting there.' Wrapping his arms around her so her head was snuggled against his chest, he said, 'We've had a good talk about things. I didn't mention it before because Loukas was there but we went to see Katerina earlier. They've both agreed to name me as legal guardian should they ever be unable to care for Loukas themselves again.'

'Do you think it will come to that again?' she asked softly.

'I hope not. Katerina's looking better but she still won't admit she has a problem. Right now she can't drink but they're talking about letting her go home in a couple of weeks. That's when we'll know if she's got a mind to kick the alcohol.'

'Will she come back to Diadonus?'

'No, she'll live in their apartment in Athens. It'll be better for her there as she'll have quicker access to the hospital if she needs it. The medical centre here is good but it doesn't cater for everything. Her sister's going to stay with her. Yanis and Loukas will visit regularly but will stay here for a few weeks while Yanis gets used to civilisation again.'

'Fingers crossed everything works out for them all.'

'I feel more hopeful than I did a couple of months ago. Yanis is resigning from the Timos board. I've been telling him for years to do it but he was worried he'd feel even more like a failure for it. Now he can see it's for the best. He doesn't know what he'll do but without the pressure and stress of a job he hates and having to deal with our parents on a daily basis, he'll have a much stronger footing to stay clean.'

She sighed into him and curved her arm a little tighter around his waist.

'I can't predict the future and, while I am hopeful things will work out for the best, I'm not going to lie that I think it will be easy. Which is where you come in.'

Her head shifted, her curls tickling his chin. 'Me?'

'Yanis will need a lot of support. He's dealing with major upheavals. There's no guarantee he won't slip up on occasions. Loukas is going to need a lot of support too.'

She didn't answer, so he carried on. 'I know we said that once we'd sorted out a legal agreement for Loukas to be in my care that you could go back to New York, but I would like you to reconsider.'

'You want me to stay?'

'Just for a few more months while things settle themselves down. Loukas has grown very fond of you. It will be good for him to have another constant in his life.'

She sat up, holding the sheets to her chest. 'That's all you require? A few more months?'

'Maybe longer. Let's take it one day at a time.'

To Xander's mind, this was the perfect solution. The chemistry between him and Elizabeth burned as strongly as ever. They'd resolved their differences and were happy together. He liked her being around and she obviously liked being there too. It seemed ludicrous to end it because of an arbitrary cut-off point they'd decided on before they'd become lovers again. If he was being completely honest with himself, he wasn't ready to let her go. Not yet.

Her face didn't give anything away. 'And then what? You decide everything's hunky-dory and send me back to New York?'

'I thought you'd be happy to stay a bit longer. You like it here, don't you?' To prove his point, he leaned into her neck and nipped it. 'And we can continue having amazing sex.'

She shoved him away. 'Anyone can have good sex.'

'Says the voice of experience?' It still rankled that he knew nothing of her sexual history in the years they'd been apart.

He waited for her to smile or make a quip but her lips pursed together and she contemplated him for an age before saying quietly, 'Level with me, Xander. What are your feelings for me?'

'Well…' He racked his brains, ignoring the alarm bells suddenly playing like a siren in his gut. 'You're beautiful, caring, witty, gutsy, and have the most fabulous hair, and you're amazingly responsive in bed.'

She didn't give even the flicker of a smile. 'And how do I assimilate in your world? Do you think I fit in now?'

'You fit in much better than I thought you would.' He caught a curl in his fingers and gently tugged at it. 'We suit each other very well.'

'You make it sound so romantic.'

'We did romance once and look where that got us.'

'We were little more than children then.'

He dropped her curl and twisted to look more clearly at her. 'What are you trying to say?'

'Nothing.'

But by the set look on her face it was clearly something. 'Talk to me. Tell me what's on your mind.'

She gave a slow nod, her eyes narrowed. 'Okay. But first let me make sure I've got what you're proposing straight. You want me to stay for a few more months while things settle down with your family, and then you're happy for me to go back to New York and carry on with my life without you?'

'That's a little colder than I would describe it but essentially, yes. Think of it as an extended vacation with excellent sex thrown into the mix.'

'And then we go our separate ways with a kiss and fond memories?'

'Exactly right. I'm happy to transfer the thirty million into your account now,' he added as an afterthought.

She flinched, then stared at him for another long pause. 'You know, for someone so sensitive and thoughtful to his family's needs, you can be a real insensitive bastard.'

Her words landed like a punch to his gut. 'What are you talking about?'

Her face now white, she flung the sheets off, jumped off the bed, and went through the adjoining door to her own room.

'What's the matter with you?' he demanded to know when she still hadn't answered his question.

She threw her dressing room door open. 'Where, at any point in your investigator's report on me, did it say anything about me being free and easy with my body and indulging in pointless affairs?'

'I'm not suggesting a pointless affair, Elizabeth. I just don't see why it has to end now when you staying here will be beneficial…'

'To Loukas,' she finished for him, pulling a pair of panties on. 'Where all I get out of it is *good sex*.' She grabbed a T-shirt off a shelf and shrugged it on. 'Where do my feelings come into it? What about what I want?'

'You've told me what you want. You don't believe in love and relationships.'

'And why is that?' She put her hands on her hips, eyes blazing with what he could see was incandescent fury. 'I'll tell you why—it's because you completely screwed me up when you abandoned me five days after marrying me, that's why!'

Now she pulled a pair of jeans off the rail. 'You broke my heart. Did you know that? Completely smashed it. I told myself my parents' marriage and the loathing they had for each other was just a case of bad pairing and that true love did exist, but you showed me how very wrong I was. You want to know how many men I've slept with since you left me? None. Not a single affair. You destroyed my faith in *everything* and you destroyed my hopes of love so completely that I turned my back on the life I'd always wanted.'

Xander stared at her, stunned at her outburst. She hadn't been with anyone else…?

'I thought we had a meeting of minds when it came to relationships,' he said, breathing heavily, working hard to get his thoughts into order.

She fastened the buttons of her jeans then gazed at the ceiling. 'My feelings have changed.' Then her face contorted again and the brief moment of calm was shattered. 'I don't want to be convenient. I don't want to have an affair because it's for the best. I want to be wanted for me. I never had that when I was growing up—I was always just an asset to be fought over. I wasn't loved for *me*, I was a weapon to be used. I thought I'd found love ten years ago with you but then you dumped me because I wasn't good enough.'

'You *were* good enough.' Xander swore under his breath, trying his hardest to keep his temper. 'We've been over this time and time again. What more do you want me to say? I couldn't bring you back with me. You would have been destroyed.'

'You didn't even *try*,' she cried. 'If you'd loved me then you would have fought for me. You could have moved to New York with me. You haven't cared what your parents thought about you for a long time, your brother would have understood, he might even have made the move with you! But no, you didn't do any of that and I'll tell you why, it's because that bloody business meant more to you than I did. It still means more than anything else...'

'That's crap,' he cut in heatedly.

'Really? Then why aren't Yanis and Katerina putting themselves out of their misery and getting a divorce? It's because of the potential cost to the business, isn't it? As long as Timos is okay, everything else can go to hell. You can have an affair with me now and pretend to the world we have a normal marriage without consequences because I now "fit" into your world. You don't have to make *any* concessions.'

His ears were ringing, the room losing its focus. 'You're talking nonsense.'

'Am I? I was prepared to give up everything for you because I loved you, but you...' She shook her head with loathing. 'You weren't prepared to lose your place in the company for anything as pathetic as love. Well, you're the pathetic one and I deserve so much more. I want it all, Xander. Spending time with Loukas and you has made me see how much I've denied myself and what I've been missing out on. I want a family of my own and if you tell me you want it too then we could have it because guess what? I still love you.'

Her words sent him reeling. 'You do?'

'Yep! But I am not prepared to waste another ten years of my life pining for a man who doesn't feel the same way, so I will ask you one more time—what are your feelings for me? And don't give me any crap about me being witty or any other such garbage. I want to know your real feelings or I walk out this minute.'

Xander was trapped. He didn't know what he was expected to say, his head spinning from her declaration of love. And she wanted a family with him…?

But it hadn't sounded like a real declaration. More an angry outburst, something she disliked saying as much as he disliked hearing it.

'You know how I feel about marriage. I've made that perfectly clear. I should never have married you in the first place.'

'So why did you?'

'Because I was young and stupid.'

She flinched.

'I'm sorry, Elizabeth, but you want the truth so I'm giving it to you. My feelings haven't changed. I don't want to make a commitment that ties me to one person's side for the rest of my life. I like you a lot, you know that. I care for you. But we've both seen how destructive tying yourself to one person can be. I don't believe in for ever and you *know* you don't believe in it either.'

She stared at him for an inordinate amount of time, her eyes flashing with fury and pain, but mostly fury.

'You can stick your offer where the sun doesn't shine. I'm going home.'

'Why? Because I'm not prepared to make a false promise?' Had she not listened to anything he'd said?

'No. Because your feelings for me aren't strong enough for you to take that leap of faith. Can you arrange for your crew to fly me to Athens, or do I have to steal a boat?'

She couldn't be serious. Things were great as they were between them. Why was she trying to spoil things now? Where had all this come from?

'Sleep on it. You'll feel differently in the morning. It's been a long, emotional day…'

'Do not tell me how I'm feeling or how I should be feeling. I want to go home, so are you going to help me or not?'

He thought quickly, which was hard with all the blood roaring in his head. 'I'll get them to fly you to Athens after breakfast and I'll have the jet ready to take you to New York.'

Whatever she said, she would feel differently in the morning. They could discuss it properly then, when she wasn't feeling so irrational about the situation, when she could see that taking it one day at a time wasn't a rejection but simply taking it one day at a time.

She steamed past him and opened the adjoining door. 'You can leave me alone now.'

He looked at her one last time.

'You'll feel differently in the morning,' he repeated.

The lock clicked behind him.

Xander opened his eyes, surprised to see his bedside clock reading nine a.m. He'd still been awake at five, certain he would never be able to fall asleep.

He felt sick, and not just in his stomach. Everything inside him felt twisted.

He staggered out of bed and knocked on the adjoining door. Sighing when there was no reply and the door remained steadfastly locked, he showered then headed to the infinity room for his breakfast, bracing himself for a cold shoulder.

Yanis and Loukas were at the table, already eating.

They both looked at him accusingly as he entered the room.

'What?'

'Elizabeth's gone.'

'To the beach?' She took a long walk most days. He'd put some shoes on and go find her.

'Home,' said Loukas. 'She woke me up to say goodbye.' Then he smiled. 'She's given me her email address and phone number. Daddy says I can call her whenever I want.'

The last words were faint as Xander was already heading back down the stairs.

Her main bedroom door was unlocked. He pushed it open and immediately thought they were playing with him. Her bed was neatly made and all her cosmetics and perfumes sat on the dressing table as they had done for over a month. Her dressing room was still filled with her clothes.

All her stuff was there. She couldn't have gone. They must be messing with...

And then he realised what *was* missing and his heart stopped. Elizabeth's laptop was gone. In a frenzy he opened drawers and doors, looking for the copious amounts of stationery she had filled them with in her time on Diadonus. They were all gone too.

Elizabeth put her case in the overhead locker and settled herself into the economy seat she'd purchased three minutes before the desk closed and thanked whoever was looking down and helping her that she'd managed to get a seat on the day's only flight to New York.

Gazing out of the window, she couldn't help strain her eyes for something out of the ordinary, some sign…

She'd done exactly the same thing ten years ago on her flight back to New York from St Francis. She'd hoped desperately for a miracle, for Xander to suddenly appear and tell her it had all been a mistake, that he was sorry and he did love her and they would spend the rest of their lives together.

There hadn't been anything then and nor was there anything now.

She'd caught the early morning ferry from Diadonus Town harbour and watched the island she'd come to think of as home disappear until it became a dot and then, nothing. Four hours later they'd docked in Piraeus and she'd been helpless to stop her eyes from scanning everywhere for a sign of him; if he'd wanted to, he could have easily beaten her there.

That miracle will never happen. It didn't happen ten years ago and it won't happen now. Forget him. Carry on with your life. Forget this ever happened.

Yet for all the stern words she aimed at herself, she was helpless to stop the tears pouring down her face as the plane taxied down the runway. As they became airborne and she stared like a masochist through blurred eyes for her last look at a city she had come to love, she had to stuff her fist into her mouth to prevent the pain from screaming itself out.

CHAPTER FOURTEEN

XANDER FINGERED THE NOTEBOOK one of his staff had just given to him.

It had fallen down the back of Elizabeth's dresser, lying there unnoticed while she'd gathered together the few possessions she'd arrived with.

She'd been gone for four days now. He'd felt every minute of it.

Curiosity overcame him and he turned the cover. As he took it all in it struck him that he'd never seen her handwriting before. He'd only seen her signature on their wedding licence ten years ago. The only way to describe it was neat and curvy. Not that he could see much writing on the first few pages—mostly it was filled with doodles; flowers, single eyes with thick long lashes, stiletto shoes and…teapots?

He flicked through a few more pages of doodles over which more of her curvy handwriting appeared, random sentences that didn't make sense until, after half an hour immersed in it, he realised it all connected and that she'd been working on the kernels of a storyline for a script. These were all her initial thoughts but he could see the broad strokes of what it would be. A tale of a fork in a road, one fork leading to love and redemption, the other leading to loneliness and hell.

* * *

Elizabeth had no idea how many miles she'd walked but when she found herself near the entrance of the Central Park Zoo, she figured at least four. Despite living in the city all her life, she'd only been to the zoo once, on a field trip in junior high.

She'd loved it there and had always hoped one of her parents would take her. After a while she'd stopped asking. Neither of them had any interest in her unless it involved getting one up on the other. Unfortunately for her small self, that hadn't included days out at the zoo. And then she'd grown up and spent a decade way too busy to even think of going there.

She paid the entrance fee and opened her guide map. If she started with the penguins and the seabirds, she could do a whole loop of the place. How could anyone fail to be happy at the sight of penguins?

She could.

Nothing lifted her mood, not the penguins or the thickly furred snow monkeys, not even the lemurs in the tropic zone who were showing off in spectacular fashion for their delighted audience.

Maybe that was why her mood wouldn't lift. She was surrounded by families; mothers, fathers and children, all reminding her of what could have been.

She would come back on a weekday when families would be at a minimum.

Once out of the tropic zone the chill in the air really hit her. The clouds were thick above her and within minutes a snowflake landed on her nose.

Normally she loved the snow but it was hard to appreciate it when she was pining for a sunny Greek island thousands of miles away. Only the island though, she assured herself. And Loukas. She missed him very much. Xander...

She would not think of him.

Wanting coffee and to go home, she headed for the exit. The gift shop winked at her.

After a moment's indecision, she crunched through the falling snow to it.

As she'd known there would be, the shop had notebooks galore.

Her cell rang from her purse. About to reach for it, she remembered there was nothing important she needed to answer it for. Her time was her own. She had thirty million dollars in her bank account and a big wide world to explore and write about.

For the first time in a week she felt a glimmer of light amid the darkness in her heart.

The world was hers to do as she wanted. She was *rich*. She could form her own production company and option her own scripts.

While none of this meant anything to her right now, at some point in the future, when the pain began to ease, she knew it would mean a great deal.

Wherever life took her, she would just have to make a point of avoiding Greece and its islands.

She paid for five notebooks and left the gift shop feeling more positive than she had in days.

She'd thrown her toys out of the pram the last time Xander had broken her heart and she was *not* going to do the same thing again.

Love *did* exist. It *did*. And maybe one day, when she least expected it, it would come to her and she would hug it close and cherish it with everything she had.

Xander's face flashed in her mind again.

She missed him. She ached for him. She would never see him again.

But she wouldn't throw her life away because of it. Not again.

The snow fell thick and fast around her but she wasn't tempted to jump on a bus or train or grab a cab. The snow was invigorating.

As she walked the four miles back, she was aware of her cell continuing to ring but by now all she wanted was to get home. She would deal with anything then.

Feeling like an Eskimo, she turned onto Seventh Avenue. A figure at the bottom of the stairway to the front door of her apartment block made her pause. She squinted through the snow to see more clearly.

Time itself stood still. Elizabeth couldn't move, was only vaguely aware of people bustling around her.

During all the walks she'd taken since she'd been home she'd thought she'd seen him a dozen times or more but not once had she really believed it was him. It was only her pining heart taking its time in accepting reality.

This time it really was him.

She forced her legs to keep going.

By the time she reached him she'd squashed the burst of joy, stamped it into a box and locked it away.

Yet up close, seeing him standing there, his long navy blue overcoat sodden with snow, the tip of his nose red with cold, snowflakes on his brows and lashes...

Oh, she had to try so damned hard not to throw herself into his arms.

She had to try even harder to get her throat to move but then she couldn't think of anything to say and, suddenly terrified she was going to cry, stalked past him up the steps that had been mercifully gritted, and unlocked the front door.

Stamping the snow off her boots, she grabbed her mail and then walked to the end of the passageway and unlocked her apartment door.

Xander stayed beside her the whole time. Neither of them made an attempt to speak.

Once she'd closed the door she put her back to it and faced him. 'Why are you here?'

Xander took in the tiny one-room apartment that was full of light without actually looking anywhere but at Elizabeth. He'd been apart from her for only a week but it had been the longest week of his life.

He cleared his throat and unbuttoned his coat.

'You're not staying,' she said sharply.

He'd been expecting this sort of welcome but still he winced. At least she'd let him into the apartment. He hadn't been sure she would even do that.

'I have something for you.' He pulled out a notebook from his inside pocket, where he'd kept it to keep dry. 'You left this behind.'

She stared at it with wide eyes. 'You came all this way to give me that?'

'No. I would have come anyway. It just might have taken me a bit longer.'

Her jaw clenched. She wasn't going to make this easy for him. He didn't blame her a bit.

'Look, Elizabeth, I've been standing outside your apartment for over an hour. I'm freezing. Do you have coffee?'

There was a definite flicker but she remained stony. 'I'm a New Yorker. Of course I have coffee.' And then she closed her eyes and sighed. 'Okay. I'll make you one. And then you can go.'

This was much more than he'd hoped for. 'Thank you.'

She shrugged her coat and woolly hat off and hung them in a store cupboard by the door. 'Whatever.'

The kitchen was at the far end of the open-plan living space. Knowing she wouldn't invite him to sit, he took a stool at the breakfast bar that separated the kitchen from the tiny dining area.

'I read through your notebook,' he said while she fixed the coffee, her back to him.

She stiffened a touch then opened a cupboard to remove two mugs.

'You're writing a script.'

Not a flicker of response this time.

'Second chance love.' He rubbed his jaw. 'Not about us. Not exactly. I could figure that for myself. But still, second chance love. The path to redemption and forgiveness.'

There was a long period of silence, then, her back still to him, she opened the cupboard under the sink and pulled out some kitchen roll. She blew her nose.

'Elizabeth?'

'Can you please go?' There was nothing stony about her voice now. It trembled and choked as she added, 'There's a coffee shop across the road. Please. Go. I can't see you right now.'

'Elizabeth…'

'Please?' Then she turned to face him. Tears fell down her cheeks in a torrent. 'Please, Xander, just get out. I can't bear it.'

He was off the stool and hauling her into his arms before he could blink.

Smoothing her hair with his hand, he held her tightly. 'Elizabeth, please, don't cry. Punch me or kick me, anything you like, just don't cry like this. I'm not worth it.'

She punched a fist against his chest. 'I know you're not.'

'I'm a selfish, selfish man.'

'Yes.'

'I put the business above everything else.'

She punched him again while still sobbing into the crook of his neck. 'Yes.'

'I walked away from you once because I was scared.'

She stilled.

'And then I let you walk away from me because I was terrified.'

He took hold of the hand he feared was about to thump him again and held it tight against his heart. 'You were the best person I had ever known. I fell in love with you the minute I saw you and I have never stopped loving you. I've done everything in my power to forget you but you've been living in my heart for so long you've claimed squatters' rights.'

She made a noise like a choking hyena.

He smiled and kissed her hair reverently. 'Those plans we made ten years ago, I meant every word of them. I wanted to spend the rest of my life with you and have our four babies. Samuel, Giannis, Imogen and Rebecca.'

She wriggled enough to tilt her head back and look at him with puffy eyes. 'You remember?' she whispered.

'Always.' He couldn't hold her tightly enough. What a fool he'd been. 'But you're right. I should have fought for you.'

He closed his eyes. 'I should have fought for you,' he repeated. 'I didn't. I thought I was doing the right thing. And maybe you're right that the business meant more to me than you but I didn't see it like that. The family business was my life. It was who I was. It didn't cross my mind that I could walk away from it. All I knew for certain was that I didn't want you within a thousand miles of my world. The one good person I knew from it was Ana and all I could think was if she couldn't cope with our world—and she'd been raised in it—then how could you? You wouldn't have, not then. And at her funeral I knew I'd made the right choice to leave you behind because it cut me to pieces to see her coffin lowered into the ground. If anything had happened to you it would have killed me.'

Elizabeth's eyes shone with tears but she kept them on his face, not interrupting, letting him spill his guts.

'Yanis and Katerina are going to divorce.'

'Really?' she whispered hoarsely.

'*Nai.* It is time. Yanis will have custody of Loukas but between us we'll make sure he spends lots of time with her. If and when she's better they'll look at it again but to keep Loukas settled they've agreed this is the way forward.'

She gave a tentative smile. 'What brought it on?'

'You.'

'Me?'

He nodded. 'You were right about that as well. They'd stayed together to protect the business. You made me see that my family have used the damned business as a means of controlling each other for too long. I bear guilt for that too, but it stops now. It's us, the people in the family, the people we love who matter. Yanis and Katerina will never find happiness together but I hope they will find happiness with other lovers in the future, and I hope the cycle of revenge stops now too. You said a long time ago that no one knew what was in Ana's head when she got behind the wheel. Ana made that choice and I need to let it go; the blame, the guilt, all of it, but I don't know if I can do it without you.'

He paused for breath and rubbed his thumbs across her cheekbones. 'When I read through your notebook and pieced together what your storyline would be about, that's when it struck me that you'd opened your heart again enough to be able to write about love, and if you, someone who has been through far more than me, can open your heart and take that leap of faith…I have done some stupid things in my life but denying my love for you last week was the stupidest of them all. I do love you, Elizabeth. When I walked away from you ten years ago I had to put my heart in a vice to get through it. Having you back broke it free and I didn't even realise. This past week…it's felt like all my limbs have been ripped off. I can't be without you. Please, come back to me, I beg you. I know I don't deserve a third chance but I'm lost without you and I swear on Loukas's life I will never put anyone or anything above you again, not even my own fears or pride.'

For the longest time, Elizabeth didn't say anything. And then she gave a tentative smile. 'Wow. That was some speech.'

He gave a shaky laugh. 'I've been going over and over what I was going to say to you since I left Diadonus. So what do you say? Will you give me another chance? Will you take the leap of faith with me?' He knew she loved him but was it enough for her to forgive him?

Her smile widened and she looped her arms around his neck and raised herself onto her toes to press a kiss to his mouth. 'I'll think about it.'

'Take all the time you need.'

She rubbed her nose against his. 'If you reject me again I will cut your heart out.'

'Cut it out now. It's yours. It's yours for ever.'

Now she put her lips back to his and kissed him with such sweet passion his heart soared.

'I've thought about it,' she said when they came up for air, 'and the answer is yes. You're my world. I can function without you but it's only when I'm with you that I feel whole. I don't want to be without you.'

And then her soft lips were on his again and he knew they would be the lips he kissed for the rest of his life.

EPILOGUE

ELIZABETH COULDN'T STOP SMILING. Her mouth had been curved up for so long her cheeks ached in protest. It made not a jot of difference. This was the happiest day of her life and the best bit was about to happen.

Xander solemnly took the simple gold band from Loukas and then, a grin widening on his own face, slid it onto her finger.

She would never take it off.

Then it was her turn to slide Xander's wedding ring onto his finger.

She knew in her heart he would never take it off.

The renewal of their vows done, they turned to face the congregation, who all stood in applause.

The church was jam-packed. Having done a beach-side quickie marriage the first time with only two of the hotel's bar staff as witnesses, this time they'd wanted to do it properly and exchange their vows in front of everyone they knew.

They'd chosen to do it *all* properly. Elizabeth wore a traditional white floor-length dress with a train Loukas kept hiding under, Xander was gorgeous in a black tux.

Her hand clasped tightly in his, she scanned the congregation. There was Katerina, still jaundiced but hopeful of recovery. After a horrendous relapse on the day she'd been discharged, she'd frightened herself enough to finally admit that she was an alcoholic. She'd been dry for two months and in another four would qualify for a liver transplant. All Elizabeth could do was pray she stayed dry.

In a surprise twist, Katerina and Yanis had decided to give their marriage another chance. Somewhere in all the years of pain and substance abuse, love had grown. It had taken them both getting sober to realise it.

In the front row to the left were Xander's parents, both pretending to be delighted at this renewal of vows. A declaration of peace had been issued and so far all parties were sticking to it. Elizabeth didn't believe for a minute that it would last.

Next to Mirela and Dragan sat Elizabeth's father and stepmother, who had taken one look at her mother sitting in the front row to the right, and changed pews. Elizabeth was very much looking forward to seeing how her mother and Mirela got on during the reception. Xander had started a sweepstake over which mother-in-law would 'accidentally' spill something on the other first.

She couldn't resist waving at Piper Mancini, bouncing her bonny newborn baby and looking utterly beautiful beside her handsome, protective husband Dante. Directly behind them sat Zayn and Amalia, pressed close together. Beside them were Benjamin and Julianna Carter. Rumours abounded that both Amalia and Julianna were pregnant and Elizabeth was determined to get them alone later to see if the rumours were true and share her own news—that the pregnancy test she'd taken a fortnight ago had been positive.

There was Yanis, now six months free from drugs and looking healthier by the day. There was Loukas, their ring-bearer, a happy soul unrecognisable from the scared child she'd met six months ago.

And then she turned her head to see the most important one of all. Xander. Her love, her rock, her best friend. And soon they would be parents, something that had made him spray champagne all over her to celebrate with.

As he leaned his head down to kiss her, she knew she would never regret taking this leap of faith.

* * * * *

A DEAL WITH
DEMAKIS

TARA PAMMI

For the strongest woman I know - my mother.

CHAPTER ONE

"Ms. NELSON IS here, Nikos."

Nikos Demakis checked his Rolex and smiled. His little lie had worked, not that he had doubted it. Not an hour had passed since he had had his secretary place the call.

"Instruct security to bring her up," he said, and turned back to his guests.

Another man might have felt a twinge of regret for having manipulated the situation to serve his purpose so well. Nikos didn't.

Christos, it was getting more unbearable by the minute to see his sister trail after her boyfriend, trying to make Tyler remember, and playing the role of the tragic lover to the hilt. Only instead of the usual volatility, Nikos was beginning to see something else in her gaze. Obviously he had underestimated how much power Tyler had gained over her. The announcement that they were engaged had stirred even his grandfather's attention.

Just as Nikos had expected, Savas had laid down the ultimatum. Another excuse for the old tyrant to postpone declaring Nikos the CEO for Demakis International.

Sort out Venetia and the company's yours, Nikos. Take away her bank account, her expensive car and her clothes.

Lock her up. She will forget that boy soon enough once she starts remembering what it feels like to go hungry again.

Nikos's gut roiled, just remembering Savas's words.

It *was* time to get the charming, manipulative Tyler out of her life. However, he had no intention of starving his sister to achieve that end. Nikos had done, and would do, anything for survival but hurt Venetia in any way. But the fact that Savas had not only considered it but dangled it like an option in front of Nikos, expected Nikos to put it into action, was unsettling in the least.

His expression must have reflected his distaste, because Nina, the leggy brunette he usually got together with when he was in New York, slipped to the other corner of the lounge.

"Ms. Nelson would like to meet you in the café across the street," his assistant whispered in his ear.

Nikos scowled. "No."

Bad enough that he would have to deal with not one but two emotionally volatile, out-of-control women in the coming days. He wanted to get this meeting done with as soon as possible and get back to Athens. He couldn't wait to see Savas's reaction when he told him of his triumph.

He grabbed a drink from a passing waiter and took a sip of the champagne. It slid like liquid gold against his tongue, richer and better tasting for his sweet victory. Against Savas's dire predictions that Nikos wouldn't find an investor, Nikos had just signed a billion-dollar contract with Nathan Ramirez, an up-and-coming entrepreneur, by granting exclusive rights to a strip of undeveloped land on one of the two islands owned by the Demakis family for almost three centuries.

It was a much-needed injection of cash for Demakis International without losing anything, and a long-fought chance that Nikos had been waiting for. This was one victory Savas couldn't overlook anymore. His goal was so close that he was thrumming with the energy of it.

But a month of intense negotiations meant he was at the tail end of the high. And his body was downright starved for sex. Swallowing the last sip of his champagne, he nodded at Nina. Ms. Nelson would wait.

Just as they reached the door to his personal suite, the sound of a laugh from the corridor stalled him.

He ordered Nina back into the lounge and walked into the corridor. The question for his security guard froze on his lips as he took in the scene in front of him.

Clutching her abdomen, the sounds of her harsh breathing filling the silence around her, a woman knelt, bent over, on the thickly carpeted floor. His six-foot-two security guard, Kane, hulked over her, his leathery face wreathed in concern. The overhead ceiling lights picked out the hints of burnished copper in her hair.

Nikos stepped closer, curiosity overpowering everything else. "Kane?"

"Sorry, Mr. Demakis," Kane replied, patting the woman's slender back with his huge palm. A strange familiarity with a woman he'd just met. "Lexi took one look at the elevator and refused to use it."

Lexi Nelson.

Nikos stared at the woman's bowed head. She was still doubled over, slender shoulders falling and rising. "She did what?"

Kane didn't raise his head. "She said no one was forcing her into the elevator. That's why she had me call you back asking you to meet her at the cafe."

Nikos tilted his head and studied the state-of-the-art elevator system on his right side. One sentence from her file popped into his head.

Trapped in an elevator once for seventeen hours.

Of course she could have turned around and left. His irritation only grew, a perverse reaction because her leaving wouldn't serve his purpose at all. "She walked up nineteen floors?"

Kane nodded, and Nikos noticed that even his breathing was a little irregular. "And you walked up the stairs with her?"

"Yep. I told her she was going to collapse halfway through. I mean, look at her." His gaze swept over her, a curious warmth in it. "And she challenged me." He shoved her playfully with a shoulder, and Nikos watched, strangely fascinated. The woman unfolded from her bent-over stance and nudged Kane back with a surprising display of strength for someone so…tiny.

"I almost beat you, too, didn't I?" she said, still sounding breathless.

Kane laughed and tugged her up, again his touch overtly familiar for a woman he met a mere twenty minutes ago. As she straightened her clothes, Nikos understood the reason for Kane's surprise at her challenge.

With her head hardly reaching his shoulder, Lexi Nelson was small. Maybe five feet one or two at best, and most of that was legs. The strip of exposed flesh between her pleated short skirt and knee-high leather boots was… distracting, to say the least.

Her shoulders were slim to the point of delicate, her small breasts only visible because of her exertion. Wide-set eyes in her perfectly oval face, a dazzling light blue, were the only feature worth a second look. A mouth too wide for her small face, tilted up at the corners, still smiling at Kane.

Honey-gold hair cut short to her nape, in addition to her

slim body, made her look like a teenage boy rather than an adult woman. Except for the fragility of her face.

The image of an Amazonian woman on her crinkled T-shirt—long-legged, big-breasted, clad in a leather outfit with a gun in her hand—invited a second look, and not only because of the exquisite detail of it but also because the woman in the sketch was a direct contrast to the woman wearing it.

"Please escort Ms. Nelson into my office, Kane," Nikos said. Her blue gaze landed on him and widened. "You are causing too much distraction here." Her smile slipped, a tiny frown tying her brows. "Wait in my office and I will see you in half an hour."

He didn't turn around when he heard her gasp.

Lexi Nelson snapped her mouth shut as Nikos Demakis turned around and left. He was rude, terse and had a spectacular behind—the errant thought flashed through her mind. Surprised by her own observation, she pulled her gaze upward, her breath still not back to normal. Powerfully wide shoulders moved with arrogant confidence.

She hadn't even got a good look at the man, yet she had the feeling that she had somehow angered him. She trembled as the elevator doors opened with a ping on her side. Ignoring Kane's call, she marched down the path his rude boss had taken, wondering what she had done to put him out of sorts.

She had walked up nineteen floors and had almost given herself a heart attack in the process. But she couldn't risk leaving without seeing him, not until she knew how Tyler was. She had planned to dog his New York base the whole week, determined to get answers, until she had received a call from his secretary summoning her here. The moment she had introduced herself at the security desk and asked to see Mr. Demakis, she had been herded to the elevator which she had promptly escaped from.

Lexi came to an abrupt stop after stepping into a dimly lit lounge that screamed understated elegance. High ceilings, pristine white carpets and floor-to-ceiling glass windows that offered a fantastic view of Manhattan's darkening skyline. A glittering open bar stood on one side.

It was as if she had stepped into a different world.

She worked her jaw closed, the eerie silence that befell the room penetrating her awe. While she had been busy gaping at the lush interior of the lounge, about ten men and women stared back at her, varying levels of shock reflected in their gazes. It was as though she were an alien that had beamed down from outer space via transporter right in front of their eyes.

She offered them a wide smile, her hands clutching the leather strap of her bag.

Having realized that she had followed him, Nikos Demakis uncoupled himself from a gorgeous brunette he was leading out of the lounge.

Lexi clutched the strap tighter, fighting the flight response her brain was urging her into.

"I asked you to wait in my office, Ms. Nelson."

Her mushy brain was a little slow processing his words when presented with such a gorgeous man. Dark brown eyes fringed by the thickest lashes held hers, challenging her to drop her gaze. The Italian suit, she would bet her last dollar that it was handmade, lovingly draped the breadth of his wide shoulders, tapering to a narrow waist. A strange fluttering started in her belly as she raised her gaze back to his arresting face.

Nikos Demakis was, without exaggeration, the most stunning man she had ever laid eyes on. Easily two inches over six feet, and with enough lean muscle to fill out his wide frame, he was everything she had been feverishly dreaming about for the past few months; her space pirate, the villainous captain who had kidnapped her heroine, Ms. Havisham, intent on opening the time portal.

Her heart racing, her fingers itched to open the flap of her bag and reach for the charcoal pencil she always kept with her. She had done so many sketches of him but she hadn't been satisfied.

A real-life version of Spike, marauding space pirate extraordinaire.

"Excuse me? Are you drunk, Ms. Nelson?"

Blushing, Lexi realized she had said those words out loud. There was a sly look in his eyes that sent a shiver down her spine. As if he could see through her skin into the strange sensation in her gut and understood it better than she. "Of course not. I just…"

"Just what?"

She pasted on a smile. "You reminded me of someone."

"If you are done daydreaming, we can talk," he said, pointing toward a door behind her.

"There's no need to walk away from your…party," she said, cutting her gaze away from him. *What had she done wrong?* "I just want to know how Tyler is."

He flicked his head to the side in an economic movement, and his guests moved inward into the lounge, or rather retreated from her. Even their conversations restarted, their apparent curiosity swept away by his imperious command. Her spine locked at the casual display of power. "Not here," he said, and whispered something in the brunette's ear, while his gaze never moved from her. "Let's go into my office."

Lexi licked her lips and took a step to the side as he passed her. Now that she had his complete attention, a sliver of apprehension streaked through her. She looked around the lounge. Safety in numbers. Really, what could he do to her with his guests outside the door? But the sheer size of the man, coupled with that unexplained contempt in his gaze, brought out her worst fears. "There's nothing to talk about, Mr. Demakis. I just want to know where Tyler is."

He didn't break his stride as he spoke over his shoulder. "It was not a request."

Hints of steel coated the velvety words. Realizing that she was staring at his retreating back again, she followed him. Within minutes, they reached his state-of-the-art office, this one with an even better view of Manhattan. She wondered if she would be able to see the tiny apartment she shared with her friends in Brooklyn from here.

A massive mahogany desk dominated the center of the room. A sitting area with its back to a spectacular view of the Manhattan skyline lay off to one side and on the other was a computer, a shredder and a printer.

He shrugged his jacket off and threw it carelessly onto the leather chair. The pristine white shirt made him look even more somber, bigger, broader, the dark shadow of his olive skin under it drawing her gaze.

He undid the cuffs and folded the sleeves back, the silver Rolex on his wrist glinting in the muted light.

Leaning against the table, he stretched his long legs in front of him. Whatever material those trousers were made of, it hugged his muscular thighs. "I asked you to wait."

Coloring, Lexi tugged her gaze up. What was she doing, blatantly staring at the man's thighs? "I walked up nineteen floors for a few minutes of your time," she finally said, feeling intensely awkward under his scrutiny. He just seemed so big and coordinated and thrumming with power that for the first time in her life, she wished she had been tall and graceful. A more nonsensical thought she had never had. "Tell me how Tyler is and I'll be on my way."

He pushed off from the table and she tried not to scuttle sideways like a frightened bird. Hands tucked into the pockets of his trousers, he towered over her, cramming his huge body into her personal space. His gaze swept over her, somehow invasive and dismissive at the same time. The urge to smooth out her hair, straighten her T-shirt, attacked again.

"Did you just roll out of bed, Ms. Nelson?"

Her mouth dropped open; she stared at him for several seconds. The man was a mannerless pig. "As a matter of fact, yes. I was sleeping after an all-nighter when the call came in. So please forgive me if my attire doesn't match your million-dollar decor." For some reason, he clearly disliked her. It made her crabby and unusually offensive. "FYI, you might have nothing better to do with your time than loll around with your girlfriend, but I have a job. Some of us actually have to work for a living."

Amusement inched into his gaze. "You think I don't work?"

"Then why the sneering attitude as if your time is more precious than mine? You obviously make more money per minute than I do, but mine pays for my food," she said, shocked at how angry she was getting. Which was really strange. "Now, the sooner you answer my question, the sooner I'll be out of your hair."

He shifted closer, unblinking and Lexi's heart pounded faster. A hint of woodsy cologne settled tantalizingly over her skin. She stood her ground, loath to betray how unsettling she found his proximity. "You're here for your precious Tyler. No one's forcing you. You can turn around and walk down the stairs the same way you came up."

Lexi wanted to do exactly that, but she couldn't. He had no idea how much it had cost her to come here to his office. "I had a phone call from someone who refused to identify himself that Tyler has been in a car accident along with your sister." Maybe this was Nikos Demakis's response to his worry over his sister? Maybe usually, he was a much more human and less-heartless alien? "How is he? Was your sister hurt, too? Are they okay?"

His brows locked together into a formidable frown, he stared down at her. "You're asking after the woman who, for all intents and purposes, stole your boyfriend of—" he turned and picked up a file from the desk behind him in a casual movement and thumbed through it "—let me see, eleven years?"

There was no winning with the infuriating man. "I thought maybe there was a reason you were being a grouchy, arrogant prig—you know, like worry about your sister. But obviously you're a natural ass…" Her words stuttered to a halt, the bold letters *N-E-L-S-O-N* written in red on the flap of the file ramming home what she had missed.

She moved quickly, a lifetime of ducking and evading bred into her muscles, and snatched the file out of his hands. She found little satisfaction that she had surprised him.

Cold dread in her chest, she thumbed through the file. There were pages and pages of information about her and Tyler, their whole lives laid out in cold bare facts, complete with mug shots of both of them.

Spent a year in juvenile detention center at sixteen for a household robbery.

Those words below her picture felt as if they could crawl out of the paper and burn her skin. Sweat trickled down between her shoulder blades even though the office was crisply cool. She dropped the file from her hands. "Those are supposed to be sealed records," she said, struggling through the waves of shame. She marched right up to him and shoved him with her hands, the crushing unfairness of it all scouring through her. "What's going on? Why would you collect information on me? I mean, we've never even laid eyes on each other until now."

"Calm down, Ms. Nelson," he said, his voice gratingly silky, as he held her wrists with a firm grip.

The sight of her small, pale hands in his big brown ones sent a kick to her brain. She jerked her hands back. *How dare he toy with her?*

"I'll lose my job if that information gets out." She clutched her stomach, fear running through her veins. "Do you know what it feels like to live on mere specks of food, Mr. Demakis? To feel as though your stomach will eat itself if you don't have something to eat soon? To live on the streets, not knowing if you will have a safe place to sleep in? That's where I will be again." She looked around herself, at the thick cream carpet, at the million-dollar view out the window, at his designer Italian suit and laughed. The bitter sound pulsed around them. "Of course you don't. I bet you don't even know what hunger feels like."

His mouth tightened, throwing the cruel, severe lines of his face into sharp focus. For an instant, his gaze glowed with a savage intensity as though there was something very primitive beneath the sophistication. "Don't be so sure of that, Ms. Nelson. You'll be surprised at how well I understand the urge to survive." He bent and picked up the file. "I don't care if you robbed one house or a whole street to feed yourself. Nothing in the file has any relevance to me except your relationship with Tyler."

His smooth mask was back on as he handed the file to her. "Do what you want with it."

Nikos smiled as the slip of a woman snatched the file from him. Clutching the file to her body, she moved to the high-

end shredder, ripped the pages with barely controlled vehemence and pushed them in.

With his photographic memory, he didn't need to refer
to the file, though. She was twenty-three years old, grew
up in foster care, had little to no education, worked as a
bartender at Vibe, a high-end club in Manhattan and had
had one boyfriend, the charming Tyler.

Based on the personal history between her and Tyler,
and the codependent relationship between them, Nikos had
expected someone meek, plain, biddable, easily led, someone with no self-esteem.

The woman standing in front of the shredder, while
small and not really a beauty, didn't fall into any of those
categories. The tight set of her shoulders, the straight spine,
even her stance, with her legs apart and hands on her hips,
brought a smile to his face. The fact that she wasn't exactly what he had been expecting—really, though, what
kind of a woman would be concerned about her lover's new
girlfriend?—meant he would have to alter his strategy.

She turned around, dark satisfaction glittering in her
gaze. The hum of the shredder died down leaving the air
thick with tension.

He ran his thumb over his jaw. "Are you satisfied now?"

"No," she said, her mouth set into a straight, uncompromising line. "Whatever you might have read in that file,
it should tell you I'm not an idiot. It was one paper copy I
shredded. You and your P.I. still have the soft copy."

He raised a brow as she picked up the paperweight from
his desk and tossed it into the air and then caught it. "Then
what was the point in shredding it?"

Up went the paperweight again, her blue gaze, alight
with defiance, never wavering from him. "A symbolic act,
an outlet because as much as I wish it—" she nodded at the

shredder behind her and caught the paperweight in a deft movement "—I can't do that to you."

Nikos reached her in a single step and caught the paperweight midair this time, his hand grazing hers. She jumped back like a nervous kitten. "I mean you no harm, Ms. Nelson."

"Yeah, right. And I'm a Victoria's Secret model."

Laughter barreled out of him. Her blue eyes wide, she stared at him.

She was no model with her boyish body and nonexistent curves. Yet there was something curiously appealing about her even to his refined tastes. "I think you're a foot shorter—" he let his gaze rove over her small breasts, and her hands tightened around her waist "—and severely lacking in several strategic places."

Crimson slashed her cheeks. She lifted her chin, her gaze assessing him, and despite himself, he was impressed. "Why the power play? You didn't open that file in front of me to double-check your facts. You wanted me to know that you had all that information on me. Is that how you get your kicks? By collecting people's weaknesses and using them to serve your purpose?"

"Yes," he replied, and the color leached from her face. He has no delusions about himself. He was by no means above using any information in his hands to gain the upper edge in business or life. And especially now when it concerned his sister's well-being, he would do anything. If you didn't protect the ones who depended on you, what was the point of it all? "I need you to do something for me and I can't take no for an answer."

CHAPTER TWO

DISBELIEF PINCHING HER mouth, she stared at him. "It didn't occur to you to just ask nicely?"

He covered the distance between them, shaking his head. She stepped back instantly, but not before he caught her scent. And racked his brains trying to place it. "Nicely? Which planet are you from? Nothing in this world gets done with please and thank you. Hasn't your life already taught you that? If you want something, you have to take it, grab it with both hands or you'll be left behind with nothing. Isn't that why you robbed that house?"

"Just because life gets hard doesn't mean you lose sight of the good things." Her hands tightened around the strap of her bag, her skin tugged tight over her cheekbones. "I robbed the house because it was either that or starve for another day. It doesn't mean I'm proud of my actions, doesn't mean I don't wish to this day that I had found another way. Now, please tell me what happened to Tyler."

Her words struck Nikos hard, delaying his response. The woman was nothing short of an impossible paradox. "Venetia and he were in a car accident."

Her face pale, she flopped onto the leather couch behind her, her knees tucked together. "Physically, there's not a scratch on him," Nikos offered, the pregnant silence grating on his nerves.

She pushed off from the couch again. "The person who called me made it sound like it was much worse. I kept asking for more details but he wouldn't answer my questions."

She walked circles around him, running long fingers over her bare nape. Once again, the boyish cut only brought his attention to her delicate features. Bones jutted out from her neck, the juncture where it met her shoulders infinitely delicate.

Her knuckles white around her bag, she came to a stop in front of him. Shock danced in her face. "It was your doing. You had one of your minions call me and make it sound like that. Why?"

He shrugged. "I needed you to be here."

"So you manipulated the truth?"

"A little."

Her forehead tied into a delicate little frown, she cast him a sharp look.

"I don't have a conscience when it comes to what I want, even more so when it comes to my sister, Ms. Nelson. So if you are waiting for me to feel guilty, it's just a waste of time. Except for a hitch in his memory, your ex is fine."

"A hitch in his memory?"

"A short-term memory loss." He leaned against his desk. "To my sister's eternal distress, he doesn't remember anything of their meeting, or their plans to marry."

He paused, watching her closely, and right on cue, the color leached from her face.

Her teeth dug into her lower lip. "They are engaged?"

He nodded.

She ran a shaking hand over her nape again. "I don't understand why you are telling me this."

"All he remembers is you, and he keeps asking for you. It's driving Venetia up the wall."

He thought he would see triumph, pure female spite.

Because whatever else he might think, Venetia *had* stolen Tyler from this woman. He braced himself for a deluge of tears, OMGs and "why-did-this-happen-to-me?"'s. At least, that's how Venetia had reacted, even though she had been pretty unscathed from the accident. But once the doctors had informed them about the memory loss, it had become worse as though she had taken on the leading role in a Shakespearean tragedy. And contrary to his expectations, that their relationship would lose its appeal, Venetia had only held on harder to Tyler.

Seconds ticked by. Ms. Nelson stared out through the glass windows, but the tears didn't fall. She took a deep breath, pressed her fingers to her forehead and turned toward him. "Where is he now, Mr. Demakis?"

The glimmer of stark pain in her eyes rendered his thought process still. Much as he would detest it, he wanted her to throw a tantrum. That he could handle. This quiet pain of hers, the depth of emotion in her eyes, however, he wanted no part of it.

It reminded him of another's pain, another's grief so much that a chill swept through him. He had worked very hard to keep his father's face neatly tucked away. And he wanted to leave it that way. "On our island in Greece."

"Of course, it is not enough that your sister and you are gorgeous. You have to own an island, too."

He smiled at the caustic comment, at the glimpse of anger.

"All the lengths you have gone to get me here, I'm assuming it's not for the pleasure of giving me bad news. No more games. What is it that you want me to do?"

"Come with me to Greece…take care of him. Venetia won't stop turning everyone's life into a circus until he remembers her."

"You're kidding, right?" Her gaze flew to him, shock

dancing in its blue depths. "Did I miss the memo on amnesia that says there's a switch to turn it on and off? An ex's kiss, maybe? What makes you so sure that I can just make him remember her?"

"Your ex wants to come back to New York so that he can see you," he said, joining her in the small sitting area. "Venetia won't let him out of her sight until he remembers their great love. His confusion and her ongoing drama are driving me insane."

"And I care about this why?"

Her tone was so irreverent that it was like seeing a different woman. "You don't. That's why the little twisting of the truth."

The moment he stepped into the sitting area, she tensed. Nikos could almost feel her suspended breath as she wondered if he would sit too close. Stifling a curse, he settled onto the coffee table instead. Instantly, her breathing evened out. Never had a woman irritated him so well and so easily.

"I want her future settled. More than anything else in the world. Which means, the only thing to do is for you to join them. With the long history between you two and your unwavering support now, Tyler will mend soon. He will remember his undying love for Venetia, and they can ride off into the sunset together," he said, struggling to keep the mockery out of his tone.

She settled back onto the couch, and crossed her legs. "You've got balls asking me to help you."

Nikos grinned. There was such a change in her demeanor, in the way she met his gaze head-on from the woman who had timidly followed him in. Because she knew now that he needed her, and she was adjusting her attitude based on that just as he had done. And to his surprise, he liked this gutsy version of her so much better.

"My...*manhood* has nothing to do with the matter at hand. It's something I need to do for my sister, and I'm doing it."

Pink flooded her cheeks and she averted her gaze from him as though she had just realized what she had blurted out. He had a feeling she did that at lot—spoke without thinking it through.

Scooting to the edge of the couch, she pointed a finger in his direction, her little body shaking. "Just a month ago, you had two giant brutes pick me up like I was a sack of garbage and had them throw me out, and I mean, they *literally* dropped me on that concrete road outside your estate in the Hamptons."

She had no idea how much he regretted that decision. By the time Venetia had dropped her bombshell at that very party, announcing that she and Tyler were engaged, Lexi Nelson had already been thrown out.

"You somehow bypassed security, broke into my estate and almost ruined the party, Ms. Nelson. It seems your colorful past is not as completely behind you as you would believe," he said lazily, and her color rose again. "You're lucky I didn't have you arrested for trespassing."

Her chin tilted up stubbornly. "I meant no harm. All I wanted was to see Tyler, even then."

"Ah, yes. The wonderful Tyler. For whom you will risk anything, it seems." He bent forward, leaning his elbows on his knees. "The fact that he didn't answer your million calls on his cell phone didn't alert you that he wanted to have nothing to do with you? Because you don't strike me as the particularly stupid kind," he added, more than a whisper of curiosity niggling him.

A shadow darkened her blue gaze, and he knew she was remembering her conversation with Tyler. "He was angry with me, yes. But I didn't want him to make a mistake."

"You don't really believe that even now, do you? Because that would make you the most pathetic woman on the planet."

Her blue gaze widened. "Wow, you really don't believe in pulling your punches."

"Because hearing the actual truth instead of your own romantic version sticks in your throat?" he said, a burst of caustic anger filling him. He ran a shaking hand through his hair, annoyed by the strength of his own reaction. Telling this woman that her love for that boy had turned her into a fool was not his responsibility. But making sure his sister didn't fall into the same mold was. "You're right. I don't care why you went to see him. All I care about now is that you take care of him."

"Why go there? Why not just bring him back here, back to New York? As you've already learned from that file, Tyler and I have lived here our whole lives. I'm sure being in a new country amidst strangers doesn't help."

"The answer to that question is one word, Ms. Nelson. *Venetia.* Believe me when I say that it's better for all parties involved if we do this there."

She nodded and stood up.

He studied her, her calm demeanor not sitting well with him. She was ready to abandon the sense she was born with for the man she loved, even if he had kicked her to the curb. *Was all that fire he had spied in her just a sham? And why did he care when that's what he needed to happen?* "I have already arranged for you to leave immediately with your boss at Vibe."

She met his gaze then, a quick flash of anger in hers. "Of course you have." She pulled her bag over her head and adjusted it over her breasts.

Coming to a halt at the door, she tugged it open, and leveled that steady gaze at him again. "I find it really curious. Why would you think you needed all that information on me?"

Nikos shrugged. "Let's just say I wanted to make sure you accepted my...proposal."

She didn't even blink. "And yet you were also very confident that I would come. Please tell me."

If she wanted to hear what he found so distasteful about her coming here, so be it. "I was standing in the corridor with Venetia when you managed to sneak into the party that night. I heard what he said to you."

She flinched, her tight grip on the doorknob turning her knuckles white. He couldn't contain the disdain that crept into his words nor did he want to. And the way she stared at him, focused, every muscle in her face stiff and tense, she heard it, too. "He called me a selfish bitch who couldn't stand the fact that he had found love with someone else and moved on, that I couldn't be happy for him," she recited, as though she was reading lines from a play.

"He conveniently turned his head and walked away while you were thrown on the street," he continued, refusing to lay off.

"And you thought no self-respecting woman would agree to help him after that."

He nodded. "I thought I would need some additional...*leverage* to persuade you. Obviously I don't."

She raised an eyebrow, her chin tilting up. "No?"

"You're here, aren't you?" he said, standing up. Lexi Nelson was the epitome of everything that had gone wrong in his life in the name of love. He felt a tight churning in his stomach, a memory of the grief and rage that he had propelled into the need to survive, for his sister's and his sake. "One call and barely an hour later, you come running back for him, your heart in your throat, and you walked up nineteen floors. Why ask so many questions, Ms. Nelson?

Why pretend as though there's even a doubt as to whether you will drop everything to take care of him?"

Lexi struggled to remind herself that Nikos Demakis didn't know her, that his opinion didn't matter. But the incredible arrogance in his words that she had fallen into his plans exactly as he had intended chafed her raw.

How she wished she could turn around, throw his disdain back in his face.

But this wasn't about the infuriating man in front of her. This was about her friend, her family, the one person in the entire world who had always cared about her. After Tyler's caustic words, after this last fight, she had finally accepted that whatever had been between them had never stood a chance. And she had no idea why.

It would hurt to see Venetia Demakis with him for sure. The young heiress was everything Lexi wasn't. Rich, sophisticated and exceptionally beautiful.

But what if she was being given another chance to right things between her and Tyler, to have her friend back? He had been there every time she had needed him. Now it was her turn.

The scorn of the man in front of her, however, was a bitter pill to swallow. She was going to say yes, but it didn't mean she had to do it on his conditions.

She leveled her gaze at him, stubbornly reminding herself that Nikos Demakis needed her just as much as she needed to see Tyler. And she couldn't let him forget that, couldn't let him think for one moment that he had the upper hand. "You have made a miscalculation, Mr. Demakis. I have no wish to help you or your sister."

His dark brown gaze gleaming, he neared her before she could blink.

She stood her ground, but she was too much of a chicken

to wait and hear what he would threaten her with. "Not without a price."

"What is it that you want, Ms. Nelson?"

"Money," she said, satisfaction pouring through her at the surprise in his eyes. She smiled for the first time in more than a month. Her heart thundering inside her chest, she closed the door and leaned back against it. "You have oodles of it and I have none."

The dark browns of his eyes flared with something akin to admiration. Lexi frowned. She had meant to anger him, needle him, at least. She had uttered the first thing that had come to her mind. Instead, the edge of his contempt, which had been a tangible thing until now, was blunted.

"Quite the little opportunist, aren't you?" he said, gazing at her with intense interest.

There was no rancor in his words. Struggling to keep her confusion out of her face, she smiled with as much fake confidence as she could muster. "I have to protect my interests, don't I? You're asking me to put my life here on hold and place my trust in someone like you."

He laughed. "Someone like me?"

"Yes, by your own admission, you don't have a conscience when it comes to what you want. What if things don't go your way, what if something happens that you don't like? You'll blame me…"

"Like what?"

"Like Tyler regaining his memory and deciding he didn't want to be with Venetia anymore."

A feral light gleamed in his gaze. "That would not do."

"I have no older brother to rescue me, no family to watch out for my welfare," she said, swallowing the painful truth. "For all I know, you and your sister could do untold harm to me, so I'm being prepared."

"Believe me, Ms. Nelson. Family is highly overrated.

You grew up in foster care—doesn't that tell you something?"

The vehemence in his tone gave her pause. She had wondered a million times why her parents might have given her up, wondered in the lowest times if there was anyone who thought of her, who wondered about her, too. Except for excruciating sadness and uncertainty, it had brought her nothing. "But you're here, aren't you? Taking every step to ensure Tyler remembers your sister, setting her world to rights. Making sure no one deprives her of her happily ever after."

"What if I don't agree to your condition?" He moved in that economic way of his and locked her in place against the door. His scent teased her nostrils, his size, the quiet hum of power packed into his large body, directed toward her making her tremble from head to toe. He had neatly sidestepped her question. "What if, instead, I alert your boss about your colorful teenage years?"

It took everything within her to stay unmoving, to meet his gaze when all she wanted was to skittle away from him. *Don't betray your fear,* she reminded herself, even though she had no idea if it was his threatening words or his nearness that was causing it. "You will ruin me and it will be pointless, but it won't go like that. Are you that heartless that you would wreck a perfect stranger's life because she won't suit your plans?"

"Yes, I will," he whispered, moving even closer. His palm landed on the door, near her face, his breath feathering over her. The heat of his body coated her with an awareness she didn't want. Every inch of her froze, and she struggled to pull air into her lungs. "Make no mistake about me. To ensure my sister's happiness, I will do anything that is required of me, and not feel a moment's regret about it."

Her stomach tight, she forced herself to speak. She had

no doubt that he was speaking the truth. "But it doesn't really serve your purpose, does it? Ruining me won't set your sister's world right. You need me, and you don't like it." His mouth tightened an infinitesimal amount and she knew she had it right. "That's why you collected all that information. Because you needed at least an illusion that you have the upper hand in the situation, to make sure you're the one with control."

Something dawned in his gaze and she knew she had hit the nail on its head. Her pulse jumped beneath her skin. "You have twisted something very straightforward into a game. I would have dropped everything to take care of Tyler. But now, I'll only come if you agree to my condition," she finished, every nerve ending in her stretched tight.

She was playing a dangerous game. But she would do this only on her terms, refused to let herself be bullied again. Even for Tyler.

His gaze swept over her. "Fine. Just remember one thing. I'm agreeing because this suits me. This way, you're my employee. You do what I say. You can't cry foul, can't say I manipulated you."

"Even if I did, it's not like you'll lose any sleep over it."

His teeth bared in a surprisingly warm smile. "Good, you're a fast learner. I'm the one who will be paying you. I'll even have my lawyers draw a contract to that effect."

"Isn't that a little over-the-top? I'm there to help Tyler, not for any other reason." His continued silence sent a shiver of warning through her. "Am I?"

He didn't answer her question and his expression was hidden by the thick sweep of his lashes. A knock sounded on an interconnecting door she hadn't noticed. The brunette she had spied earlier walked in, her mouth set into a charming pout. Her long-legged gait brought her to the sitting area in mere seconds while her expertly made-up gaze took in Nikos and her with a frown.

She pulled him toward her, nothing subtle or ambiguous in her intentions. "I thought you wanted to celebrate, Nikos. Are you ever going to be free?"

Her mouth dry, Lexi watched, her thin T-shirt too warm.

His gaze didn't waver from Lexi. A sly smile curved his mouth as he obviously noticed the heat she could feel flush her cheeks. He wrapped his hand around the woman's waist, his long fingers splayed against the cream silk of her dress. "I believe Ms. Nelson and I have concluded our business to mutual satisfaction. So, yes, I'm free to celebrate, Nina."

CHAPTER THREE

NIKOS CURSED LOUDLY and violently. The words swallowed up by the crowd around him didn't relieve his temper one bit.

It had been three days since Lexi Nelson had come to see him and yet the sneaky minx had avoided his assistant's phone calls. Exasperated, Nikos had been reduced to having Kane discover her shift times at the club. Thoroughly disgusted by his minions'—a word he couldn't stop using ever since she had—failure to persuade the woman to leave for Greece, he had flown back to New York.

He had arrived at three in the morning, forced himself to stay awake and arrived at Vibe five minutes after five. Only to find her gone. So he had his chauffeur drive him to her apartment in Brooklyn.

But even after a ten-hour shift, the irritating woman still hadn't returned. He had been ready to call the cops and report her missing. In the end, he had entered her apartment, barged into a bedroom and forced the naked couple in the bed to tell him where Ms. Nelson was. Her eyes eating him up, the redhead had finally informed him that Lexi had gone straight to another shift at a coffee shop around the corner.

So here he was standing on the sidewalk at nine in the

morning outside the bustling café amidst jostling New Yorkers. He was tired, sleep-deprived and furious.

He understood the need for money. He was the epitome of hunger for wealth and power, but this woman was something else.

Ordering his chauffeur to come back in a few minutes, he entered the café. The strong smell of coffee made his head pound harder. With the hustle and bustle behind the busy counter, it took him a few moments to spot her behind the cash register.

His heartbeat slowed to a normal pace.

A brown paper bag in hand, she was smiling at a customer.

Her hair was combed back from her forehead in that poufy way. The three silver earrings on her left ear glinted in the morning sunlight as she turned this way and that. A green apron hung loosely on her slender frame.

She thanked the customer and ran her hands over her face. He could see the pink marks her fingers left on her skin even from the distance. And that was when Nikos noticed it—the tremble in her fingers, the slight sway of her body as she turned.

He tugged his gaze to her face and took in the dark shadows under her stunning blue eyes. She blinked slowly, as though struggling to keep her eyes open and smiled that dazzling smile at the next customer.

Memories pounded through him, a fierce knot clawing his gut tight. He didn't want to remember, yet the sight of her, tired and ready to drop on her feet, punched him, knocking the breath out of him.

He hadn't felt that bone-deep desolation in a long time, because as hard as Savas had made him work for the past fourteen years, Nikos had known there would be food at the end of it. But before Savas had plucked them both from their old house, every day after his mother had died had been a lesson in survival.

The memory of it—the smell of grease at the garage, combined with the clawing hunger in his gut while the lack of sleep threatened to knuckle him down—was as potent as though it was just yesterday.

The bitter memory on top of his present exhaustion tipped him over the edge.

A red haze descending on him, he stormed through the crowd and navigated around the counter.

With a gasp, Lexi stepped back, blinking furiously. "Mr. Demakis," she said, sounding squeaky, "you can't be back—"

He didn't give her a chance to finish. Ignoring the gasps and audible whispers of the busy crowd, he moved closer, picked her up and walked out of the café.

Crimson rushed into her pale cheeks, and her mouth fell open. "What are you doing?"

She wriggled in his hold and he tightened his grip. "Seeing dots and shapes, Ms. Nelson? I'm carrying you out."

Weighing next to nothing, she squirmed again. The non-existent curves he had mocked her about rubbed against his chest, teasing shocking arousal out of his tired body.

For the first time in his life, he clamped down the sensation. It wasn't easy. "Stop wiggling around, Lexi, or I will drop you." To match his words, he slackened his hold on her.

With a gasp, she wrapped herself tighter around him. Her breath teased his neck. He let fly a curse. As rigid as a tightly tuned chassis in his arms, she glared at him. "Put me down, Nikos."

His limo appeared at the curb and he waited while the chauffeur opened the door. Bending slightly, he rolled her onto the leather seat. She scrambled on her knees for a few seconds, giving him a perfect view of her pert bottom in denim shorts before scooting to the far side of the opposite seat.

He got into the limo, settled back into the seat and stretched his legs. Perverse anger flew hotly in his veins. He shouldn't care but he couldn't control it. "A bartender at night, a barista by day. *Christos,* are you trying to kill yourself?"

Lexi had never been more shocked in her entire life. And that was big, seeing that she had run away from a foster home when she was fifteen, had stolen by sixteen and had been working at a high-class bar in Manhattan, where shocking was the norm rather than the exception, since she had been nineteen.

She clumsily sat up from the leather seat. The jitteriness in her limbs intensified just as the limo pulled away from the curb. "I can't just leave," she said loudly, her words echoing around them. The arrogant man beside her didn't even bat an eyelid. "Order your minion to turn around. Faith will lose her job and I can't—"

He leaned forward and extended his arm. Her words froze on her lips and she pressed back into her seat. The scent of the leather and him morphed into something that teased her ragged senses. The intensity of his presence tugged at her as if he were extending a force field on some fundamental level. Outside the limo, the world was bustling with crazy New York energy, and inside…inside it felt as if time and space had come to a standstill.

He reached behind her neck and undid the knot of her apron. She dug her nails into the denim of her shorts, her heart stuck in her throat. The pad of his fingers dragged against her skin and she fought to remain still. The long sweep of his lashes hid his expression but that thrumming energy of his pervaded the interior. Bunching the apron in his hands, he threw it aside with a casual flick of his wrist.

Even in the semicomatose state she was functioning in, unfamiliar sensations skittered over her. She had never been more aware of her skin, her body than when he was near. Noting every little movement of hers, he handed her a bottle of water. "Who is Faith?"

The question rang with suppressed fury. Lexi undid the cap and took a sip. She was stalling, and he knew it.

"Why are you so angry?" she blurted out, unable to stop herself.

He pushed back the cuffs of his black dress shirt. The sight of those hair-roughened tanned arms sent her stomach into a dive. "Who is Faith?" he said again, his words spoken through gritted teeth.

She sighed. "My roommate, for whom I was covering the shift. She's been sick a few times recently, and if she misses any more shifts, she'll lose her job. Which she will today, because of you."

He leaned back, watching her like a hawk. His anger still simmered in the air but with exhaustion creeping back in, she didn't care anymore. She let out a breath, and snuggled farther back into the plush leather. She was so tired. If only she could close her eyes for just a minute…

"What does this Faith look like?"

"Almost six feet tall, green eyes, blond."

"But she's a natural redhead, isn't she?"

Heat crept up her neck at the way he slightly emphasized the word *redhead.* "How would you know something like that?" Tension gripped her. "Nikos, you barge into my work, behave like a caveman and now you're asking me these strange questions without telling me what—"

"The last time I checked, which was an hour ago, your so-called 'sick' friend was lolling about in bed naked with a man, while you were killing yourself trying to do her job. From what I could see of her, which was a lot, she's perfectly fine."

Her cheeks heating, Lexi struggled to string a response. "Faith wouldn't just lie…"

Faith would. And it wasn't even the first time, either. Her chest tightened, her hands shook. But Faith was more than a mere roommate. She was her friend. If they didn't look out for each other, who would?

Struggling not to show how much it pained her, she tucked her hands in her lap. "Maybe it wasn't Faith," she offered, just to get him off her back.

"She has a tattoo of a red rose on her left buttock and a dragon on her right shoulder. When it was clear no one would answer, I opened the door and went right in. Your friend, by the way, is also a screamer, which was how I knew there was someone inside that bedroom."

Flushing, Lexi turned her gaze away from him. Even if she didn't know about the tattoos, which she did, the last bit was enough to confirm that he was talking about Faith. "All right, so she lied to me," she said, unable to fight the tidal wave of exhaustion that was coming at her fast. As long as she had felt that she was helping Faith, she'd been able to keep going. She pulled up her legs, uncaring of the expensive leather. "What I don't get is why you felt the need in the first place to barge into our apartment and confront her."

"You left that bar at five in the morning, and two hours later, you weren't at your apartment in Brooklyn. I've no idea how you've managed to not get yourself killed all these years."

Her breath lodged in her throat, painfully. Hugging her knees tight, she stared at him. Shock pulsed through the exhaustion. She lived in the liveliest city on the planet, and even with Tyler around, she'd felt the loneliness like a second skin most of her life. Nikos's matter-of-fact statement only rammed the hurtful truth closer.

"You don't have to worry about me. I take my safety very seriously." His anger was misplaced and misdirected. Yet it also held a dangerous allure.

His nostrils flared, his jaw tight as a concrete slab. "My sister's welfare depends on you," he said, enunciating every word as though he was talking to someone dimwitted. "I need you alive and kicking right now, not dead in some Dumpster."

"You don't like it that you felt a minute's concern for me? At least it makes you human."

"As opposed to what? Are you also a part-time shrink?"

The caustic comment was enough to cure her stupid thinking.

"As opposed to an alien with no heart. Why is this even relevant to you? Are you keeping tabs on all my friends so that you can manipulate me a little more?"

"She took advantage of you." He looked at her as though he was studying a curious insect, something that had crawled under his polished, handmade shoes. "Aren't you the least bit angry with her?"

"She doesn't mean to—"

"Hurt you? And yet it seems she has accomplished that very well."

Was she imagining the compassion in those brown depths? Or was her sleep-deprived mind playing tricks on her again? She scrunched back into the seat, feeling as stupid as he was calling her. "Faith's had a rough life."

"And you haven't?"

"It's not about who had the roughest life or who deserves kindness more, Nikos. Faith, for all her lies and manipulation, has no one. No one who cares about her, who would worry about her. And I know what that loneliness feels like. I don't expect you to—"

"I know enough," he said with a cutting edge to his words. "You haven't signed the contract yet. Now you have forced me to fly back to New York for the express purpose of accompanying you to Greece."

Way to go, Lexi, exactly what you wanted to avoid.

"I've been busy."

He leaned forward in a quick movement. For such a big man, he moved so quickly, so economically. But she must be getting used to him because she didn't flinch when he ran the pads of his thumbs gently under her eyes. The heat of his body stole into hers. "Are you having second thoughts about dear Tyler? Have you decided that he's not worth the money I'm paying?"

It almost sounded as if he wanted her to refuse to help him. Which couldn't be true.

She had been unable to sleep a wink ever since the horrid contract had arrived on her doorstep and she had taken a look at the exorbitant amount of money listed there. More than she had ever seen in her lifetime or probably ever would.

Just remembering it had her heart thumping in her chest again.

Money she could use to take art classes instead of having to save every cent, money she could use to, for once, buy some decent clothes instead of shopping the teenager section at the department store or thrift store.

Money she could use to take a break from her energy-draining bartending job and invest her time in developing her comic book script and develop a portfolio without having to worry over her next meal and keeping a roof over her head.

The possibilities were endless.

Yet she also knew that anything she bought with that money would also bring with it an ick factor. It would feel sullied.

But there had been something more than her discomfort that had held her back from signing that contract.

The man studying her intently had volunteered it happily enough. In fact, he had seemed *more* than happy to make her his paid employee.

Because it gave him unmitigated power over her. That was it.

She stilled in place, her stomach diving at the realization. That's what had given her the bad feeling.

If she had accompanied him without complaint, it meant she was doing him a favor. This way, she wasn't. It seemed he was either prepared to blackmail her into it or pay her an enormous amount of money so that she was obligated to do as he ordered.

Rather than simply ask her for help. The lengths he would go to just so that his position wasn't weak made her spine stiff with alarm.

"About that money," she began, feeling divided in half within. She couldn't even stop seeing the number in front of her, a bag with a dollar sign always hovering in her subconscious as though she was one of her own comic characters, "I was angry with you for manipulating me. I can't accept—"

His long, tanned finger landed on her mouth, short-circuiting her already-weak thought process. Her skin tingled at the barest contact. "In the week that I have had the misfortune to make your acquaintance," he said, leaning so close that she could smell his cologne along with the scent of his skin, "asking for money to look after Tyler was the one sensible, one clever thing you did."

Really, she had no idea what he would say next or what would suddenly send him into a spiral of anger.

"Don't embrace useless principles now and turn it down, Ms. Nelson. Think of something wild and reckless that you have always wanted but could never afford. Think of all the nice clothes you can buy." His gaze moved over her worn T-shirt, and she fought the impulse to cover her meager chest. "Maybe even something that will upstage Venetia in front of your ex?"

Her mouth falling open wordlessly, she stared at him. Apparently, her new, standard expression in his company. "I have no intention of competing with Venetia, not that I harbor any delusion that I even could."

Dark amusement glittered in his gaze. It was as if there was a one-way connection between them that let him see straight into her thoughts. Like Mr. Spock doing a Vulcan Mind Meld. If only it worked both ways. She had absolutely no knowledge about him, whereas he literally had a file on her.

He settled back into the seat and crossed his long legs. "You're a strange little woman, Ms. Nelson. Are you telling me you didn't think of using this opportunity to win him back? That the idea didn't even occur to you?"

"No," she repeated loudly, refusing to let him sully her motives. She would love to have her friend back, yes, but she wasn't going to engage in some bizarre girl war with Venetia to get Tyler back the way he assumed.

"Fine. My pilot's waiting. We leave in four hours."

"I can't leave in four hours," Lexi said, anxiety and the energy it took to talk to him beginning to give her a headache. "I have to find someone to sublet my room, have to get the plumber to fix the kitchen before I leave and I promised Mrs. Goldman next door that I would help her after her surgery in two days. I can't just up and leave because your sister can't bear the thought of not being the center of Tyler's universe for a few more days."

He shrugged—a careless, elegant movement of those broad shoulders. "I don't care how many things you had lined up to do for your parasitic friends or how much you were planning to bend over backward for the whole world, Ms. Nelson. I won't wait anymore."

She frowned. "I don't bend over back—"

His gaze sliced through her words. "You're the worst kind of pushover."

She slumped against the seat, bone-deep exhaustion taking away her ability to offer even token protest. She shouldn't be hurt by his clinical, disparaging words. But she was.

And the fact that his words could even affect her only proved him right.

How could she feel bad about what a stranger, someone as ruthless as Nikos Demakis thought about her?

"Your room at the apartment will go nowhere. If there's anything else you need help with—" his gaze lingered on her clothes again "—something that is solely *your* concern, *your* problem, I can have my assistant at your disposal."

"If I don't agree?"

He shrugged. "Your agreement or the lack of it doesn't play into it. The choice is whether you travel as my guest or my captive."

"That is kidnapping."

He plucked a couple of pages from his case and pushed it toward her along with a legal pad and a pen. "It's hard to admit, but I see that I did this all wrong."

"What?"

He leaned forward, resting his elbows on his knees. His gaze solemn, he blinked. Really, no single man should be allowed to be so gorgeous. "I should have appeared on your doorstep with my heart in my hands, pleaded my sister's case, begged you to help, tried to become your best friend. Maybe talk about my own horrible childhood, pretend to be on my death bed—"

"Okay, okay, fine. You've made your point," Lexi said loudly, cutting off his mocking words. She had always liked to help if she could. She would not let the manipulative man in front of her make her feel stupid about it.

Pulling her gaze away from him, she scanned the document again. She'd had the contract looked over by a paralegal friend, but there was no discounting the hollow fear in her gut.

She would be in his personal employ for two months and would be paid fifty thousand dollars for it, half now, and half when he deemed her job done, subject to his sole discretion.

She was being paid an exorbitant amount of money to spend time with Tyler on a Greek island, the likes of which she had no other hope of seeing in this lifetime.

Yet as the limo came to a stop on her street in the cheap neighborhood of her apartment complex, she couldn't shake off a feeling that there was an unwritten price that she would have to pay.

And she had no idea what that was.

CHAPTER FOUR

NIKOS CLOSED HIS laptop, and refused the stewardess's offer of a drink. He hadn't had a good night's sleep in four days now. He had finalized the deal with Nathan Ramirez; he finally had a solution for Venetia's problem. And yet he was restless with a weird kind of pent-up energy simmering just below his skin.

He itched to get back to his garage and get his hands dirty. He had been pushing himself this past month and he needed a break. Once everything was settled with Venetia, he would take her on a vacation. She had always wanted to see more of New York.

The passing mention of New York and his thoughts immediately shifted to Ms. Nelson. Not a peep sounded from the rear cabin. There was something about the woman that always left him on edge. Stepping into the cabin, he froze.

She lay on the very edge of the bed, half out, half in. Her knees tucked tight into her legs, her hands wrapped tight around herself, she slept hunched tight into a ball.

Her honey-gold hair glinted in the low lights, her wide mouth open like a fish.

Her white T-shirt couldn't hide the outline of her small breasts. A plastic watch with a big dial in the shape of a skull covered most of her wrist. A thoroughly distracting strip of her back was exposed by the scrunched-up top, above denim shorts. Delicate calves and even more delicate feet topped with toes painted black completed the picture.

Even while telling himself that he should just walk away, he stood rooted to the spot.

He usually paid very little attention to the women he slept with. What he wanted, he took and got the distraction out of the way. Because that's all anything a woman ever had been to him. Something to take the edge off the grueling hours, or the pace he had set himself to succeed.

Ms. Nelson, on the other hand, perplexed, irritated and downright annoyed him with her mere existence. There was such a mix of innocence and calculation about her that he found mesmerizing. He smiled, remembering her confusion, her beautiful blue eyes widened, her breath hitching in and out uncomfortably, when he had leaned toward her in the car.

Noticing a page peeking from under her arms, he leaned over her and pulled the rolled-up magazine.

His blood slowed in his veins to a sluggish pace as he breathed in that scent of her. Vanilla, that's what she smelled of. Simple yet fascinating, like her.

He straightened the magazine and looked at the article she had been reading. How To Use Sex to Get Your Man Back.

So the little minx did want that parasite back. Apparently, being called a selfish bitch wasn't enough of a deterrent for her. Displeasure and a relentless curiosity vied within him. What kind of a woman worried about an ex who turned his back on her, a friend who manipulated her and yet faced Nikos down when he had cornered her?

Shaking his head, he tried to stem the flow of resentment coursing through him. Because that's what it had to be. Ms. Nelson's effervescent outlook toward life and her sheer naïveté were beginning to grate on him. The sooner he got her out of his life and back to her I'm-all-that-is-love-manipulate-me-all-you-want existence, the better.

Muttering a curse, he turned around to leave when a sleepy moan rumbled from the bed. Still hunched tight, she scooted a little more over the edge. With a quick movement, Nikos caught her just as she would have toppled off the bed.

He ended up on his knees next to the bed, her slender body cradled on his forearms. Blue eyes flew open, terror cycling through them.

Before he could blink, she squirmed in his hold, throwing punches and kicking her legs. He turned his face just at the right time, and her punch landed on his jaw. His teeth rattled in his mouth. Grunting at the pain shooting up his jaw, he threw her onto the bed none too gently.

She rolled over to the other side, and stared up at him, her eyes wide and full of shock. "What are you doing?"

"What do you think?" he shouted back, running a hand over his jaw. "I should have let you fall. The bump would have given you some much-needed sense."

Theos, but the woman could throw a mean punch. If he hadn't turned he would have had a severely displaced nose.

She scooted to her knees on the other side, her movements wary and tight, her mouth pinched. "I'm sorry. I just acted on reflex."

Running a finger over his jaw, he looked at her and curbed his anger. "Would you like to explain, Ms. Nelson?"

Her hair stood up at awkward angles. Moving as though in slow motion, she got off the bed, walked around it and stopped at a good distance from him.

Her gaze was set on his jaw, her lips trembling. "I'm fine," he said, cringing at the thought that she might cry. He sat down on the bed and waved toward the empty spot. "Sit down."

Remaining silent, she slid down onto the edge of the

bed, leaving as much distance as possible between them. And it finally struck him. All the times she had scrunched tight when he came near. Even now her slender frame was coiled with tension. For some reason, the thought filled him with a cold anger.

"You're afraid of me."

Her silence rang around them.

He shoved away the questions and, of all the strangest things, the dent to his ego, aside. He might not like her but the fear in her eyes, it had been real. "I know that you think me a heartless bastard, and you are right, but I would never lay a finger on you."

She met his gaze finally. "I think I know that."

"Well, that's good, then." This time, he couldn't keep the sarcasm out.

She grimaced, and took a deep breath. "Sorry, that didn't come out right. I know that you won't harm me, Nikos, at least not physically," she added, just to annoy him, he was sure. "And it's not your intentions I'm scared of but…" Pink flooded her cheeks "But your… I mean…"

"*Theos,* Lexi! Just say it." Sitting here in the intimate confines of the luxurious cabin, he had never felt the strange energy that suddenly arced into life in the cabin.

Lexi sighed, fighting the urge to run away from the cabin. Even though the temperature was perfect, she still felt a line of sweat down her spine. And their sitting here on the same bed, even with the breadth of it separating them, it felt too intimate. Too many things, strange and unnerving, crowded in on her. But the man did deserve an explanation.

"Your size…I mean…you are a big man."

Amusement glittered in his gaze. "Yes. I'm six foot three. I am big, *everywhere.* And so far, you're the only woman who has not been spectacularly happy about it."

"What does your size have to do with women being

hap…" Heat rose up through her as she realized his meaning, tightening her cheeks, and there was nothing she could
do about it. *"Oh."*

He laughed and she couldn't help but smile back. He
looked gorgeous, down-to-earth and not at all like someone who should have scared her so much. "You gave me
the perfect opening."

She nodded, and made a movement to stand up when
he threw out his arm to stop her. He did it slowly, as if to
not frighten her again. "Once again, you've made me extremely curious. And you owe me an explanation," he said,
rubbing at his jaw.

Lexi pulled up her feet and hugged her knees. "This…it's
nothing that is useful to you," she said, dragging her feet.

He didn't bat an eyelid at the insult. "Tell me anyway."

"I was transferred to a new foster home when I was
twelve." She smiled, warmth filling her despite everything
else that had happened. "I loved it immediately because the
last one, they had always been kind to me but I was the only
kid. The new home was perfect because there were six of
us and it's where I met Tyler.

"But our foster parents had a son. Jason was almost
seventeen, older than any of us, and was this huge, burly
guy. From the day I walked in, he picked on me. Every
month, it got worse. Sometimes he would just lift me up
and throw me down, sometimes lock me in the closet. I
got pretty smart about avoiding him for the most part. For
two years, it went on but it was the place that I had been
the happiest. Except for those moments with Jason. The
worst was when…"

Nikos's hand clasped hers, his fingers strong and rough
against hers. Holding back the urge to pull away, she
took a breath. Her hand was tiny in his, but it felt good,

strong, a spark of comfort filling her up. "You don't have to continue."

Lexi looked up, but didn't let go of his hand. She hated that the shadow of that fear that had been her constant companion in those years was still there with her. She swallowed the hot ache in her throat. "No…see, I thought I was over it. But I guess, the way I've been reacting around you…" Her fingers twitched in his grasp but he held on tight. "I…I refuse to give him any power over me."

She closed her eyes and instantly she was back in that room where she had slept again, on the metal-framed bed that had creaked with Jason's weight, the scent of his sweat, and she could feel his body pressing down on hers. "One night when I was fifteen—" her words came out in a ravaged whisper "—I was sleeping and I guess, I don't know… I don't know why he lay down next to me. I had no idea that he was even back in the house. One minute I'm sleeping peacefully, and the next, I wake up, and he is all over me." She shivered and her short nails dug into Nikos's palm. "He pinned me down with his huge body, locked my arms over my head. I can still feel his breath over my face. I don't know for how long. But I couldn't breathe, or move."

"Did he—"

The utter savagery in Nikos's words broke the hold of the memory. "No. I don't know what he intended. And thanks to Tyler, I never had to find out."

"Of course." The two words were laden with a vehemence that jerked her gaze to his face. "That's when you ran away?"

"Yes. I couldn't take it anymore. Except within a week, we realized how hard it was to feed ourselves. But Tyler refused to leave me." And she wouldn't leave him now.

"Didn't the parents believe what happened?"

She felt the intensity of Nikos's gaze bear down on her

and looked up. Bracing herself, she answered, instinctually knowing that he would not like it. "I never told them."

Shock widened his eyes, he clenched the muscles in his cheeks. "Why not?"

"I didn't want to hurt them."

"Hurt them?" His words were low, and yet brimming with a savage fury. "Their son attacked you while you were under their care. Protecting you was their duty."

He vibrated with an emotion that Lexi couldn't understand. The fact that a decision she had made years ago could affect him so much…she didn't know what to make of it. Only that she wanted to explain. "They were kind people, Nikos. They gave me a home for two years. It would have broken their hearts…"

He ran his fingers through his hair with palpable fury. "It was not your responsibility to worry about their feelings. It should never be a child's burden. Once you start taking that on, believe me, there is no turning back." He stood up from the bed, a latent energy pulsing under the controlled movement. His gaze filled with barely concealed scorn, he leveled a look at her. "Your kind of innocence and goodwill, it has no place in this world. Seeking to make a place for you in others' lives, it's…one thing. But to the point of undermining yourself… And before you imply so—" a softening glimmered in his gaze "—I have nothing to gain in this. This piece of advice is for your own benefit."

Lexi stared at his back as he strode out of the cabin without another glance toward her. He was once again the arrogant, condescending stranger from their first meeting, the one she didn't like, even a little bit. And not the least because he had a way of cutting right to the heart of uncomfortable truths she didn't want to hear, making her question her choices and even herself.

* * *

Lexi stepped out of the limo and for once, remembered not to grab her luggage. Hardly two days in Nikos's company, and she was already getting used to being served hand and foot.

Fascinated as she was with the sheer, majestic decadence of the hotel in front of her, it took her a minute to realize she was in Paris. Nikos had left the private airstrip in a different limo without a word. And she had been so glad to get a reprieve from him that she hadn't even realized where they had landed.

Shaking her head, she mounted the steps of the glitzy hotel. Stifling the urge to just hang around and look at everything around her, she walked to the reception desk.

Unease settled in her gut as she looked past the vast, marble-tiled foyer. Like a space portal waiting to swallow her whole, the glass elevator doors opened with a swish.

She forced a smile to her mouth and turned back toward the counter, her heart slowly but steadily crawling up her throat. She hated the hold her fear had on her, but neither could she shake it off. Stairs, it had to be again.

Stubbornly pushing her heart back into its place, she glanced through the upscale ground floor café first. She needed a high boost of carbs if she had to walk up twenty floors again.

"Mr. Demakis has a permanent suite with us on the forty-fifth floor," the receptionist said and Lexi's heart sank. "But we received an email to say you need a suite on the first floor."

Lexi could have kissed the woman. Feeling giddy with pleasure that she didn't have to chance a heart attack again, she followed the uniformed staff and clicked Nikos's number on her cell phone.

"What is it, Ms. Nelson?" His irritated voice came on

the other line. "I gave you my number in case of emergencies. Anything else you need, just ask the hotel reception and they will provide it for you."

The bubble of her excitement deflated with a tangible hiss. She licked her lips and forced herself to form the words. "The first floor suite...I... Thanks for remembering, Nikos."

Silence rumbled down the line, heavy, awkward and utterly embarrassing. "You're doing it again, Ms. Nelson. Thinking that everyone else in the world is like you. They're not. I need you alive right now. After that, climb fifty or a hundred floors, I don't care."

"Why are we lolling around here when you were in such a rush to leave New York then?" she said tartly.

"Because I have a meeting here which I had to postpone to come to get you."

And he disconnected the call.

Lexi stared at her phone, her mouth hanging open. Suddenly she felt like the stupidest woman on the planet for calling him. Especially when he had dumped her unceremoniously in a strange city without so much as an explanation.

She thumped her forehead with her phone, furious with herself. Fat good thanking him had done her. But neither did she believe him.

He might be an arrogant, infuriating pain in the butt, but he had a heart, whatever he might like to think.

Resolving to maintain a distance from him, she made her way toward the doorway that led to the stairs.

Pulling the edges of her robe together, Lexi stumbled out of the shower. Embarrassment, sheer fury, plain terror, cycled through her in a matter of seconds.

Her robe clinging to her wet skin, she followed the six-foot French woman, who was utterly naked, into the lounge of the suite.

"Where is Nikos?" the woman said in a delicious French accent.

So that's what this was about. "This is not Mr. Demakis's suite," Lexi managed, through the shock sputtering through her.

The woman's shoulders were thrown back, a perfectly manicured hand on her hip, not an inch of the confidence with which she had simply barged into the shower that Lexi had been occupying, had left Emmanuelle at realizing her mistake.

Blinking, Lexi shook her head, the utter perfection of the woman's body etched into her mind. She hurriedly looked around the lavish suite. The woman couldn't have walked through the street and into the foyer naked, could she? Though with a body like hers, no one would blame her.

Spotting a towel, Lexi threw it at her and continued her search again.

She breathed in relief as her gaze fell on a small, silken red heap on the cream leather couch.

She pulled it up just when the door to the suite opened and in walked the man she wanted to strangle. With a keycard in his hand as if he owned the hotel. "I don't believe this. Is the whole world just allowed to barge into my suite?"

His gaze moved from her face to the red silk dress in her hand and then toward Emmanuelle whose slender frame was hidden from the entrance.

The blasted man burst out laughing. The sound punched Lexi in the stomach, knocking the breath out of her.

Shaking with anger, she threw the dress at him with as much force as she could muster. The weightless garment fell silkily at his feet. "That woman barged into the shower, naked, and gave me the fright of my life."

"Calm down, Ms. Nelson," he said smoothly and picked up the dress.

Mumbling something Lexi couldn't hear in Emmanuelle's ear, he handed the dress to her.

Who, in turn, nodded and pulled her dress on. Next to Emmanuelle, who looked just as striking in her red dress as without it, Nikos was the very epitome of dangerous sophistication that Lexi might as well be from another galaxy.

Why she even cared she had no idea. Except that he was very good at turning her inside out.

"I'm assuming seeing Emmanuelle naked has sent your nervous system into shock?" With a look that took in everything from her wet hair to the thin silk robe that she had bought in the teen section of her local department store, he marched past her.

Knowing that he would just tease her mercilessly whatever she said, Lexi clamped her mouth shut. She stood there resolutely, refusing to hide.

Emmanuelle kissed his cheek, looked past him at Lexi, threw an air kiss at her and walked out of the suite.

Reaching her, he flicked a wet strand of her hair from her face. Lexi shivered, the hint of stubble on his jaw, the strong column of his throat, a feast to her senses. That sense of being tugged toward him came again. "Are you okay, or should I call for a doctor?"

She folded her arms. The prick of her nails into her skin was the only thing that helped her to focus on his words. "Am I in a bachelor-type reality show starring you?" Unwise curiosity gnawed at her. "Does the woman in New York know about this one?"

Wariness replaced the dark humor in his gaze. "Excuse me?"

"The brunette, your girlfriend in New York?"

He settled down onto the cream leather couch with a

sigh, his long legs extended in front of him. "Nina's not my girlfriend. I don't think she would even like the term. And neither is Emmanuelle."

"She walked in here, naked," she said, her line of thinking shocking her, "and left like a kitten when you asked her to." Mortification should have turned her into a red blob by now. "What was that whole…exchange?"

Clasping his hands behind his head, he slid lower into the couch and closed his eyes. "I told her I didn't want to see her anymore and she left."

"Then that was the end of your—" she scrunched her brow "—association?"

"Association, Ms. Nelson?" He leaned forward in the couch, something restless uncoiling in him. "Have I wandered into the sixteenth century? No wonder—"

"Affair then, okay?" she said hurriedly. She didn't want another taunt about Tyler. "That was ruthless. You say it's over and she leaves. Is that how—"

"How I conduct my *sexual associations?* Yes. And stop feeling sorry for her. If *she* had wanted to end it, I would have walked away, too."

"So wherever you go, you have a girlfri…a woman for sex?"

"Yes. I work hard and I play hard."

"And you or she have no expectations of each other?"

With slow movements, he unbuttoned the collar of his shirt. "This is sounding like an interview."

It took everything she had in her for Lexi to keep her gaze on his face. But even in the confusion, she couldn't stop asking the questions. "Do you spend time with any of them, eat together, go sightseeing? Would you call one of them a friend?"

"No." He stood up from the couch and reached her. The

hard knot in her chest didn't relent. "You're feeling sorry for me."

She raised her gaze to him and saw the detachment in his brown eyes. For all his wealth and jet-setting lifestyle, Nikos Demakis and she had something in common. He was as alone as she was. Except she had no doubt he had precisely tailored his life like that. *Why?* From the little she had gleaned about Venetia and Nikos Demakis, they came from a huge traditional Greek family. "It's a horrible life to lead."

He laughed and the sarcasm in it pricked her. "That's what I think of your life." Her gaze locked with his, and for once, there was no contempt or mockery there. Just plain truth. "In my life, there are no lasting relationships, no doing favors for friends who will take advantage of me. And when it comes to sex, the women I see want exactly what I want. Nothing more. You would understand that if you had—"

"If I weren't an unsophisticated idiot?"

Rubbing her eyes, Lexi flopped onto the couch he had just vacated. Because that's what Tyler had always said to her, too, hadn't he? That Lexi needed to live more, do more, just be…more.

That Lexi was living everyone else's life and not hers. She had always laughed it away, truly not understanding the vehemence in his words.

"I was going to say if you lived your life like a normal twenty-three-year-old instead of playing Junior Mother Teresa of your neighborhood." He took the seat next to her, and the heat of his body beckoned her. "If that's how you see yourself, change it."

This close, he was even more gorgeous, and his proximity unnerved her on the most fundamental level. The constant state of her heightened awareness of him combined with his continuous verbal assault made her flippant. "Is there a market here in Paris that sells sophistication by the pound?"

"You have a smart mouth, Ms. Nelson. I think we have already established that. Sophistication, or for that matter, anything else, can be bought with money. You spent enough time looking at the shops on Fifth Avenue in New York before we left. Why didn't you buy what you wanted?"

She blinked, once again struck by how far and how easily he wielded his power. "Did your assistant give you a minute-by-minute update on what I did?"

"I was in the limo stuck in traffic and saw you. You hung around long enough in each store. Apparently, you're as different from Venetia as I truly thought."

He had an uncanny way of giving voice to her most troublesome thoughts. "I hope you'll be so busy that I don't have to see you once we reach Greece."

"So that you can spend it all with your precious Tyler?"

The man was the most contrary man she had ever met. "Isn't that the reason you're paying me that exorbitant amount of money?"

"What did you do with the first half?"

"That's none of your business."

"If I find out that you have loaned it to some poor friend who *really* needs it—" his gaze filled with a dangerous gleam "—I will bend you over my knee and spank you."

Her cheeks stung with heat as a vivid image of what he said flashed in front of her eyes. The curse of being such a visual person. "I didn't give it to anyone nor will I spend it."

"Because of your stupid morals?"

"No. I…just want to save it, okay?" Realizing that she was shouting, she took a deep breath. "If I ever lose my job—and you have proved how easily anyone with a little money and inclination can find out my background—and if

I can't find a new one, I don't want to go hungry ever again. I don't ever want to be reduced to stealing or do something wrong again." The memories of those hunger pangs, the cold sweat of stealing, knowing it was wrong, were so vivid that her gut tightened. Feeling his gaze drilling into her side, she turned and laughed. A hollow laugh that sounded as pathetic as it felt. "You probably think I'm a fool."

His mouth, still closed, tilted at the corners. The flash of understanding in his gaze rooted her to the spot. "I do," he said, his hard words belying his expression. "But not for this."

A concession, spoken with that incisive contempt of his, and yet in that moment, she believed that he knew the powerless feeling, the fear that haunted her. "That day, you said you understood it. How?"

"I have been hungry before. And I was responsible for Venetia, too."

"But your family is rich. And *you're* rich. Nauseatingly so."

He smiled without warmth. "My father turned his back on all that nauseating wealth for my mother. When I was thirteen, they died within a few months of each other. And even before he died, he was usually drowning in alcohol and no use to us. My mother's treatment was expensive. For almost a year, I did everything and anything I could to bring in money, as much as I could. And I mean *anything.*"

He delivered those words in a monotone, yet Lexi could feel the rage and powerlessness that radiated from him. She clasped his hand with hers, just like he had done. A jolt of sensation spiked through her, awakening every nerve ending.

Her touch pulled Nikos from the pit of memories he fell into. Even now, he remembered the stench of his desperation, his hunger. Still, he had rallied. Shaking it off, he met her gaze. The sympathy in her gaze, it made his throat raw.

"I'm sorry, Nikos. It was wrong of me to assume what I did."

He nodded, for once, unable to throw it back in her face. Because the slip of a woman next to him wasn't pitying him. She understood the pain of that thirteen-year-old boy. He had manipulated her and bullied her into coming with him, but she still had the capacity to feel sympathy for him.

How? How could anyone see so much hard life and still retain that kindness as she did, that boundless goodwill? What did she possess that he didn't?

Lexi Nelson, despite everything, was full of heart. Whereas he...the pain he had seen had somehow become a cold, hard part of him. He embraced it for it had driven him toward everything he had now. "Don't worry," he said, feeling an intense dislike of her stricken expression, "I survived. And I made sure that Venetia survived, too."

Curiosity flared in her gaze again, but she clamped her mouth with obvious effort. Standing up from the couch, she waited, with folded arms, for him to move.

He grinned, and didn't pull his legs back. Muttering something he couldn't quite hear, she stepped over him. The scent of her soap and skin combined wafted over him. His muscles tightened at the hard tug of want in his gut.

Why had he sent away Emmanuelle instead of taking up what she offered—easy, uncomplicated sex?

Leaning back against the couch, he slid lower and closed his eyes. Much as he tried, instead of Emmanuelle's sexy body and the pleasure she was so good at giving, his mind kept remembering stunning blue eyes and a slender body with barely there curves.

Lexi Nelson was definitely an interesting distraction. He gave her that. But nothing more.

Little Ms. Pushover, with her endless affection and her trusting heart, had no place in his life. With ruthlessness he had honed to perfection over the years, he shoved away the image.

CHAPTER FIVE

KNOWING THAT HIDING inside her bedroom was like inviting Nikos to mock and taunt her some more, Lexi dressed in denim shorts and a worn T-shirt that hung loose and ventured back to the sitting room.

She froze at the hubbub of activity. The sleek coffee table was gone and in its place stood a rack of clothes, designer if she was seeing the weightless fabric and the expensive cuts right. A tall woman, impeccably dressed in a silk pantsuit, stood next to it with a pad in hand, while another woman, probably assistant to the first, unwrapped a red dress from its tissue.

Even the sound of soft tissue sounded filthily expensive to Lexi's ears. Her heart raced in her chest, shameful and excited.

"You're practically drooling."

His lazy drawl pulled her gaze to Nikos. He was sitting in a leather recliner, his hands folded, his long legs extended in front of him. Latent energy rolled off him.

Sliding past the clothes with a longing glance, she reached him. "What's going on?"

"A little gift for you."

"A gift?" she said dully. One thing she had learned, and he had hammered it home, was that nothing he did was without calculation. "Like a 'give the poor little orphan a makeover' gift? Are my friends behind that glass waiting to jump up and down and shed tears at my transformation?"

He wrapped his fingers around her arm and tugged her close. "You've never seen your parents then?"

There was such an uncharacteristic gentling note in his tone that it took her a few seconds to respond. "No, I haven't."

"Do you think about them, wonder why—"

"I used to, endlessly." After all these years, she could talk about it almost normally, without crumpling into a heap of tears. "The first comic I ever had sketched had a little orphan who goes on a galactic journey and discovers that her parents are cosmic travelers trapped on the other side of the galaxy. One day I realized that as stories went it was fantastic. But reality, sadly, stayed the same." She jerked her hand away from him. "Now will you please tell me what's going on?"

His gaze stayed on her a few more seconds before he cleared his throat. "Venetia's life is a constant roller coaster of parties and clubs, and I'm providing you with armor so that she doesn't crush you. Think of me as your fairy godmother."

She burst out laughing. "Ple-e-e-ase. More like a rampaging space pirate."

"Like the one in the comic book you're working on now? That's what you called me that first day, didn't you?"

Shock reverberated through her at how clearly he remembered what she had uttered in a daze. He stood up and turned to the right, striking a pose with an imaginary pistol in hand. With his tall body, he should have looked awkward. Instead, he looked perfectly gorgeous.

"*Spike,* wasn't it? Did you model your hero after me, Ms. Nelson?"

She shook her head slowly from left to right, unable to

tear her gaze away from the perfection of his profile. Wishing she had a camera in hand, she studied him greedily. "Spike is the villain who kidnaps Ms. Havisham. You're not a hero, Nikos."

"Ahh…" His gaze moved over her face lazily, sliding past her chin to the shirt that hung loose on her, the vee of it, to her bare legs. "Is this Ms. Havisham a fragile little beauty that conquers his heart and teaches him how to love?"

Her heart came to a stuttering halt. Cursing herself for her runaway imagination, she smiled. There was nothing but mockery in his words. "Wrong again."

"Is the whole book done? Tell me what's involved."

A spurt of warmth filled her at his interest. "I am still doing the preliminary sketching and have written down the plot. Once I finalize the characters and the story, I'll do the model sheets for each character and the final step will be to begin inking."

"Hmm…so you do it all by hand, not software."

"Yes, mostly I'm a penciler. I like doing it by hand, getting all the expressions right and haven't really decided on an inking method for sure, mostly I'm just playing with all the techniques. Sometimes I will color, sometimes I…" She caught herself at his smile. "Sorry, I tend to get carried away on this topic."

"No explanation needed. Vintage cars give me a hard-on like that." He laughed as furious color rose through her cheeks. "It sounds really interesting. Do you have all the supplies you need?"

The small spurt grew into a gush of warmth. She nodded.

"When can I see them?"

"What?"

"Your sketches. I want to see them."

"Maybe when you learn to say please," she said, and he made a disappointed noise.

She almost liked him at that moment, *almost*. Which only proved how right he was in calling her a pushover.

He grinned in that sardonic way. "Now please, humor your boss and try that red dress on. I know you want to."

She took a couple of cocktail dresses from the woman and sneaked back to her bedroom. She wasn't going to accept any of it. But there was no harm in indulging herself, was there?

In her bedroom, she pulled off her shorts and T-shirt, and instead of the red one, pulled on a strapless sheath dress exactly the color of her eyes. It fit her as if it was made for her. Sliding the side zipper up, Lexi turned toward the full-length mirror.

Her breath lodged somewhere in her throat. Simply cut, the designer dress showed off her slender shoulders and slight build to maximum advantage, ending with a small flare just above her knees that contrasted with the severe cut.

She didn't look sophisticated as he had claimed. Maybe she never would. But better than that, for the first time since she had realized she was never going to have any curves, she looked like a woman.

A knock at the door meant she had to stop admiring herself. She stepped into the sitting area.

Nikos stood leaning against the open door, his dark gaze eating her up. A stillness came over him. The flash of purely male appraisal in his gaze knocked the breath out of her. That look…she had imagined Tyler looking at her like that so many times. It had never happened. But seeing that look in Nikos's eyes, it was as unwelcome as it was shocking.

She blinked as a sliver of tension suddenly arced between them.

"You look stunning, Ms. Nelson." He delivered those words with the same silky smoothness as when he insulted her. As if it had no effect on him. Had she imagined that look? "Your ex won't know what hit him when he sees you in it. If that doesn't bring him back to his senses…"

She didn't hear the rest of his sentence as something nauseating neatly slotted into place. The silky slide of the dress chafed her.

Her heart thumping in her chest, she followed him into the lounge and stood in front of him. "What is this really about, Nikos? Why do you care so much how Tyler sees me? Tell me the truth or I'll walk out right now."

With a nod of that arrogant head, he dismissed the stylist and her assistant. The prickly humor was gone. The man staring at her with a cold look in his eyes was pure predator. "Don't threaten me, Lexi."

Even his use of her name, given he usually patronized her with *Ms. Nelson,* was pure calculation to intimidate her. She was intimidated by everything about this man, but she refused to show it. Had she really thought him kind just because he had listened to her sob story, asked her about her little hobby? He had manipulated her from day one. "Don't lie to me, Nikos."

His silence was enough to convince Lexi of the truth that had been staring her in the face all this time. Her stomach felt as if it was falling through an abyss. "You mean to use me to separate Tyler from Venetia."

She reached for the zipper on the side, feeling as dirty as she had felt the day she had broken into that house. But her fingers shook, fumbled over the zipper. She grunted, impatient to get it off.

Nikos looked down at her, frowning. "Calm down."

"No, I won't calm down. And take this zipper off."

He did it. Silently and without fumbling like her, with his hands around her body, but not touching her. She felt enveloped by him, her heart skidding all over the place. This was wrong. Everything about this situation, everything about what he made her feel, everything about what he was using her for, they were all horribly wrong and quickly sliding out of her control. Cold sweat gathered over her skin.

The minute the zipper came down, she rushed into her bedroom, took the dress off and donned her usual shorts and T-shirt. Marching back into the room, she threw the dress at him.

"Drama, Ms. Nelson?" he said, bunching the expensive fabric in his hands and throwing it aside. "Finally, something Venetia and you have in common, other than Tyler."

"I'll scream if you call me Ms. Nelson again in that patronizing tone. You have manipulated me, lied to me and picked me up like I was a bag of potatoes. You *will* call me Lexi and tell me why you are doing this."

He took in her rant without so much as a flicker of his eyelid. "Tyler is a manipulative jerk who doesn't deserve Venetia. I want him out of her life."

"Tyler isn't—"

"Your opinion of him means nothing to me."

She flinched. "Why?"

"You're—" She had the distinct impression that he was choosing his words carefully, which was a surprise in itself. Because usually he didn't mince his words, cutting through her with his sharply acerbic opinions. "Blind when it comes to him."

Confusion spiraled through her, coated with a sharp fear. *What had she signed up for?* "Then why let her see him? Why pretend as though you support them?"

"Venetia, for all her outward drama, is very vulnerable and volatile. She never recovered from our parents' death. I'm the only one in the world who hasn't hurt her until now. I will not change that."

"So you're having me do the dirty work for you? And what do you think is going to happen to your precious sister if, heaven forbid, everything goes according to your plan?"

Distinct unease settled over his features. Granite would have more give than his jaw. "She will cry over him. I will explain it to her that you and he—" utter distaste coated his words now "—you always go back to each other, whatever transpires in between. Not unbelievable with your long history." He rubbed his jaw with his palm, his movements shaky. "I hate that I can't prevent this. But I will accept a few of her tears now than something more dangerous that she could do later when she realizes that Tyler never really loved her."

The emotion in his tone was unmistakable. His every word, his manipulations—everything had been to this end. And Lexi understood it, could almost admire him for it if it wasn't also highly misguided. "You can't protect her from everything in the world, Nikos."

"She saw my father shoot himself in the head. I failed long ago to protect her."

Lexi froze, her thoughts jumbling on top of each other. And she had thought she had been unfortunate. "Your father killed himself?"

"Because he couldn't bear to live without my mother." Ice coated his words. "Venetia was ten. She didn't even understand our mother's death. The worst part is she's exactly like him—emotional, volatile and prone to mood swings. With everything I know about your friend, I know he will walk out on my sister one day. I'm just expediting it so that the damage to her is limited."

His heart might be in the right place, but it was so twisted. Lexi walked back and forth, the gleaming marble floor dizzying her, her stomach churning with a viciousness she couldn't curb. "You can't just arrange her life to be without sorrow. It doesn't work that way. I won't do this."

"You will get your precious Tyler back. Don't tell me you haven't thought about that."

"Yes. That thought crossed my mind, but not like this." Disbelief rang in his eyes. "I don't care what it *might* mean for me. I'm out."

She turned around to do just that, but suddenly there he was, a terrifying prospect she couldn't escape. The tension in him was palpable, the rigid set of his mouth an unmistakable warning. "If something happens to my sister because of Tyler, I will hold you personally responsible. Knowing that you could have prevented it, can you handle that guilt, Lexi?"

She stilled as she saw that same guilt cast a dark shadow on his face.

There was nothing cold about Nikos. He was just incredibly good at pushing it all away, and tailoring his life to follow the same strategy. He'd put himself behind an invisible wall of will where nothing could touch him. And he wanted his sister next to him.

Her throat felt raw, her chest tight. So many people could be hurt by the path he was pushing her on. Tyler, Venetia, Lexi herself and Nikos, most of all. Nikos, whom she had thought impervious to any feeling, whom she had assumed ruthless to a fault. Only all he wanted was to protect his sister. *From what?* Another truth slammed into her. "Is this about getting Tyler out of Venetia's life or love out of it, Nikos?"

His head reared back in the tiniest of movements, his eyes cold and hard. A cold chill permeated her skin and she almost wished the words unsaid. "I'm not paying you to analyze me." His tone was low, thrumming with emotion he refused to give outlet. "I failed my sister once. And it broke her in so many ways. I will do whatever it takes to ensure it doesn't happen again.

"Call me a villain, like your space pirate. Tell yourself I'm forcing you into this if it helps you sleep better."

"My skin crawls to even think about manipulating him like that. But I just can't. If I could be some kind of *femme fatale* as you're plotting, Tyler and I would still have been together. But I'm not the kind of woman that men lose their minds over. So all this," she said, pointing to the designer clothes, "it's an utter waste. Because Tyler will never leave Venetia for me, of all people."

He looked at her with none of the resolve diminished. It was like banging her head against an invisible wall. "Don't underestimate yourself." A spark of something came alive in his gaze and was gone before she could blink. "I know how much you can mess with a man's head, and that's when you're not trying. Think of how easy your real job is now. All you have to do is convince Tyler that he belongs with you, as always."

He was not going to budge from this path.

Just thinking about what he suggested, the fact that he had paid for it, made her nauseous. But he would not rest until Tyler was out of Venetia's life. And she didn't doubt for a second the lengths he would go to. She had already seen proof of that. He would also do it in a way that caused his sister minimum pain. Which meant Tyler would suffer. And she just couldn't leave her friend at Nikos's mercy.

She would have to go with Nikos, play the part he wanted her to play. At least that way, she could find a way to protect Tyler in the meantime. Tucking her knees together, she kept her gaze studiously away from his. "Fine, I'll do it."

He stilled. She could almost hear the gears in his head turning. "You will?"

"You've left me no choice, have you?" she said, blustering through it. It was the only way to stop from going into full-on panic. "*You're* the manipulative jerk for doing this to them, but yes, I'll be your evil sidekick. And it's a NO to the sex clothes."

His gaze thoughtful, he walked away from her.

Lexi sagged into the couch, shivering. Lying had never been her strong suit. But she had pulled it off for now, managed to fool Nikos. A Machiavellian feat in itself.

She was playing a dangerous game, but she could see no way out of it.

CHAPTER SIX

LEXI WOKE UP with a start and jerked upright. The feel of the softest Egyptian cotton against her fingers, the high ceiling as her gaze flew open and the pleasant scent of roses, and curiously basil, only intensified her confusion.

Usually, all she could smell was old pizza and smoke.

The view through the French doors onto a vast island set her bearings straight. The water was an intense blue; the sand, burnished gold, a striking contrast against it. It stretched for miles, as far as she could see. And other than the lapping of the waves, silence reigned.

It was unsettling as she was used to the noisy din of her apartment complex.

Clutching the sheets to her, she took a deep breath and fell back against the bed.

She was in the Demakis mansion in her own room. On one of the two islands they owned in the Cyclades. Her heart had resumed its normal beat when the maid had said the Demakis family and the patriarch Savas Demakis lived on the other one.

She closed her eyes, but she knew she had slept for way too long already. Stretching her hand, she reached for her cell phone on the nightstand and checked the time. She jumped off the bed when she saw it was half past three.

They had arrived at the private airstrip at four in the morning.

By the time the limo had driven them through the islet, past the electronically manned estate gates, she'd had zero energy left. Nikos's curt "Tyler can survive a few more hours without you" had put paid to the thought before she uttered it.

Their flight from Paris had been filled with tense silence. She had been so wound up from everything Nikos had said, and her own impulsive decision to continue, she'd been on tenterhooks. Thankfully he had left her alone.

In fact, the chilling silence she had felt from him, the absence of those sarcastic undertones when he had spoken to her, which had been the barest minimum, had meant that she kept casting looks at him.

She had the most gut-twisting notion that he hadn't bought her easy agreement to his plan. But all she could do was to push on.

She padded barefoot to the bathroom and gasped at the sheer magnificence of it.

Done in gold-piped cream marble tiles, the bathroom was decadent luxury and could house both hers and Ms. Goldman's apartment next door. She rubbed her feet on the lush cream-colored rug, unwilling to leave dusty footprints on the marble.

The vanity on her left was a silver bowl, wide enough for her to sit in, with gold-edged lining in front of an oval mirror.

She rubbed the glinting metal just to be sure. Yep, pure silver. So everything she had heard about the Demakis wealth was true. And Nikos's father had walked away from it all.

Ruminating on the thought, she ventured farther. The silver-and-gold theme pervaded the bathroom. Having grown up in homes where shower time had been two minutes spray under cold water, the sheer beauty of the bath stole into her.

A shower stood to her right and the highlight of the bathroom was an oval-shaped, vast sunken tub, also made out of marble.

Laughing, she closed the door behind her and decided to take advantage of it. She was here, and she would do everything within her power to ensure Nikos didn't do something reckless. But she might as well get a luxurious bath out of it. Checking to see that there were towels aplenty, she stripped and got into the bath. Gold-edged silver taps and small handmade soaps in a variety of scents greeted her.

Turning on the jets, she immersed herself in the water.

She was sipping a mocktail on the glorious deck of a luxury yacht while a Greek heiress looked at her as though she wanted to reduce her to ash. If looks could throw her overboard, Lexi would have been kissing exotic seaweed on the floor of the sea an hour ago when she had stepped onto the deck by Nikos's side.

He had watched her with that inscrutable expression of his, accompanied her to the yacht and brought her to Tyler. Tyler had hugged her, his gaze curiously awkward while Venetia had been a sullen, disquieting figure behind him. Contrary to the dramatics Lexi had expected, the heiress had been all too composed, only the blazing emotion in her black gaze betraying her fury.

It hadn't been more than fifteen minutes before she had interrupted them and tugged Tyler away. Still, it was clear that Tyler had no intention of hurting Venetia by walking away, even if he had no memory of her.

Which was why he had asked for Lexi. Because he had wanted his best friend close by—to help him figure out what to do. Not the ex he had dumped for Venetia, as Nikos assumed. By the time Lexi had realized this, Nikos had disappeared.

She had been prepared to see them together, knew that whatever problems she and Tyler had, had begun before he had met Venetia. But even she, with her wishful thinking, couldn't miss that whatever Tyler and Venetia had shared was strong. Which was going to make one ruthless Greek very angry.

Lexi shivered even though the sea air was balmy. Tyler and Venetia stood on the far side of the deck surrounded by Venetia's friends. Venetia wasn't going to let Tyler even look at her tonight. Probably never, if Nikos wasn't there to persuade her.

Which made her want to find Nikos and give him a piece of her mind for dragging her into this mess.

Stepping off the deck without another glance, she refused the offer of a buggy from one of the security guards.

The warm breeze from the sea plastered her T-shirt and shorts against her. She clutched the worn-out cotton with her fingers, trying to root herself.

The wealth and the sophistication of the people partying behind her, it overwhelmed her. But that wasn't the reason for the heavy feeling in her gut.

She would not feel sorry for herself. It was a glorious island the likes of which she would never see again, and she would not let the loneliness inside her mar her enjoyment of it.

Nikos punched in the code and kicked the heavy garage door back, hot rage fueling his blood.

Once again, Savas had thwarted him. In the three years that Nikos had carved his way into the Demakis empire through sheer hard work and determination, he had brought

Savas's bitterest rival, Theo Katrakis, onto the Demakis board, despite Savas's vehement refusal, proving that it *was* time to bring new money and partnerships into the company.

And it had paid off. In two years of partnership with Theo, a shrewd businessman with a practical head, Demakis Exports had increased their revenue by almost forty percent. Nikos had no doubt he would succeed in the new real-estate venture, as well.

But Nikos's success, perversely, made Savas push him a little more.

Why else would he, again and again, deny Nikos what he wanted the most? Another board meeting, another refusal to elect him CEO.

Locking away the scream of rage that fought for outlet, Nikos stripped off his trousers and dress shirt and pulled on old jeans.

He walked back out into the hangar area of his garage and pulled the tarp off the Lamborghini Miura S that he was restoring. He was being tested, he was being punished, he was being denied his rightful place because he was his father's son.

Because Savas had still not forgiven his son, Nikos's father. The one thing Savas didn't understand was how much Nikos hated his father, too. He was nothing like his father and he never would be.

He had only two goals in life. He had hardened himself against everything else. He had driven himself to exhaustion and beyond, forgone any personal relationships, hadn't forged any bonds with his cousins, all in pursuit of being his own man, of doing what his father had failed to do.

Protecting Venetia and becoming the Demakis CEO. And he would do both at any cost.

Renewed determination pounded through his blood.

Switching on his mobile, he placed a call to his assistant and ordered him to arrange a meeting with Theo Katrakis.

"You will go blind drawing in the dark."

Lexi gasped and looked up, the growly rumble of Nikos's words pinged across her skin like sparks of fire. She did it so fast that that the pencil flew from her hand. Her legs ached under her, from their position on the hard concrete floor of the garage.

She had sneaked in, wondering what the structure was, and seeing Nikos, naked from the waist up, working with a furious energy on the car behind him, she had stopped still, feeling the familiar itch in her fingers to reach for her sketch pad. Every time he had crawled under the car, her breath had hitched in her throat.

Obviously, she hadn't realized how much time had passed.

Nikos's hand dangled in front of her. The veins in his forearm stood out thickly, his fingers shining with grease. "How long have you been here?"

With a sigh, she gave him her hand and let him tug her up. Her legs, sore from sitting in that position for so long, gave out from under her.

His arm going around her, he steadied her against his chest. Molten heat swathed Lexi inside and out. He smelled of sweat and grease, an incredibly strange combination that cut off her breath effortlessly. Sinuous muscle tightened under her fingers and she jerked back, the warmth of his skin singeing the pads of her fingers.

He looked nothing like the suave businessman that had mocked her that first day. This Nikos was more down-to-earth but no less intense.

Lean muscle covered up by glorious olive-toned skin. Tight, well-worn jeans hanging low on his hips. A chest that could have been carved from marble, despite the sprinkling of hair. Washboard abdomen and Dear God Of All Glorious Things, that line of hair that disappeared into those jeans.

Her breath came hard and fast, a permanent shiver on her skin.

His dark brown eyes glittered with unhidden amusement and something else. Something that sent hot little flares of need into every inch of her. "Would you like me to get completely naked?"

Yes, please...for my art, y'know...

Hot color rose to her cheeks and she looked away. She bent over and picked up the loose paper and pencil. A sharp knot in her right shoulder told her she had been sketching him for far longer than she had planned to. She clutched the spot with her left hand and turned back. "I didn't mean to disturb you."

His hands landed on her, gentle and light. He turned her around. And she went, without protest, her skin already singing to be in such close contact with him. "Here?" he whispered near her ear, his fingers tracing the tight knot in her right shoulder.

She nodded, her throat dry.

His warm breath caressed her skin as he rubbed at the sore spot with long, pulling strokes. He was like a furnace of heat behind her. Only it was the pull-you-into-it kind. The pressure was relieved by his fingers, only to flood the rest of her body.

"Relax, *agape mou*. Remember what we talked about?"

Lexi nodded. Because much as she puzzled about it, there was nothing sexual about the way he rubbed her shoulders. She'd seen him with the other women. He wore his sexuality like a second skin. His being sexy was like... her ability to draw. Only she had no idea how to handle the relentless assault. Her skin prickled with awareness, the rough grooves of his palm rasping against her skin.

She shivered at how much she wanted those fingers to move from her shoulders to the rest of her, how much she wanted to lean back into his body and feel the press of hard muscle.

He plucked the paper from her hand and let her go. Silence had never felt more unnerving. Slowly she turned around, every inch of her trembling.

Finally, he looked at her, turning the sheet in his hand so that she could see the sketch. "You're extremely talented. But you drew me, not your space pirate."

Lexi was incapable of muttering even a word. She glanced at the sketch and her gut flopped to her feet. Mortification beat a tattoo in her head. She had meant to draw Spike and yet...there was Nikos in all his glory.

There was physical hunger in his gaze, an elemental longing. The very thing she had imagined seeing.

"Are all your sketches so self-revelatory?"

He whispered the words, but the garage walls seemed to amplify them before sending them back. Unasked questions and unsaid answers pervaded the air.

Nooooo.

She stepped back, desperate to flee. "I shouldn't have come in here. I was...was just walking around—"

His fingers closed over her wrist. "Then stay," he said, cutting through all the confusion. "I won't bite, Lexi."

He tugged her gently and she followed, feeling divided within. She was pathetic enough to admit that she found him intensely interesting and yet...she was also scared.

Curiosity wiped the floor with her confusion.

"Did you sleep well?" he asked, wiping his large hands with a rag. "I informed the maids to not approach you when you are sleeping."

Lexi nodded, a hard lump in her throat making it hard to swallow. She wanted to be angry with him for manipulating her, for thinking so little of Tyler's feelings. And he crumbled it all with one kind thought. She understood his need to protect his sister. Just wished it didn't come at the cost of Tyler's happiness.

She followed him to where the vintage car stood and remembered his comments. "So this is like your Bat Cave?"

Turning around, he laughed. "You remembered."

She forced herself to hold his gaze, knowing that he was waiting for her to drop it, shy away like a blushing virgin. "I like you here."

He raised a brow.

"You seem nicer, calmer, less manipulative."

He stared at her without comment, a shadow dimming the amusement. Turning around, he grabbed a wrench. "Did Venetia say something to you?"

Mesmerized by the shift and play of the muscles in his back, she didn't answer.

He turned around and stepped closer. "Lexi?"

"What?" She colored and met his gaze. "Venetia... Venetia didn't say a word to me. Just glared at me, you know, like she wanted to reduce me into microparticles with her laser beam."

"Is that what Spike can do?"

"Naahhh... I think this is a new character—Spike's demon sister."

He threw his head back and laughed, the tendons in his neck stretching. "You're really tempting me, *thee mou*. So... you didn't get a chance to talk to Tyler then?"

"Not really. They left the deck. And I...I just didn't know what to do."

"You don't like parties?"

"Less than I like being amongst a sea of people who

don't even know I exist. I could fall into the ocean and no one would even know I was gone." She felt her face heat as he paused and looked at her. But she couldn't stop. "She's not going to let me near him, especially in front of her friends, Nikos. I'd rather not go to any more of these parties in the future unless you're there."

The echo of her words surrounded them followed by deafening silence. Of all the people in the world, she had to pour out her stupid fears to him? A man who had no place for emotions and the insecurities they brought.

"Go ahead. Call me a fool."

"Come here."

When she didn't move, he pulled her close to his side. He was all hard, lean, unforgiving muscle. Lexi exhaled on a whoosh, the aching lump in her throat mocking her and yet unable to resist settling against his side.

His arm long enough to wrap around her twice, was a heavy, comforting weight on her shoulders. Her skin tingled where it rasped against hers. She felt him exhale, his big body shuddering in the wake of it. "Fears are not always rational, I know that."

She pushed away from him and turned around, striving for composure. He didn't seem unfeeling right then. He sounded as though he had known fear and from everything he had told her, she believed he had.

"I thought you would be living it up at the party," she said, needing to clutter the silence.

"I'm not one for much partying, either. When I was younger, I didn't have the time, and now I don't have the interest. The party scene is nothing but a hunt for sex and I don't need it."

No, he didn't.

She tucked her legs into the couch as he settled down on the other side. He slid into the seat in slow, measured movements, and she knew it was for her. Feeling the silliest idiot ever, she unglued herself from the corner. Okay, so she didn't want to quite sit in his lap, but there was no reason to insult the man.

He noticed her effort with smiling eyes. "You're getting used to me."

The warmth in those eyes, the simple pleasure in his words lit a spark inside her. She sucked in a deep breath. "Why didn't you have time?"

He shrugged. "Until a few years ago, I worked every hour there was. I had no degree or work experience except the little I learned in my father's garage. The only way I moved up from being a line man on the manufacturing floor to a board member was by working hard."

"You didn't want to study?"

"I didn't have that choice. If I wanted security for Venetia and me, I had to do everything Savas asked me to do. Those were his conditions."

"Conditions?" she said, feeling sick to her stomach.

He stood up from the seat, as though he couldn't sit still. He wiped the immaculate surface of the hood with a rag. It was a comfort thing, Lexi realized with dawning awareness. There was something different about him today, and it was this place. He seemed comfortable here, almost at peace, a striking contrast to the man who had women in every city for sex.

"When Savas came to pick us up, he had specific conditions. If I was to live in his house, if I wanted Venetia to have everything she needed, I had to do anything and everything he asked of me."

"What did he ask you to do?" Her question was instantaneous.

He leaned against the car, his hands folded. "He told me to never expect anything that I hadn't earned. That I was his grandson meant nothing in the scheme of things. I was forbidden to mention my father or mother. Within a week, I started in his factory."

She shot up, his matter-of-fact tone riling her own anger. "But that was…unnecessarily cruel of him."

"He saved Venetia and me from a life of starvation and desperation. Only he refused to give it to us for free. It was not an unfair condition."

Holding his gaze took everything Lexi had when she was shaking with fury inside. "Yes, if he was only your employer. But this is your grandfather, your family we are talking about."

"Savas hated that my father walked out on all this. He wanted to ensure I didn't end up another fool like him."

Lexi wanted to argue some more, but the resolve etched into Nikos's face stopped her. Now she understood why he had been so ready to blackmail her or pay her, how everything was a transaction, how everything had a price in his mind.

How could he be any different when that's what he had been taught?

A thirteen-year-old boy, mourning his parents, dealing with his sister's shock, fighting for survival, and the price for it had been that he show no weakness. Could she blame him when she knew the depths to which the need for survival could push a person?

"He messed you up, Nikos." She said the words softly, slowly, burdened under a wave of sadness. Her childhood had been empty, her strongest memory was of craving for someone who would hold her, kiss her, hug her, love her unconditionally.

All she had ever wanted was to have a family.

Nikos, he had had one. And yet he had known less kindness than she had.

She heard Nikos's laugh through the filter of her own teetering emotions. It was fire in his eyes, curving that sinful mouth. It mocked her for feeling sorry for him. "Everything Savas has done has been to my advantage. Have you seen where I'm in my life right now? I will be the CEO of Demakis International in a few months, will have everything my father didn't have. Do you think I will ever be hungry again? We both know what that desperation feels like, *agape mou*. Admit it. Admit that any price is worth paying for it."

"I have seen your place in the world. I almost drowned in that glorious bathtub. Are you truly blind to what price you're paying for all this? Even sex is a transaction for you."

He hulked over her in an ever so gentle way. But his gentility, his concern, they were all lost on her. "You can dish it out, Lexi, but can you take it? Do you want to hear some truths, as well?"

Her stomach dipped and dived, her nerves pinging with a thrilling excitement that spread through her like a fever. Now she knew why she had drawn him with that look in his eyes. Being near Nikos, feeling everything she did in his presence, she couldn't spend another moment fooling herself.

She suddenly knew why her relationship with Tyler had failed on so many levels. Tyler and she had never meant to be more than friends. Ever. It was as if an invisible portal had been opened. Now she couldn't *un*believe its existence whatever she did. "You're right, I can't," she said, opting for cowardice. She wanted to run away before she betrayed herself, if he didn't know already. "I can, however, tell you that Venetia and Tyler…whatever they share is not so weak as you imagine. There's a fire between them. I've never…" She paused, the heat of his gaze lighting the very fire she had thought herself unaware of.

"You've never what?" His gaze widened with a dangerous curiosity that sent a pang of alarm through her. "With
all your antiquated notions, did you refuse to put out, Lexi?
Is that why he left you?"

Her gut flopped. She shivered, amazed at his razor-
sharp mind. He was so close to the pathetic truth. "The
P.I. couldn't figure out if I had already lost my V card?"
She was attracted to Nikos, and it was nothing like she had
ever felt before. It was intense, and it made her feel frayed,
as if she was coming apart at the seams.

Why else would his amusement hurt so much?

He grabbed her wrist and tugged her closer. "Articles in
Cosmo have nothing over practical experience."

"Are you volunteering then?" she said, before she could
lock away the thought. "Will you help me practice so that I
can then seduce Tyler away from your sister?"

A cavern of tension sucked them right in.

His dark gaze moved over her with lingering precision
from the top of her hair to her feet clad in open-toed san-
dals. There was such a jaded look in those eyes that something within her rebelled and twisted.

He had no interest in her. She had seen his type and like
every other man on the planet, it was boobs and legs. Neither of which she possessed enough to count, sadly.

For the first time in her life, she wished she had paid
more attention to her clothes, had worn proper makeup.
Because she wanted him to feel that hunger she felt for
him, she wanted him to be mindless in his craving for her.

"I'm sure I can be persuaded," he finally answered.

The color leached from Lexi's face, leaving a pale mask
behind.

Nikos instantly regretted his words.

She recovered fast, her mouth trembling with her fury.
"I'm glad I'm such a source of amusement for you, but I'd

rather be dumped by Tyler another hundred times than take you up on your *offer*. I'd rather sleep with one of the guys that frequent the club. You're unfeeling, manipulative and arrogant. You're toying with me just for the fun of it, and I don't need your pity sex."

She ran out of the garage as though the very devil was behind her. Stunned by how hard her words hit, Nikos forced himself to breathe, a storm of inexplicable emotion surging through him.

He had never meant to hurt her. He had only needled her, as he always did. His curiosity about every facet of her life, about her relationship with Tyler, it knew no bounds, shattering his usual reserve.

Had he hit the truth? Was there no end to her innocence? Why should it matter to him if she had slept with her blasted boyfriend or not? So he had covered his stunned reaction to it by needling her some more.

Are you volunteering?

Yes.

His body roared with its own answer. But he didn't want just sex, he wanted *her*. For the first time in his life, he wanted something that he didn't even understand.

He understood the pull he felt for her. It was more than just attraction; it was something as unique as the woman herself.

Her upbringing, her isolation even after the way she surrounded herself with people, her loneliness—it was like looking at an image of himself he didn't know existed. Only a better one, with compassion, affection, love.

And the fact that he was letting her burrow under his skin, blared like an alarm in his head.

Unfeeling, manipulative and arrogant.

He was all that and more.

Yet, right at that moment—with his body shuddering at

the very thought of kissing that mouth, his mind seething with hurt because she, Lexi Nelson, found him unsuitable— he was not the man he had forced himself to become. Old wounds and memories opened up, cloying through him, leaving him shaking.

The flash of pain, hot and shocking, that darted through him, forced him to focus like nothing else. He would not examine the whys or hows of it. There was nothing Lexi could offer him that wasn't easily available to him without complication.

Not her body, and definitely not her pitying, trusting, loving, heart.

It was good he had scared her off, good that he had hurt her, because he had nothing to offer her, either. Like Venetia's tears, the flashing hurt in her eyes was a price he would willingly pay.

Better she stay away from him, better she stopped analyzing him, better she stopped giving him glimpses of things he didn't even know were missing from his life.

CHAPTER SEVEN

LEXI RUBBED IN the sunscreen on her legs, loving the golden tan she had already acquired. The early-morning sun felt warm on her bare shoulders, while the cool waves tickled her toes.

A small whitewashed beach house, small compared to the enormous mansion, stood near the ocean while the Demakis residence lay almost two miles inland. Leaving Tyler to Venetia in the afternoons, she had taken to walking the two miles, enjoying the quiet.

Ten days had flown by since she had let herself be cornered by Nikos in the garage, since she had lost it in front of him like that. But instead of anger that he had toyed with her, it was the fact that he had no interest that bothered her more.

Which meant she really needed her head examined. Because with everything else going on, Nikos's lack of interest in her should be the high point of her life right now. Bad enough that she had to spend time with him in the morning, and evening, to feel his gaze on her, always a curious light in it.

Every morning brought a new facet of Venetia's wrath that Lexi was here, revealing her frustration that Tyler couldn't remember. Nikos hadn't been joking when he had warned her about his sister. But even with the elaborate schemes that Venetia hatched to help Tyler remember, Lexi only saw her gnawing fear, her love for him. Lexi understood the fear the dark emotion in Venetia's eyes caused Nikos.

Hearing Tyler's tread on the sand behind her, Lexi turned around with a smile.

Dark shadows swam under his eyes, his face drawn. She sat up straight, her stomach tight. "You remembered something?"

Sinking to his knees next to her, he shook his head. His mouth a bitter curve, he clasped her face. "How can you bear to even look at me, Lex?"

Cold fear swept through Lexi. "What are you talking about, Ty?"

"Venetia told me what I said to you when you came to see us that day."

"Why?"

"I guess to remind me how much I wanted you gone. Except, it didn't work like she wanted." He fisted his hands, his mouth tight. "I want to leave, Lex. There are so many things I have to apologize for. I don't want to be here another minute."

Stricken by the bitterness in his gaze, Lexi clasped his hand. Her throat stung with unshed tears, but she forced herself to say it, forced herself to see the truth she had been dancing around for so many days. "Listen, Ty. Yes, you hurt me. But I've no doubt that there was a reason behind it. This is you and me, Ty. We do this a lot. We fight, we yell and we make up. It's just that this time things are different."

He ran a hand through his hair, his gaze pained. "I… can't believe I said those hurtful things to you, Lex, on top of everything else…"

Lexi felt as though someone was sitting on her chest. "It's all forgiven, Ty. Truly."

His blue gaze shone with affection, his palms clasped her cheeks. The familiar smell of him settled in her gut, infinitely comforting.

"I messed up everything with us so badly. And now, I have to break Venetia's heart, too. I—"

Clasping his face in her palms, Lexi shook her head. "I have no idea what went wrong." Her breath faltered in her throat. It would never go back to what it had been. But her love for Tyler, it would never waver. Knowing that Nikos would roast her alive for it, she said the words. "You don't have to decide anything now, Tyler. About Venetia. Do you understand?"

His eyes glittering with the same pain, he shook his head. "I can't face myself right now much less Venetia. You're all I've ever had in the world, and I hurt you."

Lexi closed her eyes as he pulled her closer and pressed his mouth to hers. But the only thing she felt was a sense of comfort, and a growing desolation as an inescapable truth began to inch around her heart. It was the loss of a dream more than anything else. Had he felt this same desolation that day? Had he known that something was irrevocably wrong between them but hadn't known how to tell her?

He met her gaze, the same realization dawning in his. "We're going to be all right, Lex."

They were. Lexi curled into him and hugged him tight. He had always been there for her, had always made her feel as if she mattered to at least one person in the world, that she wasn't an unwanted orphan. They had no future together except as friends. The realization instead of hurting her only strengthened her.

She had her only friend in the world back, and she wanted nothing more.

Her skin prickled, the hair on her neck standing to attention. Without turning, Lexi knew it was not Venetia.

Nikos was close.

Bracing herself, she didn't know for what, especially because she was doing what he wanted her to do, she turned around.

And stared up at the open terrace of the beach house where Nikos and Venetia stood. They looked like a vengeful Greek goddess and god, come to cast a curse on them.

Focus on reality, Lexi.

She felt Tyler stiffen next to her and squeezed his hand. "Don't do this, Ty," she whispered in his ear, knowing that whatever her faults, Venetia did love him. "I'll always love you but there's nothing more between us. Don't ruin what you have with her."

Tyler turned toward her, a sad smile on his face. "If I really loved her enough to hurt *you,* it will come back, Lex. But no more of Venetia looking at you as if you were the cause of her problems, no more of her brother looking at you as if he wants to devour you."

Stunned, Lexi looked up.

His hand on his sister, and his gaze calculatingly blank, Nikos held Venetia there. Probably stopping her from running down the stairs to gouge Lexi's eyes out.

Lexi untangled herself from Tyler. Amnesia or not, heartbreaking realization that something between her and Tyler was right or not, she had kissed Venetia's fiancé.

Feeling as dirty as Nikos was paying her to be, she walked away.

Nikos stayed on the roof long after Venetia ran down the stairs after Tyler, tears streaming down her face.

The very tears he had wanted to stop her from shedding. He felt powerless, but he also knew that she needed to shed them now. Better she found the truth now than when it was too late, when her love had an even more powerful grip on her.

But the powerlessness he felt was nothing compared to the dark cavern of longing that rent him open at the sight of Tyler kissing Lexi.

Again, it was exactly what Nikos had wanted. He should be elated that, even now, Venetia was kicking Tyler out of her life. And yet all he could hear was the roaring in his ears, a possessive yearning to wipe the taste of that kiss from Lexi's mouth.

He wanted that hungry look in her eyes when she looked at him. He wanted to make her mewl with pleasure. He wanted to shower her with every possible decadent gift in the world. He wanted to possess her, he wanted to teach her to be selfish, he wanted to show her every pleasure there was to have in the world.

He wanted a part of her, that intangible element in her that made her *her.*

It took him a few minutes to get himself under control, to fight the urge to trace Tyler's steps and beat him down to a pulp, to shove the desire that thrummed in his blood into one corner.

The pleasure he had pursued had only ever been transient, and he had liked it that way. But now he wanted Lexi. And not just for a night. He wanted to understand what made her tick, he wanted to hold her when she cried, he wanted to show her the world.

And he would have her.

Stepping from under the lukewarm blast of the shower spray, Lexi grabbed a beach towel from the neatly folded stack and wrapped it around herself.

Wiping herself down in the deafening quiet of the beach

house, she pulled on her gym shorts and a pink tank top and threw her damp swimsuit into her bag. Venetia might have an army of servants to pick up after her, but she didn't feel comfortable leaving her dirty clothes for someone else. Even more so now that she was leaving.

A hollow pang went through her and she fought the silly sensation. She wasn't going to mope over a man who had nothing but mockery for her. And even if he did want her, taking on someone like Nikos Demakis, even for one night, wasn't something she wanted.

She had hardly handled the fallout with Tyler. Nikos would chew her up and spit her out, leaving her no place to hide, even from herself.

She pushed her feet into the flip-flops and tugged her beach bag onto her shoulder, looking around for a switch to turn off the lights around the small pool.

"Leave it on, Lexi," The words came from somewhere behind her, rendering her frozen for a few seconds.

She whirled around. "Nikos," she said stupidly, her heart still racing. "I thought you had left."

"And miss the chance to chat with you?"

In the low lights of the pool, she couldn't quite make out his features. Except for the rigid set of his mouth and the tension pouring out of him. "I really don't have the energy to argue with you, Nikos."

"You're not going anywhere until we have this discussion."

He was wearing a charcoal-gray dress shirt, the cuffs rolled back, and black trousers that hugged his hips. A couple of buttons were undone giving her a peek of golden-olive chest.

His sensuous mouth flattened into a thin line of displeasure, he leaned against the far wall, legs crossed at the ankles. But there was nothing casual in the way he looked at her.

"What happened with Tyler?"

"Venetia told him what he'd said to me that night at the party. He feels awful about it. Nikos, he—"

"Ahh…so everything is perfect in your little world again."

"What do you mean?"

"He's come back to you, just as I predicted."

Tension pulled at her nerves. He thought Tyler was done with Venetia. "You don't understand—"

"I do. Better than you think. I understand the crippling loneliness, the need to matter to someone, the need to be loved. But you are better than this, better than him. Tell me you're not going back to him."

"That's really none of your business, is it?" she said, pushing off the wall. She was goading him. But she couldn't stop. "You're not my pimp, or my boss."

And he took the bait.

He was in front of her before she could blink. His hands braced on the wall either side of her, he slanted his upper body just enough that she could smell the purely masculine scent of him, so that she could see the evening stubble on his jaw, so that she could feel the heat radiating off him and blanketing her in a sensuous swathe.

His mouth hovered inches from hers, and she wanted to close the distance between them with a raw ache that blinded her to everything else.

"Is there no end to your stupidity?"

She dragged her gaze to his, heat creeping up across her neck and into her cheeks. "Everything's going according to your sordid plan. Why do you care what I do?"

"I'm trying to protect you from yourself. Are you so infernally stupid to believe that's the real him or that he won't throw you away the moment he remembers everything? Or do you plan to sleep with him and seal the deal this time?"

"There's nothing to seal, okay?" She struggled to draw a breath, to form a coherent thought, cringing from the pain he could so easily inflict on her. "I've loved him since I was thirteen, and yes, I slept with him. But it was awful. Just as awful the next time too and then I just kept finding excuses to not do it. We had this horrible fight and he left me—he moved out. Are you satisfied? He's all I have in this world, but there's nothing left between him and me."

"You baited me." Instead of the anger she expected, a tight smile split his mouth. His gaze shone with a wicked fever. And Lexi regretted her behavior. Her attraction to him, it was frying her mind. "Why kiss him then?"

"Again. None of your business."

He tugged her close to him in a quick movement, with his hands on her hips, bringing her off the ground. With a gasp, she clutched his shirt, bunching the crisp fabric in her fingers.

His erection rubbed against her belly. It felt hard, and so unbearably, unbelievably good that she moaned loud. Arrows of pleasure sparked off every inch of her.

Her gaze flew to his, her skin on fire. "Nikos…"

"Yes, Lexi."

He was smiling, a wicked, buckle-your-knees smile. She was on fire and he was smiling. "This, you and I…I can't…this feels like…" She swallowed, barely catching the whimper of pleasure in her throat.

His hands spanning her tiny waist, he pressed an openmouthed kiss, wet and hot against the pulse in her neck. Nerve endings she hadn't known existed thundered into life. Her arms around his neck, she held on tight, every drag of her muscles against his sending a spasm through her.

His hands moved from her waist to capture her face, forcing her to look at him. Her mouth dried at the naked hunger dancing across those arresting features. There was a black, molten fire in his eyes and it was all for her. "What you do to me, it isn't amusing in the least."

The open, toe-curling want in his words set a low, pulsing ache in her lower belly. She closed her eyes and struggled to pull in air.

Nikos Demakis, the most gorgeous man she had ever seen, wanted her. That in itself had her shivering, and the storm of hunger he was holding back in his powerful body…it was as if every decadent fantasy of hers had come to life. And she…she was still just her…plain Lexi Nelson.

How was she supposed to say no to him?

Too tight in her own skin, she rubbed herself against him. Their mingled groans rent the air, the rasp of his body fully clothed against hers, pure torture. A shudder racked his powerful body, a string of Greek, curses she was sure, pervading the air.

She did it again, and he pushed her back against the wall, his hands spanning her tiny waist.

Lust stamped his features. "Don't do that, *thee mou.* Unless you want me to take you against the wall. Not that I won't oblige you if that's what you want."

"Wait." Panic bloomed in her stomach at the raw tingle that swept through her. She had to put a stop to this, now. While she still could. "Please, Nikos. Let me go."

He let her go instantly, his gaze devouring her. His silence screamed at her, his face a feral mask of control.

"I'm sorry. I didn't mean to lead… The fact that you want me, it's dangerous, it's gone to my head…." She took a deep breath. This was not fair, to him or to her.

"I don't think there's a woman alive who could say no to you. But I…"

"Every time you look at me with those blue eyes, you're wondering how it would feel to kiss me. Your body, whether you don't know it, or you know it and don't want to accept it, is crying for my touch."

She wrapped her hands around herself. "It is, but I have control over it. I won't have sex with just anyone, without involving my heart."

His mouth curled into a sneer. "No, you will only have sex with a friend, for whom you're an emotional crutch and nothing else, to stop him from leaving you, even if you don't really want it, no? You're prepared to go to any lengths, give up anything to keep him in your life. Who's using sex now?"

Every word out of his mouth was the utter, inescapable truth. Only she hadn't seen it until now. It coated her mouth with distaste, twisted the biggest relationship of her life, the only one, to a painful, jagged mass.

Was that what everything between her and Tyler had been reduced to? Had she clung to him all these years knowing that things weren't right? She couldn't bear the desolate thought. "You don't know what you are talking about. You just can't understand what the big deal is, why Venetia and I are willing to go to any lengths for Tyler. Because you're incapable of understanding it, of feeling *anything,* and it's beginning to annoy the hell out of you."

His face could have been a mask poured out of concrete. Every muscle in his face froze in contrast to the blistering emotion in his gaze. It put paid to her stupid claim that he didn't feel anything. "You little hypocrite. I saw you when he kissed you. You couldn't wait to get away and yet you clung to him. You want to know how it feels when you feel the opposite, Lexi, when you can't wait to rip off someone's clothes?"

She could have said that she already knew—that it was all she wanted to do when she was near him. But he didn't give her the chance. Pressing his upper body into hers, he nudged a thigh between her legs and claimed her mouth.

Her shocked gasp was lost in his mouth. The stubble on his chin scratched her sensitive skin, the hard angles of his body imprinted on her and she shivered as he nipped at her mouth, knocking the breath out of her.

He didn't kiss her gently like Tyler had done. It was as if the storm had burst, as if he had been waiting forever to do it, as if his next breath depended on kissing her. His hands stole under her T-shirt until his hot palms were laid flat on her bare flesh.

His tongue licked the inside of her lower lip, sucked at her tongue, stroked her to a high that she had to climb.

It was a kiss with pure erotic intent, it was a kiss to possess her senses, it was a kiss to prove his point. But he didn't know that he didn't need to. She was already a slave to her body's wants and desires when she was near him.

A moan rose through her throat and misted into the darkness as he sank his teeth into her lower lip. An electric shiver tingled up her spine as a million nerve endings sprang into life, both pain and pleasure coalescing and shooting down between her legs.

The wetness at her sex shocked and aroused her even more.

She groaned loud, a whimper to stop and a plea to continue, all rolled into one. Her knees trembled and she rubbed against the hard thigh lodged against her throbbing core, mindless with aching need.

His hands gentled in her hair, his hard muscles pulled

back from her. He murmured something in Greek. She shivered as he blew a soft breath on her throbbing lower lip. Something almost like an apology reached her ears.

He claimed her lips again, but this time, he was exploring, teasing, and it was the unexpected gentleness that broke the spell for her.

With a grunt, she pushed him back from her, her chest rising and falling with the effort it took to pull air into her lungs. "No," she whispered into the darkness. And then repeated it louder for her sake more than his. "No, Nikos."

The dark intent in his eyes scared her, her own powerlessness in the face of the blazing fire between them scared her. If he touched her again, if he kissed her again, she wouldn't say no. She couldn't say no.

He was the first man to incite knee-buckling desire in her. Why did he have to be so out of her league, so different from who she was?

And look how things panned out with your best friend, an insidious voice whispered in her ear.

She ran the back of her hand over her trembling lips. The taste of him wasn't going to come off so easily. "I don't love you. I…"

He jerked back slowly, his gaze incredulous. "Have you still not learned the lesson? Your love for Tyler blinded you to everything, crippled you into not living your life. You still want that love?"

"I don't know what you're talking about."

"Tyler had an affair with Faith behind your back. He cheated on you with your friend."

She raised her head and looked at him, fury and self-disgust roiling through her. "You're making this up… you're…"

Her desperation had no end, it seemed. If Nikos had

been angry before, he was a seething cauldron of fury now. Taking her arms in a gentle grip that pricked through her, he set her away from him.

"I'm an unfeeling bastard, true. And I've no misconceptions about what or who I am. However, I don't settle for what people throw at me. I don't let them treat me like trash."

She closed his mouth with her hand, and sagged against him. "I had no idea about Tyler and Faith. That they even liked each other that way. I…"

There it was, the tiny truth that been evading her for so many months, the last piece in the puzzle that threatened to pull her under.

She had done all this.

She finally understood why Tyler had called her selfish. Because he had felt bound to her by his guilt, because even though there had been proof enough that they could never be more than friends, she hadn't wanted to let him go, because her refusal to move on had meant he couldn't move on, either.

Because she had been the one who had gone to juvie, even though both of them had been responsible for the robbery.

All because she had been scared to live her own life.

So many times, Tyler had asked her to apply to a college somewhere else, asked her to change her job, always encouraged her to reach for more, to take a risk and she… she had been scared to leave his side, scared to venture into an unknown life, amongst unknown people because she had been terrified of being alone.

Of having no one who loved her, of mattering to no one. And so she had continued on her little merry way, clinging to Tyler, clinging to Faith, ruining all their lives in the process. She had convinced herself that he loved her, that she loved him in a way she hadn't, forced herself and guilted him.

And that's what he was doing again. He was leaving Venetia, breaking her heart because he felt guilty about how he had treated Lexi. And Lexi couldn't let him do that anymore.

She couldn't be a coward anymore.

Straightening her shoulders, she looked at Nikos. Fear was a primal tattoo in her head that she had to mute long enough to speak. For the first time in her life, she wanted something. She wanted to be with Nikos, she wanted to revel in the desire she felt for him.

She had to do it now, before she lost her nerve, before she forgot how many lives she had ruined because she had been scared, before she crawled back into her safe little place and let life pass her by.

She had to let Tyler go, she had to set herself free. If she fell, he would be there to catch her. He always would. She knew that now. Which meant it was time to start living.

"You want me, Nikos? You got me," she said, knowing that there was no turning back now.

A blaze of fire leaped into life in his gaze. He took another step closer. Instinctively, she stepped back and the wall kissed her spine. Her breath came in ragged little whispers as he placed his palm on her midriff, right beneath her breast. It spanned most of her waist. Her pulse leaped at her throat, and immediately, she closed her eyes.

His fingers moved up, traced the shape of her breasts, and she arched into his touch. "Look at me, Lexi. You don't have to hide from this."

She did, and his gaze held hers. She took his mouth in a hard kiss that stoked the flames in his eyes a little more. "I won't hide anymore, Nikos, or hold back. I want everything you can give me."

His fingers kept moving over her body, over her breasts, her hips, until they came to rest on her butt. He cupped her and pulled her close. The heavy weight of his arousal pressing into her belly, it was the most sinful sensation ever.

Every muscle in her body turned into molten liquid, ready to be molded into whatever he wanted. She gripped his nape and wrapped her legs around his hips. His breath coated her skin, his fingers found the seam of her bra all the while he nibbled at her lips.

He was everywhere, in her breath, in her skin, in her every cell, and she wanted to do nothing but sink into him, to give herself over into his hands.

Suddenly, he wasn't kissing her anymore, and Lexi whimpered. Her heart slowly returning to its normal beat, she blinked and realized why he had stopped.

Nikos's head of security stood on the other side of the pool. His thumb running over her cheek, Nikos grinned. "We're not done."

Lexi nodded and tried not to sink back into the wall. Her breathing still choppy, she moved to stand behind Nikos, heat streaking her cheeks.

She watched Nikos talk to the other man with increasing agitation, until a curse flew from his mouth that reverberated in the silence. Her gut feeling heavy, Lexi reached him just as his head of security left. She clasped Nikos's arm, despite the angry energy pouring off of him. "Nikos, what happened?"

"Venetia and Tyler have been gone all afternoon." He clicked Call on his cell and waited. "And she's not picking up."

"I don't understand. What do you mean they've been—"

He ran a shaking hand through his hair, the color leaching from his skin. "The maids saw her pack a bag. Tyler's clothes are missing, too. And apparently one of her friends picked them up in a boat. They have left." She stilled as another curse fell from his mouth, ringing with his worry.

Without another word to her, he was gone.

CHAPTER EIGHT

WHAT HAPPENED WHEN Lexi Nelson, delusional coward extraordinaire, decided to finally live her life and throw herself at a six-foot-three-inch hunk of Greek alpha male who had a woman in every city?

Said Greek stud apparently lost all interest in sex because his sister ran away to God-knows-where with her lover, who happened to be Lexi's best friend, in tow.

So instead of living her fantasy, Lexi was getting a peek into Athens's nightlife with Nikos alternately cursing and glowering at her, apparently having easily dismissed any attraction he had felt for her in the first place.

This time, she was really pissed off with the Greek heiress.

Lexi had known Venetia had cared for Tyler, but she hadn't expected her to spirit Tyler away from under her brother's nose. All because Tyler had kissed Lexi.

If only Venetia knew the truth…

In her heart, Lexi was glad Venetia had refused to allow Tyler to simply bow out of her life. If only she could take away the guilt and worry shining in Nikos's eyes…that and the fact Nikos hadn't even looked at her, much less touched her again.

Every night for the past four days, Nikos, intent on interrogating every man or woman Venetia had ever spoken to, or even looked at, had dragged her to a multitude of dazzling nightclubs and lavish penthouses, each more decadently rich and sophisticated than the last.

This view into his sphere of life had her senses spinning. For the first two days, she had been awed, almost enjoying the glimpse she was getting into a life she could only imagine about.

Except each visit had steadily chipped away at her already frayed self-confidence. Everywhere they went women—tall, beautiful and sexy—threw themselves at Nikos. She might as well have been an alien existing in a different galaxy.

Really, it was a testament to the man's focus, and his love for his sister, that he hadn't spared any of them even a second look.

She was beginning to believe Nikos might have been delirious that evening four days ago. She would have easily called herself delirious, except she couldn't forget how mind-bendingly good it had felt to be cradled against his powerful body, how the simple caress of his mouth against her neck had branded her.

Had his desire for her already cooled off? She'd braced for that to happen *after,* not before he even kissed her again. And it stung.

With a curt "stay here," he had dumped her in the private lounge of the nightclub almost forty-five minutes ago.

The nightclub was a glorious spectacle with live dancers on raised platforms on either side of the dance floor. Soft purple lights illuminated the crowd below. White couches, white columns, white tables—all soaked up the light giving a sultry vibe to the club. And having noticed the lines outside the entrance and the small crowd inside, she had no doubt it was an exclusive type.

Judging however by the curious, almost-hungry looks

thrown up at the private lounge where she was sitting, she realized it was the private lounges that were the main attraction. And she could see why.

Separated and placed discreetly above the main party floor, the VIP lounge, enclosed by glass walls on all sides, offered a perfect view of the club. She sat on the edge of the provocative sofa bed, the leather luxuriously soft under her touch.

Amidst the crowd and music, she found Nikos as easily as if he was her honing beacon.

Leaning against the wall on the opposite side of the club, he was talking to a tall, curvy blonde. Her upper body was slanted toward him in an unmistakable invitation. Despite black envy scouring her, Lexi couldn't find fault with her.

Nikos Demakis would tempt any woman.

She was about to leave the private lounge when a bartender walked in to serve cocktails. The easy smile in the bartender's eyes boosted her flagging spirit. She took a sip of the cocktail as he left, placed it back on the table and started moving to the steamy number playing softly. She was not going to let Nikos's indifference to her ruin her evening any longer.

Refusing Venetia's friend's blatant invitation, which held zero interest for him, Nikos pushed his way through the crowd. His frustration must have been apparent because more than one group of people jumped out of his way.

He had severely underestimated Venetia's determination, her envy for Lexi. Before meeting her, he would have called Tyler and his fickle mind the root of Venetia's insecurity. There was no such doubt in his mind now.

Lexi might not be gorgeous, or sophisticated, or wealthy, yet there was something about her that made one look deep inside and come away wanting. He perfectly understood what his sister must have felt.

In four days of his security team and Nikos himself following several leads, there was no information about where she and Tyler had gone. He was beginning to believe his sister would return only when and if she wished it.

In the meantime, Savas was tightening the screws further, Theo Katrakis was ready to start discussions about the board and then there was Lexi, who with her mere existence was spinning his life out of control.

Four days of Lexi, waiting alongside him worried about what Venetia would do to her blasted friend, four days of Lexi looking at him with those big, blue eyes.

You want me, Nikos? You got me.

Never had a woman's acceptance to have sex with him, which put in those base terms felt like an insult to her, never had such simple words moved through him with such power.

He walked up the steps to the private lounge. He halted outside the entrance and pushed the door open.

She was moving in time to the music slowly, her short white skirt displaying her toned legs perfectly. Soft revolving lights from outside the lounge revealed her laughing mouth and warm eyes in strips and flashes. The delicate curve of her neck came into view next, the silver of her earrings glinted.

The sleeveless black leather vest hugged her, displaying the curves of her small breasts. With her hands up and behind her head, she moved so sensuously to the music that lust bolted through him. Every time she turned, that vest moved upward, flashing him with a strip of her midriff.

A lush smile played on her lips and she was totally lost in the moment. He closed the door behind him and she turned slowly.

Her eyes rounded in her delicate face. He waited for her to drop her gaze, shy away, but she held his gaze, even as a dusting of pink streaked her cheeks. She was different, and not just because of how she was dressed, but the tilt of her chin, the resolve in her eyes.

"Did she—" Lexi nodded toward the dance floor "—know anything about where Venetia could have taken Tyler?"

"We have no idea who's taken whom."

She frowned. "Tyler is unwell, has no money or connections, and the last I saw him, he was determined to not hurt Venetia. Are you the one with amnesia or him? Because you seem to have forgotten everything that happened four days ago completely."

She walked past him and the whisper of her scent had his gut tightening in a burst of need. His body was over-sensitized to her presence, wound tight in anticipation of wanting her, driven to the edge by having her near and not taking, or touching. And yet he had stopped himself.

He had spilled Tyler's indiscretion with Faith in a perverse moment of selfishness, acting directly against his own larger purpose of having her here.

It was a weak, impulsive, juvenile, completely uncharacteristic move.

And suddenly, his control over this thing between them, his control over his spiraling desire for her, over the maelstrom of emotions she released in him, was more important than anything else.

Because even his worry over Venetia hadn't blunted his awareness of this woman. "No, I haven't forgotten."

Her blue eyes held that same shimmering honesty that he had come to expect from her. "That woman, she wanted you. Wherever we go, there is always at least one woman who wants you."

Her statement was in reality a question. For the past four days, he had been only thinking of himself.

She had obviously taken his distance to mean that he didn't want her anymore.

His desire for her was a near-constant hum in his blood. And it was the very intensity of it that had shackled him. Lust had ever been only a function of his body until now, not his mind or heart. "I don't want her or any of them." He knew what she wanted to hear, yet some devil in him wanted her to ask, wanted to hear her admit it again.

Now, when she wasn't still reeling from the truth about Tyler; now, when it was only Nikos that she saw. And nothing else.

Her teeth clamped on her lower lip, she straightened her shoulders. And rose to the challenge. "Are you still interested in me?"

He laid his palm horizontally on her rib cage, felt her heart race under his fingers. "What do you think?"

She pushed herself into his touch, her gaze challenging him. "Then what are you waiting for?"

"You want this because you're angry with Tyler, hurt by what he did."

"I'm not hurt by what he did. If I didn't have to worry about you, I could actually be enjoying this glimpse into your filthy rich life right now."

Furious surprise rolled through him. "You are worried about me?" The question hurled out of him before he knew.

"Of course I am. Anyone with eyes can see how much you love Venetia, how worried you are about her. That night after they left, you spent the whole night looking for her. And I..." She took a deep breath, "I don't want *anyone* to be hurt at the end of this. Not Tyler, not Venetia and definitely not you. And I don't know how to tell you to not worry so much, how to make you see that she's far stronger than you give her credit for. She saw me kissing Tyler, Nikos, and she didn't crumble."

"You think that's the only sign of her weakness? She saw my father shoot himself. It has hurt her in ways I can't understand."

She clasped his hand with hers, willing him to look at her. A shaft of sensation traveled up his arm. She was so tiny, so delicate compared to him. "Tyler won't let her do anything, Nikos. What happened between him and me, it was just as much my fault. He would never do anything to hurt her."

"He was ready to walk out on her. That's what I said he would do."

"Yes, but because he wanted to do the right thing by her. Doesn't that tell you something? Or are you just too stubborn to see it?"

"I'm not discussing them with you."

"Don't. Believe me, I don't want to, either. Venetia's probably having the time of her life, and here I am, stuck with you. You hold me responsible for everything that's happening—"

"I don't hold you responsible for any of this. I just don't trust you to tell me if Tyler contacts you."

Lexi clamped her mouth shut. There was no point in even denying it. He knew her too well. "Okay, fine. But I don't have a phone and I don't think I can even sneeze on the island without you knowing, so can we stop with you dragging me around like unwanted baggage?"

"Unwanted baggage, *thee mou?*"

"You look at me as though you want to open a space portal and throw me through it. Do you understand what it took for me to say those words to you last week?"

He tugged her hands higher and tighter as his lower body pressed into hers. Lexi closed her eyes and fought for some much-needed oxygen. Her skin felt as if it was on fire, her limbs molten with longing. "Ever since I realized what a pathetic idiot I have been all these years, I have also realized that I'm not completely without appeal."

He grinned and she pressed on, growing bolder. When he smiled like that, she wanted to roll over in the warmth of it. She wanted to press her mouth to his and revel in it. "I might not be packing in the boob and leg department and probably hold little attraction to a man with refined tastes like you, but there are other fish in the sea. Cute, dimpled, down-to-earth fish like Piers, for example, who find me attractive and wouldn't dream of calling me any names in a million—"

His muscled thigh lodged between her legs and Lexi whimpered. For a man so big, he was so incredibly well-coordinated. Just the thought of all that finesse and power focused on her had her tingling in all kinds of places. "Who the hell is Piers?"

"Piers is the bartender who's been serving me cocktails."

"And he likes you?"

She nodded. "Yes."

His teeth clamped tight, he nodded. And she had the strangest notion that he hadn't liked what she had said. Intensely. "So help me understand, *thee mou.* Just any man with a working…" His gaze glimmered with a dark amusement. "Any man will do for this new risk-taking life of yours?"

She pushed at him, fighting the heat spreading up her neck. She was not going to back down from this. So she just evaded. "You're being purposely crude."

"Sex is all you want from me?"

"I… Yes, of course." She was getting good at lying. But then it was easy, because she didn't know what else she wanted from him. And she didn't want to know, either. She had never feared her feelings before or what they drove her to. But with everything she had learned about Tyler, with everything Nikos made her face, she preferred to not have any feelings right now. "You said it yourself. Sex should not be complicated." And she wanted it with the most complicated man she had ever met, whatever he thought of himself.

Nikos ran his thumb over her lower lip, his gaze drinking her in. Stepping back from her, he shrugged off his leather jacket. The V-necked gray shirt stretched tight across his muscled chest hugged his lean waist. "There should be a sign somewhere here. Find it."

Frowning, Lexi stared at the door. Shaking her head, she looked around the lounge. Tension pinged across her skin as she found it.

Do Not Disturb.

Her heart jumped to her throat. She held up the matte sign just as Nikos walked back in.

Meeting her gaze, he smiled. "Hang it on the doorknob and close the door."

The cardboard sign slipped from her fingers. Her skin tingled as his gaze stayed on her, challenging. Molten heat flared through her as she realized his intentions. Her knees shook, her entire body felt like a pool of liquid longing and anticipation.

She looked around the room to the huge glass to her right that gave a perfect view of the dance floor and the crowd below. She was not a virgin. Granted, the two times she had slept with Tyler had been almost painfully awkward. But with the tremble in her knees, the soft but persistent tug in her lower belly, she might as well have been one.

"Here? Now?"

Nikos came to a halt with an arm's length between them,

his gaze devouring her. He handed her the champagne glass. "Yes, here. Now. Is there a problem?"

Suddenly, Lexi felt hyperaware of everything around her. Her skin, the ratcheting beat of her heart, her breath rushing in and out, the din of the crowd below and Nikos—tall, gorgeous and within touching distance.

He moved to stand behind her. His hands landed on her waist, spanning it with his long fingers. She could feel every finger, every ridge of his palm on her skin.

"That glass is one-way."

His words rumbled over her skin. Lexi turned to look at him. "They can't see us?"

The heat from his mouth seared through her skin, his fingers slowly kneading her hips. "No."

She sucked in a much-needed breath. His hands moved to her rib cage and held her tight against him.

"They can't see us or hear us. This is what I want, Lexi. Are you ready for it?" Warm breath feathered over her ear, before he ran his tongue over the outer shell.

Lexi clutched his forearms, a shiver running through her.

She turned in his arms and looked up at him. His brown gaze dark, his aquiline nose flared. The liquid desire in his eyes, the feel of his rough palm over her bare arms, it was everything she wanted. Slipping from his grasp, she took the sign from the floor. She had no idea how she did it with her legs shaking beneath her, but she hung the sign and closed the door.

CHAPTER NINE

NIKOS STRUGGLED TO hold the lust rocketing through him in check and failed completely. She closed the door and stood there, the line of her back an inviting temptation. The strip of flesh exposed between the hem of her short skirt and her knee-high boots was the most erotic thing he had ever seen.

A shiver took root in his muscles. His nerves stretched taut, he felt as if he was the one taking a risk, as if he was the one who was new to sex.

He settled down into the luxurious sofa bed with his back against the wall. She turned around and leaned against the wall. Pink streaked her cheeks. Her mouth pursed and then opened.

"Come here, *agape mou.*"

Her shoulders tensed, and he thought she would flee in a streak of white and black.

Instead, she walked toward him, her gaze unmoving from his.

Doubts and questions pummeled through him with every step she took. They were as strange to him as the strength of his desire.

There was no shyness in her gaze, but there was no boldness, either. This was important to her, whatever lies she spouted. And that realization tempered his desire. She didn't know how to play by his rules.

He fought the protective urge that rose up inside him, shoved it away with a ruthlessness that had helped him survive, and win, against all odds.

He needed to stop making this moment more than it was. She wanted him. He wanted her. He wasn't going to change himself, wasn't going to start wondering about her feelings just because she was different.

That was the cause for his conscience ringing like a bell inside him.

She was different from the women he usually slept with. Not one of them had made an effort to know what was beneath his ambition or his drive. Or maybe there hadn't been anything worth knowing before. She was the first person who had looked beneath the surface, who had realized that a man, with fears and wishes no less, existed beneath it all. Even after everything he had done to manipulate her, made her face, she wished him well, she worried about him.

He took her hand in his and pulled her down to the sofa. He leaned back on the wide sofa bed so that she sat between his legs. His gut felt tight with want, every muscle in him poised for pleasure and possession. He wrapped his hands around her midriff, and kissed the crook of her neck. She tasted of lemon soap and vanilla. He closed his eyes, praying for control. She was so delicate under his touch, she felt breakable in his hands. And even through the anticipation coiling within every inch of him, lust heating through his blood, Nikos admitted one thing to himself.

He didn't want to hurt her. The sentiment was both strange and strong.

The soft flick of Nikos's tongue against her neck knocked the breath out of Lexi's lungs. He was like a tightly toned fortress of need. And yet he held her loosely, as if she would break.

Every press of hard muscle, every caress of his fingers, fueled her own need. She laced her fingers through his and held on tighter. Throwing her neck back, she gave him better access, liquid longing bursting into life inside her. "Kiss me, Nikos."

With agility she couldn't believe, he flipped her easily until she sat astride him. His hands remained on her knees. She moved to steady herself, and instantly, her aching sex rubbed against the hard ridge of his erection.

The sound of their mingled moans, desire and need, lust and want, reverberated in the room around them.

His mouth found hers in a fury of want; his hands on her thighs limited her movement severely. She struggled in his hold and moved over the hard ridge of his arousal.

"No, *thee mou,*" he said, before capturing her mouth again.

He didn't kiss her like he had done at the pool. He kissed her softly, slowly, as though he had all the time in the world, as though there was no intensity to his need at all.

His tongue licked her lower lip and pressed for entry. Sinking her hands into his hair, Lexi let him in. Pleasure, unlike she had ever known before, bloomed in the pit of her stomach and arrowed downward.

Needing more than he was giving her, she clasped his jaw and forced him to look at her.

"More, Nikos," she whispered, her words falling over each other.

In response, he sucked her lower lip into his mouth with incredible gentleness. She sneaked her hands in under his shirt and found hot skin. The minute she touched his nipple, he jerked back and pulled her hands out.

Every time, she got closer to him, he held her off.

Lexi pressed a desperate kiss to his mouth and slipped out of his lap. She swayed on her feet before she found her bearings, her body thrumming with unfulfilled desire. Color streaking across his cheeks, Nikos looked up. A stamp of lust tightened his features, but it was just that. A shadow.

Because it was control that reigned over him.

Something snapped inside Lexi. She had wanted to start living her life; she wanted to take a risk. And going to bed with Nikos Demakis was one. On every level there was. He had a hundred lovers where she'd had one. But even more than that, Nikos was a risk because he refused to let her hide, because he refused to let her shrink away from the truth, he didn't coddle her.

And she didn't want that to change.

She hugged her arms, and forced the words out. "This isn't what I want."

He stood up from the couch like a coiled spring, his face a tight mask. She kept her gaze on his, amazed at how steady he looked. His jaw was granite. "We will leave immediately."

"I don't want to leave."

He covered the distance between them and smiled. With his hands on her shoulders, he tugged her closer, and smiled. "It's okay. I shouldn't have started this here. I know you are new to all this…" He pressed a furious kiss to her mouth, his lips clinging devouring, until she couldn't breathe. That's what she wanted—his passion. "It's not the end of it, either." He pulled back, and this time he didn't sound so steady.

She pushed his hands away, her heart stuttering to a halt. "Stop trying to protect me, Nikos. You're acting just like Tyler."

His gaze blazed with anger. "I don't know what you are talking about. But you should know this. No man wants to hear the ex's name and definitely not like that."

"Then stop acting like him."

A curse fell from his mouth. "Explain."

"You are doing what you *think* I want. You're not being yourself."

"That's the most ridiculous thing I have ever heard."

"I'm not going to break, Nikos. I want honesty between us, whether it is in the way you make love to me, or when it's time for you to say we're done. You are controlling yourself, wondering if I will break, wondering if you will hurt me."

He pushed his hair back, and Lexi noticed he was not as in control as she thought. This was not the Nikos that had pushed her into admitting how much she wanted him. Something had changed in him; something had changed between them, and she didn't know what.

"I won't be responsible for hurting you. Despite everything I proposed and did, I never intended to."

"Then tell me…no wait, show me what you like. Do this…" She moved her hand between them. "Make love to me the way you would do it with Nina, or Emmanuelle."

He jerked back from her as though she had polluted the air by speaking those names in this moment between them. "*Christos!* Stop comparing yourself to them. I cannot forget everything I know about who and what you are."

Lexi bit her lower lip. Warmth that had nothing to do with desire and lust flew through her veins. He was making concessions for her. She didn't want him to, but she couldn't help being affected by it, either. "You'll hurt me more if you are not yourself, Nikos. I believe that Tyler… He only slept with me because he thought it would make me happy. I can't bear the thought that you are doing the same…"

"*Theos!* I can't think straight with wanting you. I've never spent so much time thinking about it instead of just doing it."

Her heart stuttered and started. She couldn't speak for the breath caught in her throat.

She was terrified of what she was doing, of where she was going with him. But mixed in with that fear was also a sense of rightness. She covered the distance between them and pulled him down for a kiss.

His lips were soft and firm against hers, his hands on her waist lifting her off the ground. His tongue delved into her mouth, seeking and caressing, his hands on her buttocks tucking her tight against the V of his legs.

Pulling her hands up, he slowly guided her to the wall behind him. A slow smile curved his lips. "You want to know what I like?"

"Yes."

"I would like for you to tell me what you want me to do. You have to ask me for it, *thee mou.*"

Her gaze flew to him, heat streaking her cheeks. For some reason, he was pushing her, expecting her to back out of this. She had no idea why. But she wouldn't let him win. "Fine."

She unbuttoned the metal clasps on her vest and the leather fell away inch by inch to reveal her heated skin. Her fingers were steady despite the butterflies in her stomach. There were at least a hundred people on the other side of the glass. But it was the darkening of Nikos's gaze that spread desire like wildfire through her. Her small breasts felt heavy, her nipples rigid and chafing against the lacy silk of her bra.

The sound of his jagged breaths filled the room. "I can't wait to touch your breasts, Lexi. I have been going out of my mind thinking about them."

He ran his knuckle over the strap of her bra, his gaze hungry and hard. Without touching her, he bent and licked the upper curve of her breast. Lexi jerked and arched her spine greedily into his touch.

His forearm kept her against the wall, stopping her from leaning into him. "Sorry, *thee mou*. I forgot my own rules. Now if you want something…"

She looked up at him, every nerve in her tuned tight. Her mouth was dry but need triumphed over shyness. She pulled his hand to her mouth and kissed his palm. "I want—" she swallowed at the need rippling through her "—you to… touch my breasts."

A lick of fire burst into life in his eyes and a curse fell from his mouth. The sound of it cocooned them in the room.

He dipped his head again. His hair tickled her jaw, his fingers tugging the silky lace down. Rough fingers traced circles around her nipple, again and again, sending shivers of pleasure through her. Finally, he flicked the taut, aching buds, pinched them between his fingers. And the throaty sound of her moan filled her ears.

He took her mouth in a stinging kiss. "Next?"

"Suck…" She was wet just thinking it. If his plan was to drive her crazy with lust, he was succeeding.

He smiled against her mouth, before tugging her lower lip between his teeth. She clutched her legs tight together, a pulse of need vibrating at her sex. "Yes?"

She closed her eyes and shamelessly pushed herself into his touch. "Please, Nikos."

"What. Do. You. Want, Lexi?"

"Suck my nipples into your mouth."

In response, he tugged her up until she was straddling his knee. His hard arousal rubbed exactly where she needed it. She moaned and moved. And then his mouth closed over her nipple.

His tongue laved it and then he sucked it into his mouth. A white-hot shaft of pure sensation arched between her legs. She moved, needing more. He straightened his leg, and she would have crumpled to the floor if he hadn't been holding her up. She whimpered aloud, just short of begging.

"What next?"

She opened her eyes and looked at him. Twin streaks of color highlighted his sharp cheekbones, and his features were stark, his gaze ablaze with lust. He was just as far gone as she was. If she could reduce this powerful man to this, there was nothing she couldn't do. She felt absolutely, powerfully feminine in that moment. She widened her legs just a little and pulled her skirt up. "Touch me between my legs, Nikos," she said, owning the words, owning the desire she felt.

His nostrils flared, his eyes were the deepest brown she had ever seen. "No please?"

She shook her head, her pulse vibrating in her entire body. "No please anymore. You want to do it just as much as I want it."

The most gorgeously sinful smile curved his mouth, digging deep grooves in his cheeks. "Take off your panties."

She reached under her skirt and tugged her panties down.

He took them from her shaking fingers and threw them behind him, the sight of her white panties in his rough hands erotic.

She was not naked, but under his scrutiny, she felt hot and exposed and all kinds of sexy.

"Don't look down." Nikos whispered the words into the curve of her breast.

Every inch of her skin hyperaware, Lexi kept her eyes on him, the languid curve of his mouth, the tight cast of his features, the way his breath hissed in and out....

She could stand there and drink him in all night.

Slow, sinuous need tugged in her lower belly. The hot

rasp of his roughened palm on her skin was a searing brand as his fingers crawled up her thighs, his mouth trailing wet heat between her breasts. Her nipples knotted with need.

His long fingers finally found the folds of her sex. He stroked and tugged, pulled with a relentless pressure that had her moaning his name, tension coiling in her lower belly.

She clutched his shoulders and he traced slick, maddening circles around her nipple. "Now what, *yineka mou?*"

His voice was gravelly, coarse and deep with hunger. She sank her hands into his hair and pushed the words out. "I want you to move your fingers, Nikos," she whispered. Her wanton desire tightened her need.

His fingers pushed inside her and she threw her head back. It felt intrusive, erotic, nothing like she had ever experienced before.

It was unrelenting, intense. "What do you want now?" he whispered, his words abraded and slow.

"Faster, Nikos."

He laughed and increased the pressure.

Nerve endings she didn't know existed bloomed into life. He tugged and stroked her, whispered words in Greek that only added to the havoc he was wreaking on her.

He pinched the tight bundle of nerves at her sex, just as his mouth sucked at her nipple, and she came violently, the waves of her orgasm unending as he continued the combined assault of his mouth and fingers.

She shuddered against him, her breath hitching painfully in and out.

She opened her eyes and stared into eyes darkened to a molten black with desire. He licked one long finger and the sheer eroticism of the act sent another wave of jagged sensation to her sex.

She felt alien in her body, a fierce freedom running through her veins.

"What do *you* want, Nikos?" she said, more than a hint of brazen challenge in her tone.

He didn't answer her. Fingers digging into her hips, he lifted her off the ground. Her thigh muscles still quivering from aftershocks, she wrapped her legs around his waist.

She heard the sound of the zipper of his jeans, of a condom being ripped, felt the shudder that went through him as he sheathed himself.

And then he was pushing inside her with a guttural sound that seemed to have been ripped from him. She clawed her hands into his shoulders, pleasure and pain coalescing inside her, the walls of her wet sex clamping him tight.

She threw her head back and a long whimper escaped her. His breath stilled, a long shudder racking his powerful body.

"More, *agape mou?*"

How he was able to utter a single word, Lexi had no idea. "Yes," she whispered, her throat raw, her body aching for more.

He pushed in a little more, stretching her, making her achy and hot all over. He was big and she was tiny, and the most decadent pleasure pulsed through her sex.

He did something with his hips that sent a pulse of pleasure sputtering through her. And then, he was deep inside her—hot and throbbing. And it felt painfully good, intensely erotic.

She opened her eyes and caught him studying her, stark desire and something that was entirely Nikos.

His features stripped of all control, his breathing shaky, he was the most gorgeous sight she had ever seen. Every bone and muscle locked tight, his gaze devoured her. "You're so tight, Lexi."

He pressed a kiss to her forehead, and Lexi braced herself against the reverent touch. A frown rippled over his face, his shoulders hard knots under her fingers.

"I'm afraid to move."

She was hot, and tingly and possessed, and she never wanted to stop feeling like that. "I can't bear it if you don't, Nikos." She moved her hips and gasped at how deep he was embedded, at how mind-numbingly good it felt.

Clutching his shoulders tight, Lexi buried her mouth in his neck. He tasted of sweat and musk, an incredibly erotic taste. She clamped her teeth over his skin and sucked hard. Instantly, his hips moved, and an incredible fire licked along her aching core again.

His curse felt like the sweetest words to her ears.

His gaze never moved from her. His breath feathered over her, the raw sounds that fell from his mouth enveloped her. He pulled out slowly, the length of his erection dragging against the walls of her sex, teasing and tormenting her. Until she felt his instant loss, until her body cried out to be possessed again.

And then he thrust back into her. He moved slow, hard and deep, and she trembled, awash with jagged sensations, bursting to full with a raw awareness. Every square inch of her thrummed with a fever, shuddered with the influx of sensation.

And he did it again and again.

Lexi cried out his name as need coiled again and burst into a million lights. Her throat was raw, her entire body was raw.

His skin was slick under her palms, his muscles bunching and flexing, every inch of him rigid with want that was all for her. To have him inside her, to hold this powerful man shuddering in her arms, it was the most powerful, most freeing thing she had ever felt.

Every time, he thrust into her, Lexi felt his control snap, his finesse slip and his desperation take over. Until a hoarse grunt fell from his lips and he became utterly still.

Lexi pushed his hair from his forehead and pressed a kiss to his lips, unable to hold herself back. She had known that sex with Nikos would be fantastic, earth-shattering. But the tenderness in his eyes, the soft, slow kiss he pressed to her mouth, as if she had given him the most precious gift ever, seared through her.

She had no defense against it. Except to tell herself that she was imagining things, that it was her innate need to bond with him, to make this more than it was.

It was amazing sex, and she wasn't going to let her insecurities ruin it.

She could do this. In fact, she would not only do this, but she would have the time of her life doing it. Fears and doubts, regrets and tears…she would have the rest of her life to indulge in once she was back in New York.

CHAPTER TEN

LEXI HAD JUST returned to the mansion from the beach the next afternoon when Nikos returned from wherever it was that he'd been. Wraparound shades shielded his expression from her as he stilled in the foyer at the sight of her. But she still felt his scrutiny as vividly as if he had laid those big hands of his over her skin. Her neck prickled, every inch of her skin stretched taut at his continued perusal.

"I am going to the other side of the island where the new hotel is being built. If you would like to accompany me, meet me at the entrance in fifteen minutes. Ask Maria to pack a change of clothes for you."

"I can do that myself but...I... Why?"

"I might have to stay there overnight. Do you want to be here alone? If you wish to, that is fine."

"No, I want to go. I will be ready in fifteen."

She made her way to her bedroom, more confused than ever.

Instead of the smoldering sexual tension between them cooling off, it had only thickened once he had straightened his clothes and then hers last night.

She had just stood there on shaking legs, the aftershock of her orgasm still rocking through her, her body still quivering at the assault of unbearable pleasure. It was as though her brain circuits had gone haywire from so much pleasure. Only Nikos's gentle movements, as he'd held her in his arms for what seemed like an eternity had punctured the sensual haze.

The raucous gaiety of the nightclub, the quick ride to the private airstrip, she remembered nothing of it.

Her memories of last night were all of him—how he had felt inside her, how he had held her after and how he had her carried her to the waiting limo when her knees had threatened to buckle under her.

She had been glad that he hadn't commented on her silence, because she'd had no idea what she would have said. All she knew was that she had been buried under an avalanche of sensations and feelings. None of which she had wanted to examine or give voice to.

The next thing she knew, she had woken up in the vast bed in the Demakis mansion, a strange lethargy in her blood. Which meant she had fallen asleep on the flight to the island.

She walked back to the foyer and followed the sounds of the chopper. Clad in another pair of jeans and white T-shirt that fitted snugly against the breadth of his chest, he was waiting for her. She settled down in the helicopter, too absorbed in her own thoughts to complain about his silence.

His pants molded the hard length of his thighs. Those thighs, they had been like solid rock, clenching her tight, supporting her, cradling her.

A twang went through her belly at remembered pleasure.

She fisted her hands, a hint of regret swarming through her. She had been so lost in the sensations when he moved inside her, so lost in everything he had done to her, she had been nothing but a passive participant. The urge to touch the hot slide of his skin, to feel his muscles tighten under her was fierce.

The ride to the other side of the island didn't take more

than ten minutes. Blue water and golden sand stretched in every direction she looked. It was as close to paradise as she had ever seen. And a hotel would ruin the tranquility of it, bring tourists, puncture the peace.

But she kept her thoughts to herself as they landed and stepped out.

She stared around her with mounting wonder as Nikos had a word with the pilot.

The new hotel was nothing like she'd imagined. For one thing, it was, maybe one tenth of the size of the Demakis mansion. It was a simple, clean design with pristine white-washed walls, designed to reflect the Greek architecture.

She smiled at Nikos as he joined her. "It's not what I expected."

"Do you like it?"

She nodded eagerly. "I was worried that it would ruin the peaceful atmosphere, that it would be a noisy, tour-isty place."

"It's a new kind of approach to a hotel, really more of an authentic experience than just a place to stay. There are no televisions in any suite and the guests are guaranteed the utmost privacy. Even the meals are local Greek specialties. Every material that is used is environmentally conscious, and even the furniture and pieces inside are all one-of-a-kind specially made by local craftsmen using simple, organic materials. Kind of back to—"

"Basics," she finished, smiling widely.

She trailed after Nikos while he checked a few things, loving the idea more and more. There were no more than three suites in the whole building. Again, whitewashed walls created a cocoonlike environment. Each suite was open plan, divided into sleeping and living areas. Hand-crafted accessories and bleached wood furniture was everywhere. A large veranda offered a beautiful view of the Cycladic landscape.

A hammock made of the softest cotton hung in the veranda.

She went back down the steps and found the pool. Having finished his phone call, Nikos's gaze was back on her.

"I don't know the standard procedure for the morning after," she said, finding his silence unbearable. It weighed on her, poking holes in every comforting thought she came up with. "Do we shake hands and pat each other on the back for a job well done? Or is it beyond crass to mention it at all? Did I break the code by falling asleep on you in the car? I swear, I didn't see it coming. I mean, the only thing I can think of is that my body caved in at the influx of pheromones. You know, because what we did was…fantastic."

She grimaced at how idiotic she sounded as soon as the words left her mouth.

He turned toward her in the blink of an eye and clasped her cheek. "This is as new to me as it is to you," he said in a quiet growl.

The irises of his eyes widened as though he hadn't been aware of what he was going to say. He ran a hand through his hair.

"Then you better start thinking about answers. Are you done with me? Do you want me to leave and stay somewhere in the village? Was this a onetime deal? Because if it was, I would have liked some notice because there's a lot of stuff I wanted to do and I was so overwhelmed, I didn't get to do anything."

"Overwhelmed?" A curse fell from his lips, and he turned toward her. If any more hardness inched into his face, he would be a concrete bust. "Did I hurt you last night?"

"What? Of course not," she said, heat gathering like a storm under her skin.

"You were very—"

Hitching on her toes, she covered his mouth with her hand. The velvety edge of his lips was a sinuous whisper against her skin, the stubble on his cheeks making her wonder how it would feel against other places. Every little thing about the man sent her senses tingling. "I enjoyed every minute of what we did last night. The question is, did you?"

This time, a slow smile curved his mouth. "You couldn't tell?"

"Honestly? I can't remember anything except thinking I could die happily. And today, I'm drawing my clues from the fact that you've been gone all morning and now you're staring at me as though you wish I were invisible. With your wealth, you can probably make me. I did see an ad for an invisibility cloak on eBay last week, so—"

"You are talking nonsense."

"I think something in my brain got warped last night. Your presence now makes me think of nothing but sex, and I'm trying to cover that up—"

"With nonsense." He nodded. He pushed her against the wall, his jaw tight. "I had the hottest, most intense orgasm of my entire life last night. It took every ounce of self-control I possess to not wake you up just so I could have you again and again. Knowing that you had no panties on under that skirt…I don't know how I resisted you at all." The words hummed on the air around them, the feral intensity of it sending warmth stealing into places she didn't want to think of right then. His mouth took on a rueful twist. "Every time I closed my eyes since this morning, I can hear those long whimpers you make just before you come, taste you on my fingers.

"Is that clear enough for you?" He flicked his tongue

over the rim of her ear, his softly whispered words stroking her need hotter and higher.

Lexi would have crumpled to the ground if he hadn't been holding her upright. A rush of wetness gathered at her sex. And all he had done was talk. "Now if you'd just looked like a man who got laid last night and enjoyed it, then I wouldn't—"

"It was glorious sex, *agape mou*." He let her go, his mouth narrowed into a straight line. "And I feel better than fantastic given that my sister is still missing, and my grandfather is using it as an excuse to deny me what I want."

The fever he incited instantly cooled, and Lexi took a staggering step back. Of course, Venetia. Her mouth felt clammy, her stomach tying itself in knots.

I'm so sorry, Lex. Just give me a few days and I'll bring Venetia back.

The small note that had been left on her side table under a cup of dark Greek coffee fluttered in front of her eyes. The shock of finding it, especially in Tyler's almost illegible handwriting, still pulsed through her.

Having read it close to fifty times in two minutes, Lexi had torn it up into small pieces, her heart in her throat. It was obvious Venetia didn't want to return and Tyler didn't want to hurt her.

Lexi felt a flare of anger at the both of them for doing this, for deceiving Nikos and for dragging her in between. This thing between her and Nikos, it was a temporary madness, she knew that. Still, she wanted to do nothing that would hurt him.

And she had a sinking feeling that that's what was going to happen in the end.

Pushing her hair back from her forehead, she caught the

sigh escaping her lips. There was nothing to do but wait. "What is your grandfather refusing you?" she said, her dislike of Savas Demakis a bad taste in her mouth.

"He and his cronies are refusing to vote me in as the CEO. The fact that I didn't protect Venetia is a weapon Savas is wielding to its full extent."

"I don't understand. Venetia and your company are entirely different things. How does he propose you stop your twenty-four-year-old sister from living her life, short of locking her up and throwing away the key?"

His pointed gaze told her she nailed the truth on its ugly head. "He must know you would never do that to Venetia."

Nikos shrugged. "What he knows for sure is how much I want to be in the CEO's chair."

"Do you?"

"Yes. I would do anything to be there finally. Except hurt my sister. Although really, Savas's suggestions are beginning to make more and more sense. In my desire to not hurt her, I brought you into this, and probably drove her even deeper into Tyler's arms."

She felt a shiver settle deep in her bones. "So he is pitting the two things you want above everything else against each other? Hoping that you are heartless enough to hurt your sister?"

"Yes."

Anxiety rampant in her veins, she came to a stop in front of him. "Are his… Do his assumptions have basis, Nikos?"

He traced his knuckles over her lower lip, and Lexi trembled for more than one reason. "You're trembling, *yineka mou*." She tucked her forehead into his shoulder, willing herself to let it go. She was courting nothing but trouble by asking, by digging herself in. Whenever this issue with Tyler and Venetia was resolved, she would walk away. She had to.

His long fingers gripped her nape, the pad of his thumb moving up and down. "What is it that you want to know but are so afraid to hear, Lexi?"

She looked up. "I think…no, I know that you will never hurt Venetia willingly. It's a different thing altogether that, with your twisted anger toward Tyler, you are doing just that…. But for your grandfather to blackmail you like this, to pit you against your own sister, to…see if you will take the suggestion and run with it…it means you—"

"It means that I have done things to remove any obstacles from my way before, yes."

She exhaled on a long breath, bracing herself. Whatever Nikos did, beneath the uncaring facade, she knew he had paid a price. "Like what?"

"My aunt's son, Spyros, he is a few years older than me and he was my grandfather's favorite when I first met him. He was everything I was not. Well-educated, smart and best of all, obedient. More than that, Savas had been grooming him, ever since my father walked out, to take over the reins of Demakis International.

"But it was not his right. It was mine. I had already slogged for a decade with little notice or returns for it. I realized following Savas's rigid instructions wasn't going to get me anything but the bare minimums. It was time to make him take notice of me."

"What did you do?"

"Are you sure you want to hear this, Lexi?"

Say no, walk away. "Yes."

"I went digging and discovered Spyros, beneath his perfect exterior, had a little secret. He had a wife hidden away that no one knew about, and he was struggling to get out of his engagement to one of Savas's oldest friend's granddaughters. I arranged for his wife to come to his engagement party. And despite Spyros's pleas asking for forgiveness, Savas kicked him off the board."

The quiet, matter-of-fact tone in his words only amplified the chill they caused. "You knew what your grandfather would do."

His gaze narrowed into an unflinching hardness, Nikos stared at her. "Everyone knew what he would do, including Spyros. He had made his choice. I just hurried along the consequences."

"I don't get it. It's not like you don't have money of your own." She pushed off from the wall, and walked the perimeter of the pool. "That yacht, the private jet, this new real-estate deal you have with Nathan Ramirez…you have nothing to want.

"Why is becoming the CEO so important to you, Nikos?"

He gave her a long look that said he wasn't dignifying her question with an answer. "It just is."

"Why can't you be happy with what you have? Why let your grandfather push you into anything?"

"Savas didn't push me into anything. I started on this path with one goal in sight. The moment I walked in through those electronic gates, clutching my sister to me, the poor little bastard that everyone pitied, I made a promise to myself. That I would do everything I can to become the master of it all. Do you realize what odds I have surmounted to get to this stage? I started with nothing, Lexi. And I won't settle for everything that he walked away from, until I'm everything he was not."

"Until you're everything he…" Her heart sinking to her shoes, Lexi finally realized who he meant. The bitterness in his words, it was only a superficial cover on a deeper cut. "Your father? Nikos, what he did was awful, but you have to forgive him. He may have started this, but it's your grandfather that brought you to his point. With every little thing you tell me about your grandfather, have you never wondered why your father might have turned his back on all this?"

"I don't care why he did it. Even before he died, we never had anything. He struggled in that garage, he barely provided for us and he stood by like a useless fool while my mother's health degraded and she eventually died. All he had needed was to call Savas, ask for help."

That garage, those cars, didn't he realize why it comforted him so much? "Do you believe Savas would have helped him? Without conditions? Would he have welcomed your father with open arms without a price?"

Not even a little of his anger waned. "Any price would have been worth it. It was his duty to look after her, to take care of Venetia. He not only failed in that, he then went and killed himself, breaking Venetia forever."

"And you."

Nikos shook his head, despising the glimpse of pity in her eyes. "He taught me a very valuable lesson early on. Love is a luxury only fools want and can afford."

His pointed look wasn't lost on her. "I'm not saying he was right, Nikos. But Savas never even gave you a proper chance to grieve."

"There was nothing to grieve. My father was a weak man all his life. He couldn't stand up to Savas—he couldn't live without my mother. He couldn't even keep himself alive for Venetia and I. I refuse to be like him. Becoming the CEO of Demakis International is the last step in that journey. And Savas can't stop me. I will find a way to that chair."

Lexi had no chance to answer, because the sound of a chopper slicing through the wind around them reached them.

Pushing the hair away from her face, she hung back as a

man of about seventy stepped out of the chopper, followed by a young woman.

Nikos shook hands with the man, and offered a polite smile to the woman.

Lexi turned away and walked toward the hotel. Judging by the jealous rage that took hold of her insides, it was better that she stay away. Leaving her backpack in one of the smaller bedrooms, she climbed the stairs to the next floor. The corridor was whitewashed with dark gleaming wood floors, with simple handmade crafts here and there. Among all the places she had visited with Nikos, she loved this hotel the most. And under the ambition and jet-setting lifestyle, she had a feeling he did, too.

She walked out into the huge veranda of one of the suites. Her breath hitched at the beauty of the Cycladic heaven. Orange bloodied the dusky sky, casting an ethereal glow over the strip of beach and the whitewashed hotel walls.

Intensely glad that Nikos had asked her to join him, she climbed into the hammock, her mind running over what he had said to her. One way or another, she needed to bring a resolution to this thing between Tyler and Venetia. And she had to do it without hurting anyone in the process, least of all, Nikos.

It was an impossible task, but she had to do it. Even with the childhood she'd had, she had known kindness, even if it had been in snatches.

Nikos had known none. She was damned if she had to see those shadows of despair in his eyes ever again.

She would do anything to keep them at bay. Anything.

Darkness fell by the time Nikos bade goodbye to Theo Katrakis. Savage satisfaction fueled through him. Finally, things were falling into their right place. The older man had, however, surprised Nikos by bringing his daughter to the meeting.

And one look at Eleni Katrakis had sent the blood rushing from Lexi's face. Did she really think he would be interested in Eleni after last night?

He found Lexi in the hammock, the quiet rasp of her pencil against the paper in her hand the only sound for miles. The feeble light from the adjoining bedroom was nowhere near enough for her.

Shaking his head, he plucked the sheet from her hands and walked back inside. With a huff, she rolled out of the hammock and followed him in.

He stuck out a hand to ward her off and studied the sketch. Surprise flooded him, and he laughed, the sound tearing out of him. A lightness, an amazement he had never known before filled him inside and out.

The sketch was extraordinarily detailed for something created with a pencil and paper. It shimmered with life, with the unique essence of the woman who drew it.

The drawing was of a woman, almost Amazonian in her build, big-breasted with a tiny waist, her long legs muscular and lithe, her dark long hair flying around her face a striking anchor of femininity. She wore a leather sheath kind of dress, a pistol hanging from the belt. The same sketch he had seen on Lexi's T-shirt the first time she had met him, a direct contrast to the beautiful, delicate woman who had drawn her, but just as dangerous.

Her legs planted apart, the woman was staring at something, a mischievous little smile curving her lips.

Here he had assumed that he had Lexi Nelson all figured out. But he couldn't learn everything about her if he spent ten lifetimes with her. A tightness emerged in his gut and he fought to dispel it.

"That's very insulting, Nikos."

He turned toward her, leaning against the huge bed. Her arms around her waist, she braced herself.

"This sketch…" He took a deep breath, the expectant wariness in her gaze causing him to choose his words carefully. "It's the most brilliant thing I've ever seen," he said, opting for unvarnished truth.

Her mouth curved in a wide smile. "Then why were you laughing?"

He waved the paper in her direction. "This is Ms. Havisham, isn't it? Your heroine? The one the space pirate kidnapped?"

She nodded, her gaze shining with a brilliant radiance. "She is a mousy little woman when he snatches her. But this is her true form. It comes out only when she or someone she loves comes under threat."

"And the space pirate has no idea what he has taken on," he said, frowning. He had a feeling he knew exactly what the pirate was going through.

Lexi Nelson didn't have to change into anything to send a shiver up and down Nikos's spine. Warning bells clanged inside his head and he kept the sound at bay. For now.

"Yep."

Nodding, he grasped her wrist and tugged her along with him. He settled her in his lap on a wicker armchair. His curiosity was far more feral than anything else he felt right now. "So tell me. Why does he kidnap her?"

She wrapped her arm around his neck and smiled. And again, Nikos braced himself. Desire and something entirely alien descended on him. It had to be the intimacy of their positions. He had never spent more than a few minutes with a woman outside of a bed or an office.

"He learns that she has the key to a time portal. And he needs it to turn back time. But she's not exactly what he had imagined. Nor is the key so simple."

Nikos stared at the picture again and caught the hint of sadness in Lexi's tone. "She is the key, isn't she?"

Shock spiraling in her gaze, she stared at him. "How did you guess that?" She didn't know what she saw in his eyes as she continued. "She is the key. Sacrificing her life will give him the power to turn back time, go to three different times in the past once."

"What is he going to do?"

She shrugged. "Right now, he's just learned the truth and is staggering under the weight of what he has to do. Because, you see, the space pirate—"

"Is beginning to like Ms. Havisham." He finished her thought. "But the realization won't stop him. He will try to kill her."

"Unless she kills him first," she said, laughing. At his disbelieving stare, the smile slid from her face. "Maybe you understand Spike, but Ms. Havisham is not like me, Nikos. Not weak or lonely and forever needing someone to make her feel like she matters. She's strong, independent, a survivor. She has no qualms about her sexuality or her place in the world. If Spike threatens her survival, she will kill him. As she has already killed before. And have no regrets about it."

He placed the paper slowly on the nightstand and turned her until she was straddling him. Having her this close was nothing short of torture. He held off the liquid longing at bay with sheer determination. This—this sexual desire, this situation between them, it was still under his control. *It had to be.* Never before had this kind of control been so important to him. "I don't think she's all that different from you."

"I clung to Tyler all these years. I let Faith walk all over me. All for what? For a few crumbs of affection, to feel like I have someone who loves me? Ms. Havisham is—"

"She might be packing in the boob and leg department,"

he said, using her words, and she instantly smiled and swatted his shoulder. "And she might be a badass with that gun, but all those are outward things, Lexi." He placed his palm on her chest, and her heart thundered under his touch. The words flew out of him on a wave, and he could do nothing to curb them. "Here, you're just as strong as her or even more. No one else could have lived your life and retained the good you have, the warmth you have. You don't have to rewrite your story, *yineka mou*. It is already an extraordinary one."

Lexi swallowed at the raw honesty that rang in Nikos's words, the tenderness shining in his gaze. She had been drawing for as long as she could remember. It had started as a comfort, and somewhere down the line had become more than that. It was her lifeline, her way of controlling things she couldn't change, her way of righting the things that had gone wrong in her life. In her bleakest moments, it had been the only way she could hold on to a life that had been nothing but lonely and sometimes, even cruel.

She had always meant for Ms. Havisham to kill Spike. But ever since she had begun the actual sketching, the story had taken on a life of its own. And the man staring at her with liquid desire in his gaze, with a tenderness that threatened to pull her under, it was him.

He had changed the course of her story and that of her own life.

How was she supposed to remember that this was just sex when he made her heart ache for more, when he looked at her as though she was the most precious woman in the world?

How was she supposed to walk away when it was time?

She threw her hands around his neck and kissed his jaw, choking back the tears catching in her throat. She breathed her thanks into his skin, explored the tangy taste of him with her tongue. The depth of emotion roiling inside her scared her.

She took a bracing breath, willing her heart to slow down, willing her mind to take control, willing herself not to ruin this glorious moment with this wonderful man with unwanted fears.

Only then did she realize the absolute stillness that had inched into Nikos.

He was so rigid in her embrace that she wondered if he was even breathing. Pasting a smile on her face, she pulled herself back and looked into his eyes. "Sorry," she whispered, forcing a levity she didn't feel into her tone. "Talking about my stories and sketches always makes me emotional." As cop-outs went, it was a good one.

She pressed her mouth to his, not waiting to see if he believed it or not. Because the desire she felt for him, the need that was already unraveling inside her—*that* she understood and she used it to root herself in reality.

With a groan, he dragged her closer until her aching sex rubbed against his erection.

She instantly parted her legs and moved over the hard ridge, wanton hunger rising to the surface. Her time was limited with him. And it made her desperate.

She tugged her T-shirt off with trembling fingers. He threw his head back and laughed. A gravelly sound that abraded her skin. Rising to her knees, she attacked the band of his black trousers. But he stilled her hands on them.

His large hands holding her immobile, he licked her collarbone. That small, almost-there-but-gone point of contact, her whole body gathered behind it. "I want to see all of you this time."

She nodded, her mouth dry. She slid from his lap, her skin tingling at his continued perusal. "I want to see you, too. On the bed," she added, forcing the words past the thundering beat of her heart.

He stood up from the chair and neared her. His smile cut grooves in his cheeks, making him look deliciously divine.

"What? I'm being outspoken, demanding what I want from life, from you."

"I can see that. And you look gloriously beautiful doing it." He ran his finger over the edge of her pink bra, and she willed herself not to step back. It was easy to speak the words, but to match her actions was something else altogether. Because she would always be amazed that he could want her, that the blazing desire in his eyes was for her. "Did you just think that up?"

"It's like my subconscious speaks up every time I am near you. You probably think the bed is boring but—"

He covered the distance between them and picked her up. She tucked her hands around his neck and pushed herself closer. "Nothing with you is boring, Ms. Nelson. Although, I think we can make it interesting."

He threw her on the bed, and Lexi thought she would expire from how soft the sheets were. "What do you mean, Mr. Demakis?"

Unbuttoning his dress shirt, he prowled to the other end of the room and grabbed a champagne bottle from the ice bucket.

Lexi moved to her knees. The dark desire in his gaze sent a tingle from her head to toe. "You should know I'm not much of a drinker."

He shrugged off his T-shirt and took a sip of the champagne. "Who said you will be drinking it?"

With his other hand, he reached around her back and unhooked her bra, while his tongue found the exact spot on her neck that drove her out of her skin and licked it. His hands tugged down her shorts and panties next.

She was naked and twin strips of color blooded his cheekbones. "Never say you're not beautiful again, *thee mou.*"

One hand snaked around her waist, his long fingers cupping her buttocks. Her nipples grazed against his chest. Throwing her head back, Lexi groaned, shivering all over.

He kissed her mouth, his tongue swirling the tender inside, licking, nipping, her hands roaming his back, desperate for more. His fingers sank into her hair and pulled her face up for his scrutiny. "Do you trust me, Lexi?" he whispered against her skin.

Lexi nodded, no words coming to her mouth.

"Then close your eyes."

Willing to do anything he asked, she closed her eyes. Words whispered in Greek and English, wicked promises, rained down sensation upon sensation. She gasped as he bound something around her eyes, and realized it was the tie he had loosened earlier.

He pushed at her shoulders softly and Lexi fell back, every inch of her trembling. She waited, the soft breeze from the veranda touching every inch of her. Desire coiled tighter and tighter in her lower belly as she heard the rustle of his clothes. The bed dipped and Nikos's hair-roughened leg rasped deliciously against her.

She gasped as something cold, the champagne she realized with a gasp, fell in a slow trickle over her collarbone. Then over her breasts, over her trembling stomach. She fisted her hands in the sheets as the cold liquid only heated up the rest of her skin even more.

Nikos's heated breath, the warmth of his body, swathed her. His lips met hers in a fusion of need and lust, the pressure of his mouth, the silky strokes of his tongue, every sensation amplified without sight.

And then he was licking the champagne off her body

in sure, lingering strokes, setting her on fire. He licked it from her breasts, his tongue rasping against the tight nipple.

"Champagne has never tasted better, Lexi."

Now his mouth licked it off her abdomen, and she sank her fingers into his hair with a shaking moan.

Sensation on sensation piled over her, her skin crackling with pleasure. The minute she felt his breath on her inner thighs, she clamped her legs closed, heat billowing inside her skin. "I'm… Nikos…"

His fingers kneaded her hip, his mouth opening in a smile against her thighs. "I want to see you, *thee mou*. All of you."

Her thighs trembled as she let him push them apart. He didn't give her another minute to think. His fingers separating the folds, he tasted her wet sex in a leisurely lick, and Lexi bucked off the bed with a long moan.

His forearm stayed on her abdomen, the hair on it tingling against her skin. Heat gathered in her belly like a storm, as he continued his torment. He made love to her with his tongue, and she climbed higher and higher, sweat gathering on her skin, throwing her head from left to right.

She sobbed his name, again and again, in search of a rhythm, in pursuit of relief. Her breaths were raspy, her body feeling like it would implode if she didn't find release soon.

He sucked the quivering bundle of nerves and Lexi orgasmed, in a shower of pleasure that had her shivering from top to toe.

With a guttural groan that pushed her over the edge, Nikos thrust into her.

Lexi trembled violently under him, the weight of his hard body knocking the breath out of her, her body twisting as he pulled out and thrust back in, setting a rhythm that told tales about his shattered self-control.

On the next thrust in, she felt his warm breath on her breast, and then his mouth closed over the hardened peak. The minute she felt his teeth on the tautly tender bud, she came again in an electrifying wave of spasms.

She dug her nails into his back, feeling the deep ridge of his spine stiffen, the hard muscles tightening.

With another firm thrust, Nikos came, his sweat-soaked skin rubbing against hers. Slowly, his breath evened out again, but he was still on top of her. She nudged the tie away from her eyes, but kept them closed, focusing on evening her breaths out, glad that he couldn't see her expression.

Only he kissed her again. Slowly, softly. She tasted his sweat, she tasted his passion and most of all, she tasted his tenderness in that kiss. And she sucked in a deep breath, trying to stem the avalanche of feelings inside her. He moved away from her, and she instantly turned to her side, her breathing still labored, but for a different reason.

Stretching behind her, Nikos pulled her close into the haven of his body. She felt the shudder in his body as he tucked her close to him. "Are you all right, *thee mou?*"

Running her fingers over his forearm, Lexi pressed a kiss to his palm.

She could talk as if she owned this affair, but she had a feeling sex was never going to be just sex for her. She didn't know whether to be happy or sad about it. But it was the truth, and she already had had a lifetime of shying away from it. She had wanted to stop hiding from life, to stop standing on the sidelines. But it also meant accepting herself as she was.

She was in this bed with Nikos because it was him, because for all his acerbic words and unfeeling facade, she liked him. It scared her—the little fluttering in her tummy when he looked at her, the way her heart missed a beat when he smiled. She couldn't lie to herself that it was just attraction or desire.

"Never better, Nikos," she said, speaking past the thump, thump of her heart. And felt his smile against her skin.

CHAPTER ELEVEN

VENETIA AND TYLER are getting married tomorrow morning.

From the minute Nikos had received the message from his security head, only one thought resonated incessantly in his head.

Had Lexi known all this time where they had been? Her concern for him—had it all been an act?

She hadn't denied his earlier accusation that she wouldn't tell him if Tyler contacted her. And yet, he wanted to hear it from her mouth that she had knowingly deceived him.

He thanked his pilot and swung his legs out of the chopper.

Pulling his cell phone from his coat pocket, he switched it off. Savas was going to call; he knew it in his bones. And he was not ready for another one of his grandfather's ploys. Theo Katrakis was going to make his move any minute now, and then Nikos would finally have what he wanted, and this time without paying Savas's price.

Walking through the marble foyer, he shrugged off his coat, suit jacket and tie. He mounted the steps to the first floor, and stopped outside Lexi's bedroom.

It was past eleven and by the absence of light under the door and the silence, she was sleeping. The last thing he wanted to do was scare her.

He turned the knob slowly. Moonlight filled the room

with a silvery glow. His heart thumping in that annoying way anytime he was near her, he reached the bed, only to find it empty.

A hushed whisper reached him from beneath the veranda, and he took the stairs down to the pool behind. A rented scooter lay against the wall next to the ivy at the back of the house and standing by the pool was Lexi.

In her white shorts and bright yellow spaghetti strap top, she looked innocent and young, as if she was incapable of deception.

Her slender shoulders stiff, she looked up at him. There was no guilt in her eyes.

He knew, and he had accepted as much as he could, that what Lexi shared with Tyler was indescribable. That he was her friend, family, everything rolled into one. He understood their relationship had been born out of the hardest time of her life.

Having known that bone-crushing loneliness, he was only glad that she had had Tyler.

But the consequence of that was that in her loyalty, her affection, Nikos would always only come second to Tyler.

Something flashed in her gaze as she took in his scowl. Fear? Shame? "Nikos, I've been trying to—"

He didn't let her finish. "Did you know where they have been all this time?"

Her luscious mouth trembled.

"Answer my question, Lexi."

"Yes."

The one word reverberated in his ears. His gut felt strangely hollow, his throat closing in, making it hard to breathe. Shying his gaze away from her, he turned and looked out at the blue surface of the heated pool.

There was a gentle breeze around them, the sounds of

the ocean beyond the estate walls soothing, and yet inside, he felt anything but.

He felt betrayed, hurt, he realized. And yet she had made him no promise, owed him nothing.

It was his own fault for forgetting what was important. Because five days of spending time with the woman, making love to her every which way, waking up with her slender form tucked tight against him, had warped his defenses, his armor.

Every time he had made love to her, it was as though she was changing him from inside out and he didn't know how to stop it. Sex had become something else, something he had never felt before.

His hunger for her knew no bounds, but it was the little things he craved to see that lingered in him long after he was away from her, the little intimacies they shared that sent a ripple of fear to brew within.

How else had the little minx gotten him to admit that Spyros worked for him in Athens? Her soft body cradled against his, her eyes had shimmered in the moonlight as she muttered about why he wanted to paint himself in the cruelest color possible with her.

She was determined to prove that he had a heart, and a kind, working one, at that. To stop her from going on, he had said that it had been to his own advantage to hire Spyros behind Savas's back, because he knew everything about the ins and outs of the business.

To which she had smiled, looking at him as though she had discovered a treasure, and kissed him, forcing Nikos to admit that Spyros at the end of it all, had been thankful to Nikos because he would have never had the guts to stand up to Savas and admit his love for his wife.

But she had drawn the lines now, had shown him his place in her life, like everyone else he had ever cared about.

The little realization sat on his chest like a boulder cutting off his breath. For all her claims, she hadn't given him another thought, while he…he had been planning to ask her to stay as long as she wanted, he'd had a studio prepared for her, he…

Hurt gave way to bitter anger that he had to choke back to speak. "Have you just been manipulating me, hoping I would learn about them too late?"

She looked at him with a stricken expression, shaking her head. "I didn't tell you when I thought they just needed time. I have been trying to rack my brain about what is best for everyone—"

"You mean what is best for *him*." The words barreled out of him on a wave of emotion that suddenly he had no control over. "Because everyone and everything else is secondary to you."

"This whole week…I've never felt more alive, I've never been happier. How dare you taint it with your ridiculous accusations?"

She sounded so uncharacteristically ferocious that Nikos stilled, his heart thundering loudly in his ears. Her gaze blazed with pure fury. "Then why didn't you…"

Tyler stepped out from behind the wall. Fierce emotion flooded through him, washing away the hurt, the anger, and he stood shaking in its wake.

Theos, what was happening to him?

Lexi clamped his fingers tight, refusing to let him retreat. "I know how much she means to you, Nikos. I… The moment I learned what Venetia was proposing, I have been going crazy with worry. I spent all morning trying to contact Tyler. I begged him to come clean with you."

He couldn't look away anymore. Their gazes met and the depth of feeling there rocked him to his toes. No one had ever considered his feelings before in his life, no one had ever wondered if he was in pain, that he could hurt and bleed just as anyone else, that he wanted to be loved and cherished and even protected.

Not his father, not Venetia and not Savas.

Until, one day, he had stopped feeling at all. He had turned himself into stone, starving everything else but his ambition. And he hadn't even realized until Lexi had showed up.

This feeling…it was gratitude, it was fear, and it gripped his body and wouldn't let go. But as warm and excruciatingly real as it was, he didn't want it. The only thing he understood, the only thing he could handle was his desire for her.

Nothing more.

"I care about Venetia," Tyler said, approaching him, his eyes welling with emotion. "And I don't know how to say no to her without hurting her, Nikos. But I can't marry her like this, not when I don't remember her, not when I have messed up every important relationship I've ever had." He took a step closer to Lexi and planted his hands on her shoulders, as though drawing strength from her.

Nikos had the most atavistic urge to push his hand off Lexi, to tell him that he had no rights to her. That she belonged to Nikos now.

There was such a ringing clarity to the thought that Nikos fisted his hands to not follow through on it.

"I trusted Lexi's word that Venetia's well-being is important to you, too," Tyler said in a gruff tone, "that you can find a way out of this without hurting her. I know you want me out of her life, but all I want is her happiness, Nikos. Venetia might very well hate me for this."

"Nikos? Please say something. This is the only way I could think of to—"

Nikos nodded, not trusting himself to say anything right.

He didn't know what was right or wrong right now. Only that the expression in Lexi's eyes—concerned, expectant— would stay with him forever. He held the answering desire in him at bay through sheer will.

"Where is my sister now?"

"At the inn. She was getting overexcited about the wedding tomorrow, and extremely anxious about not telling you, so I suggested she take a sleeping pill and take it easy for tonight. She is out like a light," he said with a wince.

Nikos nodded, once again surprised. Whether Tyler loved Venetia as he claimed or not, Nikos couldn't know. But he could clearly handle her well. "Go back to the inn now," he said, considering several scenarios one after the other. "Don't say a word to her about being here. I will be there in the morning at the inn. I was this close to locating you both anyway."

"And the wedding?" Tyler asked.

Lexi had been right. His sister was stronger than he had given her credit for. "I will convince her to not go through with it. For now. Which means I have to give her my blessing about you."

Lexi looked up at him. "Do you?"

He gave in to the urge and tugged her to his side, unable to keep himself from touching her. Her apparent happiness at the very thought, the depth of her goodwill toward two people who had caused her immense hurt, it was hard not to be transformed in a little way by it.

"I won't ask you to leave immediately," he said finally, meeting Tyler's eyes. "My sister has already suffered a lot. I don't ever want to see her hurt."

Tyler met his gaze unflinchingly. "Neither do I. Nor do I want to marry her until I remember everything, until I'm worthy of her. All I ask is that you give me the chance to try."

Still clasping her wrist, he pulled Lexi along with him. "You have it," he threw at Tyler, who stood looking at them with a nonplussed expression on his face.

Did she leave now?

The innocuous question attacked Lexi as Nikos pushed her into her bedroom and disappeared to answer a phone call. She knew the question had been coming, but she had shoved it away while figuring out how to handle what Tyler had told her this morning.

Now that everything between Tyler and Venetia was resolved, at least for now, the fact was that what she had come to do was no longer valid.

Tyler didn't need her anymore. Which meant her deal with Nikos was done.

Her stomach twisting into a painful knot, Lexi got off the bed and walked to the connecting veranda. She didn't want to sit there and let Nikos see the confusion in her eyes.

Because she didn't want to leave, she didn't want to walk away from Nikos. Not yet.

If ever, a sinuous voice whispered. Rubbing her clammy hands on her T-shirt, she leaned against the wall, fast tears gathering in her throat.

She would not cry, as much as it hurt. She needed to be grown-up about it. Deal with it like a holiday fling.

"Lexi?"

She heard Nikos's tread in the bedroom, drew in a deep breath and ventured back in. Feeling as though she was marching into battle.

Nikos stood beside the bed, his knees propped against it. Undoing the cuffs of his shirt, his gaze traveled over her pale face with increasing curiosity. By the time he was done, wariness entered his face. "I thought this was what you wanted for them—a real chance."

She wrapped her arms around herself, feeling inexplicably cold. "It is."

"It would have never worked out between you and him," he said in a soft voice full of emotion.

"What?" she said automatically, frowning. Realization dawned. "Nikos, I'm not moping over Tyler."

Reaching her, he took her hands in his. Her hands were the size of his palms, the rough grooves and ridges now as familiar to her as her own. She trembled as he ran one finger over her cheek and the circles under her eyes. "Thank you for trusting me with the truth today."

She smiled up at him, wondering if everything she felt was written in her eyes. And if he would run if he saw it. "I think you like deluding Venetia, your grandfather, and even yourself into thinking that you don't understand love or affection or any matters of heart. But I know that you do. I believed that in the face of Tyler's honesty, you would give him a chance."

He inclined his head and smiled. The warmth of it enveloped her. "Then why that look in your eyes?"

She tried for casual nonchalance and utterly failed. "You don't need me here anymore. It's time I returned to New York."

"Ahhh…so you won't want this then?" With his hand on her wrist, he tugged her from the room, giving her no chance to answer.

They walked through the corridor, went down the steps, through the lounge into one of the rooms to the side. It was the room she loved most in the villa. Very sparsely furnished, and during most of the day, sunlight filled the room.

They came to a stop in front of the closed door.

"Open it."

Her heart in her throat, Lexi pushed the door. Nikos

switched on the lights behind her. Tears clogged her throat, her stomach a mass of flutters at the sight that greeted her.

A huge drafting table stood at one corner, with a detachable drawing board set up on top, slightly angled and perfectly positioned for her height. A sleek silver laptop sat on a table next to it with a printer/scanner, a filing cabinet next to it. Reams of four-by-six paper, magnetic draw/erase boards, paintbrushes and boxes, pencils in every brand and size, erasers, everything and anything she could ever want was in the room.

It was a studio he could have plucked from her dreams.

Her mouth dried up, her chest filled with a lightness that should have made breathing easier.

Nikos stood leaning against the door, drinking in every expression on her face.

"Do you like it?"

"It's perfect," she whispered, her pulse hammering in her throat. "I… You have thought of everything. But I… It's just always been a hobby."

"Why is it just a hobby?"

She couldn't even answer for a few minutes for the tumult of feelings that flew within her. For years, she had wished for someone to think of her, to care about her. And in his own way, she realized, Nikos did.

"Your talent is beyond average, Lexi. You should finish your graphic novel and submit a proposal."

Her heart slammed against her rib cage. "For what?"

"For publishing it."

Trepidation swirled through her. He caught her hands in his, his fingers drawing circles on the backs of her palms.

"Or you can just scan a few teasers, and put it up on the web. There's a large community online that's much less scary if that's what you—"

"Wait. How do you know all this?"

"I've been researching it. People are going to love your work. Compared to everything that's out there, I have no doubt your work will stand out. The second way, you create a reader base, and the best thing about it is, knowing that people want to read it will motivate you to keep going."

Lexi blinked, unable to formulate a response. The fact that he had put so much thought into this, that he had researched it, the fact that he understood her trepidation, it sat tight on her chest. "I just… It's not going to be like Superman or Spiderman, you know. And I'm not that ambitious really, either. I just want to be able to do it more and support myself."

His long strides swallowed up the distance between them. His gray V-necked T-shirt delineated that broad chest gloriously. His long fingers clutched her shoulders as he looked down. "Then stay here."

"What?"

"Stay for as long as we both want this. It seems even your friend is going to be here for a while, right?"

She laughed at that last incentive and liked him a little more. He was making it so hard to say no to him, to refuse this chance. The little resistance she might have had was crumbling before his thoughtfulness.

"I can't accept all this…" She colored furiously. "I can't just live off of you, Nikos. That would just taint everything we have. Please try to—"

"I will respect your wishes," he said with such easy acceptance that shock robbed her of words. "The second half of your payment should be debiting even as we speak." He laid a finger on her mouth. "Before you argue, I am… I was the boss. All I wanted was to stop my sister from getting hurt. I think you did a great job. With that money you have, all I am offering you is a place to stay. It's nothing less than what I would do for a friend."

She scrunched her nose at him. "You don't have any friends."

He ignored her little quip. "Apart from this studio, I won't force anything else on you. You can even put in a few hours at the hotel when they need some help."

She thought her heart might burst open from her chest. It took every bit of self-possession she had to remain still. "This is what you want?"

He bent his head and kissed her nose. She smiled at the gesture. Over the past week, she had realized that while being an extremely physical man with an insatiable sex drive, Nikos really didn't do the little things like touching, or hugging outside the context of sex.

So every moment he touched her, or kissed her like this, was a precious gift she hugged to herself. "I want this, too…but I won't to be your sex stop of Greece." In this, she would not relent. She fought to force casualness into her tone. "I grew a monstrous, scaly, green head when that woman was touching you the other day. I'm not sophisticated like your other—"

His hands moved to her buttocks and tugged her off the floor until she was cradled against his groin, his arousal a hard, pulsing weight against the V of her legs. "I haven't looked at another woman since you began messing with my head. I don't want anyone else but you."

Something colored his voice—a resigned acceptance that this was different—and she smiled. It was not only her that was venturing into new territory.

She ran her fingers over his jaw. The rasp of his stubble against her palm was an intimacy that left her shaking. Equal parts excitement and fear raced through her veins. How long would they last? What happened when he was through with her? Wouldn't it be better to walk away now?

She hid her face in his chest, fighting the swarm of questions, fighting the urge to ask them. His heart thundered under her cheek.

He smelled like sex and warmth and…even with all his contradictions, he made her happy.

Being with Nikos made her happy, made her feel alive for the first time in her life. It was as simple as that.

Of course, there was her fear that he would end this suddenly, that she was already in too deep…and that gut-wrenching feeling in her stomach every time he reached for her in his sleep.

It was the time her every defense, her carefully constructed attitude to keep this uncomplicated, collapsed like a pack of cards. Just as she did then, she pushed away the fear again.

Nikos liked her. Every action of his made up for words he didn't speak. And that was enough for her.

When she was with him, she believed she was beautiful, that she was courageous and that she deserved the best that life had to offer. She loved what she became when she was with him.

She wouldn't let her worry about the future destroy her present like she had done for so long.

He had taught her to live, and live she would. She wound her arms around his lean waist. The hard muscles tightened for a second, but she held on, knowing that he was new to this kind of intimacy.

She looked up at him and smiled. "I'll stay."

He rubbed his thumb over her lower lip, his gaze full of…warmth and a light she had never seen before. "That's good." He spoke the words in a matter-of-fact voice, but the depth of emotion he was struggling to contain and failing to was enough for her.

A hundred things could go wrong in a day. But this moment with this man was perfect. She stood on tiptoes and pressed a hard kiss to his mouth. Teeth and tongues tangled against each other, and they were both out of breath in ten seconds flat.

Breathing hard, she laughed. "Can I give you my gift now? It finally got delivered yesterday, and I've been dying to show it to you."

"A gift?" He said the words as though she had pointed a gun at him.

She nodded, embarrassed. "It's not something as grand as this studio, but I thought—"

He cut her off with a finger on his lips. "Go bring it, *thee mou.*"

It took her all of two minutes to go upstairs, grab the package from her closet and run back down to him. She clutched it tight in her hands, suddenly feeling stupid. She had thought it a riot at the time.

But then what did she have that she could give him that he didn't have?

She had a gift for him. It was what normal people in normal relationships did.

Nikos stared at the colorful, cheap packaging in her hand and struggled to remain still against the shudder that racked his body.

He had lived through the most painful moments in his life without falling apart. He had cradled his mother's weak body, seen the life go out of it while his father had cried Nikos's tears, he had held Venetia through her silent screams when she found their father without succumbing to the grief and fury that had roiled inside him.

And yet that small package in her hands, the expectant expression on Lexi's face—it was the most dangerous moment he had lived through. Cold sweat drenched him inside out. He wanted to walk away from it, never lay eyes on the package even as another part of him was dying to see it. Like a child that he had never been.

Without another thought, he plucked the package from her hands.

"I used the scanner in your office upstairs."

Nodding, he tore the packaging aside and a T-shirt fell out. It was plain white, made of cheap quality cotton. He unfolded it and froze.

It had a sketch of the space pirate Spike imprinted on it. Like the one Lexi wore of Ms. Havisham, but this one was colored in, a contrast of black and white.

Spike wore black leather pants and a sleeveless leather vest. A gun hung from the holster on his side. It was again incredibly detailed but it was his face that caught Nikos's attention.

An arrested expression covering his features, Spike was looking at something in the distance. It was the moment when he found that Ms. Havisham was the key that would open the time portal—Nikos knew it.

He felt as if someone had pushed a hand into his chest and given his heart a quiet thumping to get it going. It slammed against his rib cage now and he felt his pulse everywhere in his body like a savage drumbeat. His breath choked in his throat, and his chest hurt.

It was the most precious thing anyone had ever given him and the most dangerous. Words failed him, and the cold dread multiplied a few hundred times. Suddenly, he had the most incredible urge to possess that time portal in his own hands, to turn back everything he had said to her in the past hour, to turn back to the time before Lexi had even entered his world. Before his emotions had been safely under lock and key, before he had begun to look beneath his bitter anger for his father. He fisted his hands and let a curse loose.

"Nikos?"

Shaking himself out of it, he looked at Lexi.

Her lower lip caught between her teeth, she didn't meet his eyes. She pounced on him, to grab it probably and he tugged his arm out of her reach just in time. "It was just a silly idea."

The wariness in her eyes propelled him out of his pensive mood. He would not shatter this moment for her. It was the only reason he was doing this. The thought rang flat and false within him.

Holding his arm out to ward her off, he pulled off his shirt. Her gaze followed the movement as he pulled the T-shirt on.

Warmth shone in her blue eyes. And something in him instantly recoiled against it.

"Perhaps Spike should kill Ms. Havisham," he said, emotion roiling in his throat. It was a warning, for himself and her. "He is a heartless pirate, isn't he? He's not going to miraculously fall in love with her and want to save her."

Something flashed in her gaze. "I never said they'll have a happy ending, Nikos. And as to whether Spike will kill her, I'd say you still underestimate Ms. Havisham. She's not going to let anyone kill her, least of all Spike."

Standing back, she held the edge of the material in her hand and pulled. "It's too tight, isn't it? I should have gone for XXXL instead of XXL." She winked at him and started pulling the T-shirt up. "Now it's going to be really hard to get it off."

He swallowed at the lick of desire in her blue eyes and at the relentless shiver that took hold of his skin. And let his own desire for her mute the warning bells clanging in his head.

CHAPTER TWELVE

IT WAS A whole week before Nikos had finally untangled himself from Lexi and made it to a meeting aboard his yacht with Theo Katrakis. A meeting that Theo had requested days ago. Nikos had deliberately locked himself out of any business matters but for the most important. Walking over to the glass bar that was the pride of the main deck, he was about to reach for whiskey when he saw an ice bucket with champagne. A note said it was from Theo, which meant he had good news for Nikos.

But instead of the fierce rush of satisfaction he expected, an image of Lexi, trembling with cold champagne over her skin, little mewls of pleasure falling from her mouth, flashed in front of him. He was instantly hard as rock, the strength of his desire unprecedented. That was the word for it. His desire, this ever-growing unease he felt right under his skin, everything about the situation he created with Lexi was *unprecedented*. And through each day, Nikos felt the doubts he experienced at night with Lexi solidify into cold, hard truth.

More than once, he had caught himself, weakening, wavering and shutting out the world and even work. Postponing this meeting with Theo when he had spent more than a year carefully cultivating this association, blocking out

Savas instead of finding out what his grandfather was up to even now…when and how had he become this man?

It was like watching himself exist in a different reality, as vivid as the one in Lexi's comic book, a happy one, a parallel one that seemed as fragile as it was fantastic. The ruthless life he had carefully built into existence slowly unraveled as Lexi wove herself into the very fabric of his life.

For a man who had never had a romantic relationship that lasted more than a few hours, having one with someone like Lexi was like sitting on a box of explosives. Because that's what he was doing. Only a week ago he had asked her to stay, and yet now, he felt the iron lid he kept on his control shake loose, and everything he had ruthlessly wiped from his life creep back in.

It was when he had caught himself panicking in the middle of the night because she hadn't been in the bed, wondering if she had left him like his mother had done, like his father had done, that was when he had realized he needed to get out of there. Cold sweat had drenched him just as his darkest fear rose to the surface.

If he let himself feel so much, there would only be pain. After everything he had survived to get here in life, he didn't want pain.

Hearing a sound behind him, he turned around.

Theo walked in, a frown on his craggy, old face. Silver glinted in his hair, the warm smile he wore belying the calculatingly shrewd light in his dark eyes. Shaking Nikos's hand, he subjected Nikos to a thorough scrutiny. Nikos brought him to the deck and they settled down on opposite sides of the table.

The sun glinted off Theo's skin, shadowing his expression from Nikos. "I was surprised to learn you wanted to postpone the meeting, Nikos. Your sister, she is safe, yes?"

Gritting his teeth, Nikos nodded. He couldn't fault the man for the doubts in his eyes.

"You still want to continue this alliance between us then?"

"Of course I do, Theo. Nothing else is more important to me."

Leaning forward, Theo smiled. "Then I have three more votes on my side. They will support me without doubt. Savas does not control the board anymore."

Nikos smiled. This was it. His dream was within reach now. He would sit in that chair, claim the prize of his hard work. He shook Theo's hands, his breath ballooning up in his chest. He wanted to celebrate with Lexi, he wanted to...

"There is one condition, though."

He had been expecting this. And Nikos was prepared. "Name your price, Theo."

Theo held his gaze. "Marry my daughter, Nikos. Join the Demakis and Katrakis name forever."

A buzzing filled Nikos's ears. He shot up from his seat and grabbed the railing. The sea glimmered endlessly blue in front of him. But he heard nothing of the waves with blood rushing into his ears.

His first instinct was to scream the denial that was struggling to be let out of his throat. Distaste coated his tongue at the very thought of Eleni Katrakis. He would find a different way to the CEO's chair. He couldn't even indulge in the idea of looking at any other woman except Lexi, he couldn't even...

All his thoughts came to a suffocating halt, his gut twisting into a hard knot. A chill broke out over his skin, despite the sun shining down. Was he actually considering walking away from his life's mission because of one woman? Turning his back on everything he had worked toward? To give in to the unknown, unnamed sensation in his gut that filled him with fear over tangible prize? To follow in the same path his father had trodden, leaving nothing but destruction in his wake.

Nikos did not want that life; he had done everything he could to get away from it.

He had nothing to give Lexi, not the kind of woman she was—kind, generous, affectionate. The sooner they moved on with their lives the better.

It was an affair—they both had known that from the beginning. And all affairs, at least his, came to an end.

Lexi had never felt more intimidated in her life. Even though, for once, she was wearing the right clothes, shoes and even makeup.

The blue cocktail dress was strapless and hugged her chest and waist and then fell to her knees in a playful skirt. Her hair was combed back and piled high, thanks to the stylist that Nikos had insisted on, leaving her nape bare. She had thought the classic lines of the dress would clash with her boyish haircut. But as the stylist had claimed, the blunt haircut made the small planes of her face stand out.

The inaugural party for the hotel on the other side of the island, the same hotel she and Nikos had christened so colorfully just two weeks ago, was open as of tonight. And from what she had overheard from Nikos's assistant, booked for the next five years through, just as Nikos had predicted. Apparently there were a lot of high-profile celebrities who were really into low-key vacation spots that were a slice of paradise.

Even the party today, set up under an elegant marquee on the beach was a low-key one. Lexi had spotted a celebrity chef that she was dying to tell Tyler about and even a famous underwear model. But more than the international celebrities, it was the presence of Savas Demakis that unsettled her.

With her heated imagination, she had imagined Savas to look cruel and scary. But he looked like any other man here tonight for the most part. Except when he had stopped in front of Lexi fifteen minutes ago and fired off questions without so much as a greeting, as if it was his privilege to be answered.

Cowed by his presence, Lexi had automatically answered. He clearly didn't like her presence here tonight, but she refused to hide like a dirty secret. With a sigh, she realized that more of Savas's guests had begun casting looks in her direction, their curiosity blatant.

She would have left for the villa on the other side if it hadn't been for the fact that she hadn't seen Nikos in three days. He had spent a week with her and Venetia and Tyler; curiously they had made a very peaceful foursome at the villa before urgent business had called him away. From the way his eyes had lit up, Lexi had known it had to do with the vote for the CEO position on the Demakis board.

She had wished him luck. Only he had told her that he didn't need luck. And he hadn't returned or even called her. She had swallowed her disappointment but couldn't stay away tonight.

According to Venetia, the board was present and was going to make an announcement. Her heart raced as Lexi heard the sounds of a helicopter. She dug her heels into the carpet laid on the beach, fighting the urge to go to Nikos.

She took a champagne flute from a uniformed waiter and joined Tyler and Venetia at their table. The moment Nikos appeared in front of the small dais, people mobbed him from every side.

Glad that she was sitting, Lexi took a sip, just to give her shaking hands something to do.

Surrounded by powerful men and women, Nikos seemed far from the man who had surprised her with the studio.

His gaze raked the crowd, and finding her, settled on her. Across the distance separating them, Lexi felt the weight of it as if he had walked up to her and touched her.

An older man claimed Nikos's attention and the moment was gone.

A few minutes later, the guests began to settle around the tables under the artistic handmade paper lanterns hanging from the roof of the marquee. And the speeches began.

She had expected Nikos or the American entrepreneur Nathan Ramirez to be giving the speech, but it was the older man who had come to see Nikos on the island a couple of weeks ago. He introduced himself as Theo Katrakis, a board member of the Demakis Board. He went on at length describing Nikos's achievements, and how his leadership had pumped Demakis International with new blood and money and that congratulations were due to Nikos.

Lexi's heart thumped hard. Finally, Nikos had what he had worked so hard for.

Nikos was the new CEO of Demakis International. The older man laughed and cracked a joke that Lexi didn't understand exactly but got the gist of when he invited his daughter Eleni Katrakis to the dais along with Nikos. With Nikos and Eleni on either side, Theo Katrakis beamed and made a comment to Savas.

The broad smile on Savas's face drove the truth home for Lexi.

Nikos was engaged to Eleni Katrakis.

Lexi's heart shattered in her chest, her breath hitching in her throat. Her head felt as if it was stuck in a space warp—all sounds and sights warbled in the background against the whooshing in her ears, against the chill on her skin. Like Tyler's curse and his hands gripping her, Venetia's shocked glance shifting between her and her brother. But they were all muted against the savage gleam in Savas Demakis's eyes.

He had stopped history from repeating itself.

He had demanded Nikos pay his price to be the CEO, and Nikos had paid it with his heart. And hers, too.

Because, despite her every effort, she was in love with him. It was the most terrifying truth yet that she had to face. Fear was a physical fist in her gut, a hollowness in her chest.

She had felt like this once before. The memory hit her hard, more sensations and feelings rather than tangible details.

She had been five and after her first day in the public school, she had realized that every other kid in her class had parents. That they didn't get shuffled from home to home, that they were loved. And that, her parents, for whatever reason, had given her up.

She had cried until her head had hurt, and Mrs. Nesbitt had hugged her hard and washed her face. That's how she felt now.

Like she had lost something valuable, something precious that she had never had in the first place.

Of all the times to realize how much she wanted him to love her, to hope that he had chosen happiness—hers and his—of all the times to realize that she would forever be alone in this world because she would never stop loving him.

Spike should kill Ms. Havisham.

He had told her how this was going to end.

She blinked back the searing heat behind her eyes. She couldn't bear to look at him, couldn't bear for him to see how much she loved him, couldn't bear for him to see how much he was hurting her.

She wanted to slink away and hide. She wanted to fly

back to New York this minute. If she saw him, she would surely break down, would probably beg him to love her as she did him.

Because she couldn't be sophisticated enough to not let this hurt, because she couldn't pretend, even for one second, despite his every warning, that she hadn't fallen in love with him.

She breathed in a deep gulp of air and fought the desperation.

She wasn't going to take it lying down. If she was going to lose him anyway, she was going to make him face what he had done. She was going to find the man who'd been kind under the brutal honesty, the man who had shown her what it was to live and make sure he understood what he was giving up.

It was hours before Nikos had been able to extricate himself from the night's activities. Every board member wanted to congratulate him; every investor wanted a piece of him. Through every minute of it, he had pushed himself to stay, told himself that this was the moment he had worked to achieve for almost fifteen years.

He searched for words to say to her, wondered about what to say and how to do it without hurting her. Like he had done for three days.

He had seen her, sitting quietly at a table at the back, dressed in blue silk that made her look as breathtakingly lovely as she was on the inside. Nothing else had registered in his mind until Theo had made the announcement.

She had looked shattered, and his throat, it had felt as if he had swallowed glass. Only then, did he realize what he had set in motion.

He stood outside her studio now—it would forever

be that in his mind—stunned to see her curled up in the recliner.

He had thought she would have fled in disgust. Maybe even hoped for it, like a spineless coward. He was about to step back out when her eyes fluttered open and instantly focused on him. Her knees tucked to her chest, her hands crossed over, she looked tiny, breakable in the huge recliner.

She offered him a small smile, nothing but sadness in her blue eyes. "Congratulations, Nikos."

"You're wearing the dress I picked."

She looked down and ran a hand over the silk. Moonlight threw just enough light to bare her slender shoulders to him. She met his gaze and the intensity of emotion in it skewered him. "I wore it for you. It made me feel different, confident. I wanted to look beautiful tonight. I had a feeling it was going to be special."

His heart beat a rapid tattoo, a part of him telling him to stay at the door, to not go to her, to act with honor. What little he had left. "I've never seen anyone more beautiful."

She took a deep breath as though to contain herself. "For once, I believe that."

Shrugging off his coat, he stayed leaning against the door. "I…had no idea Theo was going to announce it tonight."

Resignation curved her mouth. "Have you already slept with her?"

The profanity that flew from his mouth should have created a frost in the air around them. But it didn't wash away the bitter need inside to explain why he had agreed to this. He looked at her, and she seemed different. "*Christos,* I have no interest in her. I haven't even looked at her."

"Is that supposed to make me feel better?"

At his silence, she smiled. It was the most cynical thing

he had ever seen on her innocent face. And he was responsible for putting it there.

"Say it, Nikos. Tell me to be gone. Tell me to my face that you're done with me, that our little affair has come to an end. Tell me that you're moving on with more important things in your life."

"You know it's not—"

She shook her head and the words halted on his lips. Not that he had any idea what he was going to say. "Don't you dare say it's not like that. People have affairs with each other, and then move on, right? Whisper those little words you whispered to Emmanuelle that day. Tell me it is time to pack up my things. Do I get a goodbye gift?"

"*Theos,* Lexi. What are you doing?"

Hugging her midriff, she cast a furious look at him. Her face alight with color, her mouth mobile, she looked like an angry tigress and nothing like the woman he had expected. "Were you hoping I would just slink away in the night, heartbroken and pitiful? Or were you thinking I would be so desperate to be loved by you, that I would take you any way I got you, that I would accept what little you offer me?"

"I had to make this choice. This marriage is nothing but an agreement."

His jaw was tight like a vise, his cheekbones sticking out making him forbidden and stark. But Lexi wouldn't back down. The hurt continued to splinter inside her as if there was no end to it. As if this moment needed to be entrenched inside her, as if she needed to be changed.

Anger, red-hot and roiling, it was the only way to survive the moment and she clutched it to herself.

Because if she didn't, she would hear that voice inside her head. That little girl filled with hurt, filled with fear, the one that so desperately wanted to be loved.

The only way to drown out that pathetic voice was to

ride the storm of anger. "You think I can find solace in the fact that you're ruining your life along with mine?"

He shifted back, the expression in his eyes cycling from fury to desperation to a terrifying emptiness within seconds. "Don't say another word," he said through gritted teeth, every syllable bellowing around them.

"I won't stop." She wiped her tears and looked up at him, her heart breaking in her chest. "You have no idea how much the very thought of leaving you terrifies me. I can't breathe if I think about not seeing you ever again." She covered the distance between them, and he braced himself as if she was a weapon that would cause him damage. She reached for his face, and he immediately bent his head, his gaze a glittering pool of anger and something else.

Standing on her toes, she kissed his cheek, and he shuddered. Burying her face in his chest, she hugged him tight, learning and memorizing the scent and feel of him.

"I'm petrified that I will never see you again, that I'll never hear your voice again, never kiss you again. That no one will ever think me beautiful—" Her voice broke. "That no one will ever tell me to stand up for myself, that no one will ever think I'm extraordinary. I've never been more terrified that I'll never be loved, Nikos."

She pressed another kiss on his palm, and looked up at him. The pain she saw in his eyes stole her breath, knuckled her so hard in the gut that she swayed. But she didn't relent. She would say this to him, for herself. "I'm in love with you. I think I'll always love you. If you weren't so blinded by your ambition—"

Pulling his hands from her, he stepped back, a vein pulsing in his temple. "I've told you things that I haven't told anyone. This is not about ambition or greed. You have to understand…"

She wanted to shake him; she wanted to hit him for not seeing the truth that was right in front of his eyes.

"You still think this is victory over your father? Because it's not."

He flinched. The flash of pain in his eyes would have stopped her before, but now, she was filled with pure fury. He had shown her what it was to live and then he wanted her to go right back to being half-alive.

"This agreement you have made, it's your victory over your fear that you are like him. *Because you are,* despite your every effort to not be. You are his son...you feel something for me." She poked him in the chest. "You feel it here. You're getting attached to me. And it terrifies you.

"It terrifies you to realize that you might be exactly like your father, that you have the same weakness as he does, that if you let this small thing for me take root, if you accept it and let it grow, it will devour you from the inside, and that you will have no control over yourself.

"And your grandfather offered you the best way to beat it back, to keep it in its place, didn't he?"

"For the last time, Savas had nothing to do with this."

"Savas has everything to do with this. You and he are both terrified of the same thing. This way, you can tell yourself that I'm secondary to something else in your life, that your emotions have no power over you.

"You are breaking my heart and burying yours. And I hope to hell you've just as miserable a life ahead of you as I do."

CHAPTER THIRTEEN

NIKOS SAT IN the leather chair in his new office in the Demakis International tower in Athens. He had been in this
room countless times, stood on the other side of the vast
desk as Savas spelled out more and more conditions that
defined Nikos's survival.

And he had conquered every obstacle Savas had thrown
his way. This moment, this chair was his prize after years
of painstaking hard work.

Except it didn't feel like a moment of triumph. It felt
hollow…it felt tainted. Frustration boiled inside him. He
didn't want to think of Lexi.

He had thought she understood why he needed this. He
didn't need her any more than he needed her analy-
sis. Wherever she went, or whatever she did, she would
be loved. It was a matter of comfort and intense envy inside him.

He picked up the champagne bottle from the ice bucket
and popped the cork just as Savas walked in. Curiously, he
had stayed away from Nikos since the party a week ago.
As if he knew that Nikos had been like a wounded animal,
rearing to attack anyone who ventured close.

But he couldn't. Savas understood nothing of emotions.
He shouldered enormous responsibility without complaint.
Nikos's father had been a late child, and by the time he had

turned his back on this wealth, Savas had already been close to sixty. But Savas had gone on with his life, with his duty, shouldered his company, his family.

"Congratulations," Savas said, taking the champagne flute from Nikos. "You've proved yourself worthy of the Demakis name."

Nikos nodded and took a sip. But one question lingered in his throat, clawing its way to his tongue, refusing to be silenced. He had never before asked Savas about his father. Ever.

There was no need to do so now. Yet the words fell from his lips and he didn't stop them. Maybe if he asked, maybe when he knew, there would be no more wondering. He could put all the dirty questions Lexi had raised to peace finally.

"My father...did he come to you for help when my mother was sick?"

His eyes widened under his dark brows for an infinitesimal moment before Savas could hide the flash of emotion. But Nikos had seen it. "You gain nothing by delving into the past, Nikos. You have done remarkably well until now, beyond my expectations. Don't look back now."

Nikos dropped the flute onto the table, his heart slamming against his rib cage. Savas turned around, leaning heavily against his cane.

Panic robbed his breath from him; his gut heaved. Nikos planted himself between Savas and the door. "Answer my question. Did he come to you for help?"

This time, there was not a flicker of doubt in his gaze. "Yes, he did."

Nikos exhaled a jagged breath, pain twisting hard in his gut. Everything he had assumed about his father, it had been colored by the excruciating hurt that he hadn't hung on for him and Venetia, that he had been weak.

"What did you do?"

If he felt anything of the vehemence in Nikos's question, Savas didn't betray it by even a muscle. "I presented him with a set of conditions, just as I had done with you."

A cold finger climbed up Nikos's spine. He knew what was coming; he finally understood what Lexi had meant when she had said it was Savas that demanded a price from Nikos. A price he had paid willingly, crushing his own heart in the process. He licked his lips, pushing the words out through a raw throat.

"What were the conditions?"

"I told him I would give her medical care, enough money to live out the rest of her life in comfort. In return, he had to walk away from her. And instead of taking what I offered, your father decided to remain a fool."

Exactly what Nikos had thought him to this day.

A sudden chill settled deep in Nikos's chest, filling his veins with ice. All his father had needed to do was to walk away from his mother. And her last days would have been in comfort.

And yet, he hadn't been able to make the ruthless choice, hadn't been able to leave the woman he loved.

Had the guilt been too unbearable to live, knowing that his love for her had caused her suffering? Powerlessness transformed to rage, and Nikos turned toward Savas. They both knew he had been a weak man. "Why? Why did you ask that of him?"

Savas rocked where he stood, his head erect, his gaze direct.

"She stole him from me. My only son, the heir to my empire, and he ran away the minute he met her. She weakened him even more. And what did she gain in return? Poverty, starvation, failure?"

"She did not weaken him, Savas. He was already weak."

Savas flinched. The tiredness he must have held at bay, the pain he must have shoved aside, crept into his face. There was unrelenting grief there, and to Nikos's shock, regrets. Savas had never meant to push his son to that bitter end he had finally sought. It had been nothing but stubborn pride that had motivated Savas.

Instead, in the blink of an eye, Nikos's father's cowardly step had shattered so many lives.

"Eventually, he let her down just as he did me. And I could not let you make the same mistake. I held you at arm's length. I put you through so much—my own blood. I could not let you become weak like him, incapable of doing your duty."

And it had cost Savas to see Nikos suffer as much as it had cost Nikos himself. Nikos shuddered at the weight of that realization. "So you manipulated Theo into making a deal with me. My marriage to Eleni Katrakis—that was your idea."

"Yes. I heard about that American woman, about how wrapped up you were in her, about how she had changed your mind even about Venetia. This time, I couldn't not act."

And as before, Nikos had walked right into his own destruction. "Neither of you was right. Do you understand, Savas?

"If he was irresponsible, weak, you were bitter, abusive. When he died, Venetia and I needed your love, we needed your support. Instead you turned my anger for him to your advantage. You made me loathe my own father. But I am not weak like him or bitter like you."

And neither would his love for Lexi weaken him.

His body shuddering at the realization, Nikos sank into his chair.

He had a heart, and it hurt, and it bled, and most of all, it loved.

And he had pushed the woman who had shown him that out of his life without second thought.

Even with her heart breaking, even with the fear that she had lived with for most of her life rioting through her, she had still fought for him, for them. She had tried to show him what they had and what he was so intent on destroying. Because the love she felt for him, it had given her that strength, that courage.

I will always love you.

Now he understood how easily, how perfectly those words had come to her, and why she had been so furious about what he had chosen.

Picking up the papers of his appointment as the CEO with shaking hands, Nikos brought them over to Savas. He dropped them on the table and met his grandfather's gaze. "Whatever you did, I realize you did it out of a twisted sense of guilt and love. You sought to make me stronger than him." He swallowed the thick lump in his throat. "And I am a stronger man than he ever was. I have never shirked my duty toward my sister. I will never betray your trust in me. But Lexi…she's a part of me, Savas.

"She makes me stronger. She fills my life with laughter and joy." He took a look around the office and sucked in a deep breath.

"I have proved my worth a hundred times over to you. I deserve to be the CEO of Demakis International. But I will not pay the price you ask of me anymore. I will not lose the woman I love any more than I will shoot myself mourning her loss. You want me to run this company…you want me to be your legacy? Then I will do it with her by my side. That's the only way I can do it. I'm through living my life based on you or him. I have to be my own man now."

Without waiting for Savas's answer, Nikos closed the door behind him. Fear-fueled anticipation flew hot in his veins. He couldn't wait to see her, couldn't wait to hold her in his arms.

Because this time, he didn't feel resentment at the thought of the woman who had been through so much and yet had such a capacity to love. This time, he wanted that love. This time, he wanted to love her as she deserved to be loved.

Lexi was opening a can of mushroom soup when a knock sounded on the door. She knew it wasn't Faith, because Faith was playing the adult, much-less-fun version of hide-and-seek with her. Tired of putting up an elaborate pretense when she was already feeling fragile, Lexi had given it to her straight—everything she had learned about her and Tyler, all the lies that Faith had told her.

And then burst into tears like a raving lunatic the moment Faith had asked about Nikos. To give her credit, Faith had stayed back a full day, looking after Lexi before splitting.

Lexi knew she wasn't gone forever, and with Tyler staying back in Greece for the time being, Faith was the only friend Lexi had. But she had told Faith in no uncertain terms that she wouldn't put up with any kind of nonsense.

But rattling around in the apartment that she had shared with both Tyler and Faith all by herself wasn't helping her already-vulnerable state. More than once, Lexi had indulged the thought of calling Nikos, had wondered how he was. But the next moment her thoughts turned to his engagement, and the vicious cycle circled back to fury at him.

That fury, it was the one thing that was holding her together. She couldn't bear to think about what would be left when it was gone, too.

The knock sounded again.

With a sigh, she took a peek through the peephole and jerked back as though bitten.

Clad in a long coat, his mouth set into a tight line, Nikos stood on the other side of the door.

Her heart, if possible, might have jumped out of her chest. For a few seconds, she forgot to breathe as panic flooded her muscles. Tears hit the back of her eyes with the force of a thunderstorm.

"Open the door, Lexi. I know you're in there."

The nerve of the man to think she was hiding from him! Sucking in a sharp breath, she undid the dead bolt and opened the door.

And felt the impact of his presence like a pealing pulse everywhere in her body. His tie dangled from his throat, his dress shirt unbuttoned and crinkled. He already had stubble—which meant he had shaved only once today—the very sight of which gave her tingles in the strangest places.

She had complained once that it rasped her skin, and he had begun shaving twice. Then she had complained that she missed it. He had grown it in the next day and tickled the inside of her thighs with it.

Dear God, the man could turn her inside out.

Fighting the upsurge of color, she stood in front of the door and eyed him nervously. "If this is about me taking that laptop, I'm sorry, but I'm not returning it. Put it under damages that were due to me." She had to keep this light, self-deprecating, or she would collapse into tears right there.

"That's what you think I came over for? Because you took a laptop?" He threw her a narrowed look before striding through the small gap and entering the apartment. The quiet brush of his body against hers made her tense.

With a sigh, she closed the door and leaned against it.

Cursing, she ran a nervous hand over her abdomen. Even with clothes mussed from the flight, he looked breathtakingly gorgeous and effortlessly sexy. It was not fair that one man had everything—looks, sexuality and the arrogant confidence to carry it off so easily.

She couldn't think like this about him. He was engaged to another woman. There were a few lines she wouldn't cross, even in thought. But the sight of his sunken eyes, and the protruding cheekbones, the tired look, gave her immense satisfaction.

Really, she needed to channel Ms. Havisham more.

"Where is your fiancée?"

"In Athens, I assume, with her lover."

"If this is a pitch about sophisticated open marriages and New York sex stops—" she wasn't going to break down again, at least not until he left "—then get out. I have work to do."

He shrugged his coat off and threw it on the couch behind him. Pushing the sleeves of his shirt back, he picked up a sketch from the couch. And casually rolled the grenade onto the floor. "The engagement is off."

Her mouth fell open. For a few seconds, she wondered if she had imagined the words, if she was, once again, lapsing into an alternate reality in which he came back to her and professed undying love.

"Lexi? Are you all right?"

When she nodded, he went back to poking around the living room that she had converted into her studio. The wide wood table she had found in a flea market stood tilted to catch the sunlight from the sliding glass doors. And taped to it with a clip was the penultimate chapter of Ms. Havisham's story.

With hands that were obviously trembling, he ran a finger over the last box on the page. The one where Ms. Havisham was standing over Spike's immobile body. He looked at her then, and the stark expression in his eyes knocked the breath out of her. "She has killed him then?"

Swallowing the tears catching in her throat, Lexi nodded. "In this draft, at least."

He frowned. "What do you mean?"

She rubbed the heel of her palm over her eyes. "I can't decide on an ending. I'm meeting a freelance publisher guy in two days, but I'm still not sure. She has to show Spike what she's capable of so that he doesn't underestimate her ever again, but maybe she'll just maim him. Maybe she will turn him into her sidekick, who knows?"

He blinked. And she realized it was to shield his expression from her face. "You're enjoying this immensely, aren't you?"

"Yes. I have totally embraced the fact that Spike's life is in my hands and I can inflict whatever damage I can on him." She raised her thumbs up, a parody to cover up the misery she felt inside. "Once again, it's delusional fantasy to the rescue."

Shaking his head, he picked up the rest of the pages of the strip from the table and flicked through them. "You have done a lot in one week."

She shrugged. "The money you paid me will tide me over for a few months if I work minimal hours. I decided it's now or never to give this a proper shot."

"That's fantastic." His gaze lingered on her hungrily before he resumed pacing again, a restless energy pouring off him in waves.

She fisted her hands, stifling the urge to pummel him. How dare he just dangle the announcement that his engagement was off but not say more? But she would not ask for details.

Her sudden movement caused his hard chest to graze against her, and he jerked back like a coiled spring.

"Will you stop the pacing? You're beginning to scare me, Nikos. What happened? Is everyone okay?"

"Yes, they are all fine. Venetia is driving Tyler and me crazy planning the wedding of the century."

Lexi's heart sank. Venetia and she, despite all odds, had struck a weird sort of friendship. They both loved Tyler, and it created a surprisingly strong connection despite their different temperaments. But because of the inconsiderate, intractable brute in front of her, Lexi was missing all the fun. "They have set a date?"

"Yes. For eighteen months from now. You would think she was the first woman to get married. I have renewed respect for Tyler that he was able to persuade her at all to a date so far away."

She hadn't spoken to Tyler in a week, and even before that only to assure him that she had reached New York safely—like a flight on a private jet would be anything but—and that she was fine. He knew she was not fine. But she hadn't wanted to linger for an extra day, so she had promised him that she would take care of herself. But she couldn't talk to him over the phone. Because if she did, she was going to start crying, and she didn't want to alarm him.

Because more than the threat of loneliness, it was the shadow of the happiness, the joy she had known with Nikos that remained behind, making her ache. And now he was here again, setting her back to square one. Not that she had made much progress in moving on.

She still had a couple of weeks before she went back to work and she had been eating greasy takeout, drawing and crying herself to sleep.

"So your sister is fine, you are still the CEO—" she had

never heard so much bitterness in her voice "—then why are you here?"

He stood rooted to the spot. She watched him swallow, watched the dark shadow that fell over his face.

Suddenly she felt exhaustingly fragile. Being in love was so hard. She would have given anything to make it stop hurting so much.

Nikos was looming in front of her before she could draw another breath, running a finger over the bags under her eyes. There was such desolation in his eyes, such open need that she trembled from head to toe. "There's this tightness in my chest, *thee mou,* like someone is relentlessly carving away at it. It hurts like nothing I have ever felt before."

Lexi felt dizzy from the emotion in his words. "You don't have a heart." She wanted to sound cutting, instead she sounded immensely sad.

His mouth closed; he smiled without warmth. "Apparently I do. You kick-started it when you blazed into my life."

"I didn't blaze anywhere. You manipulated me." Tears filled her throat. "You forced the truth on me and then you—" She hit him in the chest. "I have never been so angry with anyone in my entire life, Nikos. I hate you for you doing this to me."

His arms came around her, his grip infinitely fragile. She felt his mouth on her temple, felt his sharp hiss of indrawn breath. "Not as much as I hate myself, *thee mou. Theos,* there isn't a single name I haven't called myself these last few days. I had a whole speech prepared, liberally infused with begging. And I don't remember a word of it.

"Every time I come near you, you unravel me a little more. You show me how much I can feel, how much I can hurt. It's a little scary, Lexi."

Tears came fast at her and spilled onto her cheeks. She had no defense left to fight him. Not anymore, not when he said things like that, not when the heat of his body was an incredible fortress of warmth around her.

His mouth compressed into a line of pain, he gathered her closer. And she cried. She thought it wasn't possible for her heart to break again. Apparently it still could. The pain was as sharp as ever.

"Don't cry, *agape mou*. I can't bear it." He tucked her chin up gently, a flash of indecision in his gaze. "I'm desperately in love with you, Lexi. You were wrong about one thing. This thing…it's not just taken root inside me, it's consuming me whole. My life is terrifyingly empty without you. The power you hold over me, over my happiness—I'm not scared of it anymore. I want to spend the rest of my life loving you, *yineka mou*."

Lexi's heart beat so fast she wondered if she was having a heart attack. His hands around her waist, Nikos held her tight, a shudder racking his powerful frame. "You mean it?"

Nikos nodded, his heart shining in his eyes. "I do. I can't stop giving thanks for the moment that brought Tyler into Venetia's life and you into mine.

"You are the most wonderful woman I have ever met, and I want to live my life with you. I want to have a family with you. I want to make love to you every night and every morning. I want to hear your incredible stories about space portals and time warps. I want to be the first one who sees every sketch you ever draw. I want to take care of you, and I want you to take care of me. The number of things I feel for you, they are dizzying and invigorating.

"Please tell me you don't want to have an extremely elaborate wedding like Venetia because that would just about kill me."

"What?" Her heart pounding harder, it seemed all she was capable of was asking inane questions.

His thumbs moving over her cheeks, he pressed a kiss

to her forehead. "I want to marry you, *yineka mou,* as soon as possible. We will honeymoon on the yacht, I think. I promised Savas we would return in a month so that I can officially take over and be the new CEO."

Her gaze flew to his. It was too many shocks for one day. "He agreed to this?"

"I didn't give him a choice. I told him that the CEO position meant nothing to me without you." He pushed her hands behind her with one hand and tilted her chin up. "Tell me this is what you want, too. Tell me you love me."

Lexi smiled, but she still couldn't stop crying, either. "I do love you, Nikos. You helped me discover that I'm just as cool as an imaginary action heroine with a penchant for killing. Or even better—" she choked on the tears again "—you made me want to live my life. And then you left me to do it all alone. It's a good life, I have realized. It's just that it's a lot happier with you in it, and I don't want to spend another minute of it denying myself that happiness."

He touched his forehead to hers and whispered the words into her skin. "Then you never will. Your happiness, our happiness together, that's all I want now, *thee mou.*" He sealed his promise with a kiss, and Lexi felt the stress and tension leave her body. Her heart thundered inside her chest, and she trembled in his arms, bursting with happiness. "Although I think I have to kill whoever Tony Stark is."

"What?"

"It says I Love Tony Stark on your T-shirt, *agape mou.* You're not allowed to love anyone but me."

She laughed and stepped back from him, loving the jealous glint in his eyes. She loved him like this—playful and willing to show what he felt for her. It cost him a lot, and she loved him all the more for it. "Sorry, but that's an occupational hazard of being a comic artist, Nikos. At any given time, I'm in love with at least two to three fictional heroes. Recently, it's been Iron Man. And it's not like you can compete with him, so it's better—"

She squealed and turned as he reached her in two quick steps and pressed her to the wall behind her with his huge body. She saw his hunger in the tight lines of his gorgeous face, in the way he clenched his muscles hard holding the lust at bay. "By the time I'm through with you tonight, you won't remember your own name much less another man's, *thee mou*. My name, that's all you are going to say, or scream."

She trembled at the dark promise in his words, her body already thrumming with arousal and anticipation. She choked back a laugh as he picked her up and moved toward the couch.

She shook her head and pointed him in the other direction. "The bedroom is that way."

Desire roared into life in his eyes.

"Three hundred and sixty hours and forty-three minutes."

"What?"

"Since you made love to me."

"I think you're addicted to sex, Ms. Nelson."

"Nope." She tucked herself tighter around him and smiled up at him. "I'm addicted to you, Mr. Demakis."

* * * * *

LET'S TALK
Romance

For exclusive extracts, competitions
and special offers, find us online:

facebook.com/millsandboon

@MillsandBoon

@MillsandBoonUK

Get in touch on 01413 063232

For all the latest titles coming soon, visit

millsandboon.co.uk/nextmonth

MILLS & BOON

THE HEART OF ROMANCE

A ROMANCE FOR EVERY KIND OF READER

MODERN

Prepare to be swept off your feet by sophisticated, sexy and seductive heroes, in some of the world's most glamourous and romantic locations, where power and passion collide.
8 stories per month.

HISTORICAL

Escape with historical heroes from time gone by. Whether your passion is for wicked Regency Rakes, muscled Vikings or rugged Highlanders, awaken the romance of the past.
6 stories per month.

MEDICAL

Set your pulse racing with dedicated, delectable doctors in the high-pressure world of medicine, where emotions run high and passion, comfort and love are the best medicine.
6 stories per month.

True Love

Celebrate true love with tender stories of heartfelt romance, from the rush of falling in love to the joy a new baby can bring, and a focus on the emotional heart of a relationship.
8 stories per month.

Desire

Indulge in secrets and scandal, intense drama and plenty of sizzlir hot action with powerful and passionate heroes who have it all: wealth, status, good looks…everything but the right woman.
6 stories per month.

HEROES

Experience all the excitement of a gripping thriller, with an intens romance at its heart. Resourceful, true-to-life women and strong, fearless men face danger and desire - a killer combination!
8 stories per month.

DARE

Sensual love stories featuring smart, sassy heroines you'd want as a best friend, and compelling intense heroes who are worthy of ther
4 stories per month.

To see which titles are coming soon, please visit

millsandboon.co.uk/nextmonth

JOIN US ON SOCIAL MEDIA!

Stay up to date with our latest releases, author news and gossip, special offers and discounts, and all the behind-the-scenes action from Mills & Boon...

 millsandboon

 millsandboonuk

 millsandboon

It might just be true love...

MILLS & BOON
True Love
Romance from the Heart

Celebrate true love with tender stories of heartfelt romance, from the rush of falling in love to the joy a new baby can bring, and a focus on the emotional heart of a relationship.

MILLS & BOON
MODERN
Power and Passion

Prepare to be swept off your feet by sophisticated, sexy and seductive heroes, in some of the world's most glamourous and romantic locations, where power and passion collide.